6-20 2

GHOST
DANCE

CAROLE MASO

THE ECCO PRESS

The Ecco Press
100 West Broad Street
Hopewell, New Jersey 08525

Published simultaneously in Canada by
Penguin Books Canada Ltd., Ontario
Printed in the United States of America

Grateful acknowledgement is made to *Yellow Silk* and *Sing, Heavenly Muse*, where previous versions of
portions of this work appeared.

Enormous gratitude to the Cummington Community of the Arts.
Thanks also to the New York State Council on the Arts, the Edward Albee Foundation, and the Virginia
Center for the Creative Arts.

This book is an invention, an act of the imagination, and in no way should be mistaken for reality, the
place where much good invention originates.

FIRST ECCO EDITION

Library of Congress Cataloging-in-Publication Data

Maso, Carole.
Ghost dance / Carole Maso.
p.   cm.
ISBN 0-88001-409-1 (paper) :
I. Title
PS3563.A786G5   1995
813'.54—dc20   94-43667

9 8 7 6 5 4 3 2 1

To my mother and father,
who offered me the creative dream
as if it was water or food or a place to live.
To Barbara, who encouraged me to live there.
And to Helen, who made it possible.

In memory of David Kennedy,
Kathleen McCarthy, and James Wright.

GHOST DANCE

Part One

She is standing under the great clock in Grand Central Station and she is waiting for me. She does not shift her weight from one foot to the other, checking her watch every few moments, worrying about where I might be. She is not anxious at all, in fact, but calm, peaceful, at ease. She is so beautiful standing there. People whirl around her, talking, laughing, running, but they pause for a second when they see her, turning back to look as they hurry. She focuses in the distance, oblivious, it seems, to the life of the station, and looks straight ahead at a point still some way away, where the poem she has been struggling to finish for days will fall into place. She smiles as she feels herself come a little closer and then rests; there is no forcing it, she knows. She shifts her great attention to me. "Vanessa," she whispers, and she closes her eyes. "Vanessa," she says, guiding me through the treacherous streets to her. Slowly she clears a wide path for me through the snow and, as I step safely, in her mind, from the taxi onto the street, quite suddenly the poem is complete. As she places my foot onto the pavement, puts the fare in the driver's hand, and has me enter the station, she is overwhelmed by an immense, inexplicable joy. Nothing can equal this happiness, she thinks. She looks up at the snow that hugs the high, cathedral-like windows. She is dangerously happy. The day is beautiful. There has never been a better time or place to be alive, she thinks. There is no life more perfect than her own. And she is right.

She has just gotten off the train from Maine and she carries in her body that fierce New England coastline. She is rock strong—she has cast her restlessness into the sea. For her own she has taken the large, simple faith of the fisherman. I feel her as my taxi flies through snow. She pulls me toward her, toward her harsh, clear cold, toward her wild bramble bushes; I feel her irresistible winter in my bones.

The city sparkles like a jewel in the sun. The snow is blindingly white. She is smiling. She is bathed in apricot. The poem is complete. It is true: the world is a cathedral of light.

On such a day as this, it is possible to believe that everything will be fine. We will understand our lives, we will be the best we can be. We will be brave. We will say what we meant to say.

On such a clear day it is possible to believe that we will live forever, that death was something we once invented, long ago, on a lazy summer afternoon when we had nothing better to do—a way to add texture, dimension, a way to change the pace of our lilting lives. On such a day it is possible to believe that sorrow will turn into one great vapor and blow off and be gone forever; that the childhood dream of fire will turn out to mean nothing in the end; and that our deaths, if they must be, will be timely, after eighty, and while we sleep.

As I shut the cab door and walk down the path through drifts of snow to her, I know that all of this is possible. We will have time for everything. We will say what we meant to say. It will all make sense. We will be fine.

I step into the safety of this great station and the feeling persists: it will all last forever. The building curves around me; all longings merge here. It will all go on and on: the glances, the hurried steps, the breaking voices, the tentative good-byes, the echo of joyous hellos. A young woman races across the enormous floor. In the sound of her high heels clicking, in her purse at her elbow as she buys her ticket, I know: it will last forever. She hurries on in every time, toward every life.

I smell the snow and breathe in the air of long ago. On the balcony, forty years before this, a young man all good looks and grim optimism stood smiling nervously. He stands there now, remembering his father's hesitant pride, his mother's tears as they waved him on to war. His mother wore the softest white gloves, his father a felt hat. He shakes his white head as he watches them, still waving and waving good-bye. They will wave forever, he knows. White gloves. A felt hat. They are long dead. It does not matter. This is our fate: to love too much—even the dead, who might not need our love.

We love too much—this man who cannot forget, the woman who rushes, and I who can feel her pull from the other side of the city. I see her as I run down the marble steps. Strains of classical music, the violin, the oboe come from the café at the top of the station. The light is fragile, the music is lovely, the whole station is moving and alive. There is no place more vital than this one, more exciting, more filled with promise. There is no better place on earth, nowhere else that can fill us with such hope. It will all go on. She is beautiful. People turn to look at her. The poem is complete. I run to her. There has never been a better moment to be alive. I am immensely happy. Love makes it so. We love too much and still . . .

I get closer. She is wearing a large hat. She turns to me. The vision breaks. My mother is in deep trouble.

"Mom," I say quietly, touching her shoulder. She does not really recognize me. I know not to speak too loudly. "Mom," I say, "I'm sorry I'm late . . ." My voice trails off. She is not seeing me at all. I look away from her so that she might be spared the pain of this young woman, a college student overloaded with books, who talks to her so kindly and holds her hand and brushes her hair from her face. I look back at her, straighten her hat. She smiles. "You're very nice," she says. I look away.

The sharp arms of the great clock slice into the back of her neck and she lets out a small sigh.

"Oh, Mom."

"Darling," she says, "my darling." And with these words we are back in our places—home again—back in our hard love.

"I'm sorry I'm late, Mom," I say. "The snow," I whisper. But I know that she sees no snow, feels no cold.

She touches my face, brings her gloved hands to it, gently.

"Oh, Mom," I say. I will not look away. I will see her this time.

As she takes off her gloves I see that she is wearing a ring on every finger. Each of her nails, I notice, is carefully shaped and polished. This time I hear the sound of her bracelets in my ears as she puts her trembling hand to my face again. Around her neck and waist are scarves, gold chains, lockets, ropes of silk, feathers, charms. I shut my eyes for a moment. Her eyes, shaded by the enormous flowered hat, are heavy with makeup, her cheeks are stained with rouge, her mouth a wild, brilliant pink.

She wears layers and layers of clothes, sweater over silk blouse over sweater, making her look like a bulky, large figure in the world—someone to reckon with. I should be used to this by now, I say to myself, and yet I never am. She has never looked this bad before, I think, armored in this way against simple dailiness, her protection from the world when she is not feeling well.

I take off her hat and there are dozens of braids in her hair, intricate knots, curls.

"Oh, Mom," I say, lifting the rows of chains that hang around her neck, weighing against her chest.

"What is it, Vanessa? What is it, honey?"

"You don't need all of this," I say.

"Hmm? What, dear?" Her voice tosses, rises, and falls in the ocean off of Maine. I focus on the large black tunnels that lead out to the trains.

"You don't need all of this."

She looks around as if I am talking about the station. She nods.

"Oh, they will tear this place down, too, I suppose," she says with a sigh.

I turn away from her again. I am so afraid. I should be used to this by now.

I turn my fear into one pure, intelligent motion and finger one by one the tiny clasps at the back of her neck, lifting the gaudy neckpieces away from her, taking the feathers and charms, the chains, away from her chest where they weigh so heavily. I would like to pluck from her face the moody emeralds that have made her look so strange to me.

"You don't need all this, Mom."

She clings to my words like a child. I slip rings from her fingers. I gently lift her arm up and take it out of the sweater. Slowly, carefully, I undress her in the center of the station as if we were the only ones there.

"It's the Topaz Bird, isn't it?" I say to her in a whisper as I unknot the scarves at her neck and waist. We are both children now. She nods. The Topaz Bird was the creature of my bedtime stories, invented by my mother so that I might better understand her shifting moods, her inexplicable sadness or rage or joy. It had become, in the years since I was grown, our code word for when she was not feeling well.

I slide the large silver Elsa Peretti bracelet down her smooth arm. I open her purse and place the eyeglasses she wears at these times back into their leather case. She does not need glasses.

"Yes," she says and tries to smile, "the Topaz Bird." She tilts her head back and looks up at the starry green ceiling. I can see the line where her makeup ends.

"Silly," she whispers, still looking up. "Silly," she says, shaking her head miserably.

"We'll just have to put some of this away," I say, putting more and more into her enormous purse. "You don't need all this, Mom."

I look up, too, and imagine the Topaz Bird there—its terrible claws, its beak curved and sharp, its feathers brutal, sharpening into points. It grows huge. It devours mice in front of me. It lands on my mother's head like a spiked crown, drawing blood from her scalp.

"How's my makeup?" she asks. She hands me a tissue. I wipe away layers of color.

"There. There now. You look good. You look great, Mom. Everything's fine." As I speak I look down to the floor and see that hundreds of tiny gold chains encircle her ankles. I cannot control the surge of emotion that grows and breaks in me. It will not be fine.

"Mom," I say, "let me come back home with you." I have just come in by bus from a long Christmas break and am on my way back to college for the second semester. "I can take a train to school tomorrow. Really. It doesn't matter when I go."

She shakes her head tentatively at first, then decides. "No."

"Please."

"Vanessa."

I look at her hand, clenched in a fist. "No," she says, "I'm all right."

"What is it, Mom?" I ask. "What's in your hand?"

"Silly," she says, looking up to the cavernous ceiling where the Topaz Bird flies. "Silly. Silly," she says, biting her lip and trying not to cry, following my example.

She opens her hand and shows me a crumpled paper, something wounded in her palm.

"What is it, Mom? Do you want me to read it?" I ask her.

"Yes, would you?" she says, staring at my mouth, focusing hard.

I uncrumple the piece of paper. My hands are shaking. I see that it is in her handwriting. "Be careful," she whispers, "please."

I nod. For a while I simply stare at the piece of paper, looking at her handwriting, the swirls and dips, the flourishes, the looping *l*'s and *p*'s, and it gives me the courage to read. It says "New Year's Resolutions," and I cry with relief at my mother's earnest list.

"Don't cry," she says. I bite my lip and read them aloud:

1–Enjoy life more.

2–Work fewer hours. Relax more.

3–Take fewer trips/pack fewer clothes.

4–Spend more time with the children.

5–Help the unfortunate.

I laugh and laugh and she laughs with me. "They are good ones, I think," I say.

"Yes," she says, "I miss more things now," and she gazes off, lost in all that means to her.

"I like this one," she says. "Take fewer trips/pack fewer clothes. What do you think?" We try to pick up the two enormous suitcases at her sides and pretend we cannot.

"Really, Mom, how long was it you were gone for?" I ask.

"Oh, about a week, I think," she says, and we laugh.

"You're all grown up," she says, looking at me like the college student she remembers herself being. "I realize now how much living we've missed together. But for now—you'd better go—your train."

"No, Mom. I don't want to leave you."

"Vanessa, yes," she says.

"You'll need help with your suitcases," I say. I am still smiling.

She shakes her head no.

"Please go now," she says, and I recognize the tone of her voice. It means she is not going to change her mind.

"But—"

"Please go. You'll miss your train."

"I'll call you Sunday," I say.

"Oh, don't forget to call." She is taking the Elsa Peretti bracelet from her bag.

"Mom," I say, "are you all right?"

"Yes," she nods. "I'm fine."

I turn and begin to walk away from her, then turn back. "Mom!" I shout. I can't bear to say good-bye yet.

I am some distance from her. The snow presses against the high semicircular windows. I feel it hugging us, pressing us, telling us to part, parting us. Her face has changed. Her voice now, as she begins to speak, is not raised but still somehow separates itself from the noise of the station. I can hear it perfectly. She looks up at the snow, then to me. She is focused and clear now, lucid in this last moment.

"I have loved you my whole life," she says.

She lifts her beautiful braceleted arm into the air. "Go now."

She waves good-bye.

"You must never forget, Vanessa," my mother told me over and over through the years I was growing up, "that the Topaz Bird means us no harm." This is how she would always end her final story of the night just as I was falling into sleep.

"You must never forget," she would whisper, leaning over my bed as she turned out the light and covered me with night, as she kissed me hard on the forehead, "it means us no harm."

She would enter my large, odd-shaped room, sometimes ecstatic, sometimes exhausted, sometimes sad and afraid, but the story never changed and it seemed to calm her. She would rest in the telling of it. I helped her, too, I think, in my half-sleep, dreaming the bird with her, inventing it over and over, reaching for it, reaching, my whole body straining to see it.

"Only the luckiest people," she'd begin, "are born with a bird flying over their lives."

"Only the very luckiest," I'd say back to her, she leading, I following her through the story I knew by heart. She would start a sentence, and I would complete it. At times we talked together, our voices weaving in and out of each other's. We were like lovers drifting off to sleep together, whispering in the dark. I loved her voice at these times, it was so sweet and peaceful. It was the voice of an angel, the voice of a star.

"Only the luckiest people are born with a bird flying over their lives. It's no ordinary bird, mind you," she'd smile.

"It's not a green parrot," I said.

"Oh, no!" she said. "Not a green parrot."

"It's not a cardinal."

"It's not a dove either. It's not . . ."

"A pink flamingo," I'd say.

"Or a toucan," my mother would say.

"No, it's not a toucan."

"It's more beautiful . . ." My mother closed her eyes. "It's even more beautiful than a swan."

Her golden robe shone in the dark room. She was asking me to see the Topaz Bird with her. But I could not imagine a more exotic creature than my mother. I would have been happy to have lived in a world defined solely by the parameters of her arms, to have sunk into her large, soothing voice and stayed there, safe in her dark love, but even before I could get comfortable in her lap she had begun telling the story and pointing my head away from her, asking me to look upward, to grow wings though I had just barely learned to walk.

"It's even more beautiful than a swan," we said in unison. "I call it the Topaz Bird," she sighed. "A bird that shines like topaz. A bird so beautiful that you scarcely can bear to look at it." I knew what my mother meant. I felt I could barely look at her straight on, most times.

"But when you do, once you finally get the courage, your eyes begin to shine, bright, bright."

"To become the Topaz Bird somehow," I said, pausing for a moment trying to picture this. "It has the most magnificent—"

"Plumage," my mother said. I loved the way she said plumage, the beautiful mouth she made for the word plumage.

"Plumage," I said, trying to imitate her.

"And you must follow it—wherever it takes you. You must not be afraid," she whispered. "It means us no harm."

I love her in the deepest cells of my sleep. I feel her warm breath as I descend into sleep and hear her voice long after she has left the room. The Topaz Bird sings in her throat. The Topaz Bird flies from her mouth. I could almost see it those nights. There was such longing there in the dark.

I would love to follow that bird through my moody half-sleep. "My precious, precious," I would say, reaching, straining.

She kisses me on the forehead and shuts off the light. I have never seen the Topaz Bird but I feel that something of it forms with the part of my mother I keep after she has left the room—her smell on me still, her kiss resting on my forehead. Each night, I take the simple, strange story into sleep and dream it.

I will find that precious bird. I build a nest in my ear for it. I prepare a place. I make a circle of my forefinger and thumb and fill it with something soft. I open the palm of my hand and offer it.

Oh, if I saw that bird—

Oh, if I saw that bird I would not hesitate to follow. The kiss lingers . . .

Though I am nineteen years old now, I have never seen that precious bird, but the kiss lingers. "Mom," I say.

She is so far away.

Mother, here are the parts of the story you forgot to tell, the parts of the story I learned in my sleep.

When the Topaz Bird finally appeared after hundreds of years, your mother recognized it, even before opening her pale eyes, and through the layers of her fatigue she let out a small cry. Her family had waited so long and intently for that mythic creature to appear again that she could hardly fail to see it, even in the dark, even through her lidded eyes, as it flew past the hospital window at the hour her first child was born.

The doctors had advised my grandmother, a young woman with a rheumatic heart, not a grandmother at all then, not to have children; the consequences would be grave. But, holding in her arms her healthy baby, which felt quite strong, she knew it had been the right thing. "I will have children," she had told the doctors, "there is nothing you can do about it." The bird flew by again. She opened her eyes. She saw only a blur but she knew what it was, and the pain from childbirth was mingled with an enormous joy. So the bird was the Bird of Luck, she thought, and of Good Health.

She heard its song. No one as far as she could remember, not even George, had ever mentioned its song. She wondered whether anyone had ever heard it before. She did not know if it was a happy song or a sad song—that was the way she was accustomed to thinking—but its beauty brought tears to her eyes, and she would write in her diary often of the haunting melody that followed her up and down the sloping terrain of her illness.

As she sat up in the white bed holding her daughter close, the melody grew louder. She struggled to get up so that she might see the bird clearly at last. When she finally reached the window and looked out into the snow, she gasped, for she saw exactly what she had pictured since she had first heard the story as a little girl. It was perched on the bare branch of a chestnut tree. It was tiny, tiny, a sort of hummingbird, she thought, with a few crimson feathers, green at the throat, and possessing an all-over topaz glow. It *was* beautiful, even more beautiful than they had said, and the young mother and her daughter stood drenched in its magnificent light.

Grandma Alice knew right away that her life was a bordering life, that the bird was not really hers to see, and she wondered, looking at it, what transformations the Topaz Bird had made on that journey from the branch of the chestnut tree to her brain. She was aware that she was probably not seeing it clearly. She held her daughter up to the glow and watched her new eyes turn from pale blue to violet to deep blue to turquoise then back to pale blue again. What did the bird, here on this first day of March, mean for her sweet, smiling little girl?

She held my mother at the window for what seemed a long time. The Topaz Bird continued to sing and did not move from the tree, and my grandmother, too, standing in the brilliant light, felt only an hour old. She felt as if the world were only beginning for her, too. In fact my grandmother *was* entering a new stage as she stood before the Topaz Bird, having brought it back, after so long, with her daughter's birth: it was the beginning of the end of her life.

Chased back to bed by the nurses, the Topaz Bird flown off, the baby back in the nursery, my grandmother had a chance to think now for the first time about what was happening. There, as she drifted in and out of sleep, each member of the Hauser family appeared before her, perfectly clear against the hospital white. So the dead are even more detailed in appearance than the living, she sighed, looking at the knotted hands, counting the wrinkles, noting the many tones that made up the color of hair. She felt exhausted.

They were still searching for the Topaz Bird as she conjured them. Since the reunion in 1900 when they were alerted of the bird's existence, each Hauser had searched for it, dreamt of it, convinced they would see it if they were diligent, patient. In the middle of many nights they had opened their eyes, positive that the bird would be there, only to see empty space, a straight-backed chair, a bowl of fruit. A few had written through the years of a glowing feeling, a sudden flush on their faces, a strange fluttering in their chests, the bird apparently caught in the human rib cage with no way out.

I imagine my grandmother must have felt the Topaz Bird near her her whole life, that presence having grown stronger and stronger with each month of pregnancy. Perhaps it was the Bird of Death after all, she thought through those months, as the doctors had said. But no, now she saw that it was not. Her baby was healthy and she felt fine.

Whatever it meant, she had prepared for it, knowing it was getting closer and closer, and so she was not surprised to see it at the birth of her daughter Christine. Yet despite her preparation, she was frightened a little, she didn't know why, and she wrote later in her journal of that fear. What did it mean for her perfect, healthy daughter? In the family folklore the bird was rumored to be the Luminous Bird of Genius.

In the long history of the Hauser family the Topaz Bird had been sighted only twice. The first time was in Germany by George Hauser, a pianist and composer. He had had a glimpse of it, the story goes, while out for his mid-morning walk. "A piece has broken off the sun and taken the shape of a bird," he told his wife Hannah, breathlessly, upon his return. But at this point Hannah was no longer a good listener. She shook her head; her large arms shook as she kneaded the bread. So I have married a crazy man, she thought. This vision of a bird only reinforced what she already knew. On endless staves he furiously wrote notes, but what came out was not music, everyone agreed about that. What came out, despite all the notes he wrote, the neat clefs, the rests, was not music. It was noise, anarchy. He looked so much like a composer as he wrote. Oh, that was the worst part; he looked so serious, so concen-trated, so wrapped in it, but it was all nonsense. There was no discernible order. Everyone said so. And order was everything in Germany in those days.

What he heard no one else would hear for hundreds and hundreds of years.

The second time the Topaz Bird had been seen was in 1803 when Eva Hauser saw it one afternoon on the bough of a pear tree in Cummington, Massachu-setts. Later, in her diary, she wrote, "All my art has been an attempt to recap-ture one image, that of a topaz bird I saw for one hour outside my house as a child. It refreshes me to think about and urges me on. Though I am already forty-five, my eyesight is still good and I have not given up the hope of seeing it once more." She wrote this in 1837, having failed to make the gold leaf that would perhaps have approximated that vision. "It would have been easy to confuse it with the light of the sun and to have shaded my eyes or looked away, but it was a bird and I could not take my eyes from it."

In the last years of her life, Eva, in an attempt to capture the Topaz Bird's magnificent flight, found it necessary to add to her paintings snippets of paper, foreign stamps, pictures from tobacco packages, wood fragments, bits of glass, broken plates, photographs. "The audacity," people said, "the audacity of this Eva Hauser." But the women of the sewing circle gathering each week to make patchwork quilts were gentler; they felt sorry for Eva. "Let her be," they whispered to their families, "let her just be." She was mad, they knew, to see things that way, but "let her be." And so they did. Eva was found dead in 1865, dried flowers, French stamps, corn husks, yarn, and scraps of paper surrounding her on the bed.

In the next century both Eva and George were treated more seriously by a nephew, Karl, who was studying the Hauser history. "It shall be very significant indeed," he said, at a family gathering in 1900, "whoever sees the Topaz Bird next. It shall be very significant. This time we will know not to ridicule or humiliate. We know more now."

So generation after generation of Hausers began to look into the air. People mistook them for snobs because their heads were always raised, but what they were looking for, of course, was that elusive bird. The tale was passed from father to son, mother to daughter. Filtered through time and various personalities, the interpretation changed. "It is the Bird of Truth and Light," one man said. "It is the Bird of Supreme Sacrifice." "The Bird of Insight." "When it returns, it will be the Bird of Ultimate Pleasure." During World War II, the Hausers, now real Americans, decided it was the Bird of Absolute Power, the Bird to Wipe Out Hitler. "No, it is the Bird of Peace," another said.

Unbeknownst to them, the Topaz Bird was in Paterson, New Jersey, following a small girl as she went to school.

And so my Grandma Alice, though not surprised to see the bird outside her hospital window, must have smiled to herself, thinking of her family through time. And it must have occurred to her, remembering George and Eva, that they had only seen the bird for a short time, a moment really, and here it had lingered already all afternoon around her sweet but rather ordinary daughter. What could this mean, she wondered that night, as the nurse brought her baby to her. She held her tightly and felt her own heart give way. She would not live to read a single poem of her daughter's or to find out what the Topaz Bird really meant.

What she knew was that the bird that followed my mother was precious.

I hope my young grandmother could fall a bit easier into death knowing that this special bird, years in forming, would always be with my mother. I hope she knew that it meant her no harm.

It was the Bird of Genius, Grandma Alice.

The wild, brilliant Bird of Imagination.

The Bird of Great Invention.

Invention was everything to my mother and in that quiet, dark house I too learned how to fill empty space and dispel silence.

In that house where she was so often absent, I learned how to conjure her back a little. Silence would give way to footsteps, shadows would lighten, and she would come a bit closer. I could see her stepping momentarily into light; I could see her gray gaze and the beautiful bone structure of her face. "Mother," I would say, and she would turn to reveal the tendons in her neck or a curl that encircled her ear. I would see some familiar motion of hers and it would become new. I would see something more than I had before and I would understand her a little better.

I learned to halve the distance, then make smaller divisions. I might suddenly smell rain though the day was sunny, feel the texture of her hair, wild in such humidity, or watch her walk in moonlight as she followed a premonition, a strand of long hair in the rain, a scrap of voice, a melody, down a dark street in Nice.

And in that house Father, who was always so silent, would come clearer, too. I could invent the stories behind his cloudy glances, the hesitations in his speech. I could understand his hands finally, the mysterious way they moved from object to object but never landed. I could remember for him what he said he could not. I could easily fathom the great depths of his love for my mother and his loneliness because of it. Longing in me took shapes, but I think my father saw nothing when my mother was away—or what I imagine nothing to be: fields and fields of black or dark green or blue.

I was never lonely. In my house the darkness always gave way.

In my house, Grandma Alice is alive. She grows old. She has a long gray braid down her back. She has trouble reading the fine print. She watches my mother and me out in the garden. She sits with me on the porch and tells me the story of the Topaz Bird. She hugs me with her woolen arms. She never tires. "Tell me about Eva again," I beg, and she always does.

My house whirls and whirls with mist and moonlight and lovers. On hot summer nights a handsome stranger from Spain plays the guitar and a slow fan turns within me.

In my house there are dresses of twilight, and snowstorms, and towers and castles, and music and laughter.

In my house there are intricate scenarios. I have seen a beautiful bride whispering her marriage vows in the white curtains that flutter in the wind. I have seen the groom in the dark door step forward, then back. In my house there are racehorses and flowers and satin and my mother is a little girl there, drifting off to sleep, dreaming of flowers and horses.

In my house the sun constructs perfect golden rectangles on the ceiling; they clang together, making lovely music. In my house there is always music: Mozart and Vivaldi and Bach.

And in my house there is order. In my house there is sense. In my house the father who is so remote smiles finally, as the crime he has brooded over for years, the crime he has carefully outlined on the table with his finger, finally falls into place. Everything has an explanation, a reason. Why the mother seems always to be leaving for France becomes clear.

In my house I can hear my grandfather two states away walking on the crackling earth, listening for water. In my house I can hear a clock ticking. It grows louder and louder and larger and larger as she stands under it, bathed in apricot light. In my house I hear her bracelets clinking; I hear the bright laughter of two women.

I move slowly through these fall days. In my heavy house, which I carry on my back like a turtle, a dark-eyed woman weeps for someone who is permanently lost to her.

But they are not lost to me. In my house, which is vibrant and alive, my Grandma Alice does not die before I am born. In my house there is love and there is mystery and there is longing. In my house my mother is a little girl, a college student, a woman reclining on a pink couch, sipping a cool drink and reading the poems of Rainer Maria Rilke.

In my house there are love and violence and wonder—full orchestras, huge chandeliers, and champagne. In my house she is always there, next to me.

My mother is in a black cocktail dress and pearls. It must be about 1960. She twists the black phone cord in her hand. She is so beautiful standing there in the hallway, talking in French to the woman across the ocean before she leaves for the party.

He lives in another country but it doesn't matter, we see each other often—he wants me so much. No matter what the weather, how difficult the trip, the number of stops, the price of the fare, somehow he always gets to me. I know this and so do not worry. For coming such a long way, he is reliable, hardly ever late; pure desire keeps him from harm as he races through the city streets to me, asking directions in broken English if he must.

He glides into the room as if he hears music, Jacques Brel perhaps or Piaf. His black beret, the baguette under his arm, these let me know that tonight the distance he has come from is named France.

He pours two glasses of wine—Beaujolais-Villages. He closes his eyes, breathes me in. I lower my mouth; this wine, this music, this man—it is all perfect. He tears the bread. "Le beurre," he says, "la confiture."

We gaze at each other and our hunger grows. Outside it has begun to rain. There is a swell of music. He takes out a package of Gauloises; I recognize the light blue color, the wings on the package. Before he opens them our clothes are off. Our bodies are lovely—all perfect, graceful arcs. We perform our slow sexual ballet flawlessly, mouth to mouth to mouth. Afterwards we smoke a cigarette and it is piano music we hear now, Chopin or Poulenc. In his face I detect some waywardness. The camera that records our every move pulls closer. It means he will die soon. It brings further romance, an urgency to our next embrace when it comes, a meaning to the silence. I close my eyes, naked, twisted in the perfumed sheets. In a few hours he will be returning to a country I cannot really picture at all—mythic, far away, filled with beautiful women, I suppose.

"It's just like a film," I whisper: the rain, the wine, the stranger from France. "Le cinéma," he says. His voice is deep and tragic. "Au revoir, je t'aime," I say, as he slowly puts on his clothes and I look on, smoking his last cigarette.

"Au revoir," he sighs. A tear falls from the corner of my eye. Then the final credits.

Sometimes I will notice, while sitting in the kitchen eating lunch, that the trees outside the window are moving, slowly at first and then more and more quickly. By now I recognize this movement—it is a ride I love: the linen; the silver; this most elegant of dining cars; the scent of cologne, of fresh flowers;

the clinking of fine china, of crystal; the pale rose in the pewter vase; chicken in wine with mushrooms; the French countryside.

"You must watch for small bones," the handsome waiter whispers in my ear, and I can feel his whisper lingering somewhere near my throat as he pours me a glass of champagne.

"Champagne in the afternoon makes me dizzy," I smile. A few tables over, two women in hats begin to blur. "Meet me in the back car in five minutes," he says, his body covering mine in shadow.

"Vanessa," my brother shouts, finishing his lunch next to me. "Vanessa." The man in white in the back car lights a cigarette from the blue-winged package. "Vanessa, come back," Fletcher says.

Yes, it is probably best—leave him there for a while, smiling, loosening his tie in the last car.

"Are you dreaming again?"

I watch the landscape slow down outside the window, then stop.

"What is it?" I ask.

"Are you dreaming again?" Fletcher says.

"Do you think Mom will ever take me to France with her?" I ask Fletcher, who smiles, happy to be able to answer anything for anyone.

"Yes, I do," he says. "Sure. Why not?"

My father walks into the kitchen carrying an empty soup bowl.

"Do you think Mom will ever take me to France with her, Dad?" I ask.

He runs his hand along a copper pot that glints in the half-light.

"Oh, probably," he says finally. "Someday," he sighs.

My father is far away. His silence is so deep and seductive that it seems he has had to travel a great distance to the surface to form even these few words. He does not buoy up to the surface like a swimmer or some other temporary guest of water. His life is down there—in deep blue, in gray, in green, in tangled plants, in dim light.

Still, I would like to rescue him. I put on a black bathing suit. A silver whistle hangs around my neck. My eyes are clear and focused, my body is muscled, much stronger than my ordinary body, set for the task.

I would like to dredge him up from those depths, breathe my life into him, beach him on some even shore. I dive once, twice, hold his head in the air, push water from his lungs.

He turns on the faucet and submerges his soup bowl in warm water. "How about a movie?" he asks in his dreamy, underwater way. He is back in the air again. I have succeeded in some small way, I think.

"Sure," my brother and I say in unison. "What movie?" My father shrugs. "Whatever you like," he smiles.

Father's love of the movies always reassured us; it made him seem like other fathers to us.

"Oh, any movie will do," he says gently, helping us on with our coats. But I wondered a little, as we drove into the afternoon without any idea of where we were going or what time it was, whether even the movies meant something different to Father than they did to us.

Grace Kelly turns to say good night to Cary Grant at her hotel room. A faint smile drifts across her face and she slides her pale arms around his neck.

My father gasps in the front row and sinks into his plush, red seat in the tiny theater at the edge of campus in Princeton, New Jersey. He looks through his fingers as she presses her mouth to his.

I imagine my father spent many afternoons peering through his fingers, marveling at the great and not so great movies of the 1950s in that dingy theater with its lobby of fake ferns, its big old stage, its touches of gold and brocade. Bits of plaster and paint would fall into his dark hair from the ceiling, and, looking up, he would see on either side of the stage an artist's version of royal boxes, made from plasterboard, red painted curtains pulled back to reveal an attentive king and queen.

"What a dive, Louie," my father must have said affectionately to the apathetic owner, wiping what he imagined was the dust of centuries from Louie's bald head, pulling candy wrappers and gum from the bottoms of his own shoes. "What a dive."

Dive or not, my father never missed a movie and indeed saw most of them at least twice. I can imagine him sitting alone in the front row, devouring popcorn and waiting for the masks, one of tragedy and one of comedy, pinned to the musty velvet curtain, to part and the screen to light up. In that final second before the first reel began, he must have felt a small thrill in the pitch black, his whole body weightless with anticipation. There were newsreels then, and before *To Catch a Thief* or *The Country Girl* he could watch his lovely Grace Kelly of Philadelphia, Pennsylvania, in real life, on the arm of Clark Gable or Oleg Cassini. "Oleg," he thought, chuckling to himself, "what a great name." He watched as she took the arm of Prince Rainier III of Monaco. My father witnessed it all. He saw Rainier visit Grace's home. He saw the Kelly family, blond and athletic, smiling and waving for the camera, Grace off to one side, unlike them, distant and mysterious. He watched as tons of flowers rained down on her from Aristotle Onassis's private plane as she stepped from an ocean liner onto Rainier's yacht.

My father sighs. Her eyes are shaded by dark glasses. She is a million miles away, he thinks, walking down the aisle to the popcorn stand as Khrushchev and Eisenhower eye each other on the screen.

My father was probably not a very popular person at Princeton. He had many annoying qualities even then. He studied little and did exceptionally well, which his classmates found distressing, especially those sons of Princeton alumni who had to struggle to keep up or lose their lives. My father was also exceedingly modest about his achievements, and his modesty irked them.

He never really fit in anywhere. He was not a pusher, a striver, a tweed bag, a jock, or a lounge lizard. He was not even my father yet, or my mother's husband. He did not join clubs. He would not give the password. He would not shake secret handshakes. He never went to a football game. He never sang the Princeton song or wore a black and orange scarf. He never pinned a pennant on his wall or gave a stuffed Princeton tiger to a woman. Women liked him for no reason, certainly through no effort on his part. They must have thought him dark and romantic. They liked him even despite the vague smell of popcorn and Baby Ruths that seemed to follow him everywhere. But my father had little interest in real-life women; after all those years in the front row, they must have seemed too small to him.

I can imagine my father sitting by himself in front of a large black-and-white television in his dorm, watching Grace Kelly the film star become Princess Grace of Monaco. "She will be a princess twice, a duchess four times, nine times a baroness, eight times a countess," the TV commentator says. "However, since a majority of the prince's domain now exists in name only, her kingdom in reality is a small one, covering three towns and 22,000 people."

The day before, the civil ceremony was held in the sixteenth-century throne room of the palace. "Both were tense and grim faced," the smirking newsman reports, "and there was no hint of a smile through the half-hour ceremony. Twice Miss Kelly looked distraughtly at Rainier but he did not look back. He fidgeted in his chair, put a finger to his lips, or twiddled his thumbs." My father shakes his head at this.

The camera scans the church. The guests are seated. "There's Ava Gardner!" my father says to no one at all, pointing to a dot on the screen.

The prince enters, all sashes and medals; the music begins: the fifty-pipe organ, the orchestra, the choir. A chill goes up my father's back. He can feel her standing at the edge of the screen. She appears. She walks, slowly, slowly down the aisle. She is even more beautiful than in the movies. He closes his eyes and becomes the prince. She takes his arm. "Oui, Monsignor," she says when the marriage vows are exchanged.

"Oui, Monsignor," a classmate says who has just entered the room.

"Oui, oui! Monsignor!" another boy says with lust, "ah, oui!"

"There she is," Joel laughs, "the Queen of the Slot Machines!"

"Shh," my father says.

"Oh, come on," Teddy says.

There is some tension, a friction in the room that lets my father know, without taking his eyes from the screen, that the weekend must be nearing. There is a restless quality among his classmates. They shift their weight from one foot to the other as they look at the TV with my father.

"Are you ready?" they ask.

"What?"

"We're going to Vassar," Joel says, "don't you remember?"

"Oh, sure. Sure," my father says, a little dazed, looking up to see them with their overnight bags in hand, Princeton sweaters blazing. "Yeah, sure."

"Well then, hurry up, Turin. We're leaving in five minutes."

"I think I'll stay here," my father says.

"All right, we're leaving in ten minutes. Come on, Turin."

There is something in their syncopated marchlike voices that my father likes. "OK, all right," he says. They're funny, my father thinks. Everything they say sounds like a cheer.

He notices that Joel is wearing a raccoon coat though it is April and much too warm.

"What's that animal on your back?" my father asks Joel, the chubby one.

"Turin, I'm driving, so you'd better be decent to me," Joel says.

"Sure," my father says. "It was only a joke, Joel, only a joke." As long as I have known him, my father has never been funny.

"You're a real winner, Turin, you know that."

My father smiles, nodding. He never really listens much to what anyone says. My brother and I used to catch him, nodding his head and smiling, "Sure," when some more intricate answer was called for. "Sorry," he'd say in his dim way when he realized he had been caught. "Sorry. What did you kids want?"

My father is lost in the royal wedding. Walking to Joel's Buick, he sees himself in a tuxedo gliding toward a dove-gray limousine. With his gloved hands, he makes one elegant motion with his arm, allowing the others into the car before him.

"Turin, be real," Teddy says, carrying his math books under his arm, planning to get my father to tutor him in the car. This is probably why my father was invited in the first place.

"It's just common sense," my father will say somewhere on the New Jersey Turnpike. "This cancels out y, x is raised to the third power, and then it reduces on both sides, so $x = 3t - 1$. Get it?"

Though my father has taken just the minimum requirements in math, it is his true strength. He seems not even to lift the pencil from the page as he solves the problems for Teddy.

Over the car radio he hears more details of the wedding. He closes his eyes. The boys sing. My father seems to be dozing.

―――――――――

Christine pads down to the TV room in her slippers and bathrobe; Sabine sits smoking a cigarette and looking out the window, her feet up on the windowsill. "How is your hair doing?" Sabine asks, not turning around—she does not have to—she knows my mother's walk, her smell, the patterns of her breath by heart.

"All right, I suppose," my mother says, touching the hard, pink rollers.

My mother sits down, her hands deep in her terry-cloth robe.

"All this fuss, Sabine," she sighs. "Why, hmm? Pourquoi?"

She watches the TV screen dully as President Eisenhower throws out the first baseball of the 1956 season.

The camera angle changes. It's the wedding. "Fifteen hundred newsmen have gathered," the TV broadcaster says soberly, "substantially more than the number that converged on Geneva last summer when four heads of state were the center of world interest." Sabine laughs with glee. One French magazine has twenty-nine reporters on the story. There are five hundred photographers.

"After three continuous days of rain in Monaco, there is a warm sun today," one reporter whispers, as if it were necessary to whisper, as if the event required hushed, religious tones.

I imagine my mother gets closer to the set at the moment when Grace walks down the long aisle, the better to see her dress.

"Designed in Hollywood, a fact that has Paris couturiers sniffing," the reporter whispers, "it has a bodice of rare rose-point lace selected for its flower-and-wheat pattern, a full silk skirt and silk cummerbund. The net veil is embroidered with rose-point lace and reembroidered with thousands of tiny pearls. The skirt is fastened in the back with three bows. The back flares out to give a fan-shaped effect."

Grace goes to her place before the white marble altar. Despite the microphones and eighty loudspeakers, no one hears her pronounce her marriage vows. "Oui, Monsignor," is all they hear. "Oui, Monsignor."

Rainier has trouble getting the gold band past the knuckle of his bride's finger. She helps him with it.

The next scene is the couple riding through the streets in an open limousine. "The sun was shining in Monaco," the newscaster tells us, "although its warmth was tempered by a brisk wind."

They halt before the Chapel of Ste. Dévote, Monaco's patron saint, where the princess places her bouquet of lilies of the valley at the bare feet of the statue. She makes the sign of the cross and turns.

"La Côte d'Azur!" Sabine says excitedly, like a child.

My mother studies the scene closely, the too-bright sun, the too-perfect waves. She tilts her head. She can't decide what's wrong. She looks down at her hands. She looks back up at the screen.

"She will never be happy," my mother says quietly, and Sabine for no reason gets up and kisses my mother on the cheek. What does she see, Sabine wonders?

"Ah! Time to take out the rollers," she says.

"Why don't you come with me?" my mother asks her.

Sabine just laughs, tosses her pretty head, and takes my mother's hand. "And your nails! It's getting late! Vas-y, vas-y!"

They have painted their room, against the rules, pink. It is Sabine's favorite color. On the wall hang two large Vassar pennants, rose letters on a gray field. "The rosy dawning of women's education pushing through all that gray of the past—I like that," Sabine had said, hanging the pennants up at the beginning of the year after they had finished their painting.

Now, as Sabine shapes and polishes each one of my mother's nails, muttering about how neglected her hands are and how could anyone let them get that way, my mother thinks of the last time she dressed up. She had worn the same dress she would wear this night; it was a sort of mauve color with two long streamers tacked to the shoulders that flowed behind her. Though people always told her how beautiful she looked in it, she felt they were overcompensating to cover their alarm at the actual hideousness of the dress. My mother, a full-scholarship student, did not have money for dresses and could not fit into any of Sabine's, who was only five-foot-three and small boned. Deep down, my mother must have known that whatever she wore she would be beautiful; as much as she tried through the years to overlook that fact, it was not possible.

Sabine knows. Looking at my mother's sculpted features as she combs out her hair, she says, "You will be the belle of the ball. Isn't that what they say? The belle of the ball?" My mother smiles her reluctant, nervous smile and nods.

The last time they dressed up was in winter when my mother got the letter from the *Paris Review* saying that her poem had been accepted for publication. It was her first. She was just twenty years old. Years later, because of my mother's poem, that issue would sell for hundreds of dollars. That night, having drunk much champagne, which they were not used to, they ended up shedding their chiffon, which my mother said they looked absolutely ridiculous in anyway, and they ran naked, in honor of Paris, in the snow in the Vassar Quad.

"The *Paris Review*!" my mother screamed.

"How perfect!" Sabine said. "It's symbolic. Don't you see?" she said, giggling. "We French know what's good!"

"I'm *trying* to study," someone shouted from the third floor of Lathrop, clearly not having looked out the window to see the two nude nymphs.

My mother composed herself. "I can only say that I am stunned—but do graciously accept—the Nobel Prize." She was freezing and giddy.

Sabine made a large snowball and handed it to her. "L'Académie Française hails you as a genius. Incroyable!" My mother takes it, curtsies, and they both fall into the snow, shaking not from the cold, she thought, but from something else.

She could have lain there in the snow forever, looking up at the billions of stars, listening to Sabine singing "Un flambeau, Jeannette, Isabelle." "The next Edith Piaf," my mother shouted, and Sabine got up and in her big voice began to sing "Je ne regrette rien" loud enough to call the attention of the security guard.

"Quel dommage," Sabine cried, and the two bluish, naked girls were brought to the infirmary by a blushing elderly man in full uniform. My mother recited her published poem for the young nurse, and she in turn promised she would not tell anyone else of the incident, though they were lucky to be alive, she quickly added.

My mother had supposed the dress, left in the snow, was ruined, but now, stepping into it this night before the Vassar/Princeton mixer, she thinks it looks as if she has never lain in the snow, never drunk champagne, never sung French songs with Sabine.

"I just don't know about all of this," my mother says, feeling it to be a mistake as soon as she leaves the room for the dance. Even as she walks forward down the path, she is stepping inward and bowing her head in shadow.

My father might have missed my mother completely, standing against the wall, partially hidden by two larger, more aggressive members of the senior class, had he not been primed to see her, and in fact, had he not been actually looking for her. Grace, the wedding, the ocean in Monaco had buoyed him forward. Joel's filthy car plastered with Princeton stickers had become the leading limousine in the entourage, and that evening he was a prince in a great ballroom, his French was impeccable, his shoes shone, his gait was confident. He did not hesitate when he saw her.

"God, what's Turin doing?" one of his classmates says, as he sees him gliding toward my mother, the most beautiful woman any of them had ever seen.

"She was *more* beautiful than Grace Kelly," my father told me once, and there was a thrill in his voice still. As he approaches her, she turns her head to the side and he sees that classic, timeless profile. His eyes haze over. He does not dare look at her straight on, he thinks. He does not dare focus on such beauty; it is too much to bear.

"Would you like to dance?" he asks, concentrating on a space somewhere over her left shoulder. He cannot look directly into her eyes; it would be too dangerous. She would disappear, he thinks, be gone forever after one dance; he has to be careful, to watch out, for those eyes, that face could return over and over to haunt him long after she has left.

"Yes, I'd like to dance," my mother says quietly, looking at this impossibly tall, skinny man in front of her.

Through the entire first dance and then through the second and third, my father talks continuously and very quickly and still looks over her shoulder, not at her, though as the night progresses he moves his gaze slowly from over her shoulder to her actual shoulder, and then to her neck, and then to the top of her head. He closes his eyes and the dream presses close to his new suit.

He saved all his money to buy the suit he is wearing. He saw it advertised in the *New York Times* for sixty-nine dollars at Saks Fifth Avenue, and, touching it on the page, he felt as if it already belonged to him. It was his prized possession—the famous gray flannel suit Gregory Peck had worn in *The Man in the Gray Flannel Suit*, so the advertisement said. And as my mother, more beautiful than Grace Kelly, placed her silky head on my father's chest, he must have felt as if this indeed were a movie. He tries to think of the gestures of his favorite film stars but he cannot think of one. And so he keeps talking.

"He was charming," my mother told me of that night, "and more nervous than I."

It must have been hard for my father to detect any nervousness at all in my mother, for she had an innate composure and a grace that masked any uncertainty. He kept talking.

"What the hell is Turin talking about?" Joel asks Teddy. "He hasn't shut his mouth for one second."

"I've got two tickets to this new play on Broadway," my father says. "'A tragicomedy in two acts,' it's called. Would you like to go?"

"Why, yes, I suppose," my mother says softly. "Yes."

"He's an Irish writer. Lived in Paris for years as secretary to James Joyce. Bert Lahr and E. G. Marshall are in it."

"Sounds good," my mother says.

"Brooks Atkinson reviewed it in the *Times* and described it as 'a puzzlement,' a 'mystery wrapped in an enigma.'"

"Yes, yes," my mother thinks to herself.

"I was planning on going alone. I buy two tickets when I have the money because I like to have an empty seat next to me, but, well, surely you'd be much better than an empty seat."

"Well, if you're sure," my mother says, smiling.

Already my father is cultivating his numerous eccentricities, watering them, feeding them, making room for them, so that by the time I knew him they were enormous and in full, brilliant flower.

I bet my mother liked *Waiting for Godot*. I'm sure she liked the idea that my father went to plays at all—daring plays, "mysteries wrapped in enigmas." He must have seemed risky to her, exciting and intelligent and also quite handsome in his gray flannel suit—the opposite of most of the other men she had met, the presidential cabinet members and investment bankers and other miscellaneous shareholders of the future.

I hope they were happy that weekend, against that elegant backdrop of ivy and dark wood and mountains, with less than a month left until their graduation.

They dance together the rest of the night, and when my father finally looks at her full face, he is silenced by what he sees and hardly speaks at all again after that.

They must have looked lovely together as they swirled around the center of the dance floor for all to see.

"Look, Turin's stopped talking," Teddy says to Joel, and they shrug.

My father becomes even more lost as he hugs my mother and they listen to the silence outside, alone during the band's break, standing precariously on the verge of their adult lives.

The band returns for one final song. And yes, my parents indeed look lovely together—like figures of marzipan poised on the top of a wedding cake. As the heat rises, my father's new jacket blurs slightly. He seems to be melting into my mother's arms. He breathes one last deep breath and looks for the first time directly into her bottomless blue eyes. She takes him in and he holds on tightly, as the wafer-thin dance floor slowly begins to spin.

A few notes of the guitar—the bass—my father gets up, a small flurry of motion. He smiles, swings back and forth on his heels, snaps his fingers: a trumpet, snare drum. He starts to sing with Billie Holiday.

"The way you wear your hat," and he gestures to his head.

"The way you sip your tea," and he picks up an invisible cup, his pinkie in the air.

A tinkling of piano.

"The memory of all that"—and extends his arms—"no, no, they can't take that away from me"—and brings his arms to his chest.

He does a little soft-shoe on the deck of the ship. The first touches of silver gray at his temples shine in the moonlight.

"No, they can't take that away from me."

Sometimes, to get our father to speak, we would invent homework assignments in which it was necessary for him to answer questions. This to us seemed the ultimate in legitimacy, and we could not imagine how even our father could refuse under these circumstances to speak. We could not picture him standing like some fullback in the way of our educational progress. Surely, we reasoned, Father remembered the importance of homework. There were some things no one forgot.

We were wildly, obsessively interested in the things he would not talk about and, while at times I enjoyed imagining what he might be thinking as he drew lines on graph paper or lay on the floor staring at the ceiling, some things we wanted—needed—real answers to.

"Sit down, Daddy," we'd begin. "There's something we've got to ask you."

"It's important," Fletcher would say.

"Sit down, it's for school." Father seemed impatient. He smiled a little but we didn't know why. Fletcher looked behind me to see if someone else had entered the room. My father's preoccupied look always alarmed him.

"We'll *fail* if you don't help us," Fletcher said, and I knocked him with my elbow. The word *fail*, a word meant to be saved for the final summation, the best word we had, slipped out early and seemed to have no effect on him at all.

"Well, if you want the truth," I said calmly, "we may not get into college if we don't hand in this homework. That's how important it is."

My father must have chuckled slightly at this point because we weren't anywhere near college age yet. I think I was in sixth grade that year, Fletcher was in fifth. I wonder if he detected that the whole assignment had been a fabrication. I think he must have. I hope he did.

"We need to know our family history," we explained, "you know, all about the relatives, who they were, what they were like, if they had a job, what it was," we said as casually as we could. "Information. We need information."

"Make up whatever you like," he said. "Really, I don't mind." He was smiling.

Fletcher was already exasperated. "But we need the truth, Dad," he said, "or we'll fail." There was that word again. "We're serious."

My father put on his coat. "I think I'll go for a walk, children. Please," he said absently, patting our heads.

"Come on, you can tell us," we said in our friendly way, as Father knotted his plaid scarf, wishing, I think, that he had a dog he might call to his lonely side.

"What's the secret?" we yelled to him out the front door.

"Yeah, what's the big deal?" we shouted, and our voices seemed to echo against his receding body.

"Hey, you can tell *us*!" Fletcher said, but Father, a brisk walker, could not possibly have heard him. Already he was far down the hill, out of reach of our voices.

He looks to the sky, then down at his feet. He picks up a few leaves from the ground as he walks. They look to him like the hands of children, and he closes his own hand around them and crushes them.

Fletcher took out the family tree he had sent to Minnesota for. We studied it closely, each name with its own line, but finally the names were only ink on paper, they had no resonance, there was no flesh on their bones except what Fletcher and I imagined there. We stared at the page, then began our litany of questions.

"You can tell us," we said, sitting on the window ledge watching for the figure of our father to return. "Did Uncle Louie rob banks? Was Aunt Anastasia a drug addict? And Andrew here, who was he? Did he fight in the Boer War? Was he born out of wedlock? Was his real father a drunk? No, no, a man with one arm?"

"Maybe a king," I said.

"I doubt it. Father would tell us about a king."

"Right," I said, though I was not sure.

"Did Frank rape college students across the Midwest in the 1950s? Did they call him Frankie? Was Aunt Virginia institutionalized? Did she open her wrists in the bathtub? Did she leave a note? And who is this Grisetti fellow? It looks like he married his sister here," I said, pointing to a line on the chart. "He's probably a hunchback," I told Fletcher. "Look, his son only lived four years. What happened to the child? Did he wander in front of a car one day when the parents were arguing in the bedroom? What were they arguing about? Had the hunchback taken a lover? Or was it the wife who had, in some profound despair? What made them forget the child?"

We could go on and on for hours like this some days. But in the end we never felt completely satisfied. There was something missing. I would never be as good at inventing as my mother, I thought. I would never see the Topaz Bird.

The truth would be better, we thought. Inevitably though, when it came time to write my autobiography in ninth grade, mine *was* pretty good. It began:

"Aunt Anastasia, a morphine addict, looked to the sky and sighed, though her eyes were still covered by the sleeping mask she wore to bed each night. Even in complete darkness, Aunt Anastasia saw what most people never did."

I liked my autobiography but agreed with the comment scribbled in the corner by some skeptical teacher: "This is good, but it lacks authenticity." That's what all those distant family members seemed, finally, to lack. I liked Aunt Anastasia especially, but I think she came from a Bertolucci movie my father took us to one dark afternoon. They all seemed like movie characters in the end somehow—distant, too easy to love.

I suppose they will look just like everyone else when I finally see them. If they could still talk, their concerns would probably be ordinary. If they could still talk, their concerns would be of money and weather, I'm sure of it. Nothing to be frightened of, Daddy. Nothing to hide.

We are sitting in a dark room together. Outside it is always raining. We are both thinking of Mother, who is far away, but neither of us mentions her. The music seems melancholy to me. Her flight from Paris will not arrive for five days yet. He is stretched out on the couch in the dark. I am lying on the floor. Soon he will get up and begin to conduct his imaginary orchestra, so moved is he by the music. He forgets that I am in the room at all until he is back on the couch again and I speak.

"Tell me some names, Daddy," I whisper.

"Rameau," he says.
"Rameau," I say.
"Ravel," he says.
"Ravel," I say.
"Satie."
"Satie."
"Gabriel Fauré."
"Gabriel Fauré.
"Saint-Saëns."
The record ends. "Saint-Saëns," I say into the silence.

If those relatives could still talk, their concerns would be simple, Daddy. They would beg us to eat. They would tell us that everywhere there are children who are starving.

I did not mean to leave you there with the Topaz Bird flying so near, its feathers pointed, its claws so sharp. I did not mean to leave you there alone, your New Year's resolutions crumpled in your shaking hand, a pocketbook holding the whole weight of your great confusion.

After you left, Dad left, and after Dad, Fletcher, too. I never thought this would happen to us, that we would end up like this: hundreds of thousands of miles apart, flung like fish across the water, scattered like ashes.

They have already begun hanging this season's wreaths. It's hard to think of Christmas coming at all this year. You'd never know it's November, it's much too warm. Winter approaches tentatively—in a rush of cold air, a sudden chill at the back of the neck that comes from nowhere and then disappears as quickly. The last time I saw you it was January and there was snow. This year winter approaches with great awkwardness.

I would not place you in this uncertain season.

I try to picture you safe in some eternal summer—lying in a white hammock, your notebook open on your lap, above your head a slow fan blowing a cool breeze—a safe place, where a small woman brushes your beautiful hair and sings you songs and brings you tiny sandwiches to eat.

I would not place you in this dangerous city—climbing in high heels three flights to some dark hallway, or sinking into a plush rug on Madison Avenue, or crying because no taxis come.

No, somewhere you are waiting and you are safe. Martinique? Guadeloupe? Crete? Somewhere you are all right, free finally of your jewelry, free of your awful accessories—light.

What I see sometimes is my real mother looking out at me from a place where she is not crazy at all, and she talks to me. "Vanessa, don't let them put me here," she begs. But there's no convincing them. They are taking away her belt and necklaces. And we must leave her there, shivering, standing in her underwear.

From the fashion pages she reads to me of the new collections of Calvin Klein and Yves St. Laurent: the billowing sleeves, the padded shoulders, the pleated skirts. I dress her in my mind in the fashions of spring.

"And from the young designers," she reads, "three-quarter-length coats in giraffe and leopard designs and wide, western-type lizard belts. And red hats," she says, "shaped like snails!" She laughs and laughs, tilting her head back.

Although I walked through a fog of fashion, through hats and gloves, through linen, through fields of her silks, I recognized him immediately. I could not possibly have missed him; he was the man I had been looking for for so long—an enormous man, a man so large he might blot out the sun with his body, a man whose great hands might wring the world of its oceans of salty tears. Did he recognize me, too, as the person he had loved long and hard in a silent, private part of his brain? I think he did, right from the start—that was the brutal handsomeness in his face as he got closer. He knew it all: that our love was doomed and that it had been doomed from the minute we had begun to imagine each other, long ago. He stepped forward anyway and tried to forgive in advance everything he knew would happen, just as I tried, too, as he came nearer.

He sweats as he comes toward me as if it is through great fire that he walks. Still, he does not rush, he savors each slow step, and with each step I feel a rumbling in my body, a disorder. What is this disturbance, this uneasiness, not altogether unpleasurable, this feeling that there is nowhere to go, no way out? What is this surrender? He stands in front of me, not knowing either, just staring at me. Beads of sweat collect on his forehead; he wipes them away with a handkerchief.

"This mildness will kill us," he says, shaking his head, looking into the distance. He stares at a spot far off. "This haze we are forced to see everything through." His eyes return to me. He focuses in like a camera and holds me frozen in his words, his voice. I shiver.

"I have seen you here many times," he says. "I have watched you here day after day. I have spent hours and hours on trains imagining you, your life."

"I have never seen you before," I say, "I would have remembered."

"No," he says quietly, then laughs. "You could not have seen me." He laughs again. "I often imagine you are waiting for someone who will never return."

"That's not true," I say.

"I have seen you look through this station, lost in the past, no hand in the present or future. I know that look by heart. You could not have seen me through such eyes."

"I suppose you're right."

"You are waiting here for someone, for something. Am I wrong?"

I just look at him. His hands are the size of human heads. His thighs are the bodies of sleeping children.

"You never get on a train. You never rush, you move in slow motion, stand under the clock, move toward that ticket gate over there sometimes, then come back. I have invented many lives for you, made up many stories. But most of the endings are sad."

"It doesn't surprise me," I say.

"Yeah," he says, "but what you don't know, is that you can change the ending. Close up you are even more beautiful than I had imagined you would be."

I blush. I can feel his enormous body lowering onto mine, crushing me. His body could block out the sun. With his voice alone he could break apart people's thoughts, stop the flow of memory. He could turn the whole world dark.

"This mildness will kill us," he says. "November," he says, shaking his head. He lights a cigarette. The smoke does not rise. "Someone has broken your heart."

"It's a long story," I sigh.

"No," he says. The word is meant to punctuate, to put a full stop to my story. "I don't mean for you to tell me." He puts one finger to my lips. "Never tell me," he says, pressing his finger harder to my mouth.

With his first touch I begin my descent into a deep, deep valley I half hope I will not be able to rise from.

"You are one of the saddest people I have ever seen." His voice seems to waver. It has been so long since I have talked to another human being.

He speaks slowly, gently, knowing to be careful. "You are blurry with sadness," he whispers, "so passive. This face." He touches my cheek, moves slowly to my mouth where he lingers, then my chin. Softly: "Your features are lost in sorrow. You have given in and it has gladly taken you to its drowsy side."

I want him to touch me everywhere. I want his tongue to speak inside me.

His words begin to slow. His tongue grows thicker. His hands are sweating. He steps closer. He too has begun to fall. He feels this falling and allows it, following me downward into some deep sexual pit at the center of our living where there is only breathing, only blood, only sighs.

"I could love you right—"

"Please," I say.

"I've been waiting a long time for you," he says. "Come with me."

The sounds of the station have subsided. The lights seem to have dimmed. We bump into things.

"Come with me," he says.

I wait in the lobby of a hotel for him. I sit in something soft and feel the softness against my body.

"OK," he says, holding a shiny key.

Slowly we rise. In the small mirrored elevator I can feel him everywhere. The ride is seconds, hours. We step off. The hall is long and dark. The key goes into the lock. "We will make ourselves over," he says. The door opens.

The hotel room was warm. I felt dizzy, a little giddy.

"I'm going to faint," I said.

"No, no, you're not," he said, and I felt somewhat revived with his words. "Just sit down."

I sat on the bed and took off my coat and he sat in the one chair of the room, several feet away, and looked at me.

"You're trembling," I said.

"Am I? I've been waiting for you a long time," he said. He spoke very softly. "And now here you are, right within arm's reach. It's like a miracle."

I unbuttoned my shirt slowly. My breasts bloomed in front of him in the hot room. "I'm so hot," I whispered.

He closed his eyes and put his face in his hands. Finally, after what seemed a long time, he looked up slowly, careful not to move too quickly or say anything too loudly, as if I was on the verge of disappearing and this, his first look, would also be his last. If I was an apparition, then he must do nothing to dispel it from his psyche. If I was some wild animal, caught in this room, any sudden movement might frighten me. He spoke very cautiously, as if he might bruise me with his words if he were not careful. He spoke gently so that the image might hold.

"You are the anonymous woman I have seen for years." He did not take his eyes from me.

"Don't move," he said slowly. "Please don't move." He looked at my breasts as if he had not imagined that this woman would have a physical shape at all when he finally saw her—and a voice—words. "I never expected to see you," he said.

My face was flushed. The long, slow burning that had started deep within had now begun spreading from the inside out. The tips of my fingers were bright red. My eyes I knew were turning dark, dark blue.

"Please don't move," he said as he took off his shirt and his pants. He never stopped looking at me.

I shuddered to see this enormous man naked in front of me. Undressed, he seemed even larger, as if he had been in some way contained by his clothing.

"Don't be afraid," I whispered. "Don't be afraid of me."

He laughed softly.

I reached for his hand and pulled him slowly toward me.

"I've never seen a woman like you before," he said, his voice barely controlled. "I never thought—"

I guided his huge hand onto my breasts. A moan that had been stored for centuries in the darkest part of my body finally came into my throat. He looked more animal now than man as he scratched at my pants, trying to tear them from my body as if they were some second skin. "Let me—" I could not talk. He was sucking softly on my neck.

He got up and stood high over me and stared. I kicked off my pants and in one moment, as I closed my eyes to avoid his brutal stare, he plunged deep, far, hard into my body. He had fallen on me as if into a fire, howling and in terror. If he rose again he would not be the same, as one is not who has been badly burned or hurt. He would be changed forever. And I, who was the fire, grew larger and larger as he fed himself to me. I was enveloping him, his fingers, his mouth, his whole body. There was fire in his mouth, fire in his hair, the flames licking him everywhere—blue flames, orange, white—everywhere. It grew and grew. It burned all night.

The fire did not die in sleep, which came finally to us around five that morning. Now that it had been started there would be no stopping it. No long night, no water, no dream could extinguish it. There are fires like that, I am told, in California or Africa, that never end, that burn year after year, destroying everything. They burn for tens of years, every day; they never go out.

He was asleep. His glowing red hand rested on my small flame of hair. I began to move. Having thrown himself into the furnace of my body, he too was fire now. I pressed his fingers of fire into me.

"I'm burning up," he said, sweat running down his face.

I had begun to bleed during the night. He pushed his way through the thick flames of red, growing larger and larger by our union. I felt his tongue in my mouth, his lips against my lips in an exploding red kiss. We grew larger. I sighed. There was no controlling this. He reached for me through flames, feeding himself once again into the open center of the excruciating heat, and the fire spread.

"Next Friday," he said. "Meet me here—in this room," and he looked at me as if he were looking at me for the first time.

I was sweating in my black coat out in the street. "Don't leave me here alone," I said.

"Next Friday," he said. "Don't forget." He stepped away, afraid to catch onto me again and begin all over out there on the street. "Next Friday, here," I said. As he walked away, the fire continued, burning on, slower but steadily, in this ungodly, unseasonable November.

"For *this* is wrong," Rilke writes, "if anything is wrong:
not to enlarge the freedom of a love
with all the inner freedom one can summon.
We need, in love, to practice only this:
letting each other go. For holding on
comes easily; we do not need to learn it."

My mother never listened to the weather report and consequently was almost always dressed unsuitably for the ever-changing whims of the Connecticut climate. I can see her shivering in a thin navy-blue cloth jacket in November or sweating in April in her lined raincoat, her whole face flushed.

"Why didn't you tell me?" she'd ask, shedding layers of sweaters, or, hunched over in another season, her arms clutching a manuscript against her chest in an attempt to ward off wind and cold, "Why?"

"But, Christine, I did," my father would say, nearly inaudibly. It seemed to me that he suffered from my mother's discomfort more than she did. To my father, I think, my mother's problem of dressing was a symbol of all her suffering, and because of this he could hardly bear to witness these lapses in judgment.

"Why must she suffer so much?" he wondered day after endless day, night after sleepless night, as she typed. It moved him terribly to see my mother in the middle of January in a thin cotton blouse and cardigan sweater. He seemed wounded by it.

But I thought it was a good sign, a reassuring sign when my mother knew she was dressed improperly. What I feared more than anything in the world was when she felt no weather at all—no cold, no heat, no rain—when she would walk through a rainstorm, come back drenched, and sit down to work at her typewriter, without changing her clothes or even wiping her brow; when she came in from a walk in the snow in her sandals, her feet bright red and numb, and she, completely unaware of them. When she felt no weather, when weather did not matter, I knew it would not be long before the doctors would come and she would not be allowed out of bed. And so these days of complaining, of discomfort, of my mother questioning my father and Fletcher and me eased me in a strange way.

"Why didn't you tell me about this terrible heat?" she would ask again and again, taking off a sweater, cocking her head and squinting slightly as if to say, "If you told me, then why can't I remember?"

Her mind could not be trusted completely. It stopped, it skipped, it added, it forgot. It changed things.

"I did tell you, sweetheart," my father whispered into her ear. He held her in his strong arms. She would not go mad, he said to himself. She would not.

A simple thing like dressing for the weather might have made my mother feel more at home here, day to day, had she only somehow known how to listen to such things. She knew, though, that she only had so much energy and, considering the demanding nature of her mind, she could not afford to pay attention to everything, every conversation, every news broadcast. She knew how easily she tired. If she allowed herself to see and hear everything, she would not have survived, for everything to her was a challenge, imperfect, asking to be transformed, rearranged, made over. But she would not allow it; above all my mother was a survivor.

The simple task of just looking at the world was problematic; just going to the grocery store or meeting a new friend of mine wore her out. "Sonia," she'd say, looking at my new dark-eyed classmate. "Sonia," she'd say, and, if she let it, her mind could wander around that one name for an entire afternoon.

She had to learn, and she did learn, when to look away. Not to would have meant to burn up, to be dissipated—or to go crazy. She would not go crazy, she said to herself. Psychic energy had to be preserved, carefully doled out, used for her work. Emotions had to be hoarded for the work. Attention to detail, mental acuity had to be saved, then focused. Select, my mother must have told herself, select and choose. Careful—be careful. Go slowly. I think I understood. She would survive; the weather was just one of the many things she had to put aside.

"Quiet," my father said over and over through the years I was growing up. "Your mother needs quiet to work." It was the only thing he ever asked of us. "Quiet," he whispered, retreating into his soundproof room where his music played.

You tell me to think of the white at the end of the day on the stock market floor.
I like the way you put me to sleep.
I think of monuments. You whisper the names I want to hear:
Rachmaninoff
Shostakovich
Rimsky-Korsakov
Rach ma ni noff
Sho sta ko vich
Rim sky - Kor sa kov.

Looking up from our tangle of cat's cradle, I noticed that Sonia's brown eyes had turned the pale color of tea. The yellow flowers on the wallpaper in my bedroom were beginning to disappear as if they were being eaten off in some exquisite hunger. In the next room my father's bare feet blanched. The world was losing its color. Walking to the window, I noticed a few leaves on the backyard tree had shed their green, not for the brilliant, momentary oranges and reds of autumn but for some lesser shade, a sort of gray, the mark of a more troubled, internal season, more permanent than other seasons, colder.

This was only the beginning. In the days to come, the world would continue to empty itself slowly of color until finally, by the time my mother was handing her suitcase to my father at the top of the stairs, I would barely be able to see her at all, she would be so lost in white. This happened many times through the years of my childhood. The lake would gray and flatten into a pale square. The red-winged blackbird flying across the blue sky would lose its shock of red, its feathers would fade, and the white sky would devour it.

I began to be able to detect these changes almost immediately, no matter how subtle they were at first. I felt lucky that I could foresee my mother's departures so far in advance. With the first signs I would follow her more closely, sit nearer to her, watch her while she napped on the couch, etch her profile in my mind, hug her disappearing body as color drained from her lips and her blonde hair whitened. On these early days, her shadowy arm would curl around me like a wisp of smoke and she would whisper, "What is it, Vanessa?" But she knew well what it was.

Had I overheard telephone conversations, seen airplane or train tickets in advance, been privy to plans I had forgotten, or was it something else, something in my mother herself, some early retreat, a pulling back, a stepping away that made me aware that soon she'd be leaving again? I think I received my cue from some extreme inwardness in her, from the distant place she had already gone in preparation for her own departure, a place even beyond that place which was her normal domain. Yes, I was extremely sensitive to the timbre of my mother's existence. I loved her so much that days in advance I could see her departure in the face of a friend.

When everything had become white, I knew the time had come for my mother to go to the closet, drag her leather suitcase across the room, and lift it to the bed. She would call me into the room then, and we would sit there for a moment staring into the white. Then she would begin.

"I just don't know what to bring, Vanessa," she would say. What to pack always seemed the outward struggle of a much deeper ambivalence for both of us. We sat on the bed and looked into empty space.

"Maybe I'll pack nothing," she said finally. "Maybe I'll give the Henrietta T. Putnam Lecture in the nude! What do you think?"

"Yes, we'll only pack your hat," I said.

"Perfect," she said. "The fuchsia one with the feather."

It is one of those moments frozen in my mind forever: the hat, tilted to the side, covers one eye. Her hair, pulled up, falls over one shoulder. She stands in her lacy underwear, puckers her lips, and then laughs hysterically, shivering almost, in anticipation of the windy lecture hall.

I would keep her with me. I would keep the sparkle in her blue eyes and put it back into the lake, back into the sky she was about to leave behind. I would keep her laugh, her intonation, her hat with the feather, her hair falling down her back—her hair was yellower in those days and longer. She must have been very young.

I remained through the years an almost-silent witness to my mother's packing as I watched the mysterious rise and fall of hemlines on her lovely legs. I said very little, for language could only complicate the complicated feelings of my mother. She would sit back on the bed again and look at me and say, "I just don't know what to take," and soon she'd begin to cry in the white room. Holding her hand, I might then walk to her enormous closet with her and stand there looking at the bottoms of her dresses, and I too would begin to cry. Though I tried so hard at times, I would never be, as some children are capable of being, the grown-up my mother needed. I could not help thinking, through those years, that my friend Sonia would have been a better daughter altogether for my mother. Sonia, keeping the seasons straight and the occasion in mind, would have put together, from my mother's huge assortment of clothing, out-fits—one for each day she was to be away with a change of evening clothes for the nights. But not me. We would start by carefully picking and choosing, but by the end of the day we would have moved all the clothes from the closet onto the bed. We felt unselective. We could imagine needing just about anything. And my mother had so many clothes.

My mother's attempts to stay fashionable were, I think, her one concession to life as other people know it. She worked hard not to feel out of place. We would diligently scrutinize the fashion magazines, Italian *Vogue* and *Women's Wear Daily*, make obligatory trips to Saks and Henri Bendel, watch emaciated models walk down numerous runways. "Who writes this?" she would whisper to me exasperated, as some man with a microphone told us to "imagine you are in Bali and the sun is about to set."

Fashion was frivolous in a way my mother never really could be. Despite her supreme effort, my mother was not good at dressing. Her heart was simply not in it, and yet, stubbornly, her whole life she insisted on keeping up with the fashions of the day and wearing them.

"Do you like these?" she'd ask tentatively, taking lizard shoes out of a striped shoebox. "Oh, they're really quite ridiculous, aren't they?" she laughed.

There was an urgency about her dressing. I think she believed that if she stayed current she would not get lost. If she kept one high-heeled foot in the material world, all would be fine.

I can remember thinking, after one of our many shopping sprees, as we walked down a busy street in New York, impeccably dressed, that we were misfits, and that no matter what we put on, we would never fit in. My mother must have felt that, too, but tried to douse that feeling with French cologne, to disguise it with a Christian Dior coat or a suit from the House of Chanel.

She always hated surprises, and it was some comfort to her, walking down the street, that nothing in the wide world of fashion could surprise us. When paper dresses came, we were well prepared. Fish swimming in earrings were nothing to us. And when a certain faction began dying its hair pink and green we were not fazed. My mother just smiled, pleased to be on top of the situation.

But her multitude of clothes posed a tremendous problem when it came time to pack. She became distraught, unable to put things together. I could not help. To me, in my sorrow, each item looked like every other. I handed my mother the white dress, the white shoes, the white sweater, the white scarf, the white gloves. Did you know, she said to me, that in China white is the color of mourning? She must have seen white, too. I looked at the mountains of pale clothes on the bed. The Chinese are right, I thought, to make white the mourning color.

All those times sitting on her bed, buried under clothes, the suitcase overflowing, I found it easy to imagine that she would never come back again.

The last time I saw my mother she was waiting for me under the enormous clock in Grand Central Station where we met briefly, she on her way back from Maine and I on my way to college for the second semester. She did not see me as I approached her. She wore a large hat. Bewildered, she watched people pass her and stare. My mother could have worn anything and gotten away with it— paper dresses *and* fish earrings, snakeskin gloves, lizard shoes, parachutes, parasols. What other people saw when they passed was a large, beautiful, overdressed woman. What I saw, getting closer to her, was my mother, so ill at ease with her surroundings that she had to arm herself with layers of clothes and jewelry and makeup for protection. Her bulging suitcases flanked her.

"Hi, Mom," I said quietly, so as not to frighten her. "I'm sorry I'm late." She smiled broadly.

She was not really seeing me. "You're very nice," she said.

"Mom. Oh, Mom."

"Hmmm? What is it, honey? Vanessa?"

"Mom," I said gently. "You don't need all of this," I said, as I slipped rings from her fingers, slowly undressing her. She looked at me as though she were a child, this big woman. She was completely absorbed in me and what I was saying. "You don't need all this." Her eyes did not leave my mouth as she waited for meaning to come. I put jewelry into her large pocketbook. I removed the glasses she was wearing; there was nothing wrong with her eyes.

"How's my makeup?" she asked.

I wiped layers of color from her face. I felt the giant clock's sharp arm cutting into my back like a blade.

"I'll call you on Sunday," I said. There was so much snow—it pressed down on us. I turned to leave.

"I have loved you my whole life," she said. "Even when I was a little girl— even then."

When I turned back to look at her, she had already taken the big silver bracelet from her purse. She picked up one suitcase. It was so heavy she tipped over to one side, her leg in the air. She waved good-bye.

All those times, sitting on her bed, buried under clothes, the suitcases overflowing, I found it easy to imagine that she would not come back again, but I did not think of it that day when we parted in Grand Central Station, she on her way home to Connecticut and I back to Poughkeepsie.

Those days of packing always ended with Father coming in to close the suitcases that neither she nor I could manage, they were so full. He would then lower them to the floor. To me at this point she seemed already to be gone, though she'd be chatting away, knowing little work could be accomplished on a traveling day. If I could have changed shape, left my human life for the life of clothing, been fabric against fabric in my mother's suitcase, I would have— even to have been something frivolous, bought on a whim and never once worn.

My mother, now in a fitted dress, now in a billowy one, now in a hat, now in a veil, a scarf, a bit of plaid, my mother now in felt, now in lace, now in cashmere, smiles. My mother's shoe, one year a pump, one year flat, one year alligator, one year suede, pivots. She takes my hand in hers, one year polished, one year not, one year gloved, and we go down the stairs, she first, me following. This is how I remember her best: an extravagant, exotic figure, descending stairs or getting into the car, but always saying good-bye.

I borrowed from this scene, not on purpose, for what was the recurrent dream of my childhood. For years, nearly once a week I saw this in sleep: The room is white. My mother walks to the closet and drags the suitcase out—I recognize its smell immediately; it is like the smell of the interior of a new car. I feel as if it might suffocate me. "Mother," I say, but before completing the sentence she tells me to just relax. Breathe deeply. It's OK. She is so comforting at this moment, so maternal, that I can't believe this isn't her daily role. She

looks at me, her head resting on her hand. "Shh, shh. Breathe deeply. Everything will be all right." I nod. All afternoon as she's been packing she's been
uncertain, hesitant, sorrowful, but now, patting my head, comforting me, she
is stronger than anyone I have ever seen. She moves with new confidence to
one corner of the room. Her face has an exquisite pallor. Her chin is raised,
her eyes are focused. From the corner of the room she takes a large heavy piece
of white cloth and like an expert folds it into a triangle and, smiling, she gives
it to me. It calms me down and I can breathe again. From the top of the stairs
she passes the suitcase to my father. This is how I know the dream is nearly
over. At the end of the staircase there is always fog. I hug the triangle to me.
Through the fog I wait for the sound of the door closing. I can see the back of
her head perfectly, even through thick fog. I listen for the engine. The lights go
on. She turns to wave.

All night Fletcher had been awake or half awake in anticipation of his first trip
to the airport. Earlier in the day he had cut airplanes from newspapers and
magazines and tacked them first to his bulletin board, then somehow to his
ceiling. When I left him at bedtime, he was circling his room, a truck in one
hand, a giraffe in the other, learning to fly. In the morning Grandpa and I found
him asleep in his chair. He had made a cape out of a light-blue blanket which
was wound around his shoulders and knotted at his neck. He was curled up in
it, that sweet flyer, his thumb in his mouth.

My grandfather knew what Fletcher was dreaming. He had dreamt the
same things many times before his own first trip—a swirl of clouds, the sound
of engines, a lifting in the chest.

My grandfather rarely missed a chance to pick up my mother at the airport.
He seemed willing to drive any distance and was always sure to go well in
advance so as to have time to take in all the sights. He had not at that time
begun to mistake barn swallows or wasps for airplanes.

"My God, that pilot must be crazy flying so near the house," he would shout
in his last years.

"Dad," my father would say gently, "that's only a bird."

He would flush then, put on his glasses, joke about being so old, then look
again. "Well now, so it is," he'd say with a bewildered look. He was shaken by
his mistake, for he knew, of course, that it was much more than a simple failure
of the eyes. "Well, how do you like that?" he'd chuckle, looking into our faces
for any sign of alarm.

"It's OK," Fletcher would whisper to him, "really, it's OK."

Walking in the fields with me that final spring he would often say when a wasp flew by his ear, "Just listen to that engine, Vanessa. It's the modern age, all right! There's no turning back now."

I never corrected my grandfather. It seemed to me his hearing grew more and more acute as he grew older—sharper, more complex. In a wasp's hum he could hear the promise of the twentieth century.

"Are we there yet?" Fletcher said, opening his eyes suddenly, looking up to where the paper DC 10's and 727's flew.

"Not yet," my grandfather whispered, "but get up and get dressed. It's almost time to go."

Grandpa, an early riser, had already had his breakfast of melon and cereal and was dressed and all ready by 8:00 A.M. He wore a starched white shirt and extra cologne on the days he went to meet my mother at the airport, like some secret lover.

That day, Fletcher's first day, they left hours before my mother's plane was due, so as to have plenty of time at JFK. In the car, cinched in by a seat belt, Fletcher dozed, shifting in his seat, his arms now and then straightening at his sides like wings. "Zhummm," he murmured.

"Come in, copilot Turin," my grandfather would say, and my brother would relax his wings, open his eyes, and let the blue sky fill them. Afraid that he might have missed something, he looked from the sky to my grandfather worriedly.

"Relax," my grandfather said reassuringly. "When we get near, the sky will be thick with planes."

For another one of his unexplained reasons, my father did not like airports. If he believed in photographs, which he did not, we might have seen a picture of someone during wartime, waving and trying to smile from the cockpit of a bomber. A close relative who had plummeted to a fiery death? A good friend perhaps? We might have nodded at last, understanding why our father did not like planes and why, though he could not wait to see my mother, he avoided picking her up at the airport whenever possible. But there was no such simple clue. He refused to go; he never explained why.

So it had been decided: Grandpa who had made the trip from Pennsylvania the night before would go to the airport with Fletcher to pick up Mom, and Dad and I would make the welcome-home dinner. My father loved to cook. I could not, at age five, cook at all, but knew I was some special help to my father, who never liked to be alone on a day my mother was flying.

"Well, Vanessa, what shall we make?" he'd ask, early in the morning.

"I don't know, Dad," I'd say and automatically get the chair to stand on to reach the countless cookbooks he had arranged in some mysterious order on the shelf, while he dragged in piles of *Gourmet* magazines that we studied until we could decide on a menu.

I loved to watch my father cook. He was so animated on those days, so busy in the kitchen: measuring, testing, timing, my father the scientist flourishing among the food; methodical, exacting, I thought—though, occasionally, in the middle of whisking the beurre blanc or the béarnaise sauce, he would stop quite suddenly, against all rules of whisking, to squeeze my hand tightly and give me a kiss, as if he sensed air turbulence, landing gear that would not lower, a flock of birds flying towards the engine. We made intricate dinners the days of my mother's homecomings with five and six courses and desserts we set on fire. It kept Father's mind occupied. It kept his thoughts off flying. But I never worried about Mother when she was flying. I was not afraid of the air; I thought, like my father's arms, it could hold anything.

"Where are we?" Fletcher gasped, opening his eyes, sitting straight up in his seat.

"We're approaching JFK, my friend. We made good time, clear visibility, we'll be able to watch lots of planes before your mother's lands. You can hear them already," my grandfather said quietly.

"Are the planes bigger than houses?" Fletcher asked.

"Much," my grandfather said.

"Do they have lots of windows?"

My grandfather nodded.

"I bet you can see inside the clouds," Fletcher murmured.

My grandfather patted Fletcher's downy head.

"I'd like to be a pilot, Grandpa," he said. He started up his motor as my grandfather pulled the large soundless Oldsmobile into the parking lot.

"Sure, Fletcher," my grandfather said, taking his tiny hand, "you can be a pilot if you want."

The airport whirled around them. Everything seemed to be moving: ticket lines, conveyor belts, escalators, clouds. Fletcher, dizzy with excitement even before seeing one plane, dashed around madly, taking off and landing, taking off and landing until he collapsed in a plastic airport chair in a section where people were waiting to board.

I imagine the travelers as Fletcher saw them: adventurers, embarking on unknown voyages in these fantastic machines; all faith, all wonder. Fletcher must have studied them closely, the lucky children who got to go with their parents, the old people en route to warmer climates, those from other countries, the lost, the disoriented, those who had begun their trip at one time and ended up twelve hours later at the same time, somewhere across the world.

My grandfather and brother stepped onto the motorstairs and were taken to a large observatory window. Over the intercom announcements were being made, "Eastern flight 107 to Miami departing from gate 19." "National flight 53 arriving at gate 12." "Aer Lingus," my grandfather read off a flight bag which raced by. Al Italia, Air Canada, Lufthansa, Pan Am—the various stripes and colors of the airlines blurred together. The announcements continued. Propellers whirred.

My grandfather and brother were not part of the group that hurried. They floated around the airport in slow motion, it seemed, and watched stewardesses fly by, ticket agents, anxious travelers.

That day my mother's plane, Air France flight 446 from Paris, was delayed eight hours. Luckily, my father, always the one to imagine the worst, was not there. My grandfather and his small student of flight did not mind the wait at all. All day, then evening, then through the starry night, they sat in front of the large airport window pointing at the sky, getting up now and then to have snacks in the snack bar, then returning to watch the sleek bodies of planes, noting the particular angles of arrival and departure.

"There's Mom!" Fletcher said, suddenly pointing to a gigantic silver and blue plane, all lights, that seemed to appear out of nowhere.

"Yes, that's her, all right!" my grandfather shouted. Their faces glowed like the runway's guiding lights. They possessed the exceptional beauty of those who wait purely, out of love, outside the body, ready to meet the other somewhere halfway.

My grandfather thought, as he watched my mother's plane make its descent, that it was wonderful to love like this. His son in the kitchen, moving towards my mother also as he peeled the ends of the asparagus, had the same thought and for one moment in time father and son were united through love and it made each comprehensible to the other.

Inside, my mother collected the miniature jellies, tiny liquor bottles, air sickness bags, and numerous pamphlets for Fletcher. Fletcher took my grandfather's hand. "She's coming!" he gasped. The wheels came down. They took a deep breath and watched her land.

A most unlikely line will come into my head when the cockroaches gather force around the toaster or a new hairline crack appears in the plaster of my tiny, crumbling New York apartment. This is when I need Fletcher most: when an anonymous sigh, as loud as if it were my own, floats in on the breeze through an open window or a car screeches to a sudden stop, when I must face the dark water at the bottom of the kettle. Then the first sentence of a speech my brother gave at a rally here in New York returns to me. "It is no secret," he says, his voice like a trumpet, "that, with every breath, we are taking toxins into our bodies; it is no secret," he says, "that we and everything we love will die from it if we don't do something now."

My brother still believed in change then. The quality of his voice, the conviction of his meter, his simple faith prod me on when I am in trouble. Fletcher always believed that we might live in a different way and, judging from his voice as he spoke in the afternoon light to a crowd of thousands that had gathered in New York's Central Park for Earth Day, I think the dream must have seemed attainable to him, still within his reach. His voice does not falter; it does not back away.

"Look," he said, "even here in our largest city, the earth is more eloquent than I," and he pointed to the various trees and named them, the hardy wildflowers, the wonderful rock formations. I looked to my mother, who sat on one side of me, and then to my father, who was on the other side. I looked back at Fletcher. In his adulthood I could see the little boy I had grown up with. I could see what propelled his words, gave them their shape and color and momentum this day. It was the blueness of the lake, it was the woods around our house that early on he had learned he could not do without.

His voice had the clarity and depth of the lake itself. Had I been up closer, I would have been able to see that lake still sparkling in his blue eyes. There was no dispelling that first childhood notion of beauty; it persisted, against all odds, like the wildflowers around the band shell, it lived, like the city trees girdled in cement. It lived. That tiny lake, not more than a mile wide, had played a big part in shaping my brother's life, the contours of his concerns. We both doted on it, we both loved it, but it spoke to Fletcher.

A large and various crowd of people had assembled under the dark, dramatic sky. In the distance we could see the shape of the city, all rising geometry, all energy, quilted, patterned; beautiful, too, not as hard to love as one might have thought, abstractly, from a greater distance. It was beauty that united us that day. Though vastly different, we were all lovers of beauty, lovers of a place called home. An old woman several rows in front of me, trembling with emotion, began to cry. "This is our home," Fletcher said, "and despite everything we must find the way to love it, to care for it, to claim it for ourselves—to make it ours."

A division of the Gray Panthers, an activist group of senior citizens, had been bussed in from Long Island. They wore straw hats and buttons that said, "Save our children." Students, professors, lawyers, doctors, housewives, children—all these people were there. Way, way in the back, the Socialists from Union City stood on tiptoe with the curious dog walkers and the joggers who had just finished their runs. I imagine they could only see a blur where my brother stood, but they could easily hear his voice, hooked to an elaborate sound system, and they were compelled to stay.

There was a confidence in Fletcher's voice that made it irresistible, I think, to those less sure, to those whose convictions were less grand or were harder to articulate. His voice transcended language, for even the French tourists who sat next to my mother and kept asking her beforehand about "les boutiques et les cafés Americains" fell silent when my brother began, caught in that voice. And to me, who knew him, and to others, who did not, it seemed that he alone might purify the air with his tone. There was such command there that we thought he single-mindedly might take the clouds and shake them free of their filth.

We were so happy that day. It was one of the last times we would all be together. Dutifully we had dressed in white as we had been asked to "for the visual effect," Fletcher said, "something the media might easily comprehend."

The visual effect was stunning. Father dragged the television from the closet so that we could watch the coverage of the event. We wanted to see what it looked like to the world. It was eerie to have a flash of Fletcher flickering blue from the TV set, if only for a second. And in the black and white dots of the newspaper I saw for the first time the strange resemblance between my brother and my mother. I was shocked that I had not seen this resemblance before. Maybe everyone doomed to newsprint, trapped on the page, in some silent way looks alike.

"Look," my mother said, pointing to the sky just before my brother reached the podium. "A dove—a beautiful white dove." But when I followed her arm into the air I saw nothing, just the ominous gray clouds my brother was about to address, hanging like symbols in the sky.

Had a common city pigeon turned into a dove before my mother's eyes that day in the park as Fletcher got up and walked to the stage? Yes, I imagine it did. She had gasped with delight as she pointed up into the air, and it had reassured her in some way about the world. Watching her sitting there happy, content, I thought despite everything I would be privileged, I would count myself lucky to see what she saw, to be like her. I needed that dove, too, but when I looked up I saw only gray and no beautiful white bird intersecting it.

Had I missed the dove my mother saw so clearly as Fletcher walked to the stage? Had it flown away in one instant as I turned my head to see it? Or had she at that moment invented that bird as her contribution to the day? Often, I knew, she altered or remade the world, revising it, making it a more habitable place, a more bearable one, or sometimes just more complete.

"A dove," she said again, this time softer. For an artist like my mother, there is no rest from perception. It does not stop when the body is raised from the typewriter, when the hands are folded safely in the lap, the canvas left to dry, the dance steps passed to the dancer, the whole rest placed on the final staff. It does not stop. There is no rest.

She could not make it stop. "Look," my mother had said, and she seemed exhausted as she spoke. This dove accounted for her fatigue, I thought. Her head seemed so heavy she could not hold it up and her shoulders quivered as they supported the weight. No hard laborer, no farmer, no fisherman looked as weary at the end of the day as she sometimes did. It frightened me: the idea of no rest ever. Must the sky always fill with lovely birds or blossoming trees? Even beauty becomes intolerable to the lidless eye—even pleasure. She had no rest in sleep, no break. Where we saw gray, she saw shapes. When we listened to people talk, we just listened, but she changed syntax or tone or the end of the story. Those of us who loved her would have traded volumes of her work for her serenity. I looked to her. But no, it was not true that I would have traded her work. I put my arm around her and looked to the stage.

Would it all go on forever? I asked myself, and she seemed to look at me and nod. My mother accepted her life as children do, knowing no other one. She never complained. Don't cry for me, she said with her eyes, filled with wonder, for she was thrilled today by the white, the dramatic clouds, and her son, who now approached the podium. "Look," she gasped. Her voice was high and light. "Oh, look," she lifted her arm.

"There is no better life," her arm said. No, that was not it. "There is no other life." That was the terrible thrill in her voice, I thought. That is what the outstretched arm pointing to the sky said. She was frightening, I thought, this wild-haired, uncompromising woman. She was irresistible. And the words stayed with me.

"There is no other life."

But here was Fletcher. And there was Father. It was not true. People lived other lives. And then I heard it, the whole sentence, as Fletcher opened his speech and looked out at his audience: "There is no other life *for us*." And I knew she was right.

"It is no secret," my brother said.

As he spoke the sky seemed to take on a surreal hue, purplish, as if it were serving him, through some prearranged agreement, as a visual aid. It could not have done a better job had it received a copy of the text of the speech in advance. It looked suitably treacherous and, when it was supposed to, it gradually lightened and shone bright for the finale. In those days the whole world seemed to accommodate my brother, taking its cues from him. In those days he was capable of anything. People knew this somehow, and they trusted him.

My father seemed to be studying his son. It was as if he had never seen him before, as if he were going to paint a portrait of him and wanted to see his subject in motion, from afar, so as to comprehend his true nature, so concentrated was his look. Perhaps looking at Fletcher from a distance, he understood something about himself. He felt proud of him, without quite knowing why.

"This is our home," Fletcher said, "and we must ask for it back—back from Hooker Chemical, back from Johns-Mansville. This is *our* home."

As he finished his speech, an elderly couple behind us remarked that if this young man were on their side maybe there actually was a chance. And even those way in the back, the stragglers, the joggers, the onlookers, the Con-Ed executive out for a stroll with his family, mumbling under his breath, even he knew that my brother was someone to be dealt with. For Fletcher's plea was for common sense, for respect. People relied on Fletcher. They stood up and clapped. My mother's eyes clouded.

Fletcher looked tired and pale as we neared him through the crowds. Maybe we all asked too much of him, talked too much, leaned too hard, expected far more than we should have. He was my little brother. Maybe we wanted more than anyone could have possibly given, asked him to be strong once too often.

"Fletcher!" I called to him.

"Vanessa? Va-nes-sa!" he cried. "Mom! Dad! *There* you are! Over here! Come this way! Over here!" he shouted, flapping his arms around his head. He looked suddenly revitalized.

"You were great!" I shouted to him.

He too was dressed in white. He beamed at me.

Someone tapped me on the shoulder. I turned. A little Gray Panther squeezed my hand tightly. "Good luck to you," she said, "and to that fine young man."

"Thank you," I told her, "thank you very much," and, looking back to the stage where my brother still stood surrounded by people, I saw it now finally: my mother's wonderful white bird of peace.

It was Fletcher.

It is morning. The man stands facing east and watches as the sun, that great disk on the horizon, flares, rises up, and slowly climbs the enormous sky. This is what he loves: a succession of colors—deep umber, dark blue, lightening to rose, smoke gray. He lets his eye linger for a long time on the mesa, the sunlit cliffs, the loping hills. He sees many things: buffalo, bison, doe. Rabbit, quail. Dragonfly, spider. He breathes deeply, smells sweet grass and clover. He looks to the sky. Two eagles dip and spin in the morning light. The clouds live in him; the wind. The shining river runs through him. He smiles, touches his palm, and looks out at the valley.

The last time I saw my brother he was dressed in a charcoal-gray suit and following a fat man down a street in Mystic, Connecticut.

I knew nothing about this large man who came to me now more and more often, offering not comfort, I thought, not pleasure, but something else.

"Jack," I said, and as I said it I felt unsure as to whether or not that was his real name. "Why don't you ever tell me anything about yourself? I don't know anything about you. Why is it all such a big secret?"

"The facts," he laughed, "would only get in the way. What do you want to know? About my dreary life in some suburb? The name of my wife? My 2.5 children? What I do? The details only make us lazy. The details only limit us. We can be anyone we want. Don't you see that? Please," he said, "please start over with me."

"Who are you?" I whispered.

"Anyone you want," he said. "Invent me. Use your imagination. I shall not exist if you do not invent me."

"But I know nothing about you."

"On the contrary," he sighed, "already you know me too well."

He had barely been able to fit through the hotel room door. His massive shoulders had made it impossible for him to enter without turning to the side, and he had to bow his head to get in. I have never seen such an enormous man—his neck like the trunk of a tree, his head the head of an animal, a horse or a cow, his skin like leather. A man like that eats a dozen eggs for breakfast, two gallons of milk, three steaks. When he goes to the refrigerator it looks like a small white box next to him.

He moves slowly through the heat. A man like that loses his footing easily. A man like that causes a thousand small deaths without even being aware of it.

A man like that is so enormous with power that, when he dreams of a faucet dripping, a whole town is submerged under water. When he dreams of the death of a small house pet, the blood of thousands of innocent people is shed in some Latin American country. A man like that speaks softly, for he knows to raise his voice would cause the people whom he loves to go deaf.

A man like that does not fit easily into a family. His brothers are jealous of his tremendous appeal to women. His mother wonders from what love he fed to become this size. He is large hearted, too, she thinks. His father puzzles over what in him made this fantastic man. His brothers do not dare try to emulate him.

Any curious woman would want to know, need to know, what it would feel like to be crushed in his arms, in his thighs. Anyone would wonder what it would feel like to die a little under him.

"Mom," I'd yell in the dark, having woken from a nightmare. "Mom, Mom." But she would not come. She must have been working. It had been silly of my father to worry so much about keeping silence, for when she was really writing, she heard nothing.

She is not far away on the day I fall off my bicycle, my knee shredded, bits of the driveway embedded in the wound. She appears from around the corner when she hears me crying. She is wearing her gardening clothes.

She helps me up, looks at my knee, kisses me on the ear, and whispers, "Your dress is magnificent."

"*Your* dress is magnificent," I whisper back to her. I smile a little, the tears still wet on my face. My mother is inventing just for me.

"You may tell your carriage to leave," she says, and she wheels my bicycle into the garage.

"The ballroom is gigantic!" I say.

"I have *never* in my life seen a chandelier like this one before," she gasps, pointing to the sun. "Oh, have you ever in your life seen anything like it?"

"Never," I say. "Where are we?"

"Vienna, I think."

"Maybe Spain!" I say.

"Yes, perhaps you're right. Maybe Madrid."

"And the orchestra! Oh, my!"

"Listen," she says. "The oboe, the French horn! Would you like to dance?" and she takes my hand and bows before me.

"Oh, yes," I whisper. "Yes."

Blood flows down my leg like red satin. She hugs me close.

The musician glides up the stairs to my bedroom in three-four time after everyone is asleep. He is very handsome, of course, and quiet; his music speaks for him. The musician comes to me with gloved hands. "You must be very careful with the hands," he says.

"Play the fantaisie," I beg. "Play the fantaisie slowly."

He nods, smiles slightly, and sits before me. He poises his hands above me and we listen to the silence in the great hall. Then it begins. Our music fills the air. His hands rise and fall over my body; when he touches me, I make an exquisite sound. "Play on," I whisper. I know how I will disappear in the crescendo. "Play on."

And it is true: what happens at the climax is beyond all reasonable expectations. The tremendous force that has built up during the long cadence can scarcely be contained.

"Encore," I whisper. "Oh, encore."

Sometimes I did think that house was haunted, but it was my mother, that elaborate inventor, who looked squarely into the invisible and then suggested to me in her low, hushed way that there were ghosts there. I do not take credit for the vitality or the range of her imagination; it is she who did all the hard work, Fletcher and I merely assisted. We were her researchers, a role we never questioned. She was the genius and we were the servants to it, the lovers of it. Had it not been for my mother's need to see the house's prior residents, we would never have known Emily or Allison or any of the others who passed through our house with harpoons, with cats, with signs.

And so for a few weeks one summer we threw ourselves into the project with a sort of reckless zeal. Recklessness was new to us then, but we were naturals at it, welcoming the chance to hurl ourselves into the depths of our mother's heart with the fabulous details of the dead that we might accumulate. We did not hesitate, we had waited our whole lives for the chance, and we grew giddy at the thought of pleasing her. The danger, of course, was all too clear, and I shivered a little as Fletcher and I began: it might not work; our best efforts, our purest love might not begin to bridge the distance that separated our lives from hers. But danger has little meaning to those who love as we did. Nothing could stop us. We were captives of her vision. She was such a commanding figure and so rapt in the idea of retrieving the lost that in her presence we had little choice but to follow. She was capable of making the past sound like something we could not do without. We listened, mesmerized by the quality of her voice, the novelty of her ideas. What we could not do without was her.

Tales of the South, the smell of orange peel and roses flooding the room, a drawing done in charcoal that mysteriously changed to watercolors—these things are what I first imagined when I thought of having a house that was haunted. Men aging in their portraits and curtains breathing, hearts beating madly under the floor—it seemed so exciting. "Yes," my father said in his dreamy way, "a young woman carrying a cage of birds, her dress fluttering though there is no wind."

"And mandolin music!" I sighed.

"A limping man," Fletcher said, "with a long yellowed beard and a cane carved in ivory."

"No," my mother said, halting all speculation. "We must find the people who *actually* lived here. They are the ones who return." She looked around the room with specific hope.

In our short feverish search for the face of the past, we stalked the libraries, pulled apart the town archives, and ransacked the brains of the oldest people in town for clues. We became so caught in our work that we barely looked up. Day turned to night. Children began wearing sweaters in the mornings. School started. Fletcher carried a red leaf on his sleeve.

"Hadley," he said, tapping me on the shoulder. "Mr. F. L. Hadley, 35 West Maple Street."

Frederick Lawrence Hadley, easily the oldest man in town, perhaps in the state we thought, recalled nothing anymore.

"You think your life is hard now?" he said to us with raised eyebrows. "Well, it is. But if you hold out to my age, it gets a lot easier. You'll see." We nodded though we could not see ever being as old as Mr. Hadley.

"I remember nothing," he said. "It is one of the privileges of the very old, to worry only about letting the dog out or how long to cook the eggs." He gave a long sigh. It suggested to me that he was not telling the entire truth. "But try 'The Relics,' " he said. "They never did learn when to let go."

It was through "The Relics," two ancient sisters who had once lived next door to our house, that we learned the unhappy story of Ted and Evonne Osbourne who, from 1920 to roughly 1940, lived in our house, danced in our hallways, threw things from our windows, fought in our kitchen, and drank. "Drunk in the morning, drunk in the afternoon, drunk, of course, at night," the old women were saying. "Whiskey, Scotch whiskey. Day and night."

"Anything breakable they broke," the one who looked older said. The other one nodded. "Glass, furniture, everything, and they threw records out the window, too. Fine china, you name it." Their voices trembled. "There's nothing," they said together, "quite like the sound of fine china breaking."

It seemed that, when we walked in, these two women were already in the middle of a conversation about the Osbournes. It seemed that they never stopped talking about them, through meals, through tea, through naps.

"They threw books out the window and toys and lamps."

"They swore like sailors."

"And there was a child," one whispered. "It would cry all night. They would hit it."

"And they forgot to feed it and sometimes they went out and left it all alone."

The Relics shook their heads mechanically. Long ago the horror had worn off. They could no longer react genuinely to their story, but took vicarious pleasure in other people's dismay. In us they had a good and partisan audience. We held every nuance of emotion. We hung onto their words, our eyes wide, our brows furrowed.

They were caught up in the bravado of speech, in the storyteller's art, in the desire to move, to impress, but my brother's copious notetaking gave a legitimacy, a truth to their words that they were unaccustomed to. They paused and watched his hand slow.

"Well, we never actually *saw* them hurt the child. We never even saw the child, for that matter. But we heard it crying."

"And they didn't drink whiskey, I don't think. It was something clear, gin or vodka. They would pretend it was water if you ran into them in the supermarket."

The sisters were trying to come up with a version of the past they could both agree upon. There was a long pause. In it some exchange was going on between the two, impossible for us to know. After so many years they were adept at communicating without saying a word.

"Perhaps you would like some tea?" the older one said, getting up and stepping toward the kitchen.

"They tried to burn it down," the younger one whispered.

Her sister sat back down, impressed with the perfect timing. "It's true," she nodded.

"Had we not been waiting up for our cousin to arrive from Duluth—"

"We heard them arguing back and forth about who would have the honor of doing it—"

"Then, quite suddenly, we smelled smoke and the next thing you knew there were flames. I got up and called the fire department."

"Thank goodness only the garage was lost."

They closed their eyes for a moment. The sisters were exhausted. They had given up their last story. Not to embellish it had taken a discretion they had abandoned in their old age. They felt young again.

"How can we thank you?" we asked. But we already had. We had listened carefully to them, and we had believed what they told us.

"I was sitting there on that red velveteen sofa we had and the phone was there and I got up and I called the fire department."

The sisters were heroines again, and we had come a bit closer to understanding the long, troubled life of our house. Only the Osbournes suffered. Shortly after the fire, they were killed, as if not by accident, in a private plane crash, fleeing from the law.

"Let us know," the sisters said weakly, waving from the porch, "if you ever write a book."

I can see those sisters now reenacting their one great evening: putting on their bed jackets, looking out the window, closing their eyes, and saying to one another, "I could swear I smell smoke," and then getting up and reaching for the telephone, the fire department number taped to the black receiver. I wonder whether they could still be alive today. I suppose that's impossible, but if they are, it's the Osbournes that have kept them breathing. Even then it was the Osbournes who kept them vigilant, who warded off senility.

My brother and I, too, could communicate with each other without saying a word. How else to account for the similar transformations the Osbournes' story took as we drove home? In the silent zones of the brain, we had discussed and then agreed on yet another version of the truth. We thought we might make the Osbournes constructive in their afterlife. Ted could build furniture by hand and Evonne could be a glassblower. What pleasure we thought this would bring Mother. Maybe it was solely my mother's reaction that determined the version of the Osbournes' story we finally came up with, and not some real intimacy between my brother and me. Maybe it was always our mutual need for her happiness that determined our response to the events of the world. It is impossible to say what Fletcher and I would have been like without our mother at the center of our concerns; our lives as they were then and as they are now would not even be recognizable.

"I think Mom's sick again," Fletcher said as we pulled up to the house in Father's boatlike Oldsmobile. She was gardening in her fanciest clothes.

"Oh, no," I said, "you know how she likes to dress up!"

"Children," she cried, "what have you learned today?"

We always knew that the truth was useless if it did not make Mother happy. We did not want to see flames in her eyes. "How lovely," she said when she heard about the Osbournes, "how wonderful." And over and over in my mother's head for months after, the Osbournes made things—beautiful pitchers of glass, glass bowls, and tiny glass animals; smooth dark night tables and handsome chests of drawers; elegant cabinets and wing chairs—until they finally replaced all they had destroyed. It reassured my mother to know that not everyone who had lived in our house had met tragedy. She loved the Osbournes. They decorated her house. And who is to say that stepping out of the fiery plane wreckage they did not decide on this path for their next life? "We must try to forgive the dead," my mother used to say. And we did. We forgave the Osbournes, riding home that day in Father's enormous car.

Our search was like a treasure hunt; one clue led to the next. A young boy who had lost a finger in a boating accident revealed the doctor who moved in after the boy's family decided to leave for safety reasons. A dedicated bird-watcher was followed by cat lovers who had nearly twenty cats roaming the halls. A family who bred show dogs followed them. We watched everyone materialize in front of us. Even the highest-bred, best-trained dogs chased the cats. The bird-watcher, horrified that the cats might take away his identity, kept shoving them in the closets.

In another corner young Betsy Wiggins played a spinet. Her sister Martha carded wool and wove cloth in the living room. The Osbournes nipped at the sherry and carefully cradled glass baskets. Every corner of our huge house was full. I suppose we should have known that once we discovered the names of these people and invited them back again that they would be reluctant to leave. When we asked them about their lives, we should not have been surprised that after so long they could not stop talking. Still I was surprised to learn that the dead, with only slight coaxing, could fall so easily back into their old emotions. I am deeply disturbed by the longings of ghosts. I want better lives for them, less petty, more whole.

Usually I left the hard fact-finding to Fletcher, who found it rewarding. "Historical research," I think he told his friends, soberly. But whatever name he gave it, he found after a short while that it was impossible to leave it at the day's end. "Jacob Potter," he would say in his sleep, recalling that afternoon's work in the dusty Connecticut libraries, the county registers, the microfilm room. "Allison Anne Worthington," he murmured. I think Fletcher fell in love with Allison a little. "Allison," he'd say most nights, very late, "don't cry."

"I saw Allison's sweetheart last night," he said one morning, looking exhausted. "He was dressed in women's clothing, the fine women's clothing of the period, so as to trick her father. Isn't that great?" he smiled. "How sad," I said. "How sad," my mother said.

"What is that chill breath we feel brushing against our necks even in summer?" I asked. "Out in the back, behind the lake?"

"That is where Cecily Pickens and Samuel Hall secretly courted in the woods in winter and froze to death," Fletcher said.

My father finished his orange juice and stood up. "Someone keeps trying to convince me," he said, slightly irritated, "to vote for Lincoln."

My mother laughed gaily. She seemed to love them all. She savored each person, every detail, turning the stories around and around until she could see each face clearly, hear each voice.

"I've got a feeling you'll like this one," Fletcher said excitedly to my mother. But that was just the problem, she liked them too well, and the project which we intended to participate in so as to get more attention from our mother turned on us, giving us less and less. For, long after the rest of us had let these people go, free to roam the lost landscapes of their human lives, my mother held onto them and kept them with her. Weeks after we'd forgotten Jacob Potter, leaving him somewhere outside to pick wild strawberries, my mother would say, "I think Jay Potter should take a trip abroad next fall."

"And Emily Tilset," my mother continued. "Poor Emily Tilset," she sighed. "What to do for Emily?" Fiery Emily Tilset, suffragette, was even more lost than most in this century. "Why did you bring me back?" she demanded. "Women vote. Women work. Women run banks. Women smoke."

"But there is still so much to be done, Emily," I told her.

"We must go over the same ground a thousand times before it is ours," my mother said to her.

"And the ERA," Fletcher added.

But Emily just wept. "There is so much left to do," I told her again. But it must have been hard for Emily to believe. In a few years Ella Grasso would be governor of our state.

I looked at Emily's sad gray shape. It was dangerous to dedicate one's whole

life to a single thing, I thought, whether it was writing poetry or raising children or working for the rights of women. It did not matter. Things had a way
of ending or turning on you and leaving you empty.

I cannot say anymore how much of these lives were facts my brother lugged
back from the library and how much we ourselves invented. The documents
Fletcher copied, the notes he took, have all been lost. It is possible my father,
fed up with so many houseguests, threw them all out in a symbolic gesture,
hoping that if the words disappeared so would Jacob Potter and Emily and all
those dogs and cats. Even Fletcher, after listening to my mother, seemed un-
clear as to what he himself had learned and what we had all added. None of us
knew where it was that the facts had ended and we had taken over.

"What does it matter?" I asked finally. And Fletcher shrugged. For what did
it matter? Noises in the night no longer frightened us. We could easily imagine
Murphy, that eighteenth-century explorer, storming through the house looking for the lost deed to the land or hear Bernard reciting parts of *Hamlet* and
Richard III, a brightly colored scarf around his neck, his hair plastered back as
he stares into the long mirrors and weeps, so moved is he by his own perfor-
mance. Fact or fiction, we could not help but feel bad for John Cook, who
wandered in every now and then looking for his head, which was sold after his
death to pay doctor bills and used for a time in local productions of *Hamlet*.
Occasionally he'd come to check that it was not his head Bernard was using.

We were not frightened by any of them. We knew the tickling on our necks
was really Patrick Derrick whispering, "Whales, whales," under his breath,
his blue eyes fixed in the distance, an enormous harpoon in his hand. "I've got
to go now, children," he whispers. "Whales, whales."

The only one we dreaded hearing was Allison. When Allison cried I put the
pillow over my head. When Allison cried the room turned red. Lovely Allison,
the daughter of a wealthy shipping magnate, was forbidden to see the dock-
worker she loved. She was the saddest sort of suicide. All night sometimes she
sobbed. Nothing could make her stop. She cried into infinity. She came back
again and again looking for her father. She wanted to let him know, I guess,
that the life of grief is long—it lives even beyond the grave.

Twists of fate, lost love, broken trust, sudden death—all these things
haunted our house. I think my mother, whose wisdom was wide, knew from
the start the sorrow that was there, but she wanted to be sure that we knew,
too, and that we were willing to accept it, accept it all, accept it in advance.
She knew all along. She did it for us.

Last night we were all back in the house again: Fletcher and Dad and you and me. Dad built a fire, Fletcher read aloud from the *Canterbury Tales*, you wandered in and out, looking for the right word, warming your feet. Does it never end, Mother? Must it all go on forever?

I can barely see her now in this little apartment, but I know she's here. She does not need to speak and she knows it. She does not need to lift one finger or even assume her human form. She has taught me well what ghosts are about. The wind sighs for her. The trees rustle her poetry.

The rain beats hard on the windows. No snow this year—only the grayness of rain. It is Friday again. He lights a cigarette.

She is soaking wet. She has been out for a long walk without a hat or boots again. I reach for a towel but I cannot get her dry.

"The rain makes me want to make love," I say to him. When I close my eyes she is still there; she is soaking wet and begins to shiver.

"Such sadness," he says.

"I need you," I say, unbuttoning his shirt. "I need you now."

He knows that with his hands alone he can stop all this for a moment—at least, for a moment.

The rain beats harder and harder. The rain seems to beat from within. I know about the rain forests of Brazil, the cold rain of London, the rainy seasons of Central and South America where, after a while, people begin to mimic the rain with their voices, unconsciously, its strange, compelling monotony. I know about the men and women of rain who grow to incredible proportions, their heads like umbrellas, their moist skin like the flesh of fish, their movements the movements of fish.

I know about the monsoon belt of Southeast Asia, the dry winds that blow off the Gobi Desert for six months and the torrents of rain that follow from the Indian Ocean and the Bay of Bengal. I know about the great glaciers of Alaska, the century upon century of winter that has accumulated there. I know about the Alpine föhn and the vent du Midi. I know the paths of the tropical hurricane.

In the Amazon rain falls on a fixed daily schedule. Cape Disappointment, at the mouth of the Columbia River in Washington, is nearly always draped in fog. In the winter cold winds blow down from Siberia, pick up moisture over the Sea of Japan, and drop it as snow when they strike the mountains of Japan. In North Africa the dusty sirocco blows off the Sahara.

I have learned to watch the way trees bend, the direction smoke drifts. I listen to the pitch of wind chimes. I clock the velocity of clouds. My brother has taught me what a halo around the moon means, a rash of stars. I know the place where the boreal forest meets the tundra. I have drawn the horse latitudes around the globe. I have seen those ghost horses, dropped overboard in the windless night to lighten the load, rise up and trot on a watery field.

I hope she lives in some temperate zone, a place where the weather is easily predictable. I have let my eye wander across the rolling hills like a gentle wind, looking for her. I have looked to the sky many times, wondering what kind of weather she faces now. I know the altocumulus, the cirrostratus—the nimbus.

"You'll miss your train," she whispers.

I look up now and it is twenty-five years ago and my mother and Sabine are laughing as they get off the train from Poughkeepsie. Her head is tilted back and I can see her beautiful throat. Sabine takes her arm.

Once, Marta and I got off that same train. Our bags seemed weightless and our books, too, as we stepped onto the platform and into the city that promised everything.

Part Two

I live supported by the royalties from *To Vanessa*, which has just gone into its sixth printing. In the last few years there has been a great increase of interest in my mother's work. Even I have been asked for interviews, mostly by young journalists who hope through some obscure means to make names for themselves. But this is not a cause I believe in and I always tell them that I am not *that* Vanessa Turin.

I have a small apartment in New York's Greenwich Village. I have a cat named China, a lover I'll call Jack. To most it will seem that I do very little. I go to Grand Central Station looking for my mother who has quite simply disappeared off the face of the earth. It is December now, though a poor, warm excuse for one, and in January it will be one year since I last saw her. About once a week I see Jack.

I have very little contact with anyone else. Throughout the past year Fletcher has sent me postcards from various parts of the country he found bearable enough to stay in for more than a day. I write him letters but they have all been returned. "When do you think Mom is coming home?" I ask, following him across the country with the same question, but he cannot say yet. I have spoken several times by phone with Sabine, my mother's best friend, but she has become increasingly hard to reach, having become with her fifth record album something of an "overnight" sensation in France. I have little actual contact with Aunt Lucy, my mother's sister, who lives with her husband in Hartford, Connecticut, the insurance capital of the world. "Where did Mom go?" I ask them, whenever I get a chance, but I have grown accustomed to the silence that collects around the receiver in response to this question.

Once in a while I will take the train to our old house in Connecticut. I'll sit by the lake my brother loved and slowly lower my legs into the chilly water until they become blue and blurry, detached and impossible to touch.

I am alone. I have not seen or heard anything about Marta since I left her and college so abruptly last winter in Poughkeepsie. Occasionally I will smoke a cigarette or play a Billie Holiday record. Occasionally I will pick up the phone in an attempt to find out what happened to her, but I guess I am afraid to know, for I have never once dialed the numbers that could answer my question.

I spend a good deal of time reading: classics, detective novels, romance novels, science journals—anything. I like biographies; it brings me some comfort to know that no life is simple. I am now reading the biographies of Colette, Grace Kelly, and Nabokov. My grandfather gave us many books about the Indians, which I have recently begun reading again; they keep me near to him. I read American history, too, as if all the clues to these terrible disappearances are to be found in that complex, heartbreaking story. I love poetry, of course: Rilke, whom my mother loved so much; Neruda, Dickinson, Whitman, Lowell, Bishop. I can bear to read almost any book except *To Vanessa*.

The lake, despite a deteriorating pH level and a few dead fish along the shore, is still crystal blue. The fish out of water are purple and blue, armored in death, protected somehow.

The last time I saw Fletcher he was dressed in a charcoal-gray suit and following a fat man down a street in Connecticut.

I go to the movies a lot. New York is the city of movies: Buñuel, Godard, Fassbinder. Father always loved the movies. His Oldsmobile was located a few weeks ago in a parking lot outside New York harbor. I went down to identify it like a body. A brochure picturing icy fjords was found on the front seat. I imagine he sails toward some neutral country, Sweden or Norway, where they are just about to enter their season of darkness. Anyone who knows him would hope that a Mozart quintet or a Vivaldi concerto still runs through his head.

Fletcher is in South Dakota where I hope he has found some peace.

"All my letters to Fletcher have been returned, Jack." I can't help thinking that he sees them all, even touches them, without speaking—I always think of him as not speaking anymore. He points a straight arm away from his body and the letters are sent back to me. But maybe he's forgotten how to read altogether. Maybe he's left the English language behind completely. "I'm so worried about him."

"Shh," Jack says, "not here." He takes my hand. "Look," he says. "Here there are only you and I. We can do it," he whispers. "We can make the world over. Just the two of us. Right here. Right now."

It looks huge to him. He might not call it an iceberg, but simply ice. The whole world is shifting beneath him. He can't explain why anymore. He just notices.

In the world we try to make together there is a classroom, and in our classroom games Jack is always strict.

"You're late," he says, looking at me disapprovingly. "I will not stand for tardiness in my class. Do you understand that, Miss Turin?" He is wearing a suit and tie. He puts on his wire-rimmed glasses.

"I'm sorry," I say. "I didn't realize I was so late."

He checks his watch. "It's 3:12." He grimaces.

I walk into the room. He has two bright lights set up. The desk is covered with books. I sit in the straight-backed chair he has positioned for me.

"My homework," I say, handing him papers. He frowns, takes them from me, and places them on the desk.

He removes his suit jacket and rolls up his sleeves. I try to picture the strange geometry of our lives, the unlikely way we have intersected with each other, the theorems that have made this possible. But I am not that good a student.

"Page fifty-six," he says.

He draws three triangles on the blackboard. "Do the proof for problem one."

He knows I will need help, that I cannot retain even the most simple formula in my head. How do you find right angles again? He will begin to scold me soon. He will tell me over and over what the hypotenuse is and why it is so important.

"Why is it so important, anyway?" I beat him to it. He frowns. These are only the basics, he makes that clear; we cannot continue until we know these. There will be no way to move on without them, no way to proceed.

"You'll be stuck here forever," he says. "Is that what you want?"

I shake my head no.

"Then concentrate," he says. "Concentrate. Work."

He understands the importance of working hard—the importance of discipline. It is his message, his gift, the thing that he knows; he wants to give it to me.

"OK," he says, and he goes over the formulas again and again until I know them, until I am exhausted. I put my head on the desk. I move my chair closer to his.

"Chaos is subdued here," he says, as he draws shapes on the board. "Copy them down," he says quietly. Burdens lift, things simplify, reduce. "We can block out the world outside the classroom," he says, sitting down at his desk, tired, too.

"I love you the distance of the focal length squared," I tell him. When I reach for him under the desk he pulls away. He removes his glasses.

"Miss Turin," he says, "I never make love with my students. It's a rule."

I reach for him again, put my hand on his thigh. "Prove it," I say.

He stands up. I fidget with his belt. He steps back. "Prove it again," I say, unbuttoning my schoolgirl blouse.

He unties my ponytail. "It's a rule," he says. "We must be serious."

What he is teaching me is that what we must do will not be easy, and we will have to work hard to get there. We must be diligent, we must not be afraid to work, sacrifice. It will take the greatest effort even to make the slightest progress.

"Is this a metaphor for something, Jack?"

"This is math class," he says.

He buttons up my blouse, buckles his belt. I am his student today and the rules of the classroom must be respected, the lessons of the classroom must be learned. He's not ready to give up on me so soon.

"Now for a quiz," he says, drawing yet another shape on the board. He trembles, I think. We must be strong, discipline ourselves. These are only exercises, quizzes—yet preparation, nonetheless, for the real tests still to come.

"You must not be afraid, Vanessa. It means us no harm. It's even more beautiful than a swan."

I shivered. Great sadness filled the room. Her hand trembled on my forehead.

"You must fly with it—wherever it asks you.

"Sometimes," she said, holding my hand, "it will take you on its luminous back to places that seem bad—dark, cold, lonely places. But you must not be afraid. It is all for a reason. You must believe that you will come back."

"But most of the time," I said, "the places you go are filled with light, beautiful, bright, like nothing else in the world."

My mother closed her eyes. "That precious, precious bird," she whispers, "that bright bird of topaz."

She follows it into darkness. She follows it into places where nothing is familiar, no one stops to talk, and it seems she is lost. She follows it into the center of sorrow, into places of great pain. She follows it where no one else dares to go. That's when the men usually come.

She put her head on the pillow with me. "They are dressed in white," she said, "and they carry hypodermic needles. But even then I stay. They want me to look away, to leave the Topaz Bird behind. They think they can make me see what they want. But they can't. Even then I stay.

"You must not listen to them," she said, and her voice was raised. "You must not look away," my mother insisted. "There is no way to stay safe." My mother saw that I was frightened. She sat up. "You must try not to look away," she smiled. "You must try. Always remember, Vanessa, that the Topaz Bird is special and we are lucky to see it. Always remember: it means us no harm."

She looked so lovely in that last moment before folding the covers around me, right before turning out the light, and I thought, falling into sleep (or was I already sleeping?), that I would not look away if I saw it. If it would make me more like her, this magnificent woman who surrounded me with her saving breath, wrapping me in it, I would not hesitate.

When I go to Paterson in my head, when I finally get to the right street, identify the house, number four fifty-eight, and open the front door, I walk down a long, dingy hallway, past the dark kitchen and left into a small bedroom. A big man sits on a chair next to the bed in his undershirt, and I know I am in the right place. In front of him the *Paterson Sunday News* is open to the travel section. A towel is draped over the lampshade to block out excess light. A frail, blonde woman with eyes like glass sits in the bed propped up against a pillow. She looks so tired.

As I look more closely and my eyes adjust to the darkness, I see children, two children, two girls, nearly the same age, one light, one dark, huddled in a corner, their bony knees up against their chests, hair falling in their eyes.

"Where will we go today?" the woman in the bed asks; a slight smile, almost a smirk, comes to her face.

"Let's see," the man says in the dark. "How about Savannah?" And he begins to read.

"Savannah," the woman sighs. This is the last thing she will say. She is too weak to talk much. This reinforces the man's notion that women are quiet, women are always meant to be quiet. The girls, too, will just sit and listen quietly, like their mother.

Who falls asleep first, it's hard to know. He reads until each pair of feminine eyes has closed—Lucy, the dark girl, the youngest, sometimes first; sometimes the sick woman; last of all my mother, the other little girl, the light one, safe in a dream of magnolia.

The man gets up and closes the paper, leaving the sleeping room for his second job, necessary even on Sundays for heart money—medicine money.

But in my house Grandma Alice lives. She lives to take trips on planes to Savannah and Paris. She lives to watch her daughter grow famous. She lives to work with us in the garden, to dance with us under the chandelier of the sun. She helps me to see the Topaz Bird. She's the one I tell about the golden rectangle.

One afternoon in late October while looking for my snow boots I stumbled upon the great, mysterious shape of my childhood: a golden rectangle.

The snowstorm was unexpected and we were caught off guard. I could not immediately find my hat or scarf or boots and did not consider going out without them. My mother's only rule, the only thing she ever asked of us, was that we be dressed warmly if the weather was cold and sometimes even in hot weather she would wrap us in sweaters, fearful of some unaccountable chill that only she could feel. Now I had no idea where to find my boots. I looked through the whole house but they remained lost.

It was one of those rare early snowstorms that, occurring out of season, last only hours, an afternoon at most, and then are gone. The air returns to the air of autumn afterwards; the colorful leaves remain on the trees as if the wind and snow had never come at all. I looked everywhere that afternoon for those boots and found them finally way in the back of my father's dark closet.

His shoes lined neatly in a row seemed impossibly odd and large. I picked up one of his brown wing tips. The father that put on these shoes and went out into the world in them was a father I did not know. I was afraid of those shoes. They seemed to me in some way testimonies of sadness—the holes around the sole, the smell of the leather, the heels unevenly worn down. Their heaviness in my hands weighed on my heart. He must have been uncomfortable in them, I thought. He wore those shoes when he shook other men's hands, halfheartedly, I imagined, alone in their company, too. Each quiet pair stood like soldiers on a cliff in blue morning mist.

And then I saw it—the blue spiral notebook that would make me forget that somber line of shoes and my father's sadness. I never reached my snow boots that day; I missed that quick October blizzard. By the time I put my father's notebook back in the corner of his closet, a place I would return to over and over, the snow had melted and the sky was filled with stars. The snow had gone as quickly as it had come. No one would have remembered the storm at all had Fletcher not made a snowball and put it in the freezer for proof, evidence for my skeptical grandmother who lived in Pennsylvania and would want to *see* it.

I could never have dreamed what was in this unlikely notebook of my father's, dated 1958, the year I was born. It seemed amazing to me that he had a notebook of his own at all. It was my mother who kept all the journals. The only things I had ever seen him write were letters to her, which he labored over. But there it was, a notebook in his handwriting, and I was convinced that, to understand this one notebook, only a few pages of which were actually filled, would be to understand everything: my father, my mother, the world, all that would happen.

I continue to dream, even now, about the golden rectangle, which my father as a very young man surely must have believed meant something. The handwriting in that notebook was confident and convincing. There were loops and swirls in it, flourishes that have since disappeared from my father's script. The notebook has disappeared now, too. All I have is the memory of that large, hopeful penmanship and the copies I made of those pages. This is what I found there:

January 1958

The Concept of Beauty, the Divine Proportion, and the Golden Rectangle

Stravinsky discussing composition quotes Morse:

"Mathematics are the result of mysterious powers which no one understands and in which the unconscious recognition of beauty must play an important part. Out of an infinity of designs, a mathematician chooses one pattern for beauty's sake and pulls it down to earth."

It is not in the clarity of things but in their beauty and mystery that music and mathematics join.

Bartók—Crucial musical events mark divisions and subdivisions of the work into golden sections.

Hardy—In great mathematics there is a very high degree of unexpectedness combined with inevitability and economy.

The unexpectedness and inevitability of such math and music are not merely formal but ultimately reflect back to the real world. Music has a concrete emotional meaning with the capacity to change a listener's feeling. Math also has a concrete meaning. In such a reordered understanding of reality, which seems both surprising and necessary, may lie some qualities of beauty itself.

—Both are attempts to make sense of things, to shape aesthetic universes that bear directly upon our own.

Musical Qualities of Mathematics—

Hardy—"Beauty is the first test: there is no permanent place in the world for ugly mathematics."

Poincaré—"The feeling of mathematical beauty, of the harmony of numbers, of forms, of geometric elegance."

The Golden Ratio was considered by the Pythagoreans to be the most beautiful of proportions.

The golden rectangle with sides in that ratio has been linked with the proportions of the Parthenon.

Luca Pacioli—1509—*De Divina Proportione* Da Vinci

The Golden Ratio
A line is divided into a golden section when the ratio of its 2 parts is the same as the ratio between 1 part and the whole. The ratio, that is, reproduces itself within itself. The diagonals of a pentagon divide each other in this ratio.

$$[\sqrt{5} - 1] /$$

As a fraction it is composed entirely of 1's layered in an infinite series. The number becomes a sort of arithmetic "image" of the geometric property of the ratio. It is represented endlessly within itself. If a square formed by 1 side of a golden rectangle is cut off, a golden rectangle remains. If squares are continually removed, there is an infinite spiral of golden rectangles contained within each other.

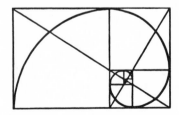

If a curve is drawn based upon the golden rectangle, it is precisely the shape of a chambered-nautilus shell. It is a logarithmic curve of continuous growth. Any two segments of the curve are the same shape; they are just different sizes.

As a snail grows, it produces shell material in the same formation. Similar curves lie in the center of a sunflower, in the shape of a fir cone, and in other natural forms that contain the golden ratio.

In the manipulation of abstract material, which reveals new relations and structures, math and music find their common formal ground.

In Beethoven piano sonatas there is the sense that a concentrated exploration of musical elements is taking place as one listens; when a theme returns in a recapitulation, it is no longer heard as it was in the beginning.

—This aesthetic has been central to the West and is implicit in the golden ratio. This concept of beauty involves proportion between various elements and a relation between parts and whole—a reproduction of macrocosm in microcosm.

I never asked my father about the golden rectangle. I wonder if he still thinks about that divine proportion now as he stares out to sea and the waves crash against his ocean liner and the sky begins to darken for what will seem like forever.

It is too late for me to ask him, and, even if he were here, I probably would not dare to. I violated his privacy that day, the method of his life. I stepped right into one of his unspoken obsessions, though I did not mean to do so. I was only a child that day looking for boots, only a curious child who loved this kind stranger called Father.

Now the dark is coming on. My father bends down and puts his hand in the frigid water. The snow starts to throw the towers and gables of the Baltic into romantic relief. Ships move about the harbor. A waltz plays. My father in a white tuxedo stares mesmerized by the dance of shadow and light.

Daddy, I would label every leaf on every tree for you. I would wedge my fingers into the wind and bring it to your ears so that you might hear what it whispers. I would build fires around your cool body and teach you to sing. I would shape your soft skull into the fleshy bulbs of lilies or tulips that bloom, then rest, then bloom again. I would make the daylight fluid and let you swim in its secrets, if I could.

"She is princess twice," my father reads from the paper, "a duchess four times, nine times a baroness, eight times a countess. However, since a majority of the prince's domain now exists in name only, her kingdom, in reality, is indeed a small one, covering three towns and 22,000 people."

He comes forward. He hesitates. He stops. He must be walking in his sleep again. He barely looks like my father. He seems shorter somehow—older. "Daddy," I say, hoping he might speak more easily in his sleep, hoping he might tell me what dream makes him this way.

My grandfather lifts his ax. When it is poised above his head, my father, just a boy, freezes the scene. He is afraid to watch the ax drop, for my grandfather is not chopping wood as one might expect. My father pulls himself from the bed and moves closer to the window. He rubs his eyes just to be sure and then he sees it: his father is cutting down the beautiful tomato plants, grown from seed, hacking them down to the ground. Earlier that season they had put up stakes together for those fragile plants to hold on to.

Is this what my father means when he says there are things it is better to forget? Is this what he is forgetting—his own father out in the garden chopping the tomato plants into pieces, insisting that they are Americans now, not Italians? Did his father announce that there will be no more Italian spoken in his house? No more wine drunk with lunch, as he burned the grapevines? Did he tell his wife there would be no more sad songs from the old country? How much she must have wept, hugging her small son to her breast!

My grandfather takes his ax from the toolshed, and when he lifts it above his head the scene freezes—but only for a moment. He hacks down those sweet tomatoes while the small boy looks on from his bedroom window and the eggplant and the peppers cower in terror.

"Vivaldi," my father says. "Albinoni."

"Albinoni," I say.

"Paganini."
"Paganini."
"Corelli."

In November the turkey industry presented a fifty-five-pound turkey to the President, but Kennedy spared its life, my father read.

"It's local fair time in Ashtabula, Ohio," the fat man reads from the newspaper, "where you will find the prize bulls, homemade pies, merry-go-rounds, animal freak shows, vegetable contests—prize pumpkins.

"Pumpkins," the fat man puzzles.

"You know, Father," the girls shout, "what we carve and put in the windows at Halloween."

He turns the page to the next article. "Ah, yes," he says.

"Alabama," the father reads.

"Alabama," Christine says. Such a pretty name, she thinks. She says it out loud, "Alabama. Alabama."

I picture my father being an avid newspaper reader once, opening it over a breakfast of cereal and eggs and folding it expertly so as not to get it in our faces. I seem to remember that: his daily origami ritual as he routinely turned the *New York Times* into a square, a rectangle, a bird, while we watched.

We had a television in those days, too, I think, and he liked to watch the news in the evenings until the news event occurred that made all other news unnecessary—the news event so great that it allowed his mind to wander around it tirelessly for years.

He sits transfixed, watching the six gray horses draw the caisson that holds the flag-draped coffin. Behind the caisson is a riderless, chestnut-brown horse. Empty boots pointing backwards hold themselves somehow in the stirrups. A beautiful mother in a black veil holds the hands of two small children.

My father moves to the piano, a giant dwarfing the keys. Hunched over, he plays the *Goldberg Variations* with a heavy-handed deliberateness. He moves back to the television.

I grew up regretting in a mild way the death of our handsome president but mourning the realization that my father was not a happy man and that he probably never had been. I have linked in my mind, unfairly, the death of President Kennedy with my father's great sadness because I never really noticed it before that day. Surely at that moment as my father sat listlessly in front of the TV set, his head in his hands, he must have abandoned the dream of the golden rectangle forever. Still—he did not destroy the notebook. It was there for me to find on that fleeting, snowy afternoon a few years later.

My father reads: "Catholics who attended the luncheon that Friday in Dallas were given a special dispensation and were allowed to eat meat."

My father reads: "The presidential office was being redecorated in red and white. The change was planned months before. The red carpet was being laid down when the news of the death was received."

My father reads that Jackie put her wedding ring on her dead husband's hand but, unable to get it past the knuckle, she left it there, halfway down his stiff finger.

My father reads that Caroline has broken a few small bones in her wrist in a fall from her horse Macaroni, a gift from President Johnson.

I am frightened when my father reads me these things.

"There are questions about the assassination that have not been answered to my satisfaction," he says to my mother over dinner one night. "I'm just not convinced." He sits there without eating for a long time and draws something with his finger on the table.

"Maria," my grandfather said one day long ago, "today your name is Mary. Today I change my own name from Angelo to Andy. Today we are real Americans."

I am forever grateful that I was not there to witness the scowl that must have appeared on my grandmother's face at this news. It must have been terrible. Of course, she never once called him Andy and the name, unused, faded. And when she refused to answer to Mary, my grandfather sadly returned to Maria, for he missed my grandmother too much. She would not look at him or say one word; he was addressing a stranger.

"I was given a name at birth and I will die with it, Angelo," she said.

"We could call the baby Mike. What do you think?"

She frowned.

"Oh, Maria, your whole family wears that frown," he said on the day he finally gave in. "Such stubbornness!" he cried. "I am sure it has ruined more than one good idea."

The evening of their second day here, my grandfather registered both of them for English classes at the local school. Right from the start he was a model student, staying late, trying to improve his pronunciation, persevering.

"I leaf in New Hope, Pencil-bannia," he said hesitantly, concentrating impossibly hard on every syllable. "I live, I live, I live in New Hope, Pencil, Pencil-vay-knee-a in the United State of America." I'm sure my grandfather smiled when he got to the America part, for he could say it perfectly. He had been saying it his entire life.

"America begins and ends with the letter *A*. America. See you too-marr-ah, too-morr-row," he said to the pretty young teacher, "American redhead. Thank you very much. Good-bye."

"The accent must go," he said each night before bed. "The accent must go," he said in the morning to his small son, Michael. "An accent is no good in this new country." Maria sighed, exhausted by so much enthusiasm. He was a teacher's dream, not a wife's. She felt lonely. The village where she was born and had lived her whole life welled in her stomach; she had to eat a lot of bread to keep it down; she had to sleep under heavy blankets.

"We need new clothes for a new country, Mary," my grandfather said. She was not answering, especially to Mary. "If you'd like to come with me, I'm going into the downtown." Still she did not answer. Meticulously my grandfather observed the dress of the people on the neighboring farms before going out to get his own blue jeans and work shirts and boots. He especially noted the dress of the Negroes whom he considered the most authentic Americans. They were new and exotic like America itself. And above all they were not Europeans. Europe became "for the birds." "Oh, Mary," he would say, "Italy is for the birds. In America there is jazz music, Charlie has told me, in a place called Harem." "Harlem," Charlie would correct him. "Yes, Harlem," my grandfather would repeat, "where women wear flowers behind their ears and the music is hot.

"I'd like to go there," my grandfather said in his halting way, something I imagine he picked up from Charlie.

"That's cool," Charlie said.

Hot and cool, my grandfather thought. "This is some country, Mary," he said, hugging her. "Hot and cool, at the same time," he said to his small son, Michael. This wonderful place, America, beginning and ending with *A*.

He felt the wind against him on the mountaintop and praised it, praised the Great Spirit, the wonderful, incomprehensible one. He looked at the stones, knelt down and touched their smooth, flat heads. He knew the oldest gods lived there in stone. He lay on the sacred earth for a long time, and listened to the stones that spoke.

"Welcome to Savannah, that sleepy southern city, that city of azaleas, lilies, camellia, dogwood, and cherry, that langorous town of balconies and secret gardens, its avenues lined with gray-bearded oak. Spanish moss. That beautiful trader's city where one can watch the oceangoing ships come up the river right beside the downtown. The City of Hope, founded in 1733 by the British general and idealist James Oglethorpe."

"Read more," the children whisper, "oh, please read more," they say, growing sleepier and sleepier.

"Wisteria and pillars . . . mansions, verandas . . . and the sea, the smell of the sea."

"The redwoods of California are the tallest living things on earth," the fat man reads in the fading light. "They live from 400 to 2500 years and may be the descendants of trees standing thirty to forty million years ago."

"I dreamed of you, of this place," my grandfather said, and he told Two Bears what he had seen. "I am here to learn."

Grandpa must have been exhausted after his bus trip. He still carried the lunch my father had packed for him days ago, uneaten.

"Speak the truth," Two Bears demanded of this little white man, and my grandfather repeated the dream.

"It is very unusual," Two Bears said, looking at him closely. "You are here from Pennsylvania because of your dream? Most white men have grown far away from the life in their sleep. They cannot remember their dreams and, if they do, they do not know what they mean."

My grandfather nodded, mesmerized by Two Bears, the music of his speech, the language of his hands. I'm sure Two Bears did not know at first what to make of this little Italian man, come all the way across the ocean, then across the country to this place.

"This is the white man's trick," he said to himself, but he invited the Italian grandfather to sit down and smoke with him anyway. And they spoke in the language of hands, my grandfather fluent from the moment he raised them.

"Maria," Grandpa said, "today your name is Wonderful Thunder." The Indians not only taught my grandfather about the secret of rain, the dances of the sun, and the earth's songs but also, after some discussion, the proper Indian name for my grandmother.

"A song from the Ohlone," my grandfather said to us, smiling:
"I dream of you,
I dream of you jumping.
Rabbit,
Jackrabbit,
Quail."

"All the trees," Grandpa said, motioning to the horizon, "and all the grass and all the stones are talking."

My grandfather, nearing seventy, was quite pleased with his version of the afterlife and took every opportunity to share it with us. As far as we children were concerned he could not tell a story too many times. We always heard something new in it or thought of something we hadn't before.

"He's better than television," we would tell our friends with pride. "He's better than 'The Man from U.N.C.L.E.'" "That's impossible," they would say, and shake their heads wildly, "impossible." We didn't care. Despite their skepticism we hardly ever let any of them meet our grandfather. We kept him to ourselves, I do not think wholly out of selfish reasons. There was something delicate about him and the nature of his stories, and our first instinct was to protect him from the crassness and cruelty of children. We feared that with public exposure he might have been misinterpreted, or abused, or questioned too literally.

We especially guarded my grandfather's story of the afterlife. We knew we could not just blurt it out any time. We had to wait until Grandmother had planned a trip into town or was going to visit friends on another farm before my grandfather would tell it. Consistent and brave, she was the watchdog of rationality in a largely irrational family, and my grandfather did not like to upset her. We did not mind waiting, the plans we had to make, the whispering; his surreptitious inflections only made the story better.

When my grandmother was safely down the road marketing or talking with the neighbors, my grandfather would begin the story. He always started in a soft voice with the best of intentions but by the end he'd be shouting as loud as Fletcher and I.

My grandfather looked forward to the day his soul would grow light and rise and he could finally dance on the surface of the sun.

"It's very hot, but your feet don't burn," Fletcher would say dreamily.

"You have no feet," I said in a high voice, "or arms or anything, but somehow you know it's you anyway."

"That's right," my grandfather said. "It's because only your soul goes."

"The soul knows things we never taught it," we said together. "The soul remembers things we didn't think we knew. It knows languages we never learned."

His hands tried to capture the movement of the soul out of the body for us. They sort of fluttered from his heart in front of our faces, and we watched spellbound as they rose toward the ceiling. Once in a while my grandmother would come in just in time to witness my grandfather standing on a chair, his arms stretched over his head, his hands beating against the rafters as the soul journeyed through the roof off into the sky. Fletcher and I would be swaying around his feet chanting something like, "The soul is a beautiful boat, the soul is a slow, beautiful boat."

It must have looked to my grandmother, blown in from the real world, like some primitive dance meant to ward off dark spirits, and in a way I guess it was. She took a deep breath. "Angelo, come down here," she'd say as quietly as she could, "before you break your neck." Once he was down she would whisper, loud enough for us to hear behind the refrigerator door where we were getting juice, "Such things to tell children, Angelo. Shame on you." She felt it her duty always to voice her opinion, to try to retrieve our lives from the dream if it was at all possible. But my grandfather smiled, just a little, as she scolded him; I think he measured the degree of success of any particular story by the disapproval in my grandmother's eyes.

"Well," Fletcher would say, quite soberly, "what do you think happens after we die, Grandma?"

My grandmother, despite years of Mass, believed that the end was the end, and since no one had come back to talk about it there was nothing else really to think. "No one *I* know of anyway," she'd say, looking at my grandfather, waiting for him to admit that he, too, did not know one person who had returned with proof.

"Proof!" he'd laugh. "Oh, my Maria, where is your faith?" Her lack of faith pained him.

"So this is it?" he gasped, gesturing out the window where a few sheep roamed against a field of brilliant green.

"As if this were not enough for you, Angelo!" she laughed.

"Faith," he said, massaging her shoulders. "Faith," he said, tickling her at the waist.

And in fact she was right. It was this world my grandfather loved—the world that held my grandmother's stern voice; the world where we stood by his side, listening to his stories, loving him; yes, the world where sheep roamed and food grew in dirt.

"But I sense there is more," he said. The gout in his hands was bothering him. "Don't you know?"

What my grandmother knew was that what always happened would continue to happen, despite what we sad humans wished for so desperately. To use our energy on any sort of speculation was to waste it. Life was short—at her age she could vouch for it.

Both my grandparents' attitudes towards the afterlife struck me as highly developed and acceptable. We spent every summer with them, and every summer I waited for the day when some philosophy might grow inside me. But the summer days with my grandparents passed quickly, like so many brightly colored playing cards being flipped in a deck, and at the end I had neither my grandfather's faith that what waited for him on that brilliant day when his breathing changed shape was heaven nor my grandmother's rational accepting eye.

What I wished for every night, staring at the ceiling before I dozed off, was a point of view, something I believed, a way to respond to the world that would be distinctly my own. Although Fletcher was younger than I, it seemed he had an opinion about everything as soon as you asked him. But any good argument—any beautiful face, a sliver of sunlight, the modulations of a voice—might alter my views or change my mind. Over and over I looked to my parents, but they were little help. All they could do was to send me back to the world; they were unwilling or perhaps unable to translate it for me.

I wonder if my parents, had they been simpler people, more predictable, more easily satisfied, would have been any better at being parents. They shrank from the parental role, uncomfortable in the authoritative stance. "Children do not grow better by themselves," my grandmother said sadly into my father's ear, and I do wonder what it would have been like to have had examples set and rules made, to have had meals on a schedule and someone who cared if you didn't do homework or missed school. No one scolded us if we forgot to brush our teeth or drank black coffee or stayed up past midnight. The idea of parents having power over their children seemed absurd to my father, and senselessness of any kind made my mother shudder.

"How do you get a point of view?" I would badger my parents. "How do you *know* something for sure?" I would ask over and over. My father would always shrug. To him it smacked of philosophy classes long ago at Princeton. And my mother, not inclined toward this sort of thought, would just laugh her long, lovely laugh. "Oh, Vanessa," she'd say, elongating the vowels, "oh, Vanessa."

The only thing that ever came close to guidance from them was my mother's cryptic instruction, "You must be able to face what you see—to let it in, whatever it might be." This advice, I am afraid, was wasted on me then. While other mothers were suggesting to their daughters what they might talk about on dates or showing them the various ways to shave a leg, my mother was telling me all she could: to trust myself and to trust what I saw. "You must be willing to live dangerously, to take risks." But to live dangerously in Mystic, Connecticut, I wondered, what did she mean? I didn't know, though I always suspected that my mother's life was very dangerous indeed.

I decided to start observing my parents very carefully to see what it was they actually meant by "to live dangerously, to take risks." In the spirit of my grandmother, I was looking for examples, for proof—a pattern, a repetition, a design of some sort. My grandmother would have called this enterprise a waste of time, and on this occasion she would have been right—no pattern ever emerged.

Still, I continued to watch. I watched them so often and so intently that soon my body assumed a position which it always took thereafter to accommodate deep concentration. One eye is squinted, my head is tilted to the side, my arms are folded across my chest. Candid photos of me at numerous occasions reveal this pose—at parties, at the zoo, at picnics, at poetry readings. Whether I am eight or ten or sixteen I always look the same: my right eye squints, my head tilts to the side, fixed in concentration, as if sheer will might expose to me the secrets of the universe. But, of course, this posture, a child's invention, never helped to unravel the intricate workings of my parents' hearts.

"You think about the strangest things sometimes, Vanessa," Fletcher said, putting his arms around me. He was worried. He couldn't understand what I needed to know so badly. For a second, I knew, he thought he was losing me to the incomprehensible world of our parents, but he should not have worried so; I would never even get close.

I will never get close. Still I have not entirely given up, even now.

I remember watching Father one night as he listened to Fletcher talk about the Civil War. I remember especially how carefully he listened to Fletcher, occasionally interjecting a comment of his own. I could tell that it brought my father pleasure to see Fletcher consider what he had said.

"It's more complicated than you make it," my father told him. "You have to let yourself really *live* in the South to understand the Confederacy," and Fletcher nodded. Then, looking down at his plate, my father would say in that voice that was half here, half somewhere else, "What fine tomatoes and fine corn this season has produced. It's been an exceptional season, I think." At this point he smiled and closed his eyes, thankful for the good food and for Fletcher's intelligence and curiosity and for his wife and daughter who on this rare occasion were all together at the same time for dinner. He looked so happy, so calm, that you would think that feeling of well-being would have stayed with him after we had all left the table.

"I'll do the dishes," Fletcher volunteered as he wandered through the Appomattox courthouse. "I'll help," my mother said.

How, then, was it that, when I followed my father out into the garden, this same man who minutes before was so content now seemed to be trembling as he turned the same black eggplant over and over in the evening light? It was a mystery to me what in the composition of this scene might turn my father into a sadder man, a smaller one. The mosquitoes at his neck? The whisper of fall in the air? The earth cooling drastically with the sunset?

"Daddy," I asked, this year's tomatoes turning in my stomach, "is anything wrong?"

"No, nothing, sweetheart," he murmured and kissed the top of my head. "Come on, it's getting chilly. Let's go inside."

And consider Mother, as we entered the house, sitting in a chair, a pencil poised in her hand, her eyes closed. What could I learn from the way she lived?

"Tell your brother that I would like to see him," she said to me one day. But when I returned with Fletcher she had disappeared, nowhere to be found, not in the house or in the garden or near the lake.

"Mother," we cried into the arms of trees. "Mother," we said, kicking up rocks as if with some small adjustment the whole world would fall into place. When I eventually learned of Virginia Woolf's death by water, I began to fear for my mother and that magnetic lake. I am grateful now that no such idea ever crossed my mind independently on those days when we searched everywhere for her to no avail.

And what was I to make of the way she would braid my hair into a thousand braids or make dandelion makeup with me or mudpacks, only to leave before she could explain, for example, what to do with the concoction she'd plastered on my face?

"Please go now, Vanessa, all right, honey?" she'd say in a voice that swam, and I walked around alone, muddy and frightened, dirt hardening, then cracking on my face.

"What on earth—?" Sonia laughed, seeing me on the way to the house. "What are you doing?" she asked, her voice excited and high with the incongruity of the idea. Dirt was to be washed off the face, not put on in thick layers. Sonia was part Russian and she felt more rational than I.

"I don't know, Sonia," I said. "It was something my mother and I—"

"It sure looks strange," she said. "How did you do it?"

"I'll show you. It's mud and clay," and I, too, felt my voice rising in excitement.

Just moments before, to get the clay my mother and I had gone down to the tennis court where we had taken all we needed. It was before tennis became obsessive in Connecticut and no one yet cared that we were making deep gouges in the vulnerable baseline. When Sonia and I returned and I saw the pits my mother and I had made a few moments before, they seemed like the saddest marks in the world. I had been so happy when she was next to me, showing me how easy it was to get the clay up, but now with her gone and only the pockmarked court to testify that she was ever there I felt like crying.

"Don't cry," said Sonia. "Your face will run."

Sonia thought my mother was wonderful. She loved coming to my house; particularly, she loved the lack of rules and regulations because her own mother had such a strange set of them.

Sonia was not allowed to leave the dinner table until she finished everything on her plate—not such an unusual rule in itself until you considered what had to be eaten. Barely disguised, it often turned out to be the brains of calves or the kidneys of sheep or some other unidentified hearts or lungs. Sweetbreads, tripe, tongue; venison, rabbits, oxtails, pigeons—every night another surprise.

Another rule was that on weekends, no matter what the weather, Sonia would be sent outside to play and could not come in until it was time for the dubious dinner to be served. We wondered what it was that Sonia's mother was doing during that time that she did not want Sonia to see. Frequently we would spy on her but never found her doing anything too unusual. We hoped she might be burning letters in the kitchen or whispering American secrets on the telephone in Russian or inviting lovers with fur hats in, but she'd always be doing something fairly routine like polishing the figurines or scrubbing the floor to classical music or sautéing some mystery meat. While we had the

Osbournes and Emily Tilset and the rest, I was relieved not to have the kinds of ghosts Sonia must have had. Though she never spoke of them, there must have been silent herds of sheep and deer, heartless and vacant eyed, roaming through her house; huge empty-headed cows must have nudged her in her sleep, breathing their terrible breaths, looking for their brains, their lost lungs.

As we blended the mud and clay and applied it to Sonia's wide forehead and high cheekbones, her pretty ears and long neck, I felt better, as if my mother were sending me a message through the earth.

We walked through town proudly in our masks and did not cower when the local boys laughed or bow our heads when the women whispered and clicked their tongues. The undercurrent of ill-willed gossip that flowed through the center of our small town would easily have been enough to drown people less preoccupied than Sonia and I. Unlike my parents, we did care what other people thought about us, but we could not hear what they whispered, so absorbed were we in our own complicated lives. Perhaps we shut them out on purpose; too fragile to hear what they really said, perhaps we magnified the sounds of the wind in the trees and the birds and the lake and the cars. If we did in fact do that, it was a good idea, and Sonia and I were far smarter than I ever thought. I have seen so many people hurt by the closed-mindedness of others that I know now it is best not to take too seriously the opinions of those you do not love or cannot ever imagine loving—finally, a point of view of my own.

After an hour we washed our faces by the lake, watching the mud and clay brown the water with its swirls and swirls.

"You are so beautiful!" Sonia gasped, looking at my new face. She touched my cheek, my hair, my smooth neck, breathlessly.

"So are you!" I cried. "You should see!"

We looked into the lake at our own reflections. Fish swam under our faces and seaweed tangled in our hair.

"We are so beautiful," we said, transfixed by our dazzling images. "We are so lovely!" we cried, thrilled simply to look into water and see ourselves.

Praise this world to the angel, not the unsayable one,
you can't impress *him* with glorious emotion; in the universe
where he feels more powerfully, you are a novice. So show him
something simple which, formed over generations,
lives as our own, near our hand and within our gaze.
Tell him of Things. He will stand astonished.

Rainer Maria Rilke

I could hear her from the hallway already beginning one of our favorite poems:

I wandered lonely as a cloud
That floats on high o'er vales and hills,
When all at once I saw a crowd,
A host of golden daffodils,
Beside the lake, beneath the trees
Fluttering and dancing in the breeze.
Continuous as the stars that shine
And twinkle on the Milky Way,
They stretched in never-ending line
Along the margin of the bay:
Ten thousand saw I at a glance
Tossing their heads in sprightly dance.

She sat on the edge of my bed and began to sing. It was barely a song at all, it was more a whisper, a prayer.

"Well, I come from Alabama," she smiled, "with my banjo on my knee." She sang it slowly, quietly. "And I'm bound for Louisiana, my true love for to see."

"Sing," she said, "come on. Well, it rained all night the day I left, the weather was bone dry. The sun so hot I froze to death, Susannah, don't you cry."

She pressed me close to her. Her voice grew softer and sweeter, and she lingered on each word. "I said, oh, Vanessa, now don't you cry for me, 'cause I come from Alabama with a banjo on my knee."

Years before the drought that would follow his death, my grandfather began his search for water.

"The sun rises every day in the East," he said. "It travels across the sky. It's a hot, fiery ball."

"Yes, Grandpa," we said. He looked at us and just shrugged his shoulders. He found himself saying odd things often these days. His life was moving in mysterious directions, there was no doubt about it, and he seemed as perplexed as Grandma by his behavior.

"You went into town yesterday, Angelo Turin," my grandmother said, "and the day before that, too. I know you better than that. Now what's going on?"

It was true—he had gone into town four times in one week; Fletcher and I had gone with him. And the strange thing was that we never *did* anything when we were in town, just followed the curve of the business district, then came home, the same way we had gone. It was not until much later that we realized it was the pond's pale oval that he had needed to pass again and again.

Other things, inexplicable at first, caused Grandma to worry. He began washing the dishes—the breakfast dishes, the dishes at lunch, the dinner dishes—each day prolonging the task and after a while taking clean dishes from the cabinets and washing them, too. His hands floated for hours under water, like a child with bath toys.

"Grandpa, let's go to town," I'd say. I did not like to see him do this. It reminded me of the days my mother stood curved like a great bird over the sink for hours and washed everything she could find in her singular fight against germs. "Let's go to town," I pleaded.

My grandfather began taking long baths, his whole day now filled with water. In between dishes and the bath we drove into town and began stopping at the pond to dangle our feet in the water. This continued, until one day, while we sat at the lake's edge, it finally occurred to him. Waves of horror passed through his body; he stood up and, looking into the water, said, "There will be a terrible, terrible drought." This was it, the farmer's nightmare. His whole life's concern surfaced finally with these words, "There will be no more water, there will be a terrible drought." It was the fear he had held in check for nearly seventy years; in Italy as a little boy, then as a young man, his whole life, it had been the same fear. But he could not hold it back any longer. It flooded his system.

We drove into town and bought notebooks. We were to record everything, the formations of clouds, the behavior of cows and sheep, the rise of pain in my grandmother's back, anything that related even vaguely to rain. Our lives took on the fluid quality of those who dream the same dream together. Our motions began to mimic each other's, and where one's thoughts dropped off another's began. We worked day after day to find the secret of rain and, as the days passed and we could find no discernible pattern, our bones seemed to fill with a strange, warm water and we grew heavier and heavier with despair.

"It is all a joke," my grandfather said one day when he could no longer stand the pictures of tortured wheat and dying animals he had in his head. "We are at the mercy of a God who does not really care if our children are thirsty or our crops die."

"Maria!" he shouted out the window. She was taking in wash from the line. "It is all a whim! We are at the mercy of an indifferent God. It is all a crazy whim!"

"Don't waste your breath!" she said. "I can't hear you from here, Angelo."

"It is all a whim!" he cried, and it was as big a revelation to him as the revelation of the drought itself. He looked at us amazed. "Children," he said, and the three of us together shouted out the window to Grandma, "It is all a whim! A whim." And this time with the force of our accumulated exasperation the word "whim" blew out the window and caught itself in the large white sheet my grandmother was taking down from the line. It was the hardest word my sensible grandmother would ever have to hear, and its deceptively light sound twisted around her with the sheet, strangling her, and she screamed and struggled to get free. I ran out to help her, spinning her around and around until she was in my arms. She looked bitterly into the dark house where she could just see the outlines of Grandfather and Fletcher standing by the window.

"I can't hear myself think anymore with your grandfather yelling his head off. I don't know what I'm going to do."

He continued his baths, hoping to find the answer through some hypnotic means. "You are becoming a wrinkled old prune from all that water," she said. "Angelo, please."

"Fool, idiot, dope," she would have said to my father or me, had we been looking for the secret of water, but with my grandfather she softened slightly. As the days passed, then the weeks, deep wrinkles of concern pleated her face, her apron, her dress. She kneaded them into the wavy dough. It was the bread we ate.

"Angelo," my grandmother pleaded. "There is plenty of water. You're making yourself sick with this."

But my grandfather continued his long walks, listening to the rumble of distant thunder and watching the mad dance of clouds. He would come in drenched, often, having been caught in the middle of a storm. Grandma hated to see him this way, but he always seemed so refreshed afterwards.

"One day you will be thankful," he said to my father, who was visiting for the weekend. "I am doing this for the children." He looked at us. He took Fletcher's hand. "So that one day they will be able to save themselves." Fletcher nodded and acted like he understood. My father, the skipped-over generation, just watched in silence and looked from my grandfather to my brother and back again to my grandfather. Some key was missing in his blood.

One evening after a solo trip to town, my grandfather came in carrying a large wooden fork. It was called a divining rod.

"It looks like a big slingshot!" Fletcher cried.

"It looks like a wishbone," I said, dreamily.

"Well, it looks like a piece of junk to me!" my grandmother said. "I'll be damned if you're going to go sticking a fork in the ground looking for water we don't need while this whole place goes to ruin."

"You don't stick it in the ground," my grandfather said softly.

"Angelo," she said, "try to be a little bit sensible."

"Oh, don't worry," he said, but already my grandfather had left behind the world of chores.

We walked day after day through the hot summer pointing the fork toward the ground and listening for a vein of water.

"Shh," he said, "we must be very quiet, it will sound like music." But we never once found even one chord of water. "There's something I'm not doing right," he said. "I don't have the thoughts right somehow." He closed his eyes and held the fork tightly.

Then one day, just as he was about to give up, the man who sold him the fork called to say there was going to be a convention. My grandmother took the call.

"I'm going to tell you what that man said on the phone, Angelo, and then I'm going to make a comment of my own, so don't interrupt me.

"There's going to be a convention for people like you on the twentieth of August. Now if you go to that convention, I swear, may the children be my witnesses, I'm going to join my sisters in California and you can fend for yourself here."

"You wouldn't really—"

"I'm serious. I'll buy my plane ticket. If you're going to go crazy, at least have the decency not to make us all watch it. We got enough crazy people in this family already. We don't need you going on us, too."

Now that she had started, my grandmother could not seem to stop. Her voice flowed like torrents of water.

"Their own mother goes away for months and months at a time and your son ignores them, sitting in some dark room with the music on. It's not right, Angelo, it's not right. These kids need you, old as you may be. Don't go senile on us now. Something just snapped—after that damned World's Fair your son insisted we go to. Unsnap it, Angelo. These kids need you."

My grandfather, standing with the fork in his hand, said nothing.

"I'll live somewhere where I'm not afraid to look around for fear I'll see you going crazy and holding that stick."

"OK," he said, "everybody up," and he marched us all out to the garbage shed. "It's gone now," he shouted, throwing it in the garbage can. "It's over. It's all over now. Are you satisfied, Maria?" he said sadly.

She did not look at him.

"All right, children, you've had enough excitement for one day. It's time for bed," my grandmother said. "Tomorrow your parents are coming for a visit." She tucked us in.

"Did you mean what you said to Grandpa?" I asked.

"Yes," she said, "every word of it."

That night Grandpa went to bed early. He was asleep, in fact, before we were. We could hear him from our rooms babbling in some troubled dialect. Fletcher thought, getting out of bed, that he might ease my grandfather's difficult sleep by slipping out to the shed and retrieving the divining rod that had promised so much. I heard him opening the door of the shed and taking the top off the garbage can. It was easy to find, right on top. He carried it into the house.

"Didn't you hear her?" I whispered. "You're going to send Grandma to California if you're not careful. Why would you want to do that?"

"I'm just going to keep it under the bed," he whispered. "No one will know."

He was right about the fork, no one ever found out about it. After a while even I forgot it was there. Fletcher did, too, I think.

That night Grandpa got up many times. I saw him go to the bathroom, fill a glass with water, drink it, fill it again, and carry it back to his room. "My throat is parched," he said to me vacantly when we bumped into each other in the hall at 5:00 A.M. "I'm parched," he said, tottering back to bed.

Grandpa did not get out of bed until late, almost eleven o'clock the next day, which was very unusual for him. Grandma paced outside the room worried.

"What's wrong?" she asked, when he finally appeared. "Are you feeling all right? Are you sick?"

"I had to finish my dream," he said.

By the time he was dressed, Mom and Dad had arrived. They looked happy, in love, like newlyweds. They held hands under the table and looked at us curiously, as if they had no children yet, only dreams of them.

"Oh, what beautiful children!" my mother said, as if we were someone else's.

"Hi, Mom," I said, kissing her, not knowing what else to say. "Hi, Daddy."
My grandfather walked in, hugged my mother, and sat down.

"I had a dream," he said, like a child who had never had one before. "I saw mountains," he said, "pitch-black mountains. I never saw mountains like this before. And on these mountains there were people who could call water from the sky at will." My grandmother gave out a sort of groan.

"Black, black mountains."

"The Black Hills?" my mother said. "The sacred land of the Indians?"

"The Indians?" he cried. "Yes, that must be it! Those people were Indians! Of course. Where are these Black Hills?"

"South Dakota," she said. It sounded beautiful when she said it: South Dakota—like a song.

My grandfather took my grandmother's hand. "I must do this," he said, "for the children."

She knew him well enough to know there was no stopping him. It was already too late. He had started off alone in the middle of last night while she slept. "South Dakota," he said. He was already halfway there, she knew, as he stood up and walked to the desk where the maps were kept.

My grandfather, whose Indian name turned out to be "Dreams of Rain," not only learned that meteorological secret but many other things as well. He went to the Black Hills over and over in his last five years and he told us everything.

" 'Moves on Water' is Father's Indian name," he told us one day. " 'Brave Ghost' is the name for your mother."

As soon as a person died, messengers were sent to summon faraway relatives. Widows or widowers singed or cut their hair and with sharp objects made long, deep gashes in their skin. Grief stricken, they would wail for days and beat their breasts with stones and pestles.

Often the ghost lingers near the place it died and for one year attempts to lure away the people it loved in life.

On a day Grandma was to be out the entire afternoon, Grandpa, in a serious mood, led us into his bedroom.

"Listen carefully," he said. "This is important. Watch carefully." From under his bed he took out a shoebox. In it were three plastic bags.

"This is black cornmeal," he said, lifting the first bag up. "After my death, pour some out into your left hand, pass it around your head four times, and cast it away. This makes the road dark. It will prevent dream visits by the spirit. Do you understand what I am saying?"

"Yes, Grandpa," we said together.

"Good. The white cornmeal comes next," he said, and he pointed to the second bag. "Take the white cornmeal in the right hand and sprinkle it, saying, 'May you offer us your good wishes. May we be safe. May our days be fulfilled.'" Fletcher wrote it down. "This," Grandpa said, "ensures the proper relation between the living and the dead. Now," his voice grew softer, "on the fourth morning after my death, leave the windows and doors open so that my spirit can leave the house for good. There," he said, pointing to the third bag— pine resin incense. "Burn this on the fourth day."

"Be nice to Grandpa," Fletcher said, walking into the room where my father stood conducting his imaginary orchestra, "because he is going to die soon."

We walked in silence, the particular silence of midsummer. Father began to hum finally. Fletcher and I pointed to peacocks in cages, to raccoons and other small animals at the wildlife center. We scattered in the tall grasses. We followed Father into the woods, we breathed deeply as we saw him do. We held his hands; he said nothing.

We walked a long time—in fields, through flowers, in heat. The afternoon seemed slow and languid, when quite suddenly Father, who was so tall, bent down and in one motion, like a giraffe eating food from the earth's floor, plucked a large, flat leaf from the ground, moved by some unknown force down and back up again.

"See this?" he said, looking at the leaf, shaking his head and laughing. "Children, look at this."

We looked at the giant leaf. I had no idea what Father might say. He plucked another from the ground, then another, and knelt down next to us, his long arms scooping us up.

"These are the leaves!" he said. "These leaves. Back in Italy when I was a little boy, my grandmother used to dip these in egg and flour and fry them!" and he turned them over in their imaginary batter. "Oh, they were quite delicious." He smiled.

"It's been a long time now," he said, gathering a few more leaves; we, too, picked them. "When she cooked them up that way they tasted just like veal." He smiled a great smile; the memory warmed him and the warmth spilled onto us.

This was one of the happiest days of my life: clutching his hand, holding close the story of how his grandmother, who had never lived before this day, changed simple leaves for a young boy into veal.

"The way you hold your knife," he sings, "the way we danced till three—the way you changed my life!" his voice rises and his heart swells. "No, no, they can't take that away from me.

"No, they can't take that away from me."

"In New Orleans there is Mardi Gras—sweet smoke and Negroes and bourbon in the streets."

"And jazz music," Lucy says.

It's so exciting. The two girls giggle. Red lights and smoke and saxophones all night long.

"Old age finally killed Charlie," my grandfather said, rubbing the ground's brown belly. "One hundred and thirty years," he said, shaking his head. "That's a long time to live.

"Natural causes, they said, killed him." My grandfather stood up. "Heart failure—kidney failure—failure failure."

"Don't forget the soul," we whispered to him.

He smiled. "Charlie could really tell a story," my grandfather said. "Oh, yeah, Charlie could really talk. We'd chew the fat all night sometimes."

I wished that I had had stories to tell my grandfather.

"You know, he's telling them now somewhere," he said as we looked down at the dirt. "Maybe in African this time around, who knows?"

Once, before his name was Charlie Jones, West Africa had been his home. Once, before the Fourth of July was his birthday, before the farmer Samuel Jones bought him, he remembered his mother taking the bones from a fish.

"Other things, too," my grandfather said. "He remembered stripes, the black-and-white stripes of the zebra, and the heat of the sun, and how fast he could run.

"They were young and strong, Charlie and his brother, and the man on the ship docked in the Liberian port saw that and tricked them with a story about how there were fritter trees on board and lots of syrup.

" 'I never saw any of it again: not my mother, or the zebras . . . ,' Charlie said, 'except here, Angelo,' and he pointed to his head."

My grandfather tucked the Charlie stories, the stories of riding with the Jesse James gang, the stories of going off with Billy the Kid to get the man who killed Garfield, he tucked them all back in his head. The stories seemed shifting and vulnerable, unstable when compared with this burial scene. My grandfather thought of the fluidity of stories and the dead man with his mouth closed. They lowered the coffin into the ground.

"On the day of the Emancipation Proclamation," Charlie had said, "there was nowhere to turn."

The local people had all made death wreaths. The gladiolus pressed their ears to the ground, listening even now for more. And Charlie talked on.

"Here is the time for the *sayable*," Rilke writes in the "Ninth Elegy." "*Here* is its homeland. Speak and bear witness."

Jack came on a Monday, unexpectedly, at 9:00 A.M. He was coming to my apartment now more and more often; we were leaving our hotel life behind. He had never done this though, come early in the morning, early in the week, and when I first heard his voice over the intercom I felt unsure, then frightened, then delighted, all while he climbed the three floors up to me. Such fluctuation in emotion from floor to floor was exhausting. As I opened the door I must have looked tired.

"Wake up, Vanessa! Wake up! Wake up!" he said.

"What are you doing here?" I asked cautiously, as calmly as I could.

"I couldn't stay away," he said. "Please." He looked like a boy on his first date, but it was morning, not evening, and, standing outside my door, he held a bag instead of the more conventional flowers.

"What's in the bag, Jack?"

"Close your eyes."

With my eyes closed I pictured him as he looked now standing in front of me, his arms full, a large smile on his face. I thought to myself that this was a new Jack, a different one. He looked younger today, more robust than I'd ever seen him. I suspected that a woman was involved—he had fallen in love, perhaps he had just come from her, he was being someone new for someone else. He was clear-eyed, the decision had been made: he was going to leave me, the ambivalence was over, no more debating in his head.

"OK," he said, walking in the door.

I opened my eyes. Out of the bag came croissants and brioches, smoked fish and fruit, champagne. I sighed. He smiled. Today he looked like a man any woman would want to marry, take home to her parents, spend her life with.

"Where did you buy all this?" The face of the other woman faded. The smells were of fruit and of yeast. The whole apartment seemed safe. I nuzzled up to him.

"I made it all," he said. "I've been planning it for days. I was up all night."

I looked at Jack, puzzled. I could not predict anything about this man who stood before me with a tray of salmon and pastry, his chest puffed with pride. "You *made* it all?"

He nodded.

"But there are little doilies around these fruit tarts."

"I know," he smiled. "I bought the doilies."

"You *bought* the doilies?"

He laughed.

"These crusts are perfect, Jack."

"I've been practicing. Ice water is the key."

"The cheese in this is absolutely—"

"Yes, I know."

"Everything's still warm."

He smiled and opened the champagne. The excess spilled into my mouth.

Who was he? What was he trying to do? He opened the fruit: the kiwi, the pomegranate, the kumquat. They bled on his hands. He fingered the sweet meat, placed it in my mouth.

It was easy to love Jack the cook—the way he fondled the fruit, how small and tender the peach looked in his hand. It was easy to love him—the smell of pears in his hair.

"Some ham?" he asked. I watched him carefully, his expertise at slicing, and for a moment I could picture this Jack with me for a long, long time, this sweet, attentive, undemanding Jack: Jack the pastry chef, Jack the sauce chef. I could imagine traveling with him to exotic lands for ingredients. I could picture him at the cocktail hour feeding me pitted olives from his fingers.

"I want to make things for you, Vanessa," he said. "I want to keep you warm and safe. I love you, my dumpling, my clam cake, my oyster stew."

"Oh, ham hocks," I said, "I love you, too."

Jack the drama teacher always wore a tweed jacket, had a long scarf wrapped around his neck, and sipped coffee. He taught me how to prepare for each role: how to breathe, how to relax each part of the body; he showed me the exercises to do to limber up. Jack the acting teacher gave me confidence. "There is no role you are incapable of playing, no role too difficult, no role too out of character," he said, "if you work hard, if you concentrate. Build, in your imagination, the circumstances in which such an action could take place. You can invent anything you have to, anything you want. You can do it all."

"But there are times I drift away, Jack—come in and out of my part, lose my concentration, become afraid."

"That's OK," he said. "Keep working. Stretch your body and your mind. Get in shape.

"Do what you must to get at the truth, to see what is difficult, to see what you believe you cannot bear to see. There is no substitute for the truth."

"Don't miss your train," my mother whispers. "Please go."

"There is no substitute for pain," she said. "There is no way to stay safe."

I have never been to that white house on the coast of Maine where my mother went so often. She would venture far into that untouchable country for weeks, months sometimes, with hardly a word for those of us who waited. "Do you think we'll ever get to that white house, Dad?" I'd ask, but he was not listening. I watched him as he painfully composed letters to my missing mother. He put so much effort into them—crossing out, underlining, adding paragraphs, arrows and asterisks everywhere, copying them over and over until they were perfect.

I thought of her there in those vacation towns of summer often: those towns of heat and water and bleached wood, the hydrangea bushes bowing their drowsy heads, the bicycles propped against the pale sheds; the striped umbrellas, the fish stands; the moths at the screen. A warm sea breeze blows through her hair. A beach ball forms a lovely arc behind her in the blue sky.

It was harder in winter. In winter she became lost to me. It was harder in winter to see her happy. I did not want to give her up under the hydrangeas or writing on the beach, I wanted her to stay there, but in winter it was different. In winter she probably stayed huddled next to a fire in her huge Icelandic sweater, a white mug of coffee in her hands. It must have been very cold. She was probably lonely way up there.

But I believe in that white house. I believe in those towns of perpetual summer. I believe in you, Camden, Bath, Castine, Wiscasett. I believe in your summer.

The mug turns to white flowers in her hand. The ocean wind warms. She is back in summer though it is December now. She hears the neighbors' voices far off. The beach ball bounces in the sand. We chase after it, wave to her.

"Is that my sweet pea I see?" she sang out to me through the blossoms and the leaves and the light of the garden. "My hibiscus? My wisteria? My alyssum? My primrose?

"Sweet William, is that you?" she called to Fletcher, and my brother blushed.

"Is that my daffodil?" I chirped back to her through the Queen Anne's lace she refused to weed out. "Is that my forget-me-not?" I giggled. "My lilac? My bluebell? My mimosa?"

"This mildness will kill us," Jack says, shaking his head. "This summer haze we are forced to see everything through, even now.

"Jesus, Vanessa," he laughs. "It will kill us."

I always wanted to believe that someone like my mother would know what she needed and where she could go. But arriving sometimes in Maine and parting the musty curtain, or directing a taxi in Italian to some new address, or stepping onto the pavement and hearing a strange clock toll, she would realize in one terrible moment that she would not be able to stay. She was afraid, uncomfortable, and she would be unable to work. Many times she'd turn right around and travel hundreds of miles, thousands of miles, back home.

"It was a foolish idea," she would say to my father over a dinner it seemed he always had waiting for her. He never knew quite when to expect her, and I think he always hoped in part that she would stay where she had decided to go and in part that she would come home. She was a solitary traveler, her expectations rising high as she left the house, only to have the message reiterated: there are limits, places the architecture of your brain will not permit you to stay, to experience. It was a terrible message, she thought.

"You must have known from the beginning, Michael," she sighed. My mother trusted my father implicitly and depended on him for advice of all kinds. "It was just another of my crazy schemes. You should have told me; I would have listened." But she would not have listened, my father knew. He shrugged his shoulders. "It doesn't matter, Christine," he said, smiling at her. He had let sadness go. He was happy just to see her sitting before him. She was back. He squeezed her hand. She was back.

But she is not back, Jack seems to be saying as he steps into the room. If a pen or a paper knife or a scissors had been handy, I think I would have killed him right there as he smiled and put the newspaper down in front of me.

From the paper I read that "despite the warm temperatures now, meteorologists say this will be the coldest winter in hundreds of years" and for some reason I believe it. "One theory is that volcanic eruptions in Mexico will have a drastic effect on the temperature. And," it says, "it is a fact that months ago jet streams failed to migrate toward the Arctic and dissipate.

"There is cold water all over the Pacific," I read to him, "from Japan to Alaska. And this configuration carries certain implications."

Jack just moans. "I don't know, Vanessa," he says. His voice is thick and slow, a mirror of the weather. He puts his enormous hand gently on my neck, then smoothes the hair back from my face. He is sweating. He shakes his head. "Your mildness will kill us," he whispers in my ear.

From the east came the men with faces and hands the color of snow. The men were ugly. Hair covered their faces and bodies, and when Drinks Water saw them he thought of the hairy water monsters who drew swimmers into their mouths by making waves. He worshipped the large boulder for strength. They came riding Shoon-ka wah-kon, fearful, mysterious dogs—wonderful dogs, fast as the wind. Drinks Water offered a pipe to these men and they let him touch the beautiful dogs. Trust us, they said to Drinks Water and they passed the pipe back and forth.

Drinks Water dreamt with his eyes open as the men sat with him in a circle. Already he could hear the ringing of their axes in his ears. As they inhaled the sacred smoke he saw them building small, gray boxes, and beside those boxes he watched his people die.

The water rushes around the rocks in wild, violent circles. He looks at it with a scientific eye. Here chaos begins, he thinks to himself.

My mother cannot stop walking. She goes from one room of the big house to another, then outside, one state to the next, then across the ocean.

"A body breathes under the earth," she moans. "Its lungs are filled up with dirt."

My father talks under his breath. "This is the hardest part," he says, and he is right—when she hears and sees what is not there.

It is not there, he is sure of it and tells her so.

"How can you be so sure, Michael?" she asks over and over, and he says it again with an authority he does not often call up.

"I am sure. Believe me." And he holds her shoulders and looks into her eyes. This is the worst part, we children think, watching her from a far corner. I wonder to myself whether she will ever be well, and Fletcher somehow knows this and puts his hand on my shoulder and whispers, "It will be fine." I want to know where his faith comes from, his eyes that shine confidence as she begs us to come to her, calling us out from the shadows.

"Mom," he says, hugging her with the whole of his strength. He is so little still.

"Tell me the weather, Fletcher," my mother says. But before he can tell her of the cold spell we are in, the temperatures below freezing each day, no sign of a break, she says, "I wish there were tulips here," and brushes his head. She picks up the phone, books a flight to the Netherlands—then cancels it— books it again.

"Tulips," she says again and again, "tulips," until somehow she sees the heads of her children, our heads, blossom red and yellow, and she is satisfied.

"Oh, my!" she exclaims. "You two are so beautiful!" To see our heads blooming in brilliant color makes us dearer to her; she understands us better in that moment, loves us more. I will gladly make my head a petaled top for her, I think, my arms the green leaves of tulips, my body a stem she might pluck and hold close to her breast; something she needs, finally.

Sometimes I think I have heard the fluttering of wings. Sometimes I think I have seen something: a tip of a tail, a piece of beak, a leg, one thin leg of that incredible bird. Sometimes I see the bare branch of a tree swaying in slow motion in my sleep and I know what that means. I try to get myself past the tree to see what's beyond it—the field that opens like a great hand, the wide breath of sky. I search for a trace of the Topaz Bird. Only moments before it was perched on that bobbing branch. I am getting closer. I follow the horizon line of my dreams. I watch. My mother's robe is shining and gold. I listen. Her voice is sweet and low. I close my eyes in the dark and feel her warm breath. I try to picture that bird in my mind. But it's so tiny, so hard to see.

"You must not be afraid," she says in her lovely night voice. But still I must be. Still I can't see it, not even now as I fall into this twenty-year-old sleep, this grown-up sleep.

"Mother," I whisper, though she is far away now, "help me, please."

I wait for the leap—the way to see past the tree to that place—her voice. I will wait forever, if I must, for that wonderful flapping, and me right there, on the wings of it.

"Gently," her biography reads, "gently in recollection, Colette led her visitor to the bedroom she had known as a child; she showed him the cat-door, through which at dawn, the vagabond cat had ambled in and fallen on the bed, 'cold, white and light as an armful of snow.' Finally she led him into the garden."

Her voice sails on the air, skimming it. "Quelle surprise, Sabine!" she says. She is delighted to hear from her friend who is so far away. It is a miracle, she thinks—and she says so—how one can sound so near, how one can be so far and so near at the same time.

My mother's voice is a small boat being tossed on the waves. Giddy and light. It gets bigger and moves steadily through the water. "Absolument," she says, "oh, absolument."

She is so charming. "N'est-ce pas?" she laughs. "Evidemment. Oui, maintenant, je suis très heureuse—oui." She is glowing. She laughs again. I close my eyes and pretend I am the woman on the other end of the phone. I concentrate on her voice. She is so delightful. "I would not hesitate to love her," I say to myself. "I would not hesitate to love that voice."

"They dined on mince," she sang, "and slices of quince—" Her eyes lit up. "Which they ate with a runcible spoon," we said together. "And hand in hand, on the edge of the sand, they danced by the light of the moon, the moon. They danced by the light of the moon."

"The waves beside them danced, but they
Outdid the sparkling waves in glee:
A poet could not be but gay,
In such a jocund company,
I gazed—and gazed—but little thought
What wealth the show to me had brought."

" 'The Daffodils!' " I yelled.
"By whom?" my mother asked, smiling.
"Wordsworth!" I screamed.

"For oft when on my couch I lie
In vacant or in pensive mood,
They flash upon the inward eye
Which is the bliss of solitude;
And then my heart with pleasure fills,
And dances with the daffodils."

"You must never forget," she would whisper, leaning over me, after all the bedtime poems had been recited, all the bedtime songs had been sung, as she covered me with her night and shut out the light and kissed me on the forehead, "that the Topaz Bird means us no harm."

"It's even more beautiful than a swan," I said, my head feathery with sleep.

"We are lucky to see it," she said. "You must not be afraid."

The women wake early. It's misty; there's a smell of dew, of damp mushrooms, of nuts—chestnuts. They lie in the wet herbs, say nothing, listen to the odd two-note whistle of a bird. It's spring.

Slowly the garden awakes, the world awakes—le jardin, le monde. They look down the Rue de Beaujolais where the milkman comes in his cart. Christine frames him with a stone wall off in the distance, puts lilacs in the foreground, a border of lavender.

They drink café au lait from cracked pink cups and eat tiny blocks of chocolate. They pet the cats. They open *Le Matin* and *Vogue*. Sabine looks up.

"Grand-père laid slabs of wet chocolate out on the roof at night to dry," she smiles, "and in the morning there would be the most wonderful flower-petal designs on them." She giggles. "They were the paw prints of cats!"

In the distance they can see the sunlit slopes where the grapes that have been in Sabine's family hundreds and hundreds of years grow. It's fall now. All is burnt orange, and yellow, and scarlet. The earth smells so lovely—the smoke, the leaves. The silence is thrilling. They walk into the dark woods together, pretending it is a virgin forest that no one has ever dared walk in, though an hour before they watched the woodcutter disappear into that leafy darkness.

"I'm cold," Christine says.

"Maman used to carry a small metal box of coals and ashes to school to keep her warm," Sabine says, running through the leaves in her boots. They laugh and laugh at the thought of Sabine's mother and hug each other, fall into the leaves, get up and run back to the house for sweaters. "There were always wonderful winter roses on the Christmas table," Sabine says, rosy cheeked, smiling, looking around the room. "Maman always saw to it."

"Come with me," she whispers, taking Christine's hand. Slowly they descend the dark steps to the apple cellar. The smell fills them. They lie on the cool dirt floor. My mother takes off her thick sweater. Their breathing grows heavy. They move closer. They close their eyes.

After a long while Sabine opens one eye. From a small window she sees the face of a young goat looking in at them. "Look!" she cries, and they are doubled over in laughter. It seems that they have never seen anything funnier in their whole lives.

"Enough of this!" Sabine says, running up the apple cellar stairs. "A Paris," she writes on blue paper and leaves it on the table of the winter roses.

"Paris," Sabine sighs, "finally!" They make a stop for cologne, a stop for blue paper, stamps, cherries, champagne.

"Oh, Paris!" my mother sighs. "Les fêtes, les soirées, les salons." "Et beaucoup de femmes!" Sabine laughs. "Grand-mère told me that Mata-Hari danced her Javanese dances entirely in the nude once, for the women. Can you picture it?" She laughs and laughs.

My mother walks slowly, dropping her gloves, catching a falling scarf, stalling for time. Beautiful, vibrant Paris turns to watercolor sadness.

"Don't worry," Sabine pouts, "one day when we are very old we'll join a traveling circus and be together forever." They embrace, kiss good-bye for the thousandth time.

"Au revoir, ma Paris. Au revoir, ma Sabine," Christine says. She walks slowly, turns once more.

"We'll be tightrope walkers," Sabine says.

My mother smiles and waves good-bye.

She is dozing off now with the other little girl, her sister, in the cramped room. The fat man reads about New Orleans to them from the newspaper's travel section.

"New Orleans—that sounds, that sounds," she murmurs, falling asleep. What she means to say, what she would have said, was "that sounds so nice."

In her dreams the notes of a saxophone slide out of the windows and she is sure she has never heard anything like it before.

Creoles—was that what those people were called? There are feathers and fans, men dressed as women, women dressed as lizards and birds, laughter, and a drink called bourbon. All of it follows her into her dreams.

And the fat man, too, leaving for work, dreams his way into the dark mill.

"The rainbow-colored Painted Desert of Arizona sweeps in a great crescent from the Grand Canyon southeast along the Colorado River to the Petrified Forest."

"The Petrified Forest!" Lucy cries.

"Go now," my mother says. "There is no other way."

The apartment is warm and dark. I turn in bed toward the wall and hug the cat. "But Mother," I say.

"Go," she urges me.

But I hesitate here. I would prefer to forget.

"There is no other way," she says.

And so I go, in my mind, back to college where I will spend a little more than one semester. First to that strange, sad room, then to the beautiful library, and then beyond that, too.

"It's time," she says. And I know she is right.

Part Three

I decided to forgo all the initiation rites of freshmen and went instead to the library. Eleanor Cove, the librarian, in response to my question, lifted her arm, pointed to the stacks on the second floor, and looked up. In her raised face I saw what I had seen so often in my mother. Here was a lover of books, a woman dizzied by them, transformed in some way. She smiled. Quietly she explained to me how things were arranged, where the periodicals were located and the reference room. I thanked her and climbed the stairs.

The library was empty. Classes had not yet begun and people were still stuck somewhere in summer, I assumed—on the wavy lake or the tennis court with its green hum.

It was cool and dark and I felt safe here. In the context of such coolness and sense and order it seemed that the events of the night before could not have happened; walking to the shelves I felt strangely free of them: that odd room on the top floor, Marta and her sad, sad story, and the needle I watched sink into my arm. I had changed into a long-sleeved shirt before going to the library, hoping to disown that arm somehow.

I loved the order of libraries. I felt at ease here among the old and new books, lined and numbered on the shelves. I found what I was looking for easily. When I was done I would put those books back in the same place, and on another day I would be able to find them again. Most people would think little of such a simple thing, but this afternoon the thought of every book having its place and no book being lost gave me an overwhelming sense of pleasure.

It was the pleasure of square dancing with my brother at the Blue Goose in Moose Point, Massachusetts. We loved the reliability of it, the certainty. We knew when we unlocked hands to allemande left or turned our backs on each other to honor our corners and do-si-do we were not losing each other; we would reunite in the end—it was in the design of the call—and it made letting go possible. We always knew that for the final promenade we would be together.

I lined up the books on the table, starting with the earliest—the first book on the left and, six books later, the last one on the right. I turned them all over so that I could see the photographs of the writer, my mother. Watching my mother slowly age on the back of her books always had a calming effect on me. I wanted to linger this afternoon at each stage, tracing the shape of the years. I had studied these photos often, but now, missing her more than I ever had, I wondered what secret her face might give up. *She* had always left *me*—trips to France, summers in Maine, readings all over the country—but this time I was the one who had driven away, and it was she who stood at the edge of the driveway, stationary, growing smaller and smaller, and it made my longing more acute. Over the years I had stayed home from school often, not wanting to leave her. And when the young teachers came, as they inevitably did, I would run and hide.

"Vanessa?" my mother would say to those earnest women, "why, Vanessa could be anywhere. I can't keep track of her." And then she'd whisper, "She's like the air, you know," and motion out into the world and laugh her long lovely laugh.

The photo of my mother on the back of her first book remains the most constant in my mind. It is the one least altered by memory for I cannot ever remember my mother looking the way she does there. I love to look at her at twenty-three: the yellow-blonde hair, the smooth egg of a forehead, the softness of her face which, at this age, still seems to be forming. She looks like someone else almost, a young beauty, an actress perhaps, caught strangely off guard in the moment before she raises her hand to block her face from the camera or to put on sunglasses, shielding herself from a demanding public. She looks unfocused, nervous, as if she has already lost her way, though she has just barely begun. She seems to be moving slightly in the frame, but she does not know where she is going or why.

At times when I look at that photo of my mother on the back of *Winter*, her first book of poems, I think I can see Sabine, who took that picture, reflected in my mother's eyes. "Smile," Sabine is saying. "Don't be so hard on yourself. This won't hurt at all." I imagine she lifts her polka-dotted dress to her thighs, bends her knees slightly, and does a little dance for my mother. Other times when I look at this photograph I think I can see a shadowy figure, quite small, standing behind my mother, caressing her shoulders, dark eyes lowered; and that, too, is Sabine.

Every time I look at this picture of my young mother I see what drew people to her and held them so long. Looking at her that afternoon in the library, I thought, we're nearly the same age—and I studied her closely, as if with enough concentration I might see what to do next.

The second portrait of my mother is the most troubled. She is thirty-two here and it has been a long time between books. In that time Fletcher and I have been born. She carries our births in her face in baffled, dramatic lines. I know just by looking at her here that loving us was never easy for my mother. In this photograph, though it ends at the shoulders, I see Fletcher asleep in her arms and myself curled around her leg like a cat. My mother looks impatient, her eyes are more heavily lidded than before, and her face is strained. She could never have guessed that it would take so long to go such a short distance. As a child, this is the face I memorized. I knew every line, the way her hair curved around her face, the eyes, always dissatisfied, and the pale color of despair that, no matter how much praise she received or how many awards she won, never left her. In her poems she was interested only in saying what could not be said. "There must be a way," I would hear her say to Sabine long distance, half in English, half in French.

She looks out from this book vacantly at an audience she can neither see nor imagine. She's too tired. It's been so hard.

The few people in the library were leaving now for dinner. The quiet seemed to deepen. I felt alone with my mother here where she herself might have sat years before, reading or staring out into the pines.

I was well accustomed to quiet. The word itself carried great significance, for it was nearly the only instruction ever given in our house. It had the gravity of a sole reprimand. We grew to accept it as one of the necessary ingredients of creativity. We respected it, lived in it. "Quiet," my father would say, "your mother is working. Don't forget, it's very important. Your mother needs quiet."

My father was comfortable in the quiet. It made the silence in him seem not so strange. People thought he had cultivated it, worked on it, restrained himself because it was so necessary for my mother. But that was not the case. Had loquaciousness and vivacity been demanded for my mother to write, my father could not have done it. For years his speechlessness, his hushed tones, his silence have been legitimized by my mother's art. It was not a heroic effort; he never even tried to talk to us.

I looked to the third photograph in an attempt to quiet my brain's unexpected noise.

On the book jacket of *To Vanessa* is my favorite picture of my mother. She is in profile and she looks as serene as I have ever seen her—content, happy. The light is beautiful and she is smiling. I would have stopped her in my mind in this position forever if I could have, but that is the photographer's art, not the daughter's. My mother cannot stay still in my mind. A lovely profile turns full face, slowly the smile dissolves, and the vision breaks. Her hair grays, then changes back. She grows young, wanders through the quiet house of her childhood in Paterson, New Jersey, a little girl on tiptoe, looking in on her own sleeping mother or sitting in the dark listening to the Sunday stories of her father. I looked again at her smiling profile on the back of *To Vanessa*, my book. She will not hold still for me.

I remember the picture on the back of her fourth book being taken on the front porch of our house in summer. This must be the reason I cannot see the photo more clearly. I keep seeing beyond the picture's perimeters, beyond the reach of the lens. I know what my mother saw the moment the shutter clicked. I see the lilac bush just feet away from her. I smell the honeysuckle still. I hear bees, a whole sweet tree buzzing. The photographer, talking to her in his quiet way, lifts her chin and says, "You have lovely children, Christine," and she, looking absently in our direction, says, "Yes, I suppose they are."

My father turns the glass knob of the porch door and comes over to where Fletcher and I stand, looking on, and we all wave to her. She sits still as a stone and smiles back.

On her latest book her face seems to have completed itself. There on her brow her first and last poems meet. The difficult second book has brought severe lines around her eyes. The middle work hollows her cheeks. The latest poems chisel her features, refining them. This was the mother I had left for college. She looks weary, I think, preoccupied, lost in her solitary craft.

I want to look like her: the high forehead, the feverish, full lips, the wild, graying hair.

Dreamy, she stares back at her invisible audience. We can't know what she's thinking. We look harder. We try to see how she gets where she goes and, every time, she loses us. The watery eyes seem to float back away from her face into her luminous head where something opens, and she sees far, far off. We pursue her and she eludes us.

"Mother," I whisper into the glossy photo, into the fresh ink, the cool, smooth page, "take me, too." Her pale eyes surface, her pupils open, overflowing with love, it seems.

"Yes," she says very quietly, reaching for me through the terrible distance. "Come then," she says, "follow me." Louder this time, "Vanessa, yes."

In what is called "real life," I have only passed once through Paterson, New Jersey, the place where my mother grew up, but I have been there many times in dreams. Some people would say that is the safer way to go to that sad, violent city, but I would not agree with them. What I have imagined from casual remarks made over the years by Aunt Lucy after too many brandies or by my mother, who on occasion tucked a childhood memory into a bedtime story, is just as dangerous, if not more.

Christine and Lucy are huddled in one corner of the sickroom. It is dark and quiet—dark even though it is summer, quiet even though the children are out of school. The house holds the family's pain in its wooden hand. Though it is hot they seem to be shivering, the two little girls and the mother who is so sick. "Why are you this way?" Lucy wants to ask but does not. "What makes you this way?" The girls crumble into each other; the house crumbles into the gray dust. I have seen houses like this before—in downtown Poughkeepsie. They are furnaces in summer. People hang out their windows or sit on the broken-down front porches fanning themselves, on the steps of August, music blaring from transistor radios, dogs tied with chains in the backyard. I have always been frightened of these houses, where I think I can see my mother barefoot, back by the fierce dog, or peering out from an upstairs window—a little girl. She will not hold still.

There are no curtains on the windows of my mother's house. There is little furniture. At night you can look straight through to the other side. There is nothing to obscure the strangeness of the fact that we live in boxes made of wood. A whole family lives in this sad box—though the father is not home much, has never been home much. He works at the silk mill, two and three shifts a day. The mother's medicine is expensive and without it the doctors say she will die.

"Don't die," Christine whispers at the edge of her mother's bed as she sleeps. "Please don't die."

"Tell me a story," her mother asks when she finally opens her eyes. My mother takes her mother's pale hand. Words are good, she thinks. Words are medicine, too. With her words she makes curtains for the windows. Light weaves through the little girl's lacy tales. She crochets beautiful bed linen. She makes elegant nightgowns for her mother. With words she wraps her, with words she makes her mother smile. She would save her life; she would make her well—with words.

"What made you this way, Mama?" Lucy finally does ask. Their mother who has been so sick for as long as the girls can remember, too weak to talk much now, moves her hand toward her heart.

"It's my heart," she whispers. "As a child I had rheumatic fever and now I have a damaged heart."

"Rheumatic," Lucy says, writing it down, sounding it out, "room-attic." How terrible.

On the day their mother died the girls were only eleven and twelve years old. Their mother was thirty-five.

"Room-attic," Lucy said over and over again. "Room-attic. How terrible."

And it was only months after their mother was gone that my own mother came running into the death house after school, crying out to her younger sister, "I'm dying, too." She hurried Lucy into the dingy bathroom and said, "Look, just look," and she pulled down her underwear to show the blood that had stained them and continued to flow from her.

"It won't stop, Lucy. I'm just like Mom." And she began to sob.

"Don't cry," Lucy said, stroking her sister's head. Something occurred to her. "Wait. I'm not positive," my eleven-year-old aunt said, "but I think this is supposed to happen."

"This is no time for jokes, Lucy," my mother yelled. She sat at the edge of the bathtub and wept. Blood ran down the inside of her thighs. Bright red blood fell to the tiled floor, flowing harder, the harder my mother cried. Her sister sat on the edge of the tub and began wrapping toilet paper into a little pad which she put in a clean pair of underwear to absorb the blood.

"Here, put this on," she said. "Don't worry. I'll think of something."

But secretly Lucy was worried indeed. She looked up blood in the encyclopedia. She looked up cut, bruise, scrape. She looked up every possible spelling of rheumatic but found nothing. Maybe it was true: they were marked for death in advance, as Christine said.

"Mother!" Lucy said, growing impatient, stomping her feet on the street and looking up into the sky. "Tell us what is happening!"

But their mother was dead now and she had been too ill to hold the words of life in her mouth that would have prevented this scene.

Wandering desperately through the drugstore, trying to find the courage to approach the pharmacist who had known their mother so well and to tell him the terrible news, Lucy found the clue she was looking for on a box. The box was lavender and had flowers on it and a woman about the age of their mother smiling. Another box was pink with a sunset and a bird flying across it.

"You're men-stroo-ate-ing," my aunt said proudly.

"That sounds bad," my mother said softly. "How long do I have?"

"No, you don't understand. It *is* supposed to happen. And everyone is smiling on the boxes like they have a secret."

"What boxes?"

"The napkin boxes."

"The napkin boxes?"

"Sanitary napkins." And Lucy presented Christine with her own box. "They catch the blood."

"Did Mother have this, too?"

"Yes, I think she did."

"Everybody gets it?"

"Only girls do, when they become women."

"I'm a woman?"

"I guess so."

My mother cried with relief. But she also cried, I think, because she was a woman and she did not want to be one yet. For some reason she knew that a woman's life would not be an easy one. Her mother, the only woman she really knew, was dead; she did not know where to turn. Lucy, soon to be a woman too, began to find consolation in boys who, by some predictably fitting quirk of fate, did not have to be men when girls had to be women.

Soon Lucy would never be home anymore either. She would get a job in the drugstore selling Hazel Bishop lipsticks behind the cosmetics counter, the same drugstore where she had discovered, not so long before, the secret of menstruation. The rest of her time she would spend at the local soda fountain or "having adventures" as she liked to call them. She would be a wild teenager, riding motorcycles with boys in leather jackets, jumping from planes in parachutes, teetering on the edge of the Great Paterson Falls. What was my aunt wishing as she looked down at the jagged rocks, the rushing water? I don't know what would have happened to her had the man in the suit and tie carrying the briefcase not shown up and offered his hand and said in his optimistic way, "I hope you have a good life plan, young lady."

"Huh?" Aunt Lucy must have said.

"I said you should be protected by a comprehensive life-insurance policy," he shouted over the water.

"Life insurance!" she said to the man. "Life insurance?" She was only sixteen.

When Philippe Petit, a celebrated tightrope walker and bon vivant, would cross the falls in the early 1970s, Aunt Lucy, in her nurse's uniform, taking the afternoon off from St. Joseph's hospital, would be in the front row with Uncle

Alex, her neck craned, pointing, closing her eyes, visualizing herself up there, too, next to Philippe, umbrella in hand, remembering her own days of daring at the edge of these same falls.

The insurance salesman proposed marriage when Aunt Lucy was seventeen, and that year she entered nursing school and put her old life behind her. She would learn what made her mother so sick in the first place and why nothing could be done about it. I can see her today. When my brave aunt puts a steady hand on a patient's forehead in Beekman General in Hartford, Connecticut, or speaks softly to a sick child, or cradles a postoperative woman in her arms, I know it is really her mother she hugs and whispers comfort to, her mother's forehead she touches. Daily she saves Grandma Alice's life as she checks a pulse, measures temperature, takes blood pressure. Over and over again for thirty years—she continues even now.

And what of Christine, my mother, a young woman left all alone in that silent house? Motorcycles, parachutes, souped-up sports cars—these things frightened her. All the risks my mother took were mental. Her high dives, her balancing acts, her fiery leaps were in the imagination. Every day of her teenage life she tried to imagine her way free—to find somehow the shining door inside her that would provide the escape from this Paterson and their poor life and no mother. Escape it with words; change it with words. Words—she looked tirelessly for the words that might bring back her mother if only momentarily or the words that might make some sense of things. She invented the versions, pictured the scenes where her mother still lived, finding a way to continue.

She looks still, wherever she is, I'm sure of it. She searches for that pale quiet woman, wrapped in blankets. She writes, helping her up from the bed. She writes, getting her back, recovering her from the dark.

This is their favorite day of the week. The children sit quietly in the room and wait for their father to come home. The mother, who is so sick, sleeps, preparing for his arrival, too. When he comes in at twelve from a morning of overtime, he will have with him flat bread and poppy-seed buns from the Armenian bakery, and the Sunday paper. They will sit together in the bedroom and all afternoon he will read to them of exotic places from the paper's travel section.

"Where are we going today?" Mother asks. She has not left her bed in weeks.

"Let's see," Father says. "How about Savannah?"

"Oh, yes," little Christine says. "Let's go there!" Savannah—they all sigh and he begins to read. He reads to them all afternoon. Savannah first, then Niagara Falls, then Taos, then San Francisco, then Savannah again, until the sky grows dark.

"It's pitch black out!" Lucy says.

"We could be anywhere!" Christine whispers.

As they grow sleepy in the scent of Savannah, of jasmine, of magnolia, Father flips to his favorite section—sports, where he reads the horse-racing results out loud.

"They run fast as the wind," Lucy says.

"Like the wind," Mother says, and her voice wavers, "the wind."

"Yes," Father says, "as fast as the wind." And with those words they are asleep. Her father closes the paper and leaves the house for the night shift.

She could dream of petting one. She could dream of running her hand down its smooth, broad nose, between the large, brown eyes—the gentlest of all eyes. She could touch its coarse mane, put her arms around its tremendous neck. She could hear its heart, its loud, huge heart, kept in the wide silky box of its chest.

She watches it play in a field of sweet clover—its rounded haunches, its curving neck, in the golden light of day. She says the word *graze*; it sounds good to her.

If she had one she would offer it apples and feel its square nose flatten her hand. She would make it a soft bed of hay. She would cover it with a red blanket, put fresh water in the drinking trough, put feed in a jute and burlap sack.

At night she would stay with it in its stall. If she saw an animal like that she would never leave its side. She could feel its large, warm breath in the dark, making a veil of protection, a home of breath. She would put her mother in that safe, warm tent where she might live forever.

Now he turns to the sports section in the drowsy room. He gets out his wallet and hands his wife and his two daughters two dollars each. They sit straight up and listen with great care as he begins to read the litany of names: Bride-to-Be, Let's Go Stella, Off the Sauce, Lunar Landing, French Lace—

"Lunar Landing!" Lucy says, "I want that one to win!"

"French Lace," my mother sighs, claiming her horse.

Their father marks off their choices on the newspaper. They consider nothing but the sounds of those names—not the jockeys or the trainers, not their racing records or the conditions of the track or the odds.

"Double or nothing," the father says, or "Miguel Hernandez will be riding." Their mother, Alice, picks "Christmas Bells." Father picks "Chrissy the Wissy" because of his daughter, Christine.

She loves the language of horses her father can speak. "It's the Perfecta," he says, "the Daily Double—the purse of a thousand dollars." She thinks what she would do with that much money. She closes her eyes and sees the jockey in satin bouncing up and down, up and down—the reins, the whips, the numbers; the horseshoes of flowers; the arms of roses. She spins garlands. She places laurels of her own making around their thick necks.

She could dream of riding one, feel her legs gripping its powerful sides. "They go as fast as the wind, Lucy." She could dream of never coming back.

She would ride as fast as the wind, feel the great heart pumping, the lungs breathing, the fierce neck straining, she straining too toward the finish, their bodies yearning toward home. She looks to her sleeping mother, squeezes her pale hand—aching—kisses her on the cheek—striving.

She joins her mother in a green pasture of sleep where they walk together longing for those horses. She knows how much they need them. They grow large in her dreams. She says the word *graze*. It sounds good to her. Each horse floats in ghostly procession in front of them, countable as sheep. Giants, they pass in slow motion, the sound of their hooves magnified a hundred times. An endless procession, one by one they lope over the hill and are gone. She names them as they pass her: Bluebell, Hibiscus, Daffodil, Mimosa. They walk, they prance, they canter, they gallop—they never tire. This is what she must do. This, she knows, is what she has to do: help her mother onto the floating back of one of those gentle ghost horses, make the trip as easy as possible for her— over the green hills, into the blue sky.

I know when she shuts off her light. I know when she shifts in her sleep or when, unable to sleep, she walks in her high rubber boots through fields of snow near our house. Her restless body plows through my every dream, my deepest sleep.

My mother raises her arm, bends her knee. The pasty dance instructor yells in a shrill voice, "One, two, cha-cha-cha. Three, four, cha-cha-cha. Head up, cha-cha-cha. Smile, smile, cha-cha-cha. Good, good, cha-cha-cha."

The sun is a steady drone in the sky. She covers her eyes as she ascends toward it. Her ears flood with the melancholy voice of the pilot. He sounds like a skinny man, she thinks, with no family. She laughs. To him she has given her ridiculous life, filled with gravity.

The steward offers after-dinner drinks: amaretto, Kahlua, Cointreau. The plane shifts its path. She wants nothing but to see Natalie in France again. Even if Natalie whispers lies, even if she talks about someone else's dark eyes, she will allow it; she would allow Natalie anything. "I will," she says to the woman fastened securely next to her. "I will see her again."

"Natalie," she whispers in the tiny, steel bathroom. "You would like this, you would really like this." She smoothes the lining of her coat and adjusts her belt, which is heavy with hash, with cocaine. "If only you were here," she thinks, looking at the tanned arms Natalie once said she loved so much.

Her name is Marta. She is not on her way to meet Natalie. She is not going to France. She is going, of all places, to Poughkeepsie, New York, back to college for her senior year. Alone, she thinks she will watch her body grow white without sun in the Hudson Valley winter. The small toilet spins like the empty cylinder of pills she holds so tightly. Dizzy, she kneels on the floor. She is caught in its circular motion as if it were a tornado, as if it could carry her away and when it stopped she would be safe finally. If she could only keep the pills down, she thinks. But her body has its own logic. It pumps out the poison, insisting on life. She vomits again and again, expelling the small ovals of white. She drops the bottle, disgusted, it having taken her nowhere.

"Natalie, did you forget our plan? The Rive Gauche, Capri, London? Have you forgotten everything? The way we carved our promises into one another's arms, slowly, deeply, so we might never forget? And how much we bled? Has the skin grown back so thick over those words?"

Blood flows up from the toilet: clouds, mangled birds, hands—Natalie's hands, her punctured arms, Natalie's blood, dark and purple—a storm—Natalie's blood. She leaves the bathroom, looks out the window. The sky is covered with it. She will see her again. The whirling wind will take her there, she tells the woman next to her. She smiles and sucks in the sweetness of high altitude. She is spinning, she is turning, she is moving away, far above the troubled earth, to Natalie.

I do not think he could help but let the past back in as he drove down Raymond Avenue and we approached Vassar College where my mother had gone to school, where he had first seen her that night at the dance, and where now I, their daughter, would be. Though he had not been back in years, he was probably not surprised at how little it had changed. There were places like that, he thought. I imagine, as we approached the main gate, that he could still see my mother there, sitting on the bench in a cotton dress and a straw hat holding a small suitcase and waiting for the bus. As we passed the library, which he pointed out to me, his eyes seemed to linger there as he watched her under that huge tree, reading Baudelaire and Rimbaud to him tentatively in French.

Perhaps once these images started coming they did not seem so dangerous to him and he no longer fought them off. I would like to think that in the consistent Vassar air he could go back easily in time and feel comfortable there.

I was to live in Main Building, where she had once lived. As my father drove home on the curving Taconic Parkway, perhaps this made some sort of lovely sense to him and he said to himself, "Life works"—said it out loud alone in the car, "Life works; things turn out," and for a moment he felt at ease in the deep green of late summer in the Hudson Valley. I'd like to think that he took a deep breath and was happy to be alive—and that the world loved and accepted my father as well. For an instant, as my father drove back to Connecticut, the future must have seemed manageable to him. I want to believe that that night my father saw in his mind my mother and me in that great building together at the mouth of the campus, and that his complicated emotions simplified and things fell into place and he smiled to himself.

Much later, when I would try to picture the two white headlights careening into the back of the car, I would think of that early morning when my father turned on the headlights of the Oldsmobile so that we could make our way to it, through rain, in darkness.

"Everybody up," my father chirped like a songbird early that morning, coming into my bedroom first, then Fletcher's, then to the guest room where my grandparents were asleep. "Come on, come on," he said with an unrecognizable zeal that woke Fletcher and me almost immediately with its strangeness.

"It's four in the morning," I heard my grandmother say.

"That's right, it's four in the morning—it's time to get dressed." He was already dressed as he walked back and forth from room to room. He had slept in his clothes, I was sure. They were wrinkled and tired on his body. His hair stuck up in strange places.

"It's four in the morning and it's pouring rain," I could hear my grandmother saying over and over.

My mother floated into the room wordlessly and looked out the window into the darkness. She went to my closet and picked out a yellow plaid dress for me to put on. She would choose red overalls and a striped shirt for Fletcher. My mother liked to dress us in bright clothing. She always believed, I think, that if we were dressed inappropriately for the receipt of bad news, we would somehow be spared it. She herself, when she was finally ready, wore a pink suit and a large white hat, her hair pulled away from her face.

My grandparents, the first to respond to Father's wake-up call, were the last to be ready, and, as we sat on the love seat in the hallway, my mother, Fletcher, and I, holding sweaters and raincoats in the dark, my father paced back and forth.

"Where *are* they?" Father muttered under his breath.

"Grandpa is trying on bow ties," Fletcher said, as if he could see through the walls to the guest room.

"How do you know?" I whispered, but he just shrugged his shoulders. He was wearing brown and white saddle shoes and his feet swung back and forth in the air. They did not nearly touch the ground. He looked ahead unblinking.

"Give them another minute, Michael," my mother said.

"Here they come," said Fletcher, in his strange way, and Grandpa appeared, like magic, on the arm of his dour wife. He looked fresh and bright and wide-awake. In spite of our great curiosity and our cheerful attire, we looked like sleepers next to him.

"Well, finally!" my father said, clapping his hands double time. In his head he heard the music that would move us bravely forward. It was so unlike him.

"In the rain," my mother sighed, as if she had just noticed it.

"Rain is good luck, Christine," my grandfather winked. My grandfather's whole posture suggested that he thought this was going to be one of the great-est days of his entire life. He had chosen a yellow bow tie with maroon spheri-cal shapes on it. He was putting rubbers over his best dress shoes.

"OK, is everybody ready now?" my father said, chirping again and clapping his hands. "Are you ready, Mother?" he asked. "Put on your coat."

Grandma, who long ago had stopped loving my father, just looked wearily at him without saying a word. Withheld love had aged her. My father stood momentarily paralyzed in the bitterness of her stare, but somehow clapped his hands and began to lift his feet like some college bandleader, whistle in mouth, baton in hand, finally gathering the momentum to break from her and lead his colorful, sleepy parade out into the dark, wet springtime.

"But we can't see anything, Daddy!" we screamed with a thrill. Bad weather had blindfolded us. The wind was spinning us around and around. Father ran ahead to turn on the headlights of the car for us. Without sight we could hear better, and we listened to his footsteps racing across the wet gravel of the long driveway that wrapped around our house. Fletcher took my hand. Grandfather put his arms around us, stooping with care so as not to let any part of his pants touch the grass. We looked at him through the windows of our rain slickers and smiled at his infectious smile. The lights went on. My mother, off to one side, held a large umbrella over her head and, even at five in the morning in the rain, she was an image of such beauty that I felt out of breath just looking at her and had to take off my hood.

Grandma just sighed, standing on the porch watching us in the black grass.

"It's going to be a long day," my grandmother said, though even she with her "negative thinking," as Grandpa called it, could not guess how long. Right from the beginning, as my father got into the car and fumbled with the keys, my grandmother was suspicious. She had a right to be, I suppose. My father had mysteriously asked them to come from the farm in Pennsylvania to join him on a very important trip, but he had neglected to say where they were going or when they might be back. Fletcher and I, typically good-humored children and always poised for adventure, did not care so much about the details; we just watched Father, who did not seem like our regular father. For everyone but Grandmother it was enough to see the amazing color in my father's face that this trip, wherever we were going, had produced. Anything we were about to do seemed certainly worth it to see Father this way.

Sliding into the passenger's seat and looking over at him, my mother seemed overcome with nostalgia. She must have thought to herself that his eyes looked as they once had, long ago, focused and clear. And for a moment my grandfather, getting into the back seat with my grandmother and Fletcher, looked up, as if he were wondering who this wonderful young man was who was driving his family in the dark, for my father was a son my grandfather had never seen before. He was taking charge. He was going somewhere.

"We're really on our way now!" my grandfather said, adjusting his bow tie and patting my grandmother on the back.

"There are no sandwiches," Fletcher whispered in my ear, leaning forward from the back seat. It was a sign we were not going far, for Father always made sure there was something to eat. He always fixed us the most elegant lunches to bring to school, chicken and pineapple salad, cucumber sandwiches, cinnamon and apple tea or hot chocolate with orange peel.

My father drove wildly through the early morning, flying down the suburban streets much faster than he had ever driven before, until the passengers began to complain.

"Michael, please," my mother said quietly, "please, not so quickly."

Taking her cue from my mother, my grandmother began in her solemn voice, "I don't know why you feel we have to leave at this unreasonable hour but if you don't slow down, I'm getting out right here and you can forget the whole thing. Why you need us all here in the first place I'll never understand."

"Just close your eyes, Maria, and enjoy the ride," my grandfather said. But he, like the rest of us, must have wondered exactly what it was that my father was up to.

I sat between my mother and father in the front seat and noticed that he lifted his foot slightly from the accelerator in deference to his passengers, but after a while he seemed to forget and I watched his foot sink back down onto the pedal.

Everything out the front window of the Oldsmobile was an intense blue at that hour, as we neared the highway. My mother, opening her eyes, held my hand and together we looked out on the blueness of the world.

I began to worry about my father and indeed about all of us, when, with the light growing paler, I could see the expression that was on his face, and when, staring into the blue out the window, I realized where we were going.

My father had mentioned the blue to me several days before. "It will be bathed in blue light," he had said, and from his intonation I could not tell whether he thought that was a good or a bad thing. I shivered now, as I thought of all the hours he had spent dreaming of this day. My father had always considered me not so much a daughter as a partner in sorrow and so had seen fit to share with me the details of the long journey of Michelangelo's *Pietà* from the Vatican in Rome to the New York World's Fair.

"The *Pietà* is being insured for five million dollars," he read to me from the newspaper one day.

"A Rome newspaper is urging the Vatican not to send the *Pietà*," he told me.

"The *Pietà* has been successfully moved from its pedestal to a packing case," and he showed me a picture of Christ up to the waist in little styrofoam pieces.

"The *Pietà* leaves the Vatican and arrives in Naples."

"The *Pietà* is placed in a watertight steel container and lashed to the deck of a ship."

"The *Pietà* will be unveiled Thursday."

And now it was Thursday. It would be bathed in blue. It would change our lives.

He turned on the radio and the back seat jumped awake. The sky was growing light. "Goddammit," my father, who never swore, said, "we should have started earlier." Someone on the radio was saying that massive traffic tie-ups were expected on all major routes to the World's Fair. A stall-in initiated by the Congress on Racial Equality meant to dramatize the Negroes' dissatisfaction with the pace of civil rights progress was planned, despite a court injunction.

"The stall-in is on!" declared a deep, resonant black voice from what seemed the center of the Oldsmobile. I did not so much understand the words as the tone. It was angry and sad, energetic and weary, loving and hostile, all at the same time. "Brutality, segregation, discrimination, neglect," the voice said. It was a call for fairness. "We are responsible," the voice bellowed. "We have a right to protest. What happens to us is unimportant. The stall-in is on!" We listened closely and looked out the windows.

My grandmother closed her eyes and put her hand on her forehead as if she already had a massive headache. My grandfather and Fletcher sat straight up at attention. "The World's Fair?!" Fletcher screamed with glee. "We're going to the World's Fair!?"

"In the rain?" my grandmother said. "Why are we going to the World's Fair in the rain, Michael?"

"Mother, please," my father said.

"I was at the 1939 World's Fair!" my grandfather cried. And his thoughts raced ahead of his words. "I remember Big Joe," he said, "the giant steel guy who stood for Soviet man! I ate caviar and drank vodka! I saw television for the first time. Television didn't *exist* before that fair! I saw a collapsible piano made for a yacht! And they put a time capsule in the ground right here in New York! And these," my grandfather said, plucking my grandmother's stockings from her legs, "I saw these invented!"

"Stop, Angelo!" my grandmother shouted, slapping his hands.

"They put all kinds of things in that time capsule—nylons, for instance," and he pulled my grandmother's stockings again, "a can opener, a hat, cigarettes. It's supposed to be opened in the year 6000 as a record of our time."

"Six thousand!" we shouted. "But it's 1964 now."

"One thousand nine hundred and sixty-four," my father said.

"Oh!"

"One thousand, two thousand, three thousand," Fletcher counted.

"And I remember a row of beautiful women dancing a fan dance," my grandfather continued.

My grandmother shook her head.

"Four thousand, five thousand, six thousand."

"And another girl wearing the tiniest bathing suit I've ever seen was put inside a block of solid ice!"

"There will be no girls in ice this time," Father said sternly. My father was the first feminist I ever met.

"Why must we go in the rain, in a civil rights demonstration?" my grandmother asked.

"Maria!" my grandfather shouted.

My mother was not sleeping but her voice was muffled, as if she spoke from some distance. "Please don't fight," she said, "there will be enough of that when we get there."

My father looked at her.

"It will be OK," he said. "Don't worry."

My mother smiled one of her wise smiles. "Fletcher," she said, "there's so much sun around you this morning, I think you may just clear away the rain for us." My brother blushed.

When we got to the highways that were to be choked with cars, there were no cars, just large expanses of gray and long white lines. Father had set aside many hours for sitting in traffic and without it we found we were in Flushing, Queens, just after sunrise, hours before the fair was to open.

When we passed Shea Stadium and my father did not so much as turn his head toward it, as other fathers would have, I knew that we would never be the kind of family that followed baseball scores and owned dogs and went on vacation to Florida. I would like to have asked him just once, when I was eighteen, how the Yankees were doing this year and he in some chummy, sporty sort of way would say, "Well, you know, they're slow starters, but September is their month." But this, of course, would never be.

We parked the car in the vast World's Fair lot and listened to the rain that was beating harder now on the car roof.

"Well, we'll just have to nap a bit," my father said, "and then when we get up it will be time to go in."

"Oh, boy," my grandmother said, closing her eyes.

Who can know what each of us dreamt that early morning in the World's Fair parking lot? I can guess. My father—that's easy: in his dream a grieving mother cradled her dead son's body in silence. It was one constant image, like a slide on a gigantic screen that kept coming into sharper and sharper focus.

My brother must have dreamt of great inventions—weather or time machines, space ships blasting into the black sky, or capsules being plunged into the damp earth.

Grandfather shifted around a lot that morning in the back seat: his long dream of the fair of 1939 suddenly broken by the deep voice from the car radio, taking shape in his sleep.

My grandmother insisted she never dreamed, but I saw her as she slept swatting the air as if shooing away flies, or swatting at my grandfather who she thought still plucked at her brand-new nylons.

It was my mother's dreams that were impossible to know. They were so tangled. When I would try to comb them, they would cascade like her hair, folding and unfolding and folding again, wrapping around each other in complicated tendrils. Does my mother drift through the rain of her dreams until she finally reaches shelter? Do her eyes fix on some simple object, something I'd never think of, a window or a wheel—or some other shape where she finds some psychic comfort? I do not know.

In the middle of his blue dream of bones, my father suddenly woke up and nudged me. "It's almost time, Vanessa," he whispered. He looked feverish and pink, and when I put my small hand to his forehead in what I had seen as adult behavior, it was burning.

"Just wait, just wait," he said to me quickly in a rasping voice.

I looked back and noticed my grandfather, too, was now awake. He looked at me and shrugged his shoulders. Italy did not interest my grandfather anymore, not even Michelangelo and his *Pietà*; America was everything now, but he had never seen my father so consumed. "Dad," my father said, "just wait."

We were nearly the first ones into the fair, and there was no line when we got to the Vatican Pavilion. "This is important," I kept thinking to myself as Father handed us our tickets. My mother took a deep breath, Grandma grimaced, and Grandpa stared straight ahead. "This is important," I thought, "this means something," but I could not for the life of me figure out what about this large sculpture, behind glass, lit in blue, moved my father to tears that day, standing between his parents, hugging them to his side on the moving conveyor belt we all stood on. My father was not, as far as I knew, a religious man. He had hardly ever stepped into a church. But this was important to him, and for no real reason I felt Father's tears in my eyes. My father whispered when we got outside that he would like to view the *Pietà* "a few more times" and then we could head back home.

"But, Dad!" Fletcher said, pointing to things so new he had no names for them yet: spheres, domes, disks, cubes, pylons.

"Oh, we're just going for a short walk, Michael," my grandfather said, running off with Fletcher.

"Meet us back at the Vatican Pavilion," my father yelled to them. "Don't forget!"

"We won't," they said, disappearing. "We won't forget."

My father and I spent the whole rainy morning in front of that sad sculpture. My mother, after two viewings, drifted through the fair alone. I would have joined her had she asked me, but she didn't. She had been quiet the whole trip and, though I sat most of the ride with my head on her pink shoulder or my arm around her arm, she was miles away; it was like holding onto outer space.

I wonder what became of Grandma in those hours. I would like to think that she enjoyed the fair, that she bought a sombrero, that she ate moussaka, that she went to the Clairol Pavilion and saw herself as a blonde or a redhead, but I suppose it's quite unlikely.

I know, though, exactly what my grandfather and Fletcher did after leaving Father and me. Sometimes I think my brother told that story too many times. Sometimes I feel it is too big to live next to. This is how it goes. In the rain, Fletcher and Grandpa watched the opening day parade go by: governors and beauty queens passed them; a steel band, African drummers, Spaniards with guitars; hula dancers shivering on the Hawaiian float; Miss Louisiana in a soaked sequined gown; Montana cowboys and the University of Pennsylvania band, the governor's daughter bravely holding the U. They saw Miss America, Miss USA, Miss Alaska, Joan of Arc on a white horse, one hundred Japanese girls in silk kimonos, and marching red umbrellas. The Watusi royal dancers danced by, and the Lippizaner stallions.

When the parade ended they walked down the Avenue of Research where GE was putting on a fusion display. They passed Indira Gandhi who was presiding over the opening of her country's modern two-story rectangular stone building. They stopped every few feet and witnessed some other miracle, each seemingly greater than the one before: they saw water screens and shadow boxes, undulating roofs, floating cement carpets—until something broke that dream. All of a sudden they saw in front of them a two-hundred-and-fifty-pound black man being lifted by two police officers into a van. The man spoke as he was being carried away. That man was James Farmer, the man whose voice had come from the center of the car and had followed my grandfather into sleep as he waited for the fair gates to open.

"Be gentle with him," my grandfather said out loud, and Fletcher looked up.

"What did he do?" Fletcher asked my grandfather, and my grandfather, who always had an answer to everything, even if it was made up, held my brother's hand tighter and whispered back, not taking his eyes from the scene, "I don't know, Fletcher." And he knelt down so as to look into my little brother's eyes and said again, "I don't know what that man did."

They continued on. They passed pavilions shaped like butterfly wings, like hats, like eggs. They saw the Santa Maria, they saw a gigantic electric map put up by the Equitable Life Insurance Company that lit up every time someone was born or died in the United States. They saw Burundi drummers who had never seen stairs before, let alone stairs that moved, travel them, lying down. They tasted English teas and sushi.

But they could not entirely forget the sight of that enormous black man being lifted into the police wagon. The unlikely image had attached itself to the back of their brains; the sound of that deep, passionate voice clung to their hearts and would not let go.

"Freedom now" was the call through the fair, as my grandfather and Fletcher watched demonstrators dragged through the mud by the legs or the arms or the hair. They were lying in front of buildings and blocking stairways.

"It is a symbolic act," my grandfather explained. "They are blocking the doors in the same way Negroes are being blocked from jobs and houses and schools." And Fletcher nodded.

It must have seemed to my grandfather that he had conjured, through his musings, Abraham Lincoln when he suddenly saw him standing on a stage, large as life. He must have seemed like some hallucination brought about by thinking too long and hard about the Negro man. My grandfather pointed speechless at the tall, brave president from Illinois. "Look," he said finally, hoping that at least Fletcher saw him, too.

At that very moment, a voice over a loudspeaker said that this was a mechanical effigy of Abraham Lincoln, "an audio-animatronic" made by Walt Disney, and that when the electronics were working Mr. Lincoln would walk and talk, would deliver the Gettysburg Address, and even give a flesh-warm handshake. But that day the great emancipator refused to move or talk. Mechanical types were fidgeting with him and with an electronic control board. But Lincoln just stood there, still as a statue, with a look of grave disappointment on his face.

"Come along, Fletcher," Grandpa said hurriedly, walking very quickly now as if he knew exactly where he was going. Nearing the Ford Pavilion he saw that it had been closed by a sit-in. My grandfather watched the small crowd of people who sat on the floor in front of the two escalators that led to Ford's Progressland.

"We want freedom," they shouted.

"When?"

"Now!"

"We want to see the show," the visitors shouted back.

"When?"

"Now!"

"You struggle all you want, you sons of bitches," a fat man in a cowboy hat with two children said.

"Ship 'em back to Africa," a woman sucking on a cigarette shouted.

"It's horrible," another woman about my grandfather's age said, "that something the whole world is looking at today has to be spoiled like this."

And then the cry that propelled my grandfather forward rose high above the crowd. "Get the gas ovens ready!" it shouted. And the whole group cheered. My grandfather felt a wave of sickness pass through him. "No," he said, shaking his head back and forth in disbelief and looking at the ground in shame. "No," he said, holding my brother's tiny hand, and he suddenly felt the need to disassociate himself from the people he stood with and, still holding my brother's hand, he crossed the line and lay down with the demonstrators.

"Freedom now," he shouted.

Freedom now.

It must have been a curious sight. Even the demonstrators must have been suspicious of this unlikely pair: a bow-tied grandfather and his little accomplice.

A young woman and her child came forward, trying to pass the demonstrators. "When I say step on them, I mean step on them," she said, scolding the child. And the little girl gingerly put her patent-leather shoe on my grandfather's chest. Fletcher began to cry. "Don't cry, Fletcher, it doesn't hurt," my grandfather whispered. "Please don't cry."

"You should be ashamed of yourself," the woman said to my grandfather. "And involving that little boy in this, too! You should be locked up!"

"We are not ashamed," my grandfather said.

"What are you? Nigger-lovers, is that what you are?"

"Nigger-lovers," the visitors shouted to my grandfather and Fletcher. "Those two are nigger-lovers," and they laughed.

The newspapers would read, "The oldest and the youngest to be arrested at the civil rights demonstration on the opening day of the New York World's Fair were from the same family. Pictured here, Angelo Turin, 67, and his grandson Fletcher, 5, being taken away by police."

"Careful with the kid and the old man," one policeman said, shaking his head as he put them into the paddy wagon, as my grandfather called it. "You feel OK, Pop? You know what you're doing?"

"Yes, we know exactly what we're doing, thank you. Don't we, Fletcher?" And Fletcher nodded.

They were thoroughly drenched. The rain had not let up much all day. A whole truckload of black men and women, young white people, and my grandfather and Fletcher were taken to some invisible part of the fair grounds.

At the makeshift jail they were an immediate attraction. "Are you for real?" a man said, coming up to my grandfather and seeing that he was quite real indeed, shaking now uncontrollably from the cold.

A few beatniks immediately befriended my brother. "You're lucky," a girl in sunglasses said to him. "You should see *my* grandfather."

When we finally realized that Fletcher and Grandpa were not going to come back, my father grew panicky. "We never should have come," Grandma said. "Opening day in the rain!"

"Perhaps they've gone back to the car," my father said, his voice so nervous that it seemed to divide into two voices.

But it was my mother who finally spoke up. "Come with me," she said. "I know where they are."

We watched as my mother walked in the rainy half-light up to a policeman who began pointing this way and that, but who finally volunteered to take us there in the police car.

She was right, of course.

As we got nearer we could hear a large group of human voices, chanting. The chant grew louder and louder. "Jim Crow must go, Jim Crow must go" was the message rising from the soaked earth.

"Hey, there's Mom!" Fletcher screamed, high and sweet, and he broke away from the group and ran into her arms. He was muddy and drenched, and Father took off his jacket and put it around him.

"Where's Grandpa?" we asked Fletcher and at that moment we heard Grandma's long, low "oh, Angelo!" She had spied him standing in a semicircle of people, dripping wet. They were looking at photographs.

"These two are ours," my father said. "This one and that one over there in the bow tie."

"Not so fast, Mister," a red-faced officer replied. And he took him into a glass office in a green building where I could see Father signing things. My grandfather waved at us but continued talking to the men, and Fletcher began telling the day's story. He was so excited and spoke so quickly that his sentences ran together.

"OK," my father said, coming out after a while, "everything's taken care of," and he went over to get my grandfather, who introduced him to his new friends.

"Grandpa," Fletcher said, "tell them about the paddy wagon!"

"Oh, I will," my grandfather said. He looked very tired, and, moving away from the makeshift jail, he grew quiet, withdrawn almost, as if with one moment of reflection he could see clearly what had happened. Having seen injustice, smelled it, and been touched by it, he felt alone with it. He spoke only once on the long walk back to the car, and it was in a whisper to my father.

"Michael," he said, "they showed me pictures—of ghosts, a secret society of ghosts. Well, they looked like ghosts, but their heads were pointed and they carried earthly weapons, torches and lead pipes."

"I know," my father nodded. "It's the Klan," he said very quietly. "You're wet, Dad. You're going to be sick." But my grandfather was not listening.

"Criminals," my grandmother hissed as my grandfather and brother got into the car. "I won't sit with criminals," she said, getting into the front seat, and so I sat in the back with them.

As Father started the car, we were not aware that back at the fairgrounds Grandfather and Fletcher had joined that part of the population whose names have been permanently on a list.

Turning around in the parking lot toward home, we noticed that the lights had come up. There were a multitude of colors: reds and blues, greens, glowing whites, domes illuminated by yellow, turquoise, and magenta beams. On the gigantic unisphere, continents and oceans and islands were lit in purple and white. Dots of white marked the world's great cities.

It seemed impossible to me that, in this awesome, shining world of light, evil could exist at all.

In front of us, atop the Kodak Building, a luminous Kodachrome Emmet Kelley gestured for us to come forward. To our left rose the Federal Pavilion glowing yellow and red and blue. Far off we could see the green egg of the International Business Machines Corporation, casting its pale hue. And, most magnificent of all, across the Grand Central Parkway stood the two largest buildings of the fair, drenched in white light—the pavilions of the General Motors Corporation and the Ford Motor Company.

My grandfather thought, looking at this exquisite show, that we had traded something important for all of this. Primitive man was better, he thought. He could not help but think that, along with the beautiful lights and the sports cars and the stairs that moved and the fusion display, we had invented a system of hatred and fear so elaborate and so subtle and efficient—in short, so perfect—that it would be nearly impossible to crack. Everything he saw suggested it.

The Pool of Industry exploded with fireworks and fountains of color and light as we watched.

"Primitive man was better," he said out loud.

I looked at my grandfather and saw the imprint of a young girl's patent-leather shoe emblazoned on his chest.

Fletcher was already asleep. I put my head on my grandfather's lap, closed my eyes, and listened to the droning of the rain on the windshield as we pulled away.

My grandfather turned around for one last glimpse of the fair.

In 1939, FDR opened the fair in New York as a symbol of peace. But nothing, of course, could stop what had already begun to happen, and before even one season was over, world war was declared and the lights in many foreign pavilions went out.

The World of Tomorrow was the fair's theme and, standing there on opening day, the sixty thousand who gathered to hear the president must still have been filled with dreams when thinking about the future.

But they could hardly have imagined what tomorrow would bring.

My grandfather turned his back on the lights finally and shook his head with the tremendous sorrow of someone who has been betrayed at the core. I watched him as he closed his eyes and extinguished, one by one, every beautiful light in the fair. He patted my head. "Everything's going to be all right," he whispered, but his voice cracked. And with those words on that April night, suddenly gone dark, in 1964, he began his journey back through time, to a simpler place, where he would live the last years of his life.

Falling Water, the holy man, spoke slowly and with difficulty in the bright light. The young man who listened felt a terrible yearning as he attempted to stop the fall of those words. "Falling Water," he said, "why must this be?"

"I see the circle being broken. I see the sacred hoop pulled apart," Falling Water said. "I see the white man everywhere I look.

"They kill everyone—our women and children, too. They give us a magic water to drink that makes us crazy.

"I see caravans of them moving across our land and making us sick with their diseases and taking away our homes."

"Say this will not happen," the young man cried. "Say you have made a mistake."

Falling Water shook his head. "They will put us into camps."

"We will fight them," the young man said. "We will fight them forever—our best warriors."

"We will die in the snow," Falling Water whispered.

"No," the young man said.

"Great roads like rivers will pass across the landscape and they will build roads in the sky as well. They will talk to each other from great distances through cobwebs.

"I have seen many wars," he said. "White men in gray coats and white men in blue coats will kill each other. And a terrible war will be fought under a black and red symbol of the rising sun." Falling Water looked straight ahead. He did not flinch; he did not look away.

"I see one last thing."

"No, Falling Water, say that is all."

"It is said by the Great Spirit that if a gourd of ashes is dropped upon the earth, then the most hideous of all events will occur. I have seen the gourd suspended in the blue sky, tilted, about to spill over. I was once the eyes of my people. But now I can see nothing beyond that great gourd.

"I am old and tired. This was once my home. But now I go to a different place, far south, into the grandfathers' country, where I will leave my good breath. Do not forget what I have told you."

Fletcher became, as he grew up, our ambassador from the outside world, and he traveled a long way back into the shadows to bring us news. Mother would listen for hours, asking endless questions, engrossed, it seemed, in the details of residential zoning or a new mash being fed farm animals or the latest dance steps or the infant mortality rate in the inner city. She watched him like a tourist, trying to hold onto the dizzying ride of another language, breathless, her eyes wide. I imagine that my face looked the same. We both held on tightly to Fletcher's stories, held on for life.

Father never shared the outside world with us. I imagine he walked through the world of stocks and bonds painfully. He was so vague when it came to his workday that I often wondered whether he really went to a job at all. I could never visualize him there. He could not possibly have chatted with other people on the train or had drinks at lunch with his fellow stockbrokers. Perhaps he did what he did at home—drew endless lines on graph paper alone in a dark room with the radio playing. He never spoke of his office or what he did there. That world must have seemed nonexistent, unreal, when he walked in the door at the end of the day and saw my mother. Everything next to her must have been pale to him, unmentionable.

But, like some foreign correspondent, Fletcher reported everything to us. He lingered on every detail and we would drift in and out of his wonderful stories and their implicit message; everything he said indicated it: the truth was something you could get at. The pursuit of it was a noble ambition. The world was a good enough place to live. Anything was possible.

Yes, anything might be possible, we thought—with hard work, with faith like Fletcher's, with love. Rivers could be cleaned up. Whales might survive. Children might sleep in warm beds having eaten a decent meal. Each house, every apartment in New York might have a warm glow. The children of Vietnam might walk straight and live. Shrapnel would be dug from their legs and they might get up and run. It did not seem so impossible.

Yes, I thought, looking at his face. The smallest efforts made out of love every day mattered. Fletcher was proof of it. He spoke softly and slowly. I listened carefully. He was the crystal in a brooding, murky family. He was my clearing in the woods, my friend, my great friend.

"Talk to me, Vanessa," he would say, even when he was busy designing banners, looking up addresses in the phone book. "Come on," he'd say. He would not allow me to become completely like Mom and Dad. We would talk. We would not lose each other.

My tenacious brother.

"How beautiful the birds must sound to one another," he said, taking a deep breath one afternoon as we walked by the lake. What a lovely day it was. I looked out onto the shining water where it seemed to me that the flat bodies of lily pads or angels floated, giving off their pale light. Fletcher looked out, too. "Vanessa," he said, shaking his head.

"What is it?" I asked, but he was already knee-deep in water, spouting blue and gold and green: my marble boy, my fountain of light.

"Hey, come here," he shouted, and in his hands he held something that glittered; his whole body seemed to glow.

They were fish. Hundreds of them floating on the calm surface. "Sewage overflow," he said. "That's what's killing them." He piled them into my arms. "Hold these," he said. He filled his arms, too, his jacket, his pockets. "Let's go," he said.

"Where?" I asked, though I should have known.

We carried those fish through the center of town and over to the mayor's office. People joined us along the way. "Come," he said, "come on, everyone. Look what's happening," he shouted through the fish stench of death.

My dramatic brother.

"This is our fault," he said to those who looked on. The rotting, open-eyed fish clung to my body, changing me, the shape of my arms, making me understand: it was my fault, too.

"This is what we're up against," he said, coming into my bedroom late one night when he could not sleep and showing me what I could not help but see ahead of time in his eyes: a fox, a bear, a dog, a raccoon, their legs in steel-jawed traps. Some of them had died there finally. Others had gnawed off their own legs to get free. He made me look at every picture.

"This can be stopped," he said. That he believed so fervently that it could be stopped prevented him from being consumed with rage. "It will stop because it must," he whispered. My just brother—my restless brother.

Each day Fletcher lived life with the strange urgency of someone about to leave it forever. It should have exhausted him, but he seemed only to grow stronger. My diligent, my hard-working brother—he never rested.

If college gives you direction and confidence, then Fletcher did not need it. If it keeps you sealed off from the rest of the world, then he did not want it. And when he looked into colleges he could not find one he might be interested in that did not own stock in South Africa.

Fletcher finished high school in three years and so he and I graduated together. I chose to go to my mother's college, and Fletcher that year moved into a special residence, not far from the house, where he worked with the emotionally disturbed who had been released from a nearby institution.

"I am more happy here than I can say," he wrote to me that fall at college. These are the words I love to hear—my loving brother, my patient, happy brother.

"The soul," my grandfather said, and we smiled, hoping that soon we'd be standing on chairs up near the ceiling. "The soul," he whispered. "To help make the soul pure and the body, too, the Indians have something that they call the sweat lodge ritual. Heat and steam are made by sprinkling water on huge white-hot rocks.

"They laughed when I went into one for the first time and told me stories of other white men who had stopped the ritual by standing up and tearing off the top of the lodge or by running away because of the heat.

" 'Now don't run away on us, little white man,' Two Bears laughed.

"Even before the water is sprinkled on the rocks it's so hot in there. It's impossible to lean back without burning yourself. Even as the first rock was put in, I was sweating a lot. Imagine being in there with thirty or forty of these enormous rocks.

" 'Sit by the door, little white man,' Lone Star said, 'so you can get out in a hurry if you have to.' The other Indians, sitting straight up with their eyes closed, chuckled.

" 'Too hot,' Running Antelope said, water flowing from his body as the rocks were handed in.

"Once the door is flapped closed, everything is dark except the light that comes from the rocks. I sat there with them, sweating, and they took me into their prayers. The sacred person prayed to the spirits of people who had died, of animals, of birds, calling everyone Tunkasila, Grandfather. He prayed for his people, for his family, for health, and for important decisions that had to be made with President Nixon. And he prayed for me—that I might go back home and speak the truth about what I had seen and done. 'Help the man who sits with us holding in his heart the whole burden of his race,' they chanted.

"We sang many songs," my grandfather said. "I grew large like an Indian in the steam. I sang out my sadness. Then Running Antelope sang—then Two Bears." Help the little white man, they chanted, through the unbearable heat.

Fletcher once thought he might rescue my mother from that vast country that she wandered through if he learned how to predict the weather. He did not know that, even then, years before he was grown, it was already too late.

The day the thermometer and barometer came, wrapped in brown paper from Dayton, Ohio, Fletcher stared at the package a long time, not opening it, not touching it, just staring. It seemed unlikely to me that this small brown package could change the course of my mother's life, but Fletcher was convinced that, with some personal knowledge of the weather, life would be more reliable, the element of surprise would diminish, plans could be made.

He's not made for this weather. A man like that sweats through his clothes in summer in less than an hour or two. His heart strains in his chest. It's too much.

He is bent over a counter in his small shop. He sweats. The large slow fan hanging from the ceiling is not enough. He is clumsy in such a confining space.

A man his size in New York is always doomed to be uncomfortable—small theaters, small restaurants, narrow streets, subways. It's a city of few Checker cabs, few Madison Square Gardens.

I dream that his thick fingers would know just how to touch me and that he would enter me skillfully. He is someone who is well aware of the texture and shape of muscle, the placement of bones, the flesh that surrounds them, the body's cavities. He holds the entire body of a deer in his arms, draining the blood. He knows just where to cut, just where to hold. He turns deer into venison, pig into pork, cow to beef. He cuts his brothers into pieces in order to live.

Blood covers his apron. His arms to the elbow are smeared with it. He's a little shy, but so capable, so handsome. His hair is short, much shorter than is the style of the time—anything to keep cool. He washes before coming to the front room of the shop, but under his nails I can see the browning blood still. He wipes his brow. He can't go on. It's too much.

A man as hot as that gives in easily. All you would have to do is brush against his hand when paying for veal or sweetbreads—or whisper to him, "how much," or "I need two pounds, please." Let him watch you wipe sweat from your own brow, show him your shoulder, or rub the calf of your leg. Call him by name: say, "Thank you, Jack." Invite him to your apartment just down the street—so close by, surely he'll come. He'll stoop at the doorway. He'll wipe his face on his sleeve.

My mother always looked exhausted to me. Some nights I massaged her neck for a long time just to watch those great lids of hers lower for a while. Other nights she would come to me in my bedroom, brush and hairpins in hand, and say, "Vanessa, darling, would you make me a hairdo?" It was strange to hear the word *hairdo* coming from my mother's mouth. It sticks in my mind—her saying hairdo, me dividing the hair on the sides of her head into three equal parts, braiding them and tying them on the top of her head. I can't decide now whether her hair felt heavy or light in my hands. It was wonderful hair, though, coarse and golden. It stayed exactly where I arranged it; I remember it perfectly. "Oh, another one, please," she would always say after I had finished one and she had admired it in the mirror for a long time. "It feels so good," she would say. My mother loved to feel my hands running through her hair, and I loved to see her relax there with me for a moment.

Her smile, her whole body wavers. Her eyes seem about to go out, to extinguish themselves. She looks from person to person. "You're exquisite!" she gasps, looking at a woman only a few years older than I am. "You're lovely," she whispers. She laughs her high laugh and tosses her head back confidently.

"It is not enough, Vanessa," Jack says. "A daughter combing her mother's long hair, a brother who saves animals—all these sweet memories. They are not enough. This mildness will kill you."

He hugs me close. "Don't be afraid," he says. "Try not to be afraid. There is no way to stay safe."

We walked silently on the turning earth with our grandfather. "Look," he said, pointing to the sky. "Look," he cried, "over there! Eagles!"

We looked up. I looked at my father's pained face.

"Those aren't eagles, Dad," my father said quietly. "Those are just barn swallows."

My grandfather's eyes widened. In his sky there were eagles.

"Barn swallows," my father whispered, "that's all."

In the dream the snake entered through White Feather's ear and came out her mouth. She awoke to a wailing that seemed to rise out of the earth itself. Now she could not help but hear it. It was as clear to her as if it were Dark Horse, lying next to her, who was wailing.

She rose and walked down to the brook where she sat for a while. She felt a pain in her left breast. Her son was not going to come back alive; she could see a man in a blue jacket pressing a bullet into his head. The brook flowed red. The earth's wailing rose into her mouth and filled it and became her own.

The postcards from Fletcher have stopped coming. My brother has traveled deep into the center of the country where I can no longer touch him, deep into the center of silence.

"Anza-Borrego Desert State Park in California," the fat man reads, "claims two unusual features: a limitless carpet of wildflowers and elusive bands of bighorn sheep. The wildflowers bloom in spring, drawing thousands of flower-sniffers, as the residents call the springtime tourist invasion. The wild sheep inhabit remote canyons and crags, their buff coloring blending with the landscape and making them difficult to spot."

"Look, here's a picture of them!" Christine giggles, passing the newspaper to her mother.

"Where is this?" the mother asks.

"California," Christine says.

Gershwin, Ives, Cage, Glass.

We could feel great silence moving in, and we spoke little words trying to break it.

"Does the second planting start today, Grandpa? Do you think Maizy will have her kittens soon?"

We were deep in spring and our words got caught in trees thick with bird song, in pockets of billowing clouds. Almost as soon as we spoke them, our words seemed to be absorbed by the plumpness of the vernal earth and all was quiet again. There was no dispelling the silence. Grandpa heard it best of all— it was coming for him.

I tried bigger words, greater ones, to try to break the heart of it.

"Are you dying, Grandpa?" I asked. He had not gotten out of bed for two days. "Are you going to die now?" This would scare death off, I thought—to point a finger at it, to name it.

But it did not dispel it. "Yes, Vanessa," he said, "I think I am." And as soon as we heard him say it, we knew it was true.

"Oh, it's a lovely day to die," my grandfather said. He hated to see us upset. "The weather is clear, the trip will be easy." He paused. "A cinch," he smiled.

"Don't die today," Fletcher said. His head was resting on the bedspread. He did not look at my grandfather. "Please don't die, Grandpa."

"It is not such a bad day to die," my grandfather said, turning his head toward the window.

He spoke slowly against the silence and we felt the terrible friction in his voice. It must have weighed down on him hard now. Still his voice rose. "It is not such a bad day to die, Fletcher. Everybody has to die someday."

"Please don't," Fletcher said.

My grandfather smiled weakly. He tried to lift a finger up from the bed to Fletcher but he couldn't. His fingernails were luminous, white. His hands were a deep brown.

"Don't forget about the soul, Fletcher," he whispered. Grandmother walked in. How often she had caught us standing on chairs following the flight of the soul from the body in rehearsal. "Don't forget the soul," he said again.

She shook her head. "All right, children. That's enough. Now let your grandfather get some rest."

"But, Maria," he whispered.

"Oh, no," she said, "it's time for you to rest now."

"Please, Maria. Observe a dying man's last request," and he smiled slightly.

"Be sensible, Angelo, please."

"I'm dying," he whispered.

"Oh, Angelo, do you really think you're just going to turn over and close your eyes and die? Do you really think it's that easy?"

"I'm telling you, Maria." She turned her face away from him toward the bright window and looked at the hay he had just stacked a few days before.

"Oh, Angelo," she sighed as she had sighed so many times before. "Be sensible." She put her hand on his cheek. "Please," she said. "This is no time for games."

Be sensible, she said, but this time it was Grandma who was not being sensible. In less than an hour, as he had predicted, Grandpa would be dead. She left the room. We listened to her heavy, black shoes going down the hallway—their denial of death.

"Take care of her," he said, looking to me. "She needs you."

I nodded.

Fletcher could not stand the formality of this ending. He tried to stop it with the power of his love.

"Grandpa," he said, "don't die yet." He got into the bed next to him and hugged his shrinking body.

"You're a good boy, Fletcher," Grandpa said, and he closed his eyes and watched Fletcher grow up there, the growing up he would not be alive to witness. "You're a fine young man," he said.

"Remember the shrinking story, Grandpa?" Fletcher said. "Could you tell us that story again?"

"Oh, yes, I remember—the shrinking story." He spoke slowly. "It's true. Ask your grandmother someday." He told this story now once more, for us. He saw the panic in our faces. He saw our fear. He was our friend. He was our ally; he never wanted to scare us. Don't leave us here alone, I said to myself.

The only times I ever saw my grandfather look like an old man were when he thought about us being alone, when he thought about how our parents ignored us, how strange they were, how silent. This in itself had prolonged his life, I thought. But he could hold on no longer now. His hand was smooth on the bed, a part of it.

"Yes," he said. "It's true. I used to be tall, oh, a long time ago, way before you were born. It was even before your father was born. Tall," he said, and he looked up to the ceiling, "tall as Abraham Lincoln," and his hand lifted from the bed for the first time. He was only five-foot-six now. "Old people shrink. It's a fact. We shrink. It's how everybody else gets used to the idea of us not being around anymore. I'm shrinking right now under the covers," he whispered.

"I'm afraid," I said.

"There's nothing to be afraid of, really," he said with his kind, kind voice. "It feels good to be so little and light, not so attached to the world anymore and the things we love. It makes it easier for me, too."

"Tall as Abraham Lincoln?"

"Yep. Ask your grandmother. She'll remember."

"It feels good to be so light?"

"Uh-huh."

"It's to help us get used to the idea?"

My grandfather nodded.

But my grandfather was wrong about that. Whenever I think of his shrinking story, think of him shrinking into nothingness before my eyes, I do not feel better or miss him less. I have never gotten used to the idea.

We were surrounded by silence and in that silence each of his words stood out: difficult, precious, discrete.

"Is it hard to die, Grandpa?" I asked.

"Look at me, children," he whispered. "Imagine," he said slowly, "never to smell the spring again or feel the silky hair of corn, never to hear your sweet voices. Yes," he said, "it's very hard."

Grandma walked into the room and toward the bed and took my grandfather's hand. They were saying good-bye. He whispered something I had never heard before. I had never seen his mouth form such shapes. It was Italian. He was talking in the forbidden language; the language he had given up in this country now came streaming back. My grandmother squeezed his hand. She talked back to him. He responded again. He looked at her and rubbed his face against her strong but trembling hand.

"It's got a strange, sweet taste, Maria," he said finally in English, "this dying." And he licked his lips and sucked in the sweetness as if someone had placed candy in his last mouth.

"Take care of her, Vanessa."

"I will, Grandpa."

"Don't forget about the shoebox," he said to Fletcher. "Don't forget to do everything I told you. It's important."

"I won't forget, Grandpa."

"Promise me you won't forget."

"We won't forget."

"Good," he smiled. "Good," he sighed.

It was time now. He looked out the window into the bright sunlight and his eyes grew wide. He pointed to something. "Look," he sputtered. "Look." What did he see there in the sun in these last seconds?

"Look!" he gasped. We stared into the sun, then back at him, then into the sun again, and in one moment I saw his look change, in a turn of my head, from wonder to horror. What rushed before him?

Instead of the past, the future must have flashed before his eyes. Instead of his whole life, our lives, the ones yet to come, appeared before him.

"My God," he gasped. "Dear God."

"What is it, Grandpa?"

We held onto his hands. "Oh," he sighed. We were losing him in light.

"My God," he cried.

"What is it, Grandpa?"

"Try to forgive them," he whispered.

He shook his head and looked at us.

"Try to forgive them—as I have tried."

———

My father walks down the crooked lanes, past squares. In this light the tall, gabled houses, the steeples, look eerie, bizarre. Torches are lit. He can't bear to look at them—or any fire; he turns away. A fierce wind blows off the bay.

"Try to forgive them," I whisper to my father, but he's so far away—Denmark or Sweden, or maybe Norway.

———

"Fly me to the moon," my father sings, "and let me swing upon the stars. Let me know what spring is like on Jupiter and Mars. In other words, hold my hand." The Frank Sinatra record is on. "In other words, darling, kiss me."

———

My grandfather's dream of water was not far away now.

"That fair made him crazy," my grandmother said. "He snapped there. There was too much rain or excitement or something. There's no doubt about it."

———

My brothers, the Indians, must always be remembered in this land. Out of our languages we have given names to many beautiful things which will always speak of us. Minnehaha will laugh of us, Seneca will shine in our image, Mississippi will murmur our woes. The broad Iowa and the rolling Dakota and the fertile Michigan will whisper our names to the sun that kisses them. The roaring Niagara, the sighing Illinois, the singing Delaware, will chant unceasingly our Dta-wa-e [Death Song].

My brethren, among the legends of my people it is told how a chief, leading the remnant of his people, crossed a great river, and, striking his tepee-stake upon the ground, exclaimed, "A-la-ba-ma!" This in our language means "here we may rest!" But he saw not the future. The white man came: he and his people could not rest there; they were driven out, and in a dark swamp they were thrust down into the slime and killed. The word he spoke has given a name to one of the white man's states. There is no spot under those stars that now smile upon us, where the Indian can plant his foot and sigh, "A-la-ba-ma." It may be that Wakada will grant us such a place. But it seems that it will be only at His side.

Eagle Wing

We were restless. We walked deliriously through the landscape of passion, always at the edge of breath. Our desire alone exhausted us. We sleepwalked through our days with uneven breath, hooded eyelids, lusting not only after the absent lover, the lover out of our reach, but after what we sensed was the unavailable in ourselves: the thing we could never call up no matter how diligent or attentive we were, the places we could never reach, the people we could never be.

Jack wiped his face on his sleeve as he came in the door. He was sweating heavily, his shirt was soaked through. I knew not to ask about it. He looked tired. I did not push him. He looked enormous, too large for my apartment; the ceilings were too low, the walls too close. He had to bend over to get in the doorway. "You've grown," I said. He laughed and shook his head. The half-refrigerator which he opened looked like a tiny white box next to him. I had accepted it: with Jack I knew that everything would always be out of proportion.

He took the skin off an orange, tore a piece and sucked the juice from it, then ate the pulp, doing this until he finished. I watched him cautiously from the other side of the room. I felt frightened of him, but I did not know why.

"Come to me, Vanessa," he said quietly, gently, coaxing me as if I were an antelope or a deer and in his hand were food, or kindness, some human security. I moved toward him tentatively, testing the air. It was warm, strange, but the smells reassured me, orange and tea and the salt of his sweat. I could not hear anything but his gentle voice.

"Come now," he said, "come to me." And I did after a while, though still I did not trust him entirely.

He laid his hand on my thigh, lifted it slightly, felt its weight. His hand looked swollen, his lips too looked swollen, and his words, though gentle, had a thickness to them not unlike the air. His tongue was heavy, his thoughts slowed, his pulse. He stroked my hair, massaged my neck. I blinked my eyes, stretched my back, pawed the ground with my foot. He moved his hand slowly down my chest, down my belly, then to my leg where he studied its muscles. "My beautiful animal," he whispered. He caressed my foot, outlining with his lips each toe; he held my ankle between his thumb and forefinger, a giant's hand. He applied some pressure. I sighed. I felt an aching deep within me. He reached between my legs, they opened with his first movement forward, and slowly he began revolving his hand. The room began to revolve with his slow steady motion. He had led the shy beast into a clearing. I fed from his hand. He watched my breathing change shape. Squares became circles. He moved his mouth up to meet his hand and circled his sweaty head in the same round motion. His hand slipped under my shirt. He circled my full breasts and pressed my nipples between his thick, soft fingers.

But suddenly the air changed. I sensed danger, flood or fire.

"What is it?" I said. "What?"

He looked at me like an ancient man, wild, needing food. With an enormous strength he ripped apart the zipper of my pants as if he did not know what a zipper was or how it worked. He was going back in time. He had forgotten all this. I squirmed under him. Having gotten my pants off, he pinned my shoulders down to stop my movement, bracing me, holding me tight, not knowing where we were going though we had gone there so many times before together. He was hard and large on top of me. He was something primitive, made of stone or bone, something blunt like a club. He put his hand in my mouth. I felt I might choke on it. He forced his salty fingers down my throat and pressed his way into me. I pushed my head away and sat up, feeling him in this position deep inside me where another more mysterious mouth opened and opened and howled, and he, too, began to howl, and his howls grew louder and louder, changing from the sounds we recognize as human into other sounds—sounds that had been lost at the beginning of language. I followed him backwards to the time before words, before memory, where I let go of everything, and we lay there at the start for a moment, two bodies of water, of air, breathing in the dark—for a moment.

Slowly the darkness began to give way and the land bathed in the light of dawn. He let his eye linger for a long time over the mesa, the sunlit cliffs, the loping hills. He stood facing east, watching that great red disk on the horizon flare, rise up, and slowly climb the enormous sky.

"It's even more beautiful than a swan," my mother whispers.
"That precious, precious bird," I say. She nods her head.
"You must not be afraid."

They must have looked lovely together as they swirled around the center of the dance floor for all to see.

My father was becoming even more lost as they hugged and listened to the silence outside, alone during the band's break, standing precariously on the verge of their adult lives.

The band returned—one final song. And, yes, my parents indeed looked lovely together—like figures of marzipan poised on the top of a wedding cake. . . .

Sabine opens the large windows of the house in Maine. Strangely, at the same time the air of the sea seems warm and cool. She looks out at the breast of the beach, the lovely white belly of the beach. She watches the fishermen lift their nets, come in with their catch. The air of the room is heavy, drenched with the sea, a persistent humidity. My mother's empty pages stacked in a white pile are filled up already with so much water. She, too, is filled up. She bends down. Her eyes slip slowly to Sabine's ankles. She helps Sabine pull back the heavy sheets in the languid air.

She is not so far away on that day I fall off my bicycle, my knee shredded, bits of the driveway embedded in the wound. She appears from around the corner when she hears me crying. She is wearing her gardening clothes.

She helps me up, looks at my knee, kisses me on the ear, and whispers, "Your dress is magnificent."

"The ballroom is gigantic!" I say.

"I have *never* in my life seen a chandelier like this one before," she gasps, pointing to the sun. "Oh, have you ever in your life seen anything like it?"

"Never," I say. "Where are we?" I ask. "Where are we, Mom?"

On the book jacket of *To Vanessa* is my favorite picture of my mother. She is in profile and she looks as serene as I have ever seen her—content, happy. The light is beautiful and she is smiling.

"You'll miss your train. Don't miss it," she urges. "Go now. Go."

I try to enter the sky, to force myself to become that bird. But there is no forcing it, I know.

"Do not be afraid," she whispers to me.

I watch that bobbing branch where the Topaz Bird once was. But it's so tiny, so hard to see.

"Continue the story," she prods me. "Go on."

The note asked that I come to Main Building, Room 525, as soon as possible. It was written on an index card in an impossibly small handwriting and signed by someone named Jennifer Stafford. There was nothing unusual about this note, it was just one among many instructions I found in my mailbox upon arrival at college, and yet I kept going back to it, going over the same few words. Even as I read other papers, other notes, I visualized that handwriting and that name. There was something familiar there, something that called me to it; the other papers fell to the floor.

Slowly I unpacked my clothes, savoring the mystery of the message, prolonging it. What could this Jennifer Stafford want from me? It began to sound like a command. "Stop by. Soon." Hundreds of things occurred to me as I fumbled with hangers and put away books, but none of them anticipated that room on the top floor of Main Building under the catwalk. "Come as soon as you can," I said to myself. "Jennifer Stafford." Parents still lingered in the halls. There seemed a sea of students all folding into one another, crashing on an unfamiliar shore. There were waves of color and sound all around me, but the note that I held in my hand was silent and a certain darkness seemed to collect around it. I read it once more, then again, and, using the heads of parents and the shiny black trunks of students for stones, I crossed this glittering, shouting body of water and stepped safely onto the ascending elevator.

"Come in," she said.

Walking into that room was like moving from one life into another, light into dark, air into water. With my first look inside I could already feel myself adapting, always the survivor. My body grew sleeker, my hands broader, best for swimming. My lungs expanded. I felt as if my eyes were becoming bluer so as to fathom the depths, my heart stronger because I sensed it needed to be.

The demands of this dark, vaguely sweet-smelling room were great. It asked even of its most casual visitors what no room, no place should have been able to ask of anyone. To enter the room was to surrender something, to give something up.

She seemed to be crying.

"Jennifer," I said quickly. "Maybe it's a mistake. I got this in my mailbox today. I don't know if—"

"Please," she said, as if she could not keep up with my speech. "Please, I'm not Jennifer, I don't live here, and I don't want to hear about it. Really." She read Jennifer's note, holding it up close to her eyes as if she found the size of the handwriting ridiculous. "But you've got a little note here," she smiled sarcastically, "so please come in.

"As you can see," she said, motioning around the bare room, "Jennifer has a rather modest conception of her own needs." On the floor was a mattress, a desk lamp, and a record player. In the hallway the dresser, the desk, and the bedframe stood with a note like mine on an index card to the maintenance people, asking that these items be put in storage for the year.

"She's doing her thesis now on the history of the women of her family, starting with her long-lost relative Sarah Stafford, who came over on the *Godspeed* or one of those. I think she's trying to get a little bit of the Pilgrim ship ambiance in here." She laughed and her laugh echoed in the empty, angular room.

"She doesn't ask much anymore," this strange woman said, looking directly at me, "just to be left alone."

"Perhaps I should leave," I said.

She shrugged, lighting a joint. "Regardless of its rather austere appearance, this is a room you will soon find you cannot leave," she exhaled, "ever."

I accepted the joint, but it felt like I was accepting much more. She smiled at me, knowing that already I was becoming a part of this thing.

"I think you'll probably like it here," she said.

"I don't know what you mean," I answered, but already I felt as though I was a bowl or an urn in this dark still life.

"Who are you, then?" I asked shyly.

"Oh, where are my manners?" she asked, again with great sarcasm. "Forgive me. My name is Marta Arenelle and today I commence my fourth and presumably final year at this hallowed institution where I am," she paused, "of course," she paused again, "a drama major." She smiled at her own good sense of timing. "Let me redeem myself. Here, have a drink," she said, getting me a glass from the closet and filling it with Scotch.

"Yes, but still, you say, who is this Jennifer Stafford and where is she anyway? And above all what does she want from *me?*" "Well, let's see. She's our resident feminist, Women's Center, Women's Studies student par excellence, and I don't know what she wants from you but I can certainly guess. She's in the bathtub right now." Marta laughed and shook her head. "If you want to be near Jennifer, you must be resigned to the fact that half the time you will spend submerged underwater." She laughed but the laughter went nowhere. It was a dense laugh, heavy with gloom. Like certain fogs, it felt as if it might never lift.

Billie Holiday's voice slurred through the empty room—the sad, eerie, off-key voice I would come to associate forever with this day and with Marta, who retreated into the song with her bottle of Scotch. The voice deepened the darkness, intensified it. It was difficult to breathe such mournful air.

"Dreaming, I was only dreaming," Billie Holiday sang, agonizing toward her final death. "I wake and I find you asleep in the deep of my heart, dear."

She was singing to someone Marta could see standing in front of her. Marta had made the song hers, personalized it so that it was almost unbearable to listen to.

"Darling, I hope that my dream never haunted you. My heart is telling you how much I wanted you." The song articulated her sorrow, validated it. She sank into its lowest registers. Tears filled her eyes; they would not fall.

"Please pardon my sentimentality," she said, reaching for a small bag of hashish and covering my hand with hers.

"We've been waiting for you," she whispered. "We've been waiting a long time for you." Her hand was large and strong. I did not dare look at her.

I knew some further definition of myself lay here in this room, something I had previously only glimpsed, a suggestion lost before in a change of light or a conversation that took a different direction—lost at the last minute because I had turned away in a failure of nerve or a change of heart. What was here that promised to change everything now? I wondered.

I suppose it would be easy to be carried away by the voluptuousness of the scene—the velvety darkness, the ruined voice, the sweet smell of hashish, Jennifer's conspicuous absence, and the lost person breathing shapes into Marta's full mouth. She looked at me through her tears, forcing my chin up so she could study my face.

"Why, you're just a kid!" she cried. "You're just a child!" she laughed. "What a joke!" She fell silent. It was Marta's enormous capacity for hope that had made me seem for a moment to be someone I was not. She wanted so much to believe that I, dressed in white, knocking on the door, was her angel, her miracle, but now in a moment of clear-eyed scrutiny she saw me as I must have really looked: ridiculous, silly, eighteen.

"I'm sorry," I whispered. She raised her head slowly and looked at me with contempt.

"Don't apologize to me," she said. "What do you have to be sorry about?" At that time I had never seen anyone like her—paralyzed with grief, every word colored by it, every movement determined, defined, by its cruel properties.

I could still feel myself moving in and out of the scene, one moment being able to see myself and Marta objectively, like some omniscient narrator: "Two women, one dressed in black, one in white, sat in the corner like a symbol." But the next moment I was locked inextricably in her gaze, caught in the hundreds of black curls that framed her tortured face.

"You'd never understand," she whispered, "not in a million years," but she reached for my hand and her body leaned forward and I could feel the brutal muscles of her heart contracting around me. "You'd never understand. How could you?"

"Try me," I said. I felt brave suddenly. She was driving her nails into me but I did not struggle to get free. She put her head on my shoulder and in a second my shirt was soaked. "Don't cry," I said, and I felt my courage disappear. "Can I do something?"

"No," she sighed, "unless of course you can bring back the dead."

If at that moment I had told Marta that I was capable of that feat, I think she would have believed me: she wanted so badly to believe. Desire was like magic; love was a kind of magic. The hopeless love magic the most—for a person to be sawed in half and come out whole, for black mice to disappear. "Please," she whispered.

She hardly looked up now. I think she feared what she might see in the suggestive air, though when she closed her eyes or looked out the window or glared at me, she saw the same thing, always the same thing. It was the magic of the dead: they could do anything, they could be anywhere.

"Perhaps I should leave you alone," I said. "I feel like an intruder. I should leave you."

"No," she said, getting up slowly—although to her it must have seemed quickly—"please. Don't leave." In her voice I recognized my own, many years ago, begging my mother not to leave my darkened room. "Please, don't go," she said.

"Love will make you drink and gamble," she sang, taking a large bag of cocaine from her jacket, "love will make you stay out all night long. Love will make you drink and gamble; love will make you stay out all night long." She was struggling to hold onto the melody. "Love will make you do things that you know are wrong." She smiled.

"From Venezuela," she said, holding the plastic bag in front of my eyes. "I live there."

In a minute's time Marta was back on that South American coastline. She had slipped out of her clothes. The sun beat on her body. She began to sweat. She took a deep breath and her lungs filled with the salt of the ocean. She swayed slightly as she spoke. Small salamanders darted along the sill. "Venezuela," she said, holding the words of home in her mouth a long time. "If it got too hot on the beach I could always move to the cool, blue ceramic tiles of the beach house. I loved that house. There was such peace there, such quiet. And eating fruit there," she said and licked her lips, "is like tasting it for the first time." I looked at her pink, tropical mouth.

"Mangoes," she sighed, "papaya." She was covering a mirror with long lines of cocaine. "Guava," she said. "There's nothing like it."

"But I was never really happy there," she said, snorting up the white powder. "Come on, don't be shy." She waited for me to inhale it. "Only my mother is Venezuelan. My father is American. He went down there at your age, just a boy dreaming of making a fortune in pearls, and sitting in the sun. But he never stopped talking about America. And it sounded so good when he talked about it." She inhaled again.

"I used to dream about coming to the States, where I could buy the Beatles albums as soon as they came out." She laughed. "You know, I thought I'd get to see the baseball players on the street. What a jerk I was.

"Please excuse all this," she said, disgusted with herself. She knocked over the glass of Scotch and we watched it soak into the mattress. "But when I finally did get here and met Natalie, all I wanted to do was to go to Europe. Natalie had lived in Europe. Her father was a diplomat. She was very jet set. She said it was the only place to live."

Marta sighed. The cocaine had made her energetic, but thinking about her life made her weary. She snorted more off the floor.

"To make a short story shorter, the gringo left us for diamonds in Africa. He always promised to send for me. I learned everything there was to know about the place. Fauna, flowers, exports, climate, gross national product. What would you like to know?"

"Did you ever get there?"

She laughed. "What do you think?"

"Where is he now?"

She shrugged, "Who knows? I've spent my whole life wanting to be somewhere I wasn't. It's really quite a pathetic story. Now all I want to do is die and, look, still I am alive. Though," she added, "there are some rather uncharitable people at this school who would like to dispute it. I swear I'm not high anymore," Marta said. "Let's do just a little more, OK?"

She dumped the whole bag out on the floor and then got up and went into the closet where I could hear her dialing the phone and ordering another bottle of Scotch.

"They deliver," she said from inside the closet. "They're very accommodating."

When she returned she held something wrapped in a white cloth. Slowly she unwrapped it. It was a hypodermic needle. "Cocaine," she whispered, "was not meant to be snorted. Believe me. I know."

Who had once lain in the cavity under Marta's arm? Her body draped in black looked so strong. Her dark arms were smooth, muscular. They looked like the arms of an athlete, a bearer of torches, a person no one could hurt. Who could reduce her to this? She had tried her hardest, she had done her best, only now to have Natalie—that was the word she was saying softly to herself over and over: Natalie, Natalie, Natalie. . . .

In her voice I could hear the bones of their embrace being broken apart and strewn about the room. They were everywhere—bones in the closet, bones piled up against the door.

"Make a fist," she said. She tied my arm with a rubber tube.

I shivered. Marta put the needle in my arm. The room turned blue.

"Once it goes in," she said quietly, "it never really comes out."

I imagined Jennifer who, having closed her eyes for a moment, now opened them and added more hot water to the tub.

Blood stained the window shades. Long strands of hair slept in the bed. The bones piled higher and higher.

"Marta," I said, shaking her, "I'm scared."

"Don't cry."

"I'm afraid."

"Don't be afraid."

"I think I should go now," I said, moving to the door. My legs swayed under me.

"You're my thrill," Billie Holiday sang, "you do something to me. You send chills right through me." My hand slipped from the doorknob. I turned to Marta.

"Come here," she said.

"Don't cry. Please don't cry. I can't stand to see girls cry," she said. If she had looked in her own mirror, it would have broken her heart.

"I'm scared," I said, collapsing to the floor. "I'm afraid."

"What do you have to be afraid of?" she said, but then looked away, caught in the sorrow that would not let her go. "Why? Why did she have to die? Why?" she said over and over, but the more she said the word, the more senseless it became—just a sound and no way in.

She surrendered to the question and it drove her to the ground. "Why?" she asked, bringing me down with her, shaking me, staring into the wideness of my eyes as if the body when challenged would reveal its ancient, mortal secret. "Why?" she said, pressing hard for an answer.

I was afraid of her but I extended my arm anyway and touched her lightly on the shoulder. She shuddered.

I did not know why.

And great tears fell from her eyes. All was silent, dark. Finally, after many hours, she stood up.

"Would you like to dance?" she whispers.

"What?" I say.

"Would you like to dance?" she asks again politely, lowering her eyes, bowing slightly, and offering me her hand.

"The orchestra," she says, "is so lovely. Listen." She strains to hear the opening notes—the oboe, the French horn. "And your dress is exquisite."

"Yes, oh, yes," I say. "The ballroom is gigantic!"

"And the chandelier," she says, pointing to the ceiling.

"Where are we, Marta?" I gasp.

"It's Vienna. It's Bavaria. It's Port-au-Prince, Haiti," she says. I had not heard such tenderness in a human voice before.

And for a minute I almost believe it: Somewhere we are dressed in linens and silks. Somewhere our hair is piled ludicrously on the tops of our heads and the dance steps have all been planned hundreds of years in advance for us. Somewhere we are safe in a box step, in the reliable timing of the waltz. Somewhere we are out of danger.

"It's Mykonos," she whispers. "It's Nice." Her eyes are closed; when she opens them, she is far away.

"Natalie?" she sighs. "Is that you?" She leans heavily on me. It is a terrible weight; it is the weight of the whole world. "It's Mykonos. It's Nice."

We could barely pick up our feet. "Marta," I say.

"It's Nice," she answers.

"I'm losing my balance."

"Natalie," she says, "Natalie."

"What is it? What is it, Marta?" She touches my hair. It grows long and straight in her hands. She buries her face in it.

We stumble, we bump, we collide; we trip finally on the one mattress, the one lamp, falling into the void that is everywhere.

From her upstairs window my grandmother saw the two women embrace. "I'll let it pass," she said to herself, but she could not get rid of the image of the two women touching each other like man and woman. That was in Italy over fifty years ago. Now, I imagine, she saw it again, on the farm shortly after my parents were married and were still living with them. There she saw it: Sabine and my mother while Michael was away. The letter to my father was addressed, stamped, sealed, but she waited to mail it, deliberately missing the postman; she didn't know why.

The whole world lay still. Nothing moved. I felt my gaze, too, stuck on the window of the room. On the sill the lizard stood stunned. In the sky the clouds had stopped. Not one leaf moved. No branches bobbed as branches will.

The associate professor of English sat frozen at her carrel in the library with her hand on her forehead, trying to gather the strength for a new year. The alcoholic dean of freshmen held his glass two inches from his mouth. It went no further. A student's pen slowed. She could not decide whether to take one course or another. Her mind went blank for a moment.

A red Frisbee lay in the green grass. The dog did not move to chase it.

Marta slept next to me; her body was perfectly still. She did not have the even breathing of a sleeper. Her mouth was slightly open as if she had been stopped in midsentence.

The whole world held still, it seemed, with Marta's sorrow—but not me. I took her heavy, sleeping arm from around my neck, pulled myself up, and left the room that was still dark although it was morning.

Marta had given me no facts, I thought, as I stepped into a world much brighter, more animated than I had remembered. The campus looked beautiful. I walked to the library; it seemed to call me. A small wind had started up. My mind raced, too fast. How did it happen, Marta? Was there nothing you could have done?

I look up to the top window where she lies now in troubled sleep. She does not move one muscle. My questions remain unanswered. No one hears me. How did it happen? Was there nothing you could do?

I walk faster and faster. Why? Why? In my mind I raise the Frisbee from the grass and propel it into motion. A fellow freshman catches it and smiles. The dean takes a drink. The associate professor of English, gathering up her books, leaves her carrel on the library's second floor.

The library was empty. Classes had not yet begun and people were still stuck in summer—on the wavy lake or the tennis court with its green hum. It was cool and dark and I felt safe there. In the context of such coolness and sense and order, the events of the night before seemed as if they could not have taken place, and, walking to the shelves, I felt strangely free of them: that odd room on the top floor, Marta and her story, and the needle I watched sink into my arm.

I loved the order of libraries. I felt at ease there among the old and new books, lined and numbered on the shelves. I found what I was looking for easily. When I was done I would put those books back in the same place and on another day I would be able to find them again. Most people would think little of such a simple thing, but today the thought of every book having its place and of no book being lost gave me an overwhelming sense of pleasure.

The auditorium was filling. The faculty sat on the right side in a reserved section roped off by a purple braid: formal, deathlike on this spring evening. My mother would not like this purple square, I thought. If she saw me sitting in it, she would run to me and hug me and take me away—it would be like her. I was not, of course, faculty but rather a guest of honor simply by birth, and a man who recognized me immediately, though I did not know him, led me to this distinguished corral. I sat on the aisle, one inch from the purple braid, and was careful not to touch it, as if touching it might include me somehow in its mournful darkness. We were superstitious, my mother and I. Anything could look like a symbol, a sign: a shelf of books, a glass half filled, the reserved section of a room.

Members of the faculty began to take their seats. They laughed with one another as they entered the hall. Many were coming from the dinner given for my mother beforehand. I had excused myself from that event; my mother's friends Florence and Bethany would be with her and so she did not need me so near. Still I wondered how she was doing. I hoped that the cocktail hour had not gone on too long and that the dinner had not been too much of an ordeal. Few of these dinners were in fact as bad as she imagined them before she arrived; often she would find herself having, despite herself, quite a nice time. How easily she could shift into sociability. How easily sometimes she rode the wave of conversation into the night.

Still I hoped the faculty had been sensitive, that they had not asked too much of her, that they had given her some time to herself.

How many years had I been thinking in this way, keeping her free from harm by adopting a certain mental position, wishing her well? I could not keep her safe, I could not keep her by my side, though, waiting for her in the purple square, I still thought that I might be able to protect her simply by concentrating.

At the party I imagine that the handsome host, seeing my mother a little giddy, a little breathless, offers her a room upstairs where she might lie down for a moment. She accepts and he shows her the way. "Don't go," I picture my mother saying as he turns to leave her, hating sometimes more than anything to be alone. And so he doesn't. "Hold me," she whispers, and he takes her in his bearlike arms and kisses her gently. I choose that they should make love in the large bed, that it is passionate; and that afterwards he murmurs to her what she needs to hear—that the first cycle of poems works as a cycle must, or that the final leap in her newest poem makes everything stop, as she intended; and that she rests momentarily, lies peacefully next to him while the other dinner guests drink cognac, while the coffee brews, while the Italian professor plays the piano.

That May evening my mother walked down the aisle to the podium like a queen, like a bride, focused single-mindedly on the task still ahead of her. She did not even look at the reserved purple section. She did not come to me as she does in my dreams, sensing danger or darkness, and rescue me from it, whisking me to her side, hugging me tightly. She walked straight to the front and sat in the front row and waited. The introductory speaker was late. The introduction that night would make my mother cringe: all superlatives and the facts wrong.

I could only see her from the back. She looked so animated, gulping water, flushed, chatting with her host, flanked by Florence and Bethany, her college friends, now teachers at this college. I knew that I worried about her too much. I heard her stormy, wild laugh. So many times I had seen her this way, her hands flying about her like birds as she talked. I turned away.

They teetered down the aisles at the last moment, taking seats, one next to me, one in front of me. They looked fragile, breakable, but that was not the case. They are in their own ways more capable, stronger than most of us. They teach the Victorian novel or Chaucer or the Romantic poets. They wave to their bearded friends and clutch their programs and smile in anticipation. I love these women with their eccentric hairdos: the wispy blonde bangs and ponytail, the red hair swept up with tendrils at the ears, curls cascading down the neck. I love these women with their frilly bodices or little-girl pinafores or long plaid skirts or cocktail dresses from the fifties. I love these women with their box-shaped pocketbooks, their complicated shoes, their high sexual laughs, their quirky brilliance.

They had made my mother feel less fearful. She seemed happier when she was with them, not as alone in the world. Years after she left college she would still visit with them, sit in their houses, drink with them, and relish their intricate, intelligent stories. As a famous person, my mother had met many such women living in college towns all across the country, throwing parties for Byron's birthday, dancing in spring at bacchanalias, reading Emily Dickinson by a fire. They were obsessive, unpredictable, exacting. When I got to college I recognized them immediately.

I loved them for the way they made my mother feel. All these years they had made her feel safe. What they told her was this: "Take refuge." "Step into your talent." "Apologize to no one." "Life is perplexing. Your imagination is your gift." "Do what you must." They were islands of comfort. She had swum out to them and rested on their wonderful shores.

The associate professor of English, carrying an armful of books, smiles. I pass her on the library steps. "Take refuge," she says.

"Come now, Christine," she says softly, offering her hand. "You're going to be all right. I promise."

My mother stands up and allows herself to be helped out of the ditch by the woman who is so kind. She has a long, gray braid down her back. "I promise," she says again, speaking softly to her grown daughter. They turn from the ditch. It is Grandma Alice. She hugs my mother. "Everything's going to be all right."

Marta, walking through the library, no interest in books, recognized me against the high, pine window where I still sat gazing at the many faces of my mother. She looked from the photos to me but made no connection as far as I could tell. I collected the books and put them in a pile as if I might protect my mother from Marta in this way. Though it seemed to me that Marta lived a dangerous life, something my mother had once recommended, I was doubtful that this was what she had had in mind.

I did not expect Marta to recognize me. She had barely seen me the previous night in Jennifer's room, I thought. She had barely known that I was there at all. And though she had at one point actually described my face, lingered over my features, it had not seemed to me an accurate portrait.

"Forget a face like that?" Marta laughed, tipping my head up and putting her thumb and forefinger on my chin. "No chance." I caught a glimmer of what might have been the old Marta, the Marta before Natalie, the one who laughed and wanted, without hesitation, faces like mine.

"Have you seen Jennifer?" she asked, as if we had known each other a long time, as if the face she could not forget exhausted her, bored her.

"I don't know who Jennifer is."

She looked at me as if she wondered what it would be like to be able to say that.

"You haven't met her yet?"

"No."

Marta had lost track of the days. How many had passed, she wondered, since I had arrived holding that little note?

"Well, won't that be something?" she smiled. She looked like a mischievous child: the grin, the sneakers, the mass of dark curls, the papers she held in her hand, crumpled, tear-stained.

She put her hand on my shoulder. Her touch was like no other, firm but gentle, hard but yielding, and it brought me immediately back to the night before. She was drawing me at a tremendous speed into intimacy. There was no time to waste.

"I've got a dog," she said. She was still a child to me.

"Oh?" I said.

"She's really only a puppy. I live in Cushing. She's in my room. Do you want to see her?"

"Sure," I said.

I put the books back on the shelf. On another day I would be able to find them easily, I said to myself.

"Come on," she said.

I knew what Marta wanted. It was easy to see. We left the library. I turned to look at the librarian and watched her grow small as we walked toward Marta's dormitory.

"This is it," she said as we stood in front of a large house made completely, it seemed, of gingerbread.

"This is it?" I said.

She nodded. "This way," she smiled. And I followed her up the winding stairs to the tiny room where the dead girl lived.

Each night was the same. She wore the same clothes, the black pants she had gotten in Mykonos and the cotton T-shirt of Natalie's. Every night she rubbed her cheek against her shoulder, closed her eyes, and sniffed the shirt as if fabric, like the heart, could hold a person long after they were gone, in its weave.

Two eight-by-ten black-and-white photographs of Natalie were propped on the bureau and illuminated by candles. Every night we toasted those photos of her and listened to the records of Billie Holiday. Wherever we were, if we sat in her room or if we went to classes or to the dining hall, Billie Holiday seemed to follow us. She sang as I studied those pictures of Natalie. The straight blonde hair, the long, elegant nose, the lips—too thin, I thought, cruel, somehow.

"She was a complete mystery to me, Vanessa," Marta said.

I nodded, engrossed in the photographs. Natalie seemed terrified to me, alone in that frame against a black background, lost. She carefully held the poses of a self-conscious child, though the poses, a hand on a hip, a cigarette poised between beautiful fingers, were meant to convey the opposite impression: sophistication, worldliness, maturity—Natalie in her leather pants, Natalie clutching an Italian *Vogue*. What did she see, as she looked into the glassy eye of the camera, that frightened her so?

There were pictures everywhere, propped on trunks and tables, taped to the walls, lying on top of books. In each photo she looked just as lonely, just as scared—her face always the same. There could be no touching her. She just stared. When you thought you were safe, there was always another photo; when you thought you were out of the range of her gaze, you would turn suddenly and she would be watching.

"Isn't she beautiful?" Marta said. And it was true; she was.

After many nights spent in that room with Marta I would finally dare to touch those photos, putting them together in different ways, in an attempt to animate her, to watch her move, watch her light her cigarette, watch her walk in her spiked heels, her Stetson hat, her fur coat. I wanted to see her look at Marta, then look away, watch her leave for France, try to understand what made her this way.

"To Natalie," Marta said, barely able to lift her glass at all by midnight, a toast, I imagined, that Natalie, lit by candles, being worshipped, would appreciate.

"Tell me more and more and then some," Billie Holiday sang.

"It didn't happen the way they said," Marta whispered. "Natalie did not want to die. I'm going to go there. I'm going to find out what really happened. People don't disappear like that. I never spoke with her parents. I couldn't find them anywhere. People don't just disappear like that."

Every night I listened to the stories, drank Scotch, and watched Marta toast the photos of the dead girl until they dissolved and disappeared.

"Natalie would never have killed herself," she said. Her brown eyes were black. "It couldn't have happened the way they said."

"Tell me more," I murmured. "Tell me more and more," I sang, until the candles burned out.

She had lived everywhere. She had done everything. Her father was a diplomat and she had grown up a golden girl, gleaning beauty from all the great cities of the world.

People didn't disappear like that: off the edge of some foreign country, at the phone number just beyond the reach of the voice, some operator insisting in French over and over that she has dialed correctly.

People didn't disappear that way—the final message left on the mouth of a man in a phone booth in Nice, a man with a voice easy not to believe.

Her parents are sitting suspended in air, somewhere between New York and Paris, eating the darkness, swallowing it whole, counting the miles to the man, the phone booth, reviewing the years, never once sensing something in their daughter having gone a long way off.

People didn't die that way—nothing left behind: no Calvin Klein shirts, no

Kenzo dresses; no Dior, no Estée Lauder, no Mary Quant; no Shiseido, no Nina Simone, no Gato Barbieri, no Yves St. Laurent.

They tell us she has already forgotten her entire life. We are chewing on the sharp edges of empty space. We are calling home our truant feelings.

People didn't disappear like that—no bulge in the ground, no stone to throw roses at. People that disappeared that way always came back.

My mother winds the black phone cord around her hand. She clears her throat and puts on her phone voice, the one she feels is decipherable to the real world, the world of numbers and phones, the one operators can hear. As soon as she gets Sabine on the other end her phone voice melts. "Sabine," she sighs, and her language changes.

I have heard this conversation many times. Again tonight, my mother worries. I translate the French as best I can. "I am exceptional only in appearance, only in charm," is what I think she says. I can't hear what Sabine says but whatever it is it calms my mother slightly.

"I am a coward," my mother says as she steps into her pumps, and she believes it. "I will never be good enough." She kisses the receiver twice and hangs up. I sit at her feet. "My beauty," she whispers, hugging me to her, and she begins to cry.

How she hesitated those nights she was to be at one party or another.

My mother could not understand why she caused such a commotion in people. The mere suggestion that she might attend a certain party would turn it into an event. She hated this; it baffled her, for she distrusted those who would so readily attach themselves to her.

"Clearly no one in this room understands or has even read one line of my work," she'd say after three or four drinks.

Beauty is a trap; it is its own art form. To be beautiful, it is said, is enough.

On her worst days she thought people admired her work because of her beauty, because of the person she was at cocktail parties: witty, charming, seductive, caustic, dangerous—beautiful. But it is not enough.

The centerpiece—let them have what they wanted, she thought. Let them take what was least important to her. She didn't mind. It meant nothing to her—the shape of her face, her blue eyes, her bare shoulders.

"No," she said, she was not a decoration. She did not simply sparkle. "Don't prettify me," I heard her say once to a well-dressed man at one of those parties. "Don't do it."

It was the work that shaped her life, that gave her her intense radiance and beauty. She did not want them to take that.

She was too polite, she thought. Politely she had accepted compliments, politely she had bowed her head, letting those who needed get a glimpse of her neck. "No more," she said on her thirty-fifth birthday. "Let them stare elsewhere." It had never been flattering, she had simply endured it, for reasons even she must not have been clear about.

My mother was always angry with the way she was presented to the world. "The beautiful Christine Wing will read from her newest collection at eight," she read aloud from the newspaper's society column. "As if that makes the poems any better," she'd scowl, "or any easier to write." After an interview for *Time* she found herself on the cover of that magazine with the caption "The Beautiful Poet." And when we opened to the article we found it began with two long, elaborate paragraphs describing her appearance.

She is dressed in royal blue taffeta. She looks at the young man, who stares at her, and her laugh is impossibly high. He blushes. He is very young. "My daughter," she says, introducing me, never taking her eyes from his soft mouth. "You're so handsome. What's your name again?" She turns away. "I'll be back," she promises, taking me by the hand. She looks at him again, saying nothing. Even her silences are beautiful, not at all awkward. I watch him through the night. He does not venture far from his spot on the floor.

I have seen my mother paranoid. "It's a trap, Vanessa," she'd tell me, "all the laughter, all the handsome men and women. They want me to stop writing. All of them do. Don't trust them," she hissed. "Be careful."

"There's been too much talking tonight," she'd say sometimes in the middle of a sentence, in the middle of a dinner party, and then excuse herself in a way no one but she could. But often she did not move when she might have, did not leave her throne, took in the praise, talked about nothing, gave all her profile. A slightly fearful look would pass over her face on those nights. I knew what she was thinking just by a glance or a sigh, when I was finally old enough to accompany her to those parties. Some nights she'd nod when I'd suggest we leave, as if she were just about to suggest the same thing, and she would get up shakily. But other nights she'd look at me as if I was crazy and say, "Oh, not *yet*, Vanessa," in a giddy flirtatious voice. "Please," she'd beg like a child, "not yet."

What I see sometimes is my real mother peering out from behind her illness, and she is fine. She is not crazy at all. "Don't let them put me here," she pleads, but there is no convincing them. The doctors come with their hypodermic needles, wrapped in cloth so that she cannot see them in advance. They are taking away her belts and necklaces, and we leave her standing there, sobbing, in her underwear.

The sky puts on the darkening blue coat
held for it by a row of ancient trees;
you watch: and the land grows distant in your sight,
one journeying to heaven, one that falls;

and leave you, not at home in either one,
not quite so still and dark as the darkened houses,
not calling to eternity with the passion
of what becomes a star each night, and rises;

and leave you (inexpressibly to unravel)
your life, with its immensity and fear,
so that now bounded, now immeasurable,
it is alternately stone in you and star.

"Evening" by Rainer Maria Rilke

The large, white hull of the oceanliner moves through ice. The other passengers have retired for the night: no stars tonight. My father stands on the deck and stares ahead at the land. He lifts his immense fist, which rises into the sky then sinks into the sea. "Why?" he asks over and over. The word is a jagged rock in the freezing sea. "Why?" he asks again. And the rock stands alone.

"Where did Mom go?" I ask Sabine from across the ocean. Silence wraps around the receiver.

"I don't know, Vanessa," she says finally. "Nobody knows the real answer to that."

"Sabine," I say, "you must know. Please don't lie to me." She says nothing.

My voice does not sail like my mother's once did. And the ocean crashes in my ears.

Marta lifted the domed cover from the silver server and watched Natalie closely through the steam: her eyes, their deep blue color, each eyelash—she could count them—her beautiful, regal nose, but most of all her mouth; she concentrated on it, waiting for her next words. She hung on these words, she lived for them, anticipated them through the delicious, steamy haze.

"I adore you," Natalie said emphatically, stretched out on the huge bed, unreal in her beauty. "I adore you." Marta reached out her hand but then stopped; she wanted to prolong this moment, wanted nothing to change it.

Natalie sighed. She sighed with delight at the eggs Benedict, the smoked trout, the champagne, the fresh flowers everywhere. "I wish this morning could last forever," she said, dipping her finger into the runny yolk of the egg. Marta smiled and ran her rough hand up Natalie's impossibly smooth back. Just two years ago Marta had come to college never having been loved, not by her parents, not by anyone, and now there was this—this strange, unpredictable love, but it was love nonetheless.

Natalie turned toward Marta, and Marta's hand slipped from her back. Natalie's eyes were cold and blue, her face like sculpted alabaster.

"Light me a cigarette," Natalie said sweetly, "will you?" Her face should have softened, but it did not.

"Of course," Marta said, reaching for the Gaulois. Smoke only Gaulois in New York, Natalie had insisted, smoke only Marlboros in Paris. Marta lit a cigarette from the blue-winged package, held it in her mouth for a moment, inhaled deeply, and then passed it to Natalie. The bed seemed like a large boat, and they floated on it for a long time, just smoking. The chandelier glittered in the morning light. The pale pink walls seemed to sparkle.

"It reminds me of Italian candy," Natalie said, running her hand down the glossy wall.

Natalie got up for more champagne and looked out onto New York, the city she loved. It glittered like diamonds in the morning light.

"It will be mine," she said.

Marta came up from behind holding a pink present with white satin ribbons.

"Don't touch me," Natalie commanded, not turning around.

"Natalie," Marta said.

"What do you want?" Natalie asked, turning abruptly. "What is it now?" Marta held out the present.

"For me?" she said.

"Happy birthday," Marta said, closing her eyes.

"I wish this day could last forever. Forever," Natalie said, and her voice dropped with a chilling finality.

"Happy birthday," Marta said. "Go on, open it."

She would have it all, she thought to herself. Marta poured more champagne. She watched the tiny bubbles rise in her glass. Just looking at them made her dizzy with excitement.

"It's beautiful," Natalie said, holding the shining robe up to her. "It's so beautiful."

"I want this day to last forever," Natalie had sighed, and for Marta in some ways it would—this happiness flung in her face, long after the happy times with Natalie had ended for good. She was not someone who could keep the past separate from the present. They existed simultaneously, always. If she could have dislodged it from her brain, this day, she probably would not have, despite the pain it would cause her as she sat in her room and told me the story. Every detail caused her pain. But it was a perfect memory, and for that she was grateful still.

"You're the most beautiful woman in the world," Marta said to Natalie, who had put on her new robe.

"How beautiful?" she demanded, rubbing up against her, intoxicated at the thought.

"More beautiful than Dominique Sanda?" she asked.

"Yes," Marta said.

"More beautiful than Jeanne Moreau?"

"Oh, yes," Marta whispered.

"More beautiful than Brigitte Bardot?"

"Mais oui," Marta smiled.

"Mais oui," Natalie laughed. "More beautiful than Marilyn Monroe?"

"Yes," Marta said, holding her tightly, "even more beautiful than Marilyn Monroe."

Jack looked at me, a champagne glass in the Plaza Hotel being lifted to the lips of Marta, of Natalie. He took me in his enormous hands, ran his fingers up the stem, and cradled the fragile bowl in his palm, then pressed hard, crushing the illusion to bits.

"I need you here," he said, "now."

"I need you, too," I said.

"I know," he said.

I was on the verge of tears. Whom were these tears for? Jack alone now linked me to the world, to moments in time measured by the hands of the clock. I pictured the two hands meeting like lovers at twelve and felt calmer.

"I need you here," I said. "I need you now."

The first time I saw Jennifer Stafford, it was not in that dark, heartlike chamber but in bright light, surrounded by women in the College Center. How easily the walls of her room had given in, changed size and shape in order to accommodate the contours of Marta's grief. Jennifer's own arms I assumed would be as yielding, but that was not the impression I got as I watched her putting papers into piles in preparation for the meeting. Even the simplest act performed by Jennifer commanded great attention. She did everything with such authority.

She did not look as I had imagined. I thought she would be plainer; I thought she would be more straightforward, less mysterious, but she was filled with darkness and a primitive allure, not modern in the least, though the modern world was her domain. Her hair was like the mane of a lion; her brown eyes were animal eyes; her voice was low and, since it was outside the tonal range of most voices, it distinguished itself, separated itself from others, and you could hear it though she spoke softly. She seemed distant, although she was introducing herself and welcoming the women who had gathered. She was speaking of the Women's Center. Four years ago she had rescued it single-handedly from obscurity. She alone had made it work, shaping it into a viable union. Now, this being her last year, she wanted to make sure it would continue without her. She was tired, it had all exhausted her, and she had her thesis to do now. She would have to start giving the Women's Center up, letting go. She sighed, surveying the crowd. No one immediately jumped out at her as a choice for a successor.

Though I was still there, sitting near her, I knew some part of me was already asleep dreaming of that wonderful light brown hair, that mane of a lion, following her wherever she asked me to go. To see Jennifer was to raise a hand and pledge allegiance to what she wanted.

I walked up to her after the meeting, my hand already raised. Whatever she wanted I had already agreed to it. I said nothing.

"You must be Christine Wing's daughter," she said, staring at me as she put papers into a folder.

I nodded, taking a step back. Hearing her speak directly to me and say my mother's name made me shudder with cold suddenly.

"I'd like to talk with you sometime."

Yes, I nodded.

"I've got her old room, you know," she said. "I'm a great admirer of hers."

I stared at her, wondering what she wanted of me.

"That's all," she said, motioning with her head as if to dismiss me. "Thank you."

With her voice alone she forced the season prematurely into winter.

I could not have known that my first meeting with Jennifer would be the only time we would ever speak. As simply and as strangely as she had entered my life, she would exit from it. And the place that seemed to promise so much would become off-limits to me as she grew more and more solitary, lost in the lives of the Stafford women in the room that had been my mother's.

So it was my mother who had brought me here, I thought. Because I was her daughter I was privy to a sad underworld that otherwise I would probably have never come across. It had been the reason for the small note, the reason for everything. My mother through Jennifer had brought me here—to Marta, to this sorrow. She had united us at this wailing wall, this place of the lacerated skin, the shorn hair. She had brought me here, as if she herself had taken me by the hand. She had brought me here to this universe of grief, though I did not know why yet.

It had not occurred to her while they were together that the lovely, branching line that looked like a delicate sprig of wheat was actually the life line and that it separated early, somewhere near the base of the thumb.

But Natalie had already stepped onto another continent, her arms outstretched, her doomed hands open, before Marta realized the truth etched in her palm, and by that time it was too late.

Pamela Stafford, second aunt of Jennifer Stafford, but only a wisp of a child at the time, stepped tentatively in front of the camera for her screen test at the MGM studios. She looked back at her new friend for luck and smiled. Her straight hair, which had been set on hard rollers all night, had already lost its curl. Her pink dress puffed out from the waist made her look like the most fragile of flowers.

"Go on," the smiling man coaxed. "Go on, sweetheart."

"Moon River," she sang softly off key,

"Wider than the Nile,
"I'm crossing you in style
"Someday."
She cleared her throat.
"Oh, dream maker, you heartbreaker,
"Wherever you're going,
"I'm going your way."

"What are we going to see, Dad?" we screamed.
"It's called *It's a Mad Mad Mad Mad World*," he said dreamily. "It's in Cinerama, with the screen so big that it wraps around you." He paused for a long time. "Cinerama," he murmured. "You've never seen anything like it."

On the book jacket of *To Vanessa* is my favorite picture of my mother. She is in profile and she looks as serene as I have ever seen her—content, happy. The light is beautiful and she is smiling. I would have stopped her in my mind in this position forever if I could have, but that is the photographer's art, not the daughter's. My mother cannot stay still in my mind. A lovely profile turns full face, slowly the smile dissolves, and the vision breaks. Her hair grays, then changes back. She grows young, wanders through the quiet house of her childhood in Paterson, New Jersey, a little girl on tiptoe, looking in on her own sleeping mother or sitting in the dark listening to the Sunday stories of her father. I look again at her smiling profile on the back of *To Vanessa*, my book. She will not hold still for me.

"Disneyland!" Grandpa Sarkis said. "Would you look at that?"
"The Magic Kingdom!"
"Look at that castle!" my mother cried.
"A castle for my little princesses in California!" their father said, patting their heads.
"Here's Niagara Falls!" Lucy said.
"Where lovers go!" my mother sighed.
"Listen to this," Lucy said. "About four million gallons of water per minute thunder over the lip of the falls into the Maid-of-Mist Pool!"
"Four million gallons!" my mother said.
"Per minute!" Lucy added.

My father sings loudly over the rushing water along with Louis Armstrong:

> "Two drifters, off to see the world
> There's such a lot of world to see.
>
> We're after the same
> Rainbow's end
> Waiting round the bend,
> My huckleberry friend,
> Moon River and me."

He raises a shiny trumpet to his lips, bends his knees, and blows. Beads of sweat fall down his face. He wipes his brow with an imaginary rag.

Part Four

I expect there'll be rain today," she says, flexing her arthritic fingers as we look out the back window onto the smoldering landscape.

"Oh, I don't know, Grandma." I smile at her. To me the farm sky looks like it's going to hold back, going to deny the open-throated hens, the crippled corn, the old women.

"We'll see," she says, her eyes closed. It looks as if she's trying to gather the strength to go on. In the darkness she pictures three white pillars. She opens her eyes, forcing herself back to the scene, back to the breeze and its empty promise, back to the weeping willows sucking stones from dirt, the panting dogs, the neighbor's slow gaze, the memory of water lulling everything to sleep. She clears her throat, opens and shuts her hands. It's as if those bony fingers extend out past the glass onto the earth as rows of crops. If she could only do something—she draws her fingers in, folds her hands, and puts them in her lap. The tomatoes bleed into the ground. The basil dries on its stalk. Peas shrivel. Trees shrink to shrubs. The scorpion moves in, the tortoise, the lizard glitters in the sun. Humps grow on the backs of dogs until they are camels. When I turn around, the soil has turned to sand. When I turn again, the rosebush is a cactus.

"It's so hot, Grandma. If I was a snake I'd leave my skin."

"Be sensible," she says. Her voice is as old as the sand. Her throat is the bark of oaks.

"I think I'd like to take a long, cool bath"—water gushing up to the top of the tub, overflowing when I reach for the soap; water hitting my thighs, circling my knees.

"Grandma, it's so hot. I think I'd like to go to the grocery store and stand next to the frozen foods for a while. I wish I was a TV dinner! I wish I was a fish stick!"

"Vanessa, be sensible," she says. It sounds like a plea.

My grandmother was all good sense. A beautiful plant flowered at the base of her brain: broad-leaved, hardy, dark green. If she could have seen it, it would have pleased her, but of course she could not. She did not have the eyes for it. Only at the end was it replaced by something else—something more dense, rounded, almost luminous, something harder. I watched it happen: the flower fold into itself, the leaves curl back into the seed, the seed explode. Then my grandmother, strong willed, confident, grew backward into some tentative future and was frightened. But that was only much later.

"It's too hot to argue with you today, Vanessa."

But I could not think of a time when we had argued. Our conversations usually consisted of two or three sentences, a statement by one of us and response by the other, all of which was repeated a few times over. The rest of the argument must have gone on in my grandmother's head. She always seemed more angry with me than her words had indicated.

Because I needed my grandmother most in spring, I rarely spoke to her at all then, out of fear that I might upset or alienate her. In that watery, unstable season when the whole world seemed to be changing, she did not. She was always the same: a silhouette, a dark triangle, carrying eggs and milk and wood back and forth between the barn and the house. She was a place for the wandering eye to rest. As the dogwood exploded around my head and, under my feet, seedlings sighed and gasped for air, I followed her along her hypnotic path and attempted to focus my attention, instead of letting it run on endlessly here, there, until inevitable exhaustion and then depression set in. What I was looking for was an order, and somehow I knew even then that order was the product of a self-conscious effort, it was a man-made thing imposed on the universe and involving constant exclusions. But as hard as I tried, as much as I concentrated on the print in my grandmother's dress or the gray strands in her hair, I could not forget the complex texture of the evening or the sound of the ground breaking apart. And though the transparency of spring frightened me—the chloroplasts I could see in the leaves, the worms moving underneath the dirt, and the human body looking like the plastic models in science class— I kept it all: the exposed heart, the miles and miles of purple and blue veins everywhere; I think I had no choice.

I remember how the animals howled, not just at night but all day long, too—high pitched, at the edge of control. Sex turned their bodies liquid. They seemed to swim inside each other, with their curving backs and gleaming eyes. Could you see it in me, Grandma? The sex of animals? The fur on my arms? The hair standing straight up on the back of my neck? The swollen glands? The friction under my skin? I frightened myself. But you kept walking; the chores kept you busy—the hens, the hogs. You were tireless, your head bent, your arms overflowing, insisting in your every action that life made sense, life made good sense. I thought it was wonderful that someone who had lived as long as she could still believe that. But when she was seventy, I was only twelve and just learning how the bed could float around under my hands. I noticed the sweating men in the market, their thick arms, their large muddy hands. They began to stare at me. How beautiful a young girl's neck can be, one whispered, how smooth her skin. I fingered my lower lip and pretended I did not hear. At night I could feel the weight of those words like hands all over me. Is that why she disliked me? Could she tell that one day my eyes would be able to make anyone melt? That freely, and without guilt, I'd open myself to them?

Plants pushed through the cracked earth. Fish twirled in the air, their scales reflected light in every direction. Thousands of ants moved together like black shadows across the yard.

But none of this seemed to bother her. "Dinner," she'd call from the kitchen window. "Dinner," she'd say, ringing a large bell, wiping her hands on her apron. I loved you best in spring, Grandma, if I ever loved you.

In the dreams of my grandmother the barn looks enormous—a red cutout against the stark sky. The sky itself is almost white but not quite; there's a hint of gray, a touch of blue there. Somewhere in the cloudless, birdless sky, my grandfather lies—somewhere I can't see, he's lost in gray-blue.

"How much longer?" I ask the sky. I feel myself to be an ancient instrument upon which someone's fingers play slow, sad music, hesitantly, careful not to touch the wrong note. It's something eerie and difficult, something I've never heard before, and yet I feel a part of it. The music continues as I look out the back window and see the hay he stacked in huge piles before he died, still there, about to ignite. There's a message among those brittle bales. I study them from every angle. The notes fade. Or perhaps he forgot to leave one as he moved closer and closer to the place where messages no longer count. Does a twelve-year-old girl make any difference at all to him now? Maybe in the overall pattern there's a larger truth, a design I can't yet see. He tells me something—the best way to reach him or how to live a better life. Some days I think I hear his voice coming from the center of the stacks, the voice I've kept vivid and perfect in my mind. It's softer than in life, muffled, but distinctly his. "Why do you make your grandmother walk so far?" it asks.

"Why don't we just sit for a minute, Grandma? Why don't we just rest?" I place my hands on the tops of her shoulders, wanting to push her down. Already I am as tall as she. She sits for a minute to tie her shoe. Her bones are brittle. She could break so easily under my hands.

"I can't, Vanessa. My feet won't do it." She rises. Quickly, I lift my hands up.

"Thank God I'm able," she says, as we begin the walk to the cemetery on the other side of town. I suppose she believed that soon enough her shoes would fill with dirt for billions and billions of years, too heavy to lift.

Grandma would have buried him on the farm. Wheat would have sprung between his bones. The lacy leaves of tomatoes would have formed a crown for his head. Fruit would have grown in his mouth. His fingers would have fed the flowers.

It was my father who objected when my grandmother suggested a plot of land left of the silo in the north pasture behind the barn.

"I will not," his pale hands looked like two smooth fish, "I will not eat my own father's flesh." He stared at his mother, the stare of the orphan, the stare of the terrified child left totally alone in the world—the stare that much later would become the permanent face of my father. But now the look changed: the grown man came back; his eyes grew darker; his pupils opened; his mouth seemed to curl in sarcasm or anger. Did he think then, looking at my grandmother in her yellow apron, why was it she—pacing in the kitchen, now lighting the oven and complaining about the price of oil—who continued while his gentle father in the next room could not even get up? As he sat there at the table, his eyes bloodshot and wide, did he wish to trade their deaths? Her hair that had not yet completely grayed seemed an insult, her feet that would not drag. I thought of my own tenuous position in my father's heart. He looked to me. I thought he wanted to touch me; it seemed his body moved slightly forward in my direction but then pulled back. I think he wanted to be forgiven, for he was sorry he would never be a father like his father, and he didn't know how to make it up to us. He stood up. His face went blank.

"I will not eat my own father's flesh." He turned toward the window. The wheat quivered in the wind. "Bury him somewhere else. The dead grow enormous without our help—so huge you cannot swallow them, you cannot choke them down."

Already when my father looked out onto the land that his father loved so much he could see him there, his hands folded across his chest in the slopes of the hills. When he walked on the land he thought he heard my grandfather sigh. In the cow's brown eyes he thought my grandfather watched him. In the wind my grandfather whispered requests my father could not keep.

I remember wandering into the barn one night very late and seeing him, lit by the moon, kneeling in the hay. Was I just sleepwalking? Was I only dreaming? I still do not know for sure. His arms were bent to his chest, and he held something gently, carefully, close to his heart. At first I could not see. And then he laid them down in the hay. They were two white eggs. Anyone might have thought my father crazy then. But I understood. He thought they were his own father's fragile testicles.

My grandmother shook her head the way horses do, trying to cast something off, and peered at my father as if he indeed were some stranger, not her child at all, some madman, some insult.

Although my father could never stand the slaughter of hogs, now he cried. He thought he heard his father wailing in their throats.

"I don't know where we went wrong with him," my grandmother sighed one day as we weeded the peas. "I'm afraid there's not much sense to your father."

He had perplexed her from the very beginning. She remembered the nine months he lay inside her. "In all that time," she said, "he never moved, never gave one kick, never turned. Not even I knew whether he would be born dead or alive." And then there had been, after the final contraction, that awful silence. So it was over, she thought, before it had ever really begun. My father had taken one look at the world through his mother's blood and decided he did not care to live here. Given one moment, he knew he did not want to take air into his lungs and breathe. But the young doctor, bent on preserving life no matter how reluctant his subject, saw this right away and spanked my father repeatedly until finally he gave a small yelp, then a cry of protest, and then a long full-bodied scream.

After his tentative start my father was a quiet, brainy child. He could spend day after day working on a single problem of mathematics or lose himself in a dream of fission. He could entertain himself for weeks with the details of the big bang theory or the concept of black holes. By age ten he had mastered geometry; by twelve, algebra; by fourteen, advanced calculus. He grew bored with it after that, though, and did no more—no algorithms, no studies of number theories. Mostly, he listened to music alone in his room in the farmhouse attic: Poulenc, Mahler, Rachmaninoff, Stravinsky. "Music saved my life," he confessed to me on one of the rare occasions he allowed himself to reminisce.

"He could have been a pioneer in genetics," my grandmother said.

"No, Grandma," I said, giggling at the thought of my father in pioneer clothes, sporting a rifle or a bear trap.

"He could have worked in aerospace. He could have found the cure for something."

The dream of my father's greatness was the only dream my pragmatic grandmother had ever cared to keep. After all these years, it still shone in her eyes like a light, but it served no purpose except to make the reality of my father's life almost unbearable to her. She had wanted to be intimately related to greatness and not just a mother-in-law to it.

"He could have been a chemical engineer," my grandmother whispered, "had she not been so beautiful."

"I don't think so, Grandma."

"Don't ask me why he chose to study philosophy, of all things, in college! Imagine! Philosophy! But by that time there was no talking to him." To his parents my father was a walking mystery.

And indeed, had my mother not been so beautiful, my father might have had a very different sort of life, but the minute he saw her across the hall at a college dance, he had already dedicated the rest of his life to her. Good-bye, Kierkegaard; good-bye, Nietzsche. The problem was solved. He would love her even if she would not love him back. He would love her despite every-thing—before she said one word, before he knew one thing about her and her tremendous talent and the sadness that wore everyone out. In his mind he saw himself closing the *Investigations* of Wittgenstein, Heidegger's *Being and Time*, Kant's *Critique of Pure Reason*. Au revoir, Jean-Paul Sartre; farewell, Aristotle. Good-bye—no need for philosophy anymore, no need for any of it. As he glided across the college hall he pictured himself beside the girl in the organdy dress forever.

"That dress was quite simply hideous," my mother once told me. On an-other occasion she said, "If only my mother had lived, I would have known how to act, what to wear."

"It was a beautiful dress," my father said. "You could never see a dress like that today. Its sleeves were like wings and blew in the breeze, and it was the color of the sky at certain dusks."

"He could have been a nuclear physicist," my grandmother said. To her, my mother was the worst sort of person you could be, a selfish one, for, as far as my father was concerned, she kept what could have been from being.

"He said he was happy," my grandmother said, "but I never saw it. It was as if your mother was dragging him further and further into her own private world.

"I don't think your father was ever really happy until you and Fletcher were born." Then, for a minute, my grandmother told me, things changed for him. Our small lives asked to be loved and he loved them. He left his job to care for us. He fed us, he changed our diapers, he sang to us, he made us toys, he played Vivaldi and Mozart for us.

"Your mother, it seemed, never had any time for you," my grandmother said, as if I was hard of hearing. "She was always too busy, though she never seemed to be doing anything." My grandmother kept talking and talking, but I couldn't exactly hear her.

"Yes," I finally said, wiping my brow and clenching the weeds in my fist, and responding in the best adult voice and language I could manage, "I already know that. For your information, Grandma, I'm already aware of that fact so you don't have to tell me anymore," I said, tears in my voice. "Just stop telling me that."

The pea plants looked like veins that led to some invisible heart in the ground. "Daddy," I whispered into the porous earth, "help me."

"Don't make a scene," I thought I heard my grandmother say, but when I looked up she was far down the path, her back turned away from me, guiding some plants up a fence. I was glad she had not seen me. Excess emotion always embarrassed her. She didn't know what to do with it.

At night my grandmother stands over my bed and repeats things she thinks I should know—useful things like when to sow vegetables. "Sow hardy vegetables when apple blossoms show pink, tender vegetables with the first color in lilacs. Some cucumbers retard the growth of weeds." Life is understandable was what my grandmother was trying to say. You can understand your life.

"What good are your dreams?" she asked, pushing the hair from my face. "You dream you are the water and then cry when you cannot do what the waves do, when you cannot fill any container. I don't want to see you hurt, Vanessa. It's the last thing in the world I'd want to see." She paused. "You and Fletcher—you kids are everything to me—everything. I love you kids. I do."

I nodded. "I know, Grandma." I looked into her pale eyes. Her hands were shaking. In one way or another we would both disappoint her.

Life is comprehensible: it is the clothes flapping in the wind on the line; it is how the cat bristles when frightened, how steam rises from the kettle. That was the only truth to my grandmother—the observed life. She gathered her strength from the sunlight reflected on the bread pans, the cheese grater, the butcher block, the beehive. She collected her observations like rain in a barrel and used them when she needed.

"It's so hot, Grandma."

Tiny beads of sweat form on my grandmother's forehead. Her hair is damp and sticks to her head. It's so hot.

"Grandma, imagine the snow." She is fanning herself with an important issue of *Time* or *Newsweek* that my grandfather insisted she save. John F. Kennedy is on the cover. His eyes seem to roll into his head and back out again as she waves him in the air. Her thumb rests on the base of his skull.

"Grandma, the snow is so high we can barely stand in it." I take her hand and we tumble down the hill for what seems forever. My brother Fletcher glides by. His feet are like the red runners on sleds. Snow in slow motion falls on our shoulders. Snow settles on our knees. I can see my grandmother's breath. Our hair goes white, silver white, our faces so bright. Grandma, come back. She disappears in white. Something cracks like ice. Snow piles in my throat. We fall to the ground. We sink in the snow. We move our arms and legs and make angels like the old days. Fletcher flaps wildly. I prefer a slower, more graceful technique. Our arms make the wings, our legs make the dress. And there's mother, too, from out of nowhere, right next to us now. It's snowing so hard that our angels seem to fill up even as we stand, turning to look at them. Mother shivers in the cold. The snow has soaked through her coat. "Oh! You make the best angel of all, Mom," Fletcher sighs, looking at hers, which the snow does not seem to cover over. And he, too, begins to shake. The hills swerve into us.

"Such utter nonsense." My grandmother's voice chills the air. "Where do you get such ideas?" But she doesn't wait for an answer. She's blaming my mother, I know. My mother disappears for weeks and weeks. My mother hears voices in the trees.

"That is no way to live, Vanessa."

My grandmother wished that I might take some sort of control over my life, that I not float along recklessly until death, but that I consciously choose a life and then live it. I know if she had lived to see me choose an enormous gray city to live in she would have helped me as much as she could have. First we would have memorized the thin pages of the encyclopedia under New York, learned its population and the shape of the city. She would have shown me where each borough was. We would have learned the grid system of the streets—east from west, downtown from up. She would have mastered the subway system, known that the E train crosses to Queens and the RR goes west. We would have written to the mayor and the chamber of commerce. We would have knocked on the walls to test their thickness and checked the positions of the windows and the ways of escape. We would have inspected the size of the closets, the condition of the appliances, learned something about the neighbors and the superintendent. We would have known the rights of tenants. We would have studied the lease until our heads hurt. She would have made sure that I made the most intelligent, the best choice. "Zabar's," she would have printed across a postcard or "King Tut" in a red pen. "Flower show at the Brooklyn Botanical Garden, May fifth."

Then, after I was settled, she would have found me the right job. It would have been in an office with a big view somewhere on the twenty-ninth floor of a building downtown in a large firm, taking up four floors with its hundreds and hundreds of offices, its dull carpets, and Xerox machines glowing in every corner. She would have seated me next to some computer, so cold, so terrible to the touch that my arm would jerk back into my body for protection. She would have wanted me among businessmen, among stockbrokers, in halls of finance, among corporate lawyers and their secretaries and cigarettes and air-conditioning, earning an honest living, saving my money, enduring this life, even though it is the only one I have.

The locusts grow louder and louder. It means more hot weather.

That is not living at all, Grandma.

We get the white cups down from the top shelf, fold the red cloth napkins. I place the fork on the left, the knife and spoon on the right. I take the pitcher from the refrigerator. My grandmother pinches some mint from the plant on the windowsill and puts it in the tea. It floats on the top. Because of the heat we wait to put out the butter, and we put the tea back in the refrigerator. We sit at the table and wait for the chicken to finish cooking. Her hands rest in her lap. They do not fly unexpectedly like frightened birds when the light in the room changes or a small breeze blows from the back of the house. My own hands are cold, even in this weather. "It's my circulatory system," I tell her. She smiles. I'm smart for my age. The sunlight pours in the kitchen window, making us think that it is earlier than it really is. Tomorrow I'll be back on the train to Connecticut.

"How pretty you are," she says sweetly. My grandmother looks so nice sitting there. I wish I could be more like her. She wipes her brow and leaves me seated alone. When she opens the oven, the heat is unbearable. The chicken is done. It falls apart on our forks. She stares at me from across the large pine table, which used to be an appropriate place to eat when the whole family was together.

What's wrong? I wonder. She stares at me through the pitcher of iced tea. Do I eat too fast? Is my hair not neat enough? She keeps looking at me. Grandma, don't, I say under my breath. She looks at me as if with enough concentration she could pass her brain into mine. "Grandma, don't."

She asks that I cut myself out from her, like a cookie from dough, like a dress from cloth, and that I be grown up about it and sensible and that I go quietly. She offers her hands in the well-lit kitchen, and to anyone it would look like a small gesture of love, a Mother's Day card, a painting by Cassatt, a simple movement that any grandmother might make toward her grandchild. She offers her hands like two white loaves—something good, something nourishing, necessary to accept. She offers her hands in the well-lit kitchen among the thick white cups, the fruit balanced safely on the wallpaper.

"Be mine," she whispers. "Be mine."

But she's underestimated me.

"Don't leave me. Don't. Don't go," she says quietly over and over in a voice so casual, so offhand that you might think the weather is the subject. And when we look to the sky the low clouds have begun to form, the storm not as far off as I once thought, already gathering force.

"They came in wagons—hundreds of them. They covered the land like terrible shadows. Many were sick. There were graves all along the way—white people's graves everywhere. They brought their darkness. They made us sick with their diseases. They infected us with their lies, with the way they lived. They wanted to tear apart the graves of Indians for minerals, for gold. They would pull apart their own parents. There is nothing they would not do.

"The sun seemed to be going out. They came, hundreds of them, in covered wagons. They dug under the face of my father. They made my mother's body sore. They think they can own the land. There is nothing they would not do. You cannot trade the lives of people for handfuls of gold. They came in wagons. They came to claim the land.

"But how dare they dig under my father's skin for gold? How dare they cut my mother's hair?"

Mary, I love your apple face—round and broad, smooth and shining on this late-fall afternoon. I can't stay long—this old car is not mine and I've got to get it back to the college by dark.

"Ah, yes, the college," she nods, trying to see it in her mind.

"This will be the last picking," she tells me, bending and stretching—reaching, reaching. I follow her, cherishing the movements our bodies make in their last harvest dance. We hear apples like heartbeats, falling from all parts of the orchard, the only sound. "They are picking themselves," her husband Donald laughs.

"The last time for the year," she repeats. Donald has agreed, it is time to move inside. Let the remaining fruit go untouched. Let the children come and take it for nothing. The earth gives of itself freely; it asks nothing in return. It is time to collect the wood and enter the small house, fragrant with apples at the foot of the orchard. It is time for the final weatherproofing.

She stumbles down the hill in the dusk. Her eyes are as heavy and generous as apple trees. Her apron is filled with the fruits she'll use for cider, for apple-sauce. Her rounded arms reach out to her husband for help. Apples dangle from his beard. Apples color the sound of his speech, his concerns. When will the trucks show up for a pickup? How many hundreds of bushels have been left behind?

I want to follow her into her kitchen, settle in next to the wood-burning stove, drink Gertrude Ford tea with her, separate the pumpkin from its seeds, read the *Poughkeepsie Journal*, its early snow reports, and drift into winter.

White light, bluejay, bear-sleep, split wood, apple wine, baked apple: bruised, I want to be with her now, to pass the days in her warmth, to sleep soundly through the bitter nights and dream of no one and nothing but apples.

"I can hardly find your vein," Marta said. "You've gotten so skinny."

"Please don't," I said. But I gave her my arms and, after those veins collapsed, I took off my socks and we examined the places between my toes. "Please don't," I whispered, offering her the back of my leg.

I missed her terribly even before she had gone away. I missed her as I watched her writing. I could tell she was so far away that nothing could bring her back. Watching her some nights, stretched out on the couch reading or dozing off, I missed her even then.

"Help yourself," Jack said, wiping my brow, stroking my hair.

"I'm trying," I said. "But I can't seem to get myself any further."

"Come on," Jack said. "Try harder."

I shivered. The weather turned colder.

I reach for her arm and she is strong, stronger than I could have imagined.

"Vanessa," she says.

"You've remembered my name!" I smile.

"Of course I have," Grandma Alice says. She lifts me up. "Everything's going to be all right. I promise."

"Anza-Borrego State Park in California," he reads, "claims two unusual features: a limitless carpet of wildflowers and elusive bands of bighorn sheep.

"California," he muses. "Disneyland," he says dreamily. "A castle for my princesses."

Grandpa Sarkis, born in the year of the ox, had big plans for my mother. From the first moment he saw her behind glass in the infant nursery, he knew there was something different, something special about his daughter. Girl babies in the old country were nothing to dance about, but he danced at the birth of my mother. Through drifts of cigar smoke in the maternity wing of St. Joseph's Hospital, he danced, he sang. She was beautiful; she was special. He was sure of it. Without knowing anything about the Topaz Bird, he knew. She was the most perfect creature he had ever laid his eyes on or ever would. And best of all she was *his*.

She would bring him luck. "My tamarind seed, my goat's tooth," he said to her and smiled. He was proud of her light hair that waved. He had made an American girl, with her blue eyes like the Pacific, her long graceful body—California. He had made a real American beauty. As unlikely as it seemed, he had had a part in this. His brooding dark good looks had combined with those of his frail American wife and from this hard-fought union Christine had been born.

Everyone had disapproved of the marriage, it had seemed, but especially his in-laws, William and Anne Hauser, Germans from Germany, who could not bear the thought of their only daughter marrying an Armenian, from Armenia, no less, of all places. But even they, after seeing Christine, were appeased somewhat. She was lovely, all agreed on that.

Grandpa Sarkis accepted the compliments and took all the credit he could get, but still he could not help feeling that she was the product of something else, he did not know what—something out of his reach. She felt invented to him, a product of this new country. Like the morning mist itself, rising over the land, at birth she had seemed to lift up gently from her mother's lap and float into the air—something to admire and love but belonging to no one.

Yet Grandpa Sarkis tried. "My American daughter," he said, showing her baby pictures to the men he worked with in the mill, showing them to the women in the grocery store, the family who owned the candy and newspaper store, the bakers where he bought his Armenian bread. "Isn't she beautiful?" Yes, everyone agreed. Even at two weeks old she impressed them, even at two months old; even those who did not appreciate babies appreciated Christine.

And this got Sarkis to thinking. In America it was true, anything was possible. In America even he could have a beautiful baby. In America, and the thought came out whole as he drove home from work one late night, you can make movie stars.

My grandfather, a weaver in a silk mill in Paterson, New Jersey, could not afford his wife's hospital bills. He must have lived in terror of them. He worked night and day, two and sometimes three shifts, and still it was not enough. I would like to think that it was this specific terror that made my grandfather's dark eyes, darting around the house for something to sell for money, rest on my mother asleep in her crib. In America you can make movie stars, he thought, and at six months a baby can make diaper commercials. Beautiful babies could make money just for being beautiful. This is a good country, he thought, as his sick wife called him from the other room.

"A good country," he said to his wife, Alice, and in desperation one wintry day he took the baby from her crib without Alice knowing and brought her to the commercial studios in New York City where photographers posed her in diapers, in other mothers' arms—posed her in front of fields of flowers, backdrops of spring. "My sweet little silkworm," he purred.

I hope my mother found comfort in the notion that perhaps she had prolonged her own mother's life a little, that she provided her with a nurse when she needed one, that the medicine was always there, the tank of oxygen, the way to the hospital. I hope she believed this and not the darker things which it undeniably suggested about her father. Diapers turned to pinafores. She did it for years.

As my mother grew more and more lovely, more radiant with each day, my grandfather's plans for her grew, too. He dreamed she might be a beauty queen one day and took her every year as a little girl to the Convention Hall in Atlantic City, that cake of a building, to watch those hopeful women strut down the lighted runways: laurels and crowns; banners and bounce; red, white, and blue; Miss America.

"Look at Miss Mississippi," my grandfather would say, nudging her. "Oh, Miss Florida, you're breaking my heart," he shouted. "They're like racehorses," he sighed, "thoroughbreds."

But my mother, grown out of pinafores, stepped back, away from the toothy grin, the larger than life. My grandfather did not understand. Watching her walk onto the beach off the boardwalk, he shouted for her to come back, but it made my mother, only seven years old, walk faster and faster. As she ran in the sand, my grandfather dreamed her into a Rockette. He pictured the long line of women she would be a part of, lifting their legs in beautiful unison.

"That is my daughter," he said, pointing to Christine who stood where the ocean met the beach. "One day you will see her in the Rockettes." My mother turned to see him pointing at her and ran faster along the edge of the sea, kicking as she went—a different sort of dancer.

What was wrong with Christine? Silently, Sarkis blamed his wife. "You did not talk to her enough when she was in the womb," he thought. "That's why all this fuss about books, the need for so many stories. You were too weak, and it sapped the joy from her heart. You were too sick and it brought her inconsolable sadness." Nearly immediately Sarkis regretted even thinking this, but it was too late; he could not call the thought back.

Marilyn Monroe, Veronica Lake, Jean Harlow—beautiful Marilyn Monroe, sexy, sweet Marilyn Monroe—Lana Turner, Carroll Baker, Dorothy Lamour in a sarong—these women populated my grandfather's thoughts. In America there are blonde women. In America everyone has a big car, a Cadillac or a DeSoto or a Lincoln, with fins, with wings. They are the biggest and the fastest and the most beautiful cars that have ever been made, and the blonde women sit next to you in them. The windows are rolled down and music plays on the radio. Everyone smokes cigarettes.

No one worries about cancer yet; no one wears seat belts. They cannot help this feeling: that no matter what they do, how fast they drive, nothing can hurt them. They are indestructible. This is America. Everyone will have a job. There will be plenty of money. They will bounce back when hit. Everything will be fine. When they are lonely or sad, they can call up the blonde women on the telephone and go for a ride.

My mother was not the blonde my grandfather wanted. She tied her hair back, kept her legs covered by pants, rarely smiled or spoke; still, all remarked to Sarkis what a beauty she was. He nodded proudly but received no joy from it anymore; it was not a true pride. She could not be pushed. She would not fulfill the dream.

California in those days was a long way to go, especially for a poor man. A movie filled with the stars of the day must have been playing in my grandfather's head, maybe hospital scenes spliced between the dance numbers, as he packed the car and coaxed my mother out of the shadows of the sick house.

"There is always sun there, my little songbird. You will never be cold again."

She was only ten then; by the time they reached Hollywood, she was eleven. She would be a child star, he thought, bigger than Shirley Temple, bigger than Judy Garland.

"Where are the bighorn sheep?" my mother must have demanded, looking out the window of the car. "Where are the carpets of flowers?" she wondered as they walked into MGM for her screen test. Having been powdered and crinolined, perfumed and curled, all at great expense, she looked exactly like a movie star and Grandpa Sarkis swelled with pride. "Where are the bighorn sheep?" she asked as the camera rolled, and she began to cry. Having held it in across the entire United States she could not stop.

"In the old country we drown children like you," Grandpa Sarkis muttered as they left the studio. "Turk-breath," he cursed, and my mother cried harder. "Turk-breath," he said, getting angrier and angrier until he too started to cry; just that morning he had received a telegram saying that his wife had taken another turn for the worse.

During the long, lonely trip back to Paterson, my mother sat crumpled in the back seat, barely moving, refusing to talk.

I imagine that she refused to talk. My mother never told me if this trip to California actually happened. What she did say was that they were poor and the bills were high and her father had once thought she should be a movie star. But it is not enough, Mother, what you have not said. It is not enough—your sadness with no explanation, your life of solitude, your retreats.

This must have been why my mother hated rides in the car so much. This, too, must have been why she would never go to the movies with Father, Fletcher, and me. She could still see the producer, fat forever in her mind, chewing on his cigar, whispering his rotten breath into her ear, "Don't cry, sweetie, there, there, don't cry. What the hell is this about sheep?"

I have seen my mother in a series of dime-store photographs as a teenager wearing black horn-rimmed glasses. She must have gone into Woolworth's for a pair, wishing, I suppose, to appear more studious, to be taken seriously, to change the image of herself her father had given to her, as if it were a gift. I can see her sitting alone in that black photo booth, the velveteen curtain pulled, she positioned in different somber, intelligent poses. She liked the way she looked in glasses. She looked like someone to listen to. She looked like some-one who had something to say.

My mother was always sure to tuck her glasses away in a safe spot after school so that her father, who was home by dinnertime, would not see them. But one day when he and his friends were let out early from work because of a power failure, he saw his daughter from the back on the way home from school.

"My daughter," he told the men, "my American daughter."

She was caught in a serious discussion with one of her classmates and did not see her father as he pulled up alongside her in his beat-up blue Chevrolet.

"What do you think you're doing, Christine?" he yelled from the car window as he passed her. The brakes, which did not work well, left the car a good distance in front of her. "Come here," he said in his old-world voice. His face grew red as she walked to him. "Why are you covering up those beautiful eyes?" his small black eyes said to her. "It's unheard of. It's not right what you're doing."

She stepped back, refusing to get into the car. She recalls that day perfectly: her friend, her father's angry face, the people peering out from the dark car.

"What do you think you're doing?" He could see her eyes, even behind the glasses, turning violet. Her stare was incandescent.

"It's to keep men away," she whispered, "men like your friends, men like you."

"Four weeks," he shouted to her as she ran down the street. This, she knew, meant no school, no friends, nothing but the sad, dark house as punishment. It did not matter. Her father could not hurt her anymore. She had said it. "Words," she thought, shaking uncontrollably, "words."

My grandfather knew, too, after that day that despite everything, all the dance lessons at the Y, all the trips to Atlantic City, all his encouragement, that there would be no Rockette to dance through his old age, no high kicks, no lifted bosom, no spangles or sequins to relieve sadness.

When my mother was eighteen and her sister Lucy was seventeen and their mother had been dead many years already, my grandfather left his daughters, every American hope dashed, every bloated dream deflated. The movies had tricked him. No quiet, beautiful daughter had ever resisted stardom in them. No wife died of a rheumatic heart at the age of thirty-five. No family was broken into pieces.

Does he show a photo of his American daughter in a square in Russia, in a desert in Syria, as he looks everywhere for his old Armenia? No telling. Does he dream her over? In his mind, does she dance through the sorrowful landscape, Ginger Rogers, Ann Miller, full screen, larger than life?

Does he hold her photo up to the Turks? I wonder. Can she alter the bloody past for him—my beautiful, stubborn mother? A defense against the death force? A survivor? Transformed now—proof of something.

Now you move westward, Fletcher, leaving this old life far behind, as if it were possible to do so, and for you, even now, I would like to believe that it might be. Months ago your angry messages scrawled across picture postcards of Massachusetts, of Michigan, of West Virginia stopped coming. Did your anger end finally or only change form, become wordless, incommunicable? I must say it straight out—I am lonely for you. Write to me if you still can.

I always wanted to believe you, Fletcher, wanted to think that somehow we could live side by side with the sadness. It was your example I tried to follow: you, with your blue blanket slung around your shoulders, dreaming of flight; you, fast asleep on top of your leaflets, your thousand prayers for the earth; you of the civil rights rally, the peace march; your armbands, your food for the poor, your large, burning heart.

Today you burn with a different fire, and everything you see as you cross the country burns in it. You level the land with your stare. You turn forests into ash, cities into ash, even houses where people live, even yourself.

This cannot go on, Fletcher—you, an old man carrying your bitter root across the country in a jute sack. Let it go. Bury it deep in the sand. Let it grow downward into darkness now as it curls from the bag into your arms and crawls onto your back, as it wraps all around you. I always believed you, Fletcher: that somehow we might forgive them. Now you face your greatest test, to take that faith of yours when you need it most, and use it.

Last I heard from my father he was nearing some neutral country like Sweden or Norway where they are just about to enter their season of darkness. Anyone who knows him would hope a Vivaldi concerto or a Bach fugue still runs through his head.

". . . there'd been the biggest motorcade from the airport. Hot. Wild. Like Mexico and Vienna. The sun was so strong in our faces. I couldn't put on sunglasses. . . . Then we saw this tunnel ahead, I thought it would be cool in the tunnel, I thought if you were on the left the sun wouldn't get into your eyes. . . .

"They were gunning the motorcycles. There were these little back-fires. There was one noise like that. I thought it was a backfire. Then next I saw Connally grabbing his arms and saying no, no, no, no, no, with his fist beating. Then Jack turned and I turned. All I remember was a blue-gray building up ahead. Then Jack turned back so neatly, his last expression was so neat . . . you know, that wonderful expression he had when they'd ask him a question about one of the ten million pieces they have in a rocket, just before he'd answer. He looked puzzled, then he slumped forward. He was holding out his hand. . . . I could see a piece of his skull coming off. It was flesh-colored, not white—he was holding out his hand. . . . I can see this perfectly clean piece detaching itself from his head. Then he slumped in my lap, his blood and his brains were in my lap. . . . Then Clint Hill [the Secret Service man], he loved us, he made my life so easy, he was the first man in the car. . . . We all lay down in the car. . . . And I kept saying, Jack, Jack, Jack, and someone was yelling he's dead, he's dead. All the ride to the hospital I kept bending over him, saying Jack, Jack, can you hear me, I love you, Jack. I kept holding the top of his head down, trying to keep the brains in."

Jacqueline Kennedy

"This is black cornmeal," he said, lifting the first bag up. "After my death, pass it around your head four times and cast it away. This makes the road dark so as to prevent dream visits by the spirit. Don't follow me," my grandfather said, "no matter how much I beg.

"The white cornmeal comes next," he said, and he pointed to the second bag. "Take the white cornmeal in the right hand and sprinkle it, saying, 'May you offer us your good wishes. May we be safe. May our lives be fulfilled.' Please don't follow me, no matter what.

"Now, children," his voice grew softer, "on the fourth morning after my death, leave the windows and doors open so that my spirit can leave the house for good. There," he said, pointing to the third bag—pine resin incense. "Burn this on the fourth day."

It's December. And gradually now I feel it coming on. The mildness breaks. Drafts of cold air move down from Canada. This will be the harshest winter in decades, meteorologists say.

He heard the gray screech owl and knew the cold was coming. He looked into the sky and began to count the stars, despite the legend that said to count even one would surely mean his death. He did not care. He thought he saw a great gourd of ashes in the sky about to spill over. Still counting he took the golden-haired child and pierced arrows through her eyes, then took off her scalp. It was the end.

"I know nothing about you, Jack."

"Oh, Vanessa," he sighed. "You know all that is necessary," he whispered.

"I know nothing."

"Would it help? Do you think it would really help?" He smiled.

"I don't know."

"What would you like to know?" he asked. "Where I grew up? Something like that?"

"Yes," I said.

"Detroit. I grew up in Detroit. Does that help you at all? Does that change anything that will happen here? I don't think so, Vanessa." He smiled, put on his wire-rimmed glasses, and studied my face. "Oh, love," he said, "it won't help us."

When my brother was in Detroit he sent me a postcard of the Ford Motor Company plant. Only my name and address appeared on the back.

I stumbled into the white room. The mercury fell. I hugged my black coat to me. White envelopes fell from my pockets and the package of needles. Jack looked into my eyes.

"Can't you do anything," he cried, "but surrender?"

When I think of Detroit, I do not think of the men who pull themselves from their beds each gray day to hug fender after fender until their backs curve like wheels into retirement; I think of you, Jack, just a boy surrounded by books in your father's library. You've read there all day and now your eyes are beginning to hurt. You take off your glasses and watch the afternoon as it slowly surrenders its light. I wonder where your father is—probably working on some difficult equation in another part of the house. You set up the chess set and wait for him. You have just finished reading *The Rise and Fall of the Third Reich* and wonder what it is all about. You've never heard it mentioned before, not even in passing. You punch out numbers on your father's calculator and try to count up the dead, as if you could. Is this why your father's head always seems to be bowed? Why no one speaks German in your house anymore, not Father, not Mother, not Ilse? Not the eldest Uncle Werner or the youngest cousin Christa? And Wagner, once Grandfather's favorite composer, is missing from the shelves of records now. Why? You would ask your father these questions but sense that you should not, that it would draw you even further apart. Besides this, chess requires great concentration and you must not speak. When he walks into the room you stand. His wire-rimmed glasses seem to shine in the failing light. You wonder how the equation is going but do not ask; it would be an indiscretion. Sometimes you wish you could see his brain. It must be a wonderful thing.

"Your move," Father says quietly. You are only nine but already a good match for him. As you put your hand on the pawn's carved head and move it toward the center of the board, I am just being born. You move again and I cry out. A large woman with long thick hair comes into the room with "refreshment." Her English is unsure of itself. Now and then a "wie gehts" still slips from her tightened lips. Something troubles her. Is this your mother?

"Wagner," my father says.
  "Wagner."
  "Mahler."
  "Mahler."
  "Bruckner."

"I couldn't stay away" was what he said now more and more often, coming at unexpected times, not to our hotel anymore but to my apartment where he knew he could find me. He will disappear, I thought, as simply, as mysteriously, as he has arrived, with a word about the weather, a shrug, a last cigarette. But he had not disappeared. I saw him more and more frequently. "Please," he'd say into the intercom, "I couldn't stay away."

His voice was not tender, I thought, as I pressed the button that would open the door downstairs and allow him up. No, there was no tenderness there. It was not love that brought him here; it was something else. I don't think even he could understand his own actions anymore, what it was that kept leading him here to me. He looked bewildered, angry, as I opened the door. "I couldn't stay away," he hissed.

I smiled. "Come in," I said. "Did you really miss me?" I laughed.

He took my arm. "I try never to think of you when we are apart," he said softly. "It makes me crazy. Sometimes just the idea of the force of your thighs crushes all thoughts from me. I can't remember anything: where I was going or what I wanted. This is something I did not plan on, Vanessa, something I did not foresee—your power."

"I have no power."

He laughed. "It is what you love to believe about yourself. It is what you want to believe."

"I am at your mercy."

"Ha!" he laughed.

"Who are you then?" I asked. "I don't even know your last name. I don't know anything about you—why you are here at all, what you are trying to do with all these games. That's power? I want to know where you go when you leave me. I want to know what your mother looks like. I want you to tell me things."

"You already know everything," he said. "You know me only too well."

"Just to know where you sleep when you're not here, what your days are like." I began to cry.

"What's with you, Vanessa?" he asked, taking my hand in his. "What's with you, anyway?" My hand was smooth, unlined. Like a stone it felt heavy, impossible. Jack's hand was large, rough, veined, as if it had lived a thousand lives, had a thousand stories to tell, all of them off-limits to me.

He took me in his arms. Slowly his large hands fumbled with the robe I was wearing.

"Oh, love," he whispered, "what's happening to us?"

"You think you can be free," I said, "because I know so little? Because you keep me ignorant?"

"On the contrary," he said. Anger rose in his voice. "I will never really be free of you." I stepped back.

"Don't you know that one simple thing yet?" he asked, nearing me. In one strangely gentle motion, he tied my hands behind my back with the belt of my bathrobe, which he'd hung around his neck.

"We can pretend that you are the dog—but it is only a game. Get down," he said. "Good. Now just watch me." He patted my head. Slowly he took off his clothes and folded them neatly and placed them in a pile.

He flipped me over suddenly, took his necktie and tied my feet together.

"Now," he said, "we can pretend, if you want, that you are the one who cannot move, that you are the one who is going nowhere, that you are a poor innocent victim of circumstances. This big man has come and tied your hands behind your back and now your feet together and you cannot escape."

He just looked at me lying on the floor. "Poor, poor Vanessa." He tied his handkerchief around my head so that I could not see. "You want to be the victim forever. How very dull—the one who's been wronged, abandoned." I could feel his mouth at my ear, his hot, urgent breath.

"Who hasn't been asked to suffer terribly?" he whispered fiercely. "How long can you go on like this?" he demanded. "You can get out of it if you want. Picture yourself free," he said. "Fight back." His voice sounded very sad. I began to thrash on the floor trying to get my feet loose. My arms ached.

"You have the ability to escape, Vanessa, but you don't want to."

"I want to," I said.

"Not badly enough. You are in charge of your own life. You are in charge even now."

"Help me," I said.

"How can you possibly believe that a man, a stranger really, can come in here and rescue you—help you—save you?" He laughed. "Don't buy into it, Vanessa. It is the myth of the oppressor."

"I don't care. Do what you want."

"Fight back. Save yourself."

I began to cry. "Help me," I said.

"We'll sit here all night this way."

"Please," I said.

"Be ingenious."

"Please," I whispered.

"Fight back," he said in desperation. "Don't give up." He untied the handkerchief from my eyes so that I might watch. "Please," he said. "Don't make me do this."

He took his leather belt from the pile of clothes, raised it over his head, hesitated, I thought, for a moment, then lowered it, hitting me over and over again. He was crying as he hit me harder and harder. "Say something," he screamed. He could not stop now. I felt only pain, nothing else. I could not see him, but only his motions, only his sobs.

"Why?" I cried. "Why?"

"Forgive us," he said, and I felt a great warmth flowing over me.

"Why?" I whispered, in my blood voice.

"Please, say stop," he screamed. "Please, say something." It was the last thing I heard. I must have passed out.

"Untie me," I said when I regained consciousness, "now." I could not feel my own body. He said nothing but only followed my instructions. I was covered with blood. "Lift me to the bed," I said, "gently. Be careful." Without a word he did this, too.

"Jack," I said, and, hearing his name now in my broken voice, he started to weep.

"Please. Please hold me," I whispered, "just hold me for a minute."

"Now sit in the chair," I said calmly. "Sit there and watch me sleep. Take care of me. Do you understand?" He nodded. He sat in the chair and said nothing. I slept. I could not bear to stay awake.

When I awoke, he was sitting next to the bed on the floor, his face in his hands. He had not slept. He moved his hand toward me. I pulled away.

"You have the ability to get better," he said with a huge tenderness, an impossible sorrow, "but you have to want it, you have to work at it. You can do whatever you want."

"Who the fuck do you think you are?" I said. "What gives you the right to tell me how to live, to show me the way?"

"You've suffered enough, Vanessa, enough."

"That's where you're wrong, my friend. I can never suffer enough."

"It's not your fault that your whole family is gone."

"I didn't say it was."

"Look at you, just look at you." His anger filled his whole body, the whole room. With the sheer force of his anger he pulled the mirror from the door of the bedroom and brought it over to me. "Look at yourself."

"Don't be so dramatic," I said.

"Live," he cried, "or die. Do you understand what I'm saying to you? You're going to die, Vanessa."

"Maybe," I said. "What does it matter to you?"

"Don't die, Vanessa. Please don't die," he said, and I heard a great wailing. "Invent the way to live with this. Do anything you have to," he whispered, kissing me. "Save yourself."

The day we bought the Ford the sun was shining, and the car salesman, who wore a plaid seersucker jacket, whistled "For Once in My Life" as he watched my mother slip one long leg then the other into the small red car. The glare was so great that day that my parents seemed to disappear in it when the Pinto's doors were shut and they took the car for a trial run around the block.

This cannot go on, Fletcher—you an old man carrying your bitter root across the country in a jute sack. Let it go. Bury it deep in the sand. Let it grow downward into darkness now as it curls from the bag into your arms and crawls onto your back, as it wraps all around you. I always believed you: that somehow there might be a way to live.

Back in Detroit, you, too, loved Wagner and crept to the closet at night, after everyone was asleep, to reach up for him. On those nights something stretched in me, too, and I turned in my crib and cried out. And a few years later, when you lifted your dinner of meat and noodles to your mouth, I shuddered, knowing you were somewhere, waiting for me.

Father and Fletcher sat in the front and Mother sat in the back seat where she liked it best. She closed her eyes. She would try to rest in the car, enjoy life more, spend more time with the children.

Miss Cameron, the associate professor of English, pauses in front of me and smiles, helping me to gather the strength to go on.

As she lit a cigarette from the new pack she had just bought, we tell ourselves that she wanted to live forever.

There were three phone calls that night. The first came from her mother, regal even through the dirty receiver, her image instantly conjured with the sound of her voice. She was wondering whether France, rather provincial, she thought, on her last visit, was the right place for her daughter to pursue her studies in the history of art. Florence undoubtedly would have been the more logical choice. But there was nothing to worry about, her daughter assured her, then asked about her father and promised to write. After a few more monosyllabic minutes she hung up because, as she told her mother, she feared the sound of her disembodied voice.

We know now because we know the end of the story that she will die later on in this small room, but after the second call we forget; we cannot see how it is possible. The second call was to a man, age thirty-eight, named Paul Racine, a fashion designer she had met while in Paris a few weeks before. A flamboyant man, witty, energetic, the type of person Natalie liked to be around: he forced her into animation. The conversation was long and leisurely, and they discussed many things: the upcoming fashions—the shorter skirts, the longer hair, the use of color for spring, the lines of the future, cosmetics— and her chances of being a model. It was a call made by someone who planned to see the spring, someone with plans far beyond this cold January night. "Drugs were never once mentioned," Paul said when asked afterwards.

"I want to take it back—the idea of my tongue in your mouth, the idea that I could ever love you," she said to someone whose name we cannot get—the third call.

Some time after the third call the drug was injected, we now believe. As close as we can tell, it was somewhere between nine and eleven o'clock. She then began preparing to go out, combing her hair, putting it up, loosening it, taking it down, putting it up again. She applied and reapplied makeup to her ghost face, painting on cheeks and eyes, composing a mouth. But no matter how much color she added, she remained white as the heroin climbed her arms and reached up for her. Giving up, she put a few lipsticks into her purse—an incomplete work, untitled yet.

When she gets to the bar she buys a new pack of cigarettes, which she smokes to the rhythm of French pop music, and then she fumbles across the dance floor. Two women stop her to talk. She lies clearly and without hesitation to one lover about another, loses interest in the lie midway, forgets the ending, walks away. Slowly she finds her way to the bathroom, refusing help every few steps, her divorce with the body almost final now. She blacks out several times but somehow manages to get herself home. Her dazzling eyes light the way. She moves forward, quicker than she had previously, open-armed, toward light, toward a large, white American car. She nearly runs into it, like a cat giving away its last life.

Back in the apartment she falls to the bed, farther away with each breath now from her intentions, her fingertips freed from the history of art. Who can remember now, she wonders? Longer skirts? Shorter hair? Longer hair? The color white?

Soon the police arrive—two young men. "This happens," they say, covering the body, steady as surgeons. "This happens." For them it is the only way to see such things. "This happens," they mutter to each other, looking at her long, beautiful legs, her flawless face. "It was very pure—the heroin. She probably did not know," they tell anyone who will listen. "It happens, that's all. C'est tout. C'est ça."

Later, there will be police photographers.

Later, in the mind, we will try over and over to see this—her body sculpting itself into its final position—but we cannot.

"On Natalie's behalf I quote from a Richard Brautigan poem for you," Marta said quietly.

> I don't want to see you end up that way
> with your body being poured like wounded
> marble into the architecture of those who make
> bridges out of crippled birds.

"If you feel compelled to remember, try to imagine her hunched over pin-ball."

"Imagine it differently, Marta," I told her. "Help yourself out of this." But Marta could not imagine her way through grief and past it. She sank into it and she took me, too. She had never followed the flight of the Topaz Bird. She had never even heard of it.

Natalie is lying in her apartment on the floor with her head propped against a blank wall, drawing conclusions, summing things up. "Do you think it was right," she asks herself now, "to come here to France, so far from Marta and everyone else?" She reaches across the floor for a pen but finds only pencils and with them carves a few short lines, last words, as the dresser disappears, the kitchen light dims. Her meditation is long and involved; it does not fit on the page and cannot be captured completely by the slowing pace of her hand. The complex thoughts of an abstracting mind flood her whole system.

"Do not picture it that way," Marta says, "Natalie apologizing, Natalie thanking those she'd always meant to, Natalie saying good-bye, making the ordinary, the simple gestures of love. Do not think of it that way. For some, the most simple things are not possible.

"She probably welcomed sleep, because she was so restless always and had gone without sleep for so long. She probably was thinking about the color red or a new way to cut her hair."

She probably never once thought of the growing space in front of her eyes. A song from the bar that would not leave her head was probably the last thing on her mind, locked forever inside her skull after the brain closed down. Surely, she could not have known that she was about to die.

"And if someone had told her," Marta says, "she probably would have laughed and shrugged her shoulders. She probably would not have been listening."

"My palms once said unjust criticism would follow my death. My palms are gone, their lines incorporated into the world you now see, along with all the dead."

She looked just as she looked in Marta's photographs. As in the photos, empty space enveloped her. She looked lonely out there, in need of company.

"Give me a chance," she said. "Imagine me," she pleaded, and she stepped closer, "please."

"Maybe Natalie isn't dead," I said, jumping awake. "Maybe she's still alive. What if she wanted to trick everybody? Escape her parents? Change her life? Start over? Become French or Italian? Change her name? Maybe she arranged it all with the man in the phone booth in Nice. Maybe the whole thing was set up somehow."

"Vanessa," Marta said slowly, looking at me with her flickering brown eyes, "you're so stupid sometimes." She took my hand. "These are the facts. I loved a strange and beautiful woman. I never understood her. Our time together was short. I was a season's diversion for her, a plaything—an exotic object from South America for her impressive collection. When she tired of me, she packed up and left. Do not idealize her. She was thoughtless, selfish, and vain. But I loved her anyway. She never really cared about me. She died that cold night in France. She's dead. I love her still."

"But, Marta . . ."

"There are things that can never be explained, Vanessa, things that will never make sense. I'm unlucky, I guess. I can't get around the facts; they keep coming back. Natalie is dead. She died for nothing. I can never bring her back."

Mourning clothes weigh far more than regular clothing. They are not only heavier, but they cling close to the body and they do not come off at night. I was not at all surprised by Marta's stooped posture, her rounded shoulders, her slow motion. I was impressed that she could move at all under such a tremendous weight. It must have taken great effort. She barely picked up her feet anymore; they were covered by mourning shoes.

How did we get up to the catwalk of Main those late afternoons where we stood and watched the sun sink like a heart? She could barely walk most days, but we climbed up there somehow. Where was Jennifer, I wondered, as we stared into the pink light and Marta told stories?

"Oh, off on some project, no doubt," Marta said, with disdain and affection. She laughed, picturing her friend talking in feminist to the Ladies' Auxiliary Club in Poughkeepsie or negotiating some treaty with the women at Bard College.

"You've got to give Jennifer credit," she said, exhausted just thinking of the piles of leaflets and petitions that covered the floor of her room.

I miss her, this Marta, only because I have seen her shed for a moment her mourning clothes and join some unencumbered present where she comments on a task of Jennifer's or a particular professor's eccentricities or reads aloud some ridiculous article from the student newspaper. I wish for this Marta to be with me all the time. But as quickly as she's surfaced, it seems she sinks again, so heavy in her clothes of death.

I too had grown fonder and fonder of escape. "Where is the needle, Marta?" I asked.

The Chinese are right to make white the mourning color. It is the color of the eyes rolled back in the head, the color of the blank page that is always before my mother. It is the color of cocaine—the color of heroin.

She is baklava sweet in the stale ground.

"She slipped out of the wreckage of our lives casually," Marta said, falling into sleep, "as if out of a pair of stockings."

There was no sign of turmoil on Natalie's face that day as she discussed with her adviser taking the year in France, then wrote to her parents, on vacation in Africa, for money, then made the plane reservations. She felt calm, relieved even, as if some weight had been lifted.

Not even she knew how much damage had been done. The mind can continue for days or months or years sometimes before allowing chaos in. Not everyone falls apart immediately during a crisis. Some grow stronger at first, more beautiful. The men on the plane could not keep their eyes off Natalie. She knew this, and it brought her some small pleasure as she lit a cigarette and unfastened her safety belt. They had no power over her and she enjoyed that, for she could never love a man and their lecherous and forlorn looks made her quite suddenly giddy. She was in control of her life. How easily she had made all the necessary arrangements.

What waited for her in France she was too tired even to conceive. She took from her large leather bag an Italian *Vogue*, a French dictionary, and some light-blue writing paper, which she quickly put away. She would not look back again. Gray Poughkeepsie was gone. She had made it disappear. She could do anything. Marta, too, was gone. Her French, of course, would need brushing up, she thought. Marta's had always been so pathetic, so horribly Spanish. Natalie loathed imperfection, weakness of any kind. She hated the way Marta groveled. Natalie practiced her cold, hard look on the man across the aisle. He fidgeted in his seat. Marta had become so weak. At the end Natalie could not stand the sight of her. She smiled. She had made her disappear.

I stumbled into the white room. The weather was getting colder and colder now, the mercury falling way below freezing. I hugged my black coat to me. White envelopes fell from my pockets and the package of needles. Jack looked into my eyes, rolled up my sleeves.

"Goddamn it," he said. "Goddamn it, Vanessa." He kissed me everywhere as if he might suck the drug from my system. "Goddamn it," he whispered.

"Don't do this," he said. "Save yourself."

White, too, is the color of snow.

"Crazy Horse was dead. Sitting Bull was soon to die. What Drinks Water dreamt in advance was coming true: 'they will come and they will build small gray boxes on the land and beside those boxes we shall die.' "

We walked on the farm with Grandfather. He was getting old as he spoke the story. "Let's sit here," he said, and we sat in the center of a field of wheat.

"They were being crowded into camps," Grandpa said. "Their food was being cut off and they were slowly starving to death. The land they loved was being taken away. The white men wanted to buy it. They did not understand that it was not for sale.

"It was the end. The earth was being pulled apart for coal and gold. Every promise was broken. Many, many were killed. There was no hope on earth."

"It was the end," Fletcher said. "They could not roam on the land. They were put into camps."

"But then from the west," my grandfather said, "came a dream over the plains." He made a large gesture with his arm. "And the dream was this: Christ had come back to earth as an Indian. Indians from all over went to Nevada to hear the dreamer's story. 'The dead will all be alive again,' Wovoka said. 'The earth will be green with high grass. The buffalo and elk will return. There will be plenty of food. It will be like old times.'

"They were starving. There was no hope on earth. Crazy Horse was dead," my grandfather said.

White Feather thought of her son and her heart swelled.

" 'We will walk and talk with our lost ones,' Wovoka said, 'if you do the Ghost Dance,' and he taught them how to do it. 'Everyone,' he said, 'must dance. There will be food and sweet grass. And the white man will become small fish in the rivers. Spread the word.' "

The Indians brought Wovoka's message back to their tribes, Grandpa told us, and everywhere men and women began dancing the Ghost Dance. They wore the magic Ghost Shirts that were painted with sacred symbols and impenetrable to the bullets of the white man.

There was no hope on earth.

"After doing the dance for a long time, men and women fell into trances. Many saw what had been promised. There was happiness and peace. When they came back from the trances they told their dreams to others. They had seen the dead. In the next spring it was promised there would be no more misery. They danced on and on. The white men ordered the Ghost Dancing to be stopped. Sitting Bull was taken away. But the Indians continued. 'We shall live again,' they chanted."

It was 1890 and winter was coming on.

Anne Stafford held her five-year-old son Joshua tightly in her arms as if she might squeeze the life back into him. Her heart ached so that she wished she might die with him. Cholera had broken out all along the Platte River. All day as they traveled westward in their covered wagons, they could see people burying their dead, using the side boards of the wagons to construct coffins.

"You cannot trade the lives of children for handfuls of gold," Anne cried. "One does not make up for the other."

After three days Anne's husband finally pried Joshua away from his wife, took some boards and made the second small coffin of their short voyage. Her arms were now empty of both children. One could hear her piercing cry, like that of the coyote, through the dark nights. In grief she gathered her children's toys together, glued them to a pail, and painted them blue.

Eva Hauser, sitting up in bed, moved the blue stamp from Germany from the top corner of the canvas down to the bottom. A series of pink stamps from France, cut in half, ran down the left side like a border. She sprinkled a bit of chamomile through the center. Looking at the various scraps of fabrics the women of the sewing circle had left her, she picked one and held it in her hands. She cut out a triangle from a family photograph and placed it carefully to the right. A broken teacup that her grandmother once lovingly put her lips to every day completes the piece.

"I can't live here anymore," she sighs over the phone, exhaling cigarette smoke as she tells her parents of her plans. "I can't even drive."

"Drive? What do you need to drive for?" her mother, always chauffeured, asks.

"You've obviously never come to visit me in Poughkeepsie," Natalie says. "You obviously don't know what I'm up against!"

"Your father will get you a car," her mother says.

"Yes, but I don't want a car. I want to go back to Europe."

Marta began to eat only things that crunched: carrots, celery, crackers, popcorn, apples. She did not move. I brought these things to her bed, closed my eyes, and listened to the sound of her jaw coming down on a stalk or a core. She did not speak. She was making sounds the only way she could. No more talk about Natalie's death—no more talk at all, the crunching went on all day and long into the night.

As I lie alone in my bed in New York now, I hear her crunching again, though I have not seen Marta in such a long time. Now in the middle of this lonely December she hands me a perfect, red apple. "Eat this," she tells me. "Eat this." She passes me a carrot next, a cracker, not much, but all she has.

"I miss you, Marta," I call out in the darkness where only the cat moves.

"I loved her so much," I hear her say. "It was so hard to try to live without her, to try to live after her."

She tries to help me now as a light snow begins to fall, and I realize that she has been helping me all along. The room, the candles, the photos, the—it was all part of the rehearsal. She gives me my marks on the stage now, telling me where to stand, my line cues. She hands me a ripe, red apple. "Eat this," she says, "eat this."

Before her eyes the highway opened up like a field and slowly filled with snow. She looked up at the white sky; it seemed the snow might never stop. As they neared home in the little red car, the snow fell harder, transforming the landscape.

It was one of those bright, impossibly clear spring days that had become less and less common in New York. Rain had become its weather, gray its color. A haze that would not entirely burn off seemed always to envelop the city. We had grown accustomed to it; it was how we lived. So on this day in Central Park the heightened clarity seemed strange, giving us all a sense of unreality. Things this clear did not seem true anymore.

I was unused to such a skyline. It was sharp, pointed. I felt I might pierce my hand on the Chrysler or the Empire State Building; they seemed that defined, that close. I could nearly see into them: the off-hour office scenarios: in one building a band of young lawyers working this Saturday on an antitrust case; in another building a boss taking his secretary onto his lap.

Such clarity provides information we do not know how to take in, how to integrate. Faces are more exposed, we are forced to see the hundred deaths in them. Words are more vulnerable, fragile, sounds are magnified. Everything is exaggerated. Even a piece of paper can have a wounding edge. But this was the day chosen months in advance to celebrate the earth, and on the thousand mouths of those who gathered, the words "perfect," "beautiful," "lovely," "exceptional" rose as they looked to the blue-egg sky.

My mother looked to me, then away, then back again quickly as if she saw some small feature of mine that had been hidden from her for seventeen years. My father studied Fletcher who, chosen by the high school to make a speech this day, was just approaching the podium. It seemed as if Father was seeing Fletcher clearly for the first time, seeing him with new eyes, and with these eyes he glimpsed something he hadn't been able to see before; something came clear in his own mysterious life. Staring straight ahead, he was not the man who adored my mother and lived in her shadow, he was not the father of two children whose jacket ends were tugged even in sleep. He was not the wayward son, the disappointment. Looking at his own son he was someone else, a man of nature with a destiny, a free will. It welled in his chest and filled him with a great feeling of power and momentum. For a few brief moments I saw my father this way: a free man, an immense, important figure in his own life.

But in less than a minute something happened. The wind changed direction or the public address system hissed and the spell broke. It is I who cannot sustain this vision.

Though my mother's shoulder touched mine and my father's shoulder touched my mother's, I was aware that something was already beginning to divide us, separate us. Fletcher seemed to recede before me, my parents to fall away. "Don't go," I said, but no one heard me. I knew that I would have to start talking louder, concentrating harder. Blocks of lucite or some other modern, clear material seemed to be forcing us apart. I feared it would cloud over and distort my eyesight. I feared that soon I would not even be able to shout through it. I should have investigated its terrible proportions more that day, touched its thickness and its edges before it grew monstrous, untouchable, unbreakable, without boundaries. My father, a tall man, found his knees constricted by the invisible slab. They knocked against it. Through it he looked at my mother and, sensing her uneasiness, attempted to calm her with talk. The tiniest details of everyday life could sometimes relax her. They looked at the light fixtures, changed since their last visit to the park. They noted the tourists, guessing their nationalities. They watched the colorful garb of joggers, talked about shoes, followed the horse-drawn carriages as they made their way around the park.

"That horse is so poorly groomed," my mother said, pointing to a shabby brown one. "An animal like that should be cherished, not made to pull overweight foreigners on concrete.

"Where do they keep the horses at night, Michael?" she asked, and her voice was as high and light as a child's. Once my mother got hold of an idea, she did not easily let go of it. She moved back and forth slightly in her seat. I knew as my brother neared the podium that she was imagining those old brown horses shifting from one leg to another in their tiny stalls.

"It is no secret," Fletcher said, and she jumped, looking at me with animal eyes that darted wildly as if there were fire and she was a horse. I took her hand.

"I love you, Mom," I said, and the "m" sound hung in the air. It reminded her, I think, that she was a mother, that next to her was her daughter, in front of her her son, and she smiled slightly, if only for my sake; and as I watched her smiling for my sake I knew for no particular reason that somehow this was the beginning of the end. How ridiculous, I said to myself as soon as the thought formed; I did not know what it meant, it was senseless, melodramatic, and still I believed it.

"We are each of us alone," I thought.

My grandmother, dead two years, would think that on such a bright day such thoughts were inappropriate: my brother giving a public speech, the sky an impossible blue. But my grandmother could not see beyond primary colors, and this sky had too much white in it to be a true blue. I watched Fletcher against this backdrop.

He is a little boy fishing in the lake, catching trout, then throwing them back.

He is a little boy waking early to find his turtles, which he left outside overnight in a pail of water, eaten by birds, a tiny leg there, a piece of shell, a head bitten off and left.

He is a little older, up late, caught already in the excitement of primary politics, watching the young senator win California, then moments later fall mortally wounded.

He is older, sitting in the woods collecting moss and putting it in a basket.

He is older, looking at mushrooms under a microscope.

And there is my brother, sometime in the future, slumped over the edge of a stage, dejected, but I don't know why.

He felt himself to be falling. He seemed to be struggling as he spoke to maintain his momentum, to keep up his energy. He was floundering in shallow water. He was doing all he could to stay afloat. Those who did not know him could not have realized that he was having trouble, but he was my brother and an intricate system of attachments bound us in a way not even we completely understood. He was having difficulty. My magnetic brother, the person who could convince anyone to follow him anywhere, my brother, whom hordes of people had followed wherever he asked them to go, now panicked. As he began I saw him take a deep breath and shake his head. Like an athlete he had prepared for this speech, done jumping jacks, run in place, but he was not feeling it. Something was wrong. It might all slip away as he spoke. He might wander off or his voice might falter. People would pull back. People would think him insincere or weak. This is what I detected in him. He worried through the speech that he was somehow not connecting, not getting through, holding back. Only the audience reaction, the donations of money, the number of volunteers proved otherwise. He had moved his listeners, illuminated the problems. In some new way they would see the situation. He had succeeded. He sighed. He felt such relief that tears fell from his eyes, and his arms and legs went limp.

As we neared him I could see that tiny lines had already begun forming in his face. The shadows cast in the bright sunlight were long and dramatic. Now that his speech was over, his thoughts turned inward, growing darker, and they kept him separate from his earthly vision, and his own pleasure at what he had accomplished that day was diminished. For a split second he knew it. What he had sensed somewhere in the beginning of his speech now was clear: what he hoped for with every cell of his body would not come true. He sat alone perched on the edge of the stage, a dark hawk (dark as the sky was light), inconsolable.

It is late afternoon. He is an old man. He stares at the bright orange wall of the house. His eyes burn. He looks down at his hands. His palm twitches. He knows this means he will soon strike someone or become angry.

Nothing moves—not the high grass, not the prairie dog, not the shriveled pods of yucca. All is the color of sand and dust. Rusted cans are strewn on the landscape.

Wood ages quickly here, worn by wind and rain. He looks out over the reservation and then further off at all he has lost. He sees a row of wooden boxes bleached gray. These tiny houses are like the coffins of white men: there's no air. He sends a petition to the Great Spirit. "We can't breathe in here. We lie down in here and die."

It is the end. He walks into the kitchen, turns on the faucet: sound of metal, sound of dark water. He opens the refrigerator, closes it. "The young ones tell me I've got to forget the way it was," and a smirk comes to his face. "When we forget, then surely we die. Once there were buffalo and elk and clear water. Once we roamed freely on the land.

"Give me back," he rasps, "what you have taken."

He walks into the other room. He turns on the television.

Fred Flintstone and Barney Rubble flip brontosaurus burgers on the grill in Bedrock in brilliant technicolor and plot how to sneak away to the Water Buffalo meeting without the girls finding out.

Lucy and Ethel have just begun work at a chocolate factory. They stand in front of the conveyor belt. The foreman tells them if one candy passes them and gets down to the packing room unwrapped, they're finished.

A game-show host in heavy makeup smiles madly. "What is behind that curtain?" he asks a squealing audience.

"Come on down," he calls out. "Mrs. Betty Loomis from Nashville, Tennessee, come on down! Let's make a deal."

Switch to a commercial: a woman in a nurse's uniform breathes her mouthwash breath on a young doctor.

A man offers a woman a cup of coffee by a fire. Demurely she refuses. "It's the caffeine," she says, wrinkling her brow with puppy-dog sincerity. "But it's decaf," he says. "No, it can't be. This rich?" she says in amazement, in adoration.

His voice quivers. "Give me back," he says into the false smiles, "give me back," he says into the antiseptic grins, into all the lies, "give me back what you have taken."

Now as the orange and yellow and lime-green walls start to close in on him and he is beginning to have difficulty breathing, he closes his eyes and calls up the sacred land of the grandfathers. Slowly the walls recede and disappear.

Tears fall; tears have fallen for hundreds of years. The sun drops; the clouds turn pink and purple. Once he could call rain from the sky. "You must never forget," he says.

He looks out the tiny window and sees his grandchildren reaching for the red medicine ball.

Lucy and Ricky, roses in their mouths, do the tango for the PTA at Little Ricky's school.

In this fragile light which seems to change even as he observes it, the figures of the children dissolving, as he holds them, into a dusty background—in this light he calls up Butte Mountain where he can still go whenever he has to, in his mind. He reaches for it now.

"I dream of you," he smiles,

"I dream of you jumping.

Rabbit,

Jackrabbit,

Quail."

"We are killing people. There is no other way to see this," Fletcher said in sorrow, standing paralyzed in his realization. "We fill the earth with the bones of those who beg simply to live out an average life: seventy years and the chance to work, but for many even that is not possible. This must change," Fletcher burned, looking at Bill whose lungs had filled with asbestos.

Timmy Skofield was filled with questions.

Clifford kept saying, "I quit. I quit for good." The deal he and Fletcher had made now seemed stupid. He had made the promise earlier that week that he would not quit at all for ten days and Fletcher in turn would take him out alone to any movie he wanted and afterwards for ice cream. It was the fifth day but now he kept saying, "I quit, I quit," over and over. Fletcher was leaving. What Clifford had always known was still true: there was no one who would take him seriously, no one who could be trusted, relied upon, though life in the house with the other residents and Fletcher had seemed different somehow.

Amanda began neighing like a horse the way she always did when she was upset.

And in the bathroom Debbie unrolled roll after roll of toilet paper and stuffed it into the toilet.

The whole house was in chaos, my brother having to leave the job, unexpectedly, without notice.

The first postcard came from Maine. On it a fisherman stands on a wharf holding up two lobsters. The sky is a brilliant blue, like his eyes, which shine out from a haggard face.

"Eli Lilly," Fletcher scrawls on the back, "manufacturers of the drug DES. Wrongfully marketed for use in preventing miscarriage. No preliminary lab tests done on pregnant mice. Consequences: all plaintiff's reproductive organs and more than half her vagina removed. 1953 prenatal exposure to DES, which was ingested by the mother while pregnant with plaintiff, is proximate cause of cancer that developed seventeen years after her birth."

Sarah Stafford, age twenty-two, having become accustomed to the movement of the boat, felt dizzy stepping onto the earth. It seemed to her years since she had left England; with the boat's first motion forward, the land's first tilt, she had left behind the idea of the world, and it had been oddly comforting to her. She had grown to love the oceans of blue and lavender and pewter.

Now, landing here, she could scarcely believe that this was the dream that had propelled the tiny ship forward: paradise. How the idea of paradise must have varied among the one hundred and fifty tossed through the water on the courageous *Godspeed*. Now they were here. So this was paradise: a land you could not stand on, a tangle of trees. All right, then, she thought. But it was not all right. It seemed far, far away from anything she had conjured. Her children clung to her skirt. Some of the men shouted. Others laughed with delight at their first sight of the New World. Some sighed as if with a lover. Her children began to cry. A dark shape rose in her.

My mother moves her feet across the polished floor—one, two, cha-cha-cha.

"Miami Beach," Grandpa Sarkis sighs, wiping sweat from his forehead. "There are those pink birds that stand on one foot," Lucy says, pointing to the picture on soiled newsprint. "Flamingos," her mother says to her.

"And blue dolphins," Christine whispers.

"I've heard that at the hotels in Miami Beach," the father says, "men dressed in white bring cushions out for you so that you can sit by the pool. And just for signing a paper they will bring you banana and strawberry drinks with parasols in them."

"Really? Parasols!" my mother says.

"Oh, yes," her father nods solemnly. "That's what I've heard."

The next time I heard from my brother, he was in Fall River, Massachusetts, where he continued to name names. "Johns-Manville," he wrote on the back of a postcard picturing the house of the famous ax-murderess, Lizzie Borden, "was fully aware of the hazards of asbestos in the 1930s but actively suppressed the information, making 'a conscious, cold-blooded business decision, in utter flagrant disregard of the rights of others, to take no protective or remedial action.'"

This is the part of the story Grandpa hated to tell: It was a cold night. Ice was already thick on the creek called Wounded Knee. The crystalline trees seemed to bend further and further into the earth. It was 1890 and winter was coming on.

A white flag hoisted at the center of the Indian camp promised to the white man that there would be peace, harmony, safety. But the men with faces like snow moved into the camps anyway, hundreds of them, in great drifts like sorrow.

"Everywhere the Indians are dancing," the men said, as they came nearer and nearer, mistaking the Ghost Dance for a rite of war, not noticing the white flag, not noticing that women, too, danced side by side with the men. "We begged for life, and the white man thought we wanted theirs," Red Cloud cried.

The soldiers demanded the Indians' guns, searched their tepees, spilled food from bowls, tore animal skins from sleeping children. Women screamed. Yellow Bird blew an eagle-bone whistle and told his people not to fear—they would be protected by their Ghost Shirts.

The soldiers found about forty old guns, but not Black Fox's, which he carried under his blanket. The women chanted and cried. And seeing this, all of this, Black Fox took out his gun and fired into the line of soldiers he hated.

Immediately the troops retaliated, shooting at point-blank range at the unarmed Indians. Some Indians had knives or war clubs and fought hand to hand for their lives. At this time another troop positioned up the hill joined in—

firing nearly fifty rounds a minute into the women and children who had gathered together and were standing off to the side.

Yet another ring of soldiers killed those who tried to escape into the hills. From four sides the white men fired. Within minutes hundreds were dead. Women and children who attempted to escape by running up the dry ravine were followed and slaughtered. Their bodies afterward were found for more than two miles. A few survivors, mostly children, hidden in the brush, were told they had nothing to fear. Little boys who crept out were surrounded and butchered.

Later, a member of the burial party said that many of the women were found dead with their shawls pulled up over their heads, covering their faces in that last second as the soldiers raised their guns and took aim.

They were buried in a mass grave. Most were naked. Souvenir hunters had taken the bloody Ghost Shirts from their backs. Soon after the massacre was complete, a great blizzard swept over the Plains and covered the dead with snow. It was hard to get some of them into the grave, frozen as they were into the various grotesque postures of violent death.

It was New Year's Day, 1891.

If you had listened carefully, you could have heard through the snow, some distance away, a chorus of auld lang syne.

"It was so thick on the engine-room floors that we used to walk through it like snow."

Bill had been a welder at the shipyard. He sat with us now at dinner. He was gaunt and haggard and he gasped for breath. My father put food on his plate.

"Please eat," Dad said in a whisper.

"They gave us asbestos clothes to wear for protection. In '72 they started paying us dirty money to work in certain areas."

"I've got people dying here every two weeks," the business agent for Local 24 said, Fletcher told us.

"Please try to eat something," my father said.

He was dying from a disease called mesothelioma.

I did not know then how much was ended. When I look back now from the high hill of my old age, I can still see the butchered women and children lying heaped and scattered all along the crooked gulch as plain as when I saw them with eyes still young. And I can see something else died there in the bloody mud and was buried in the blizzard. A people's dream died there. It was a beautiful dream.

Black Elk

"Johns-Manville," he carved into a postcard, "made a conscious, cold-blooded business decision, in utter flagrant disregard of the rights of others."

"A. H. Robins, manufacturers of the Dalkon Shield, an intrauterine device."

"You sip these incredible drinks through a straw," Grandpa Sarkis says, "and the men dressed in white dinner jackets pass out cards for bingo. You can play bingo all afternoon in the sun if you want—or put your chips on the Wheel of Fortune."

"The white man shall never kill me. If they try to, it is they who will die. They will fall down as if they had no bones. They will suffocate in a great landslide. They will be burned by an enormous wall of fire. They could put bullets through me, they could chop me up into little pieces, they could burn me until I glittered in the palm of their hands, and still I would live."

"We used to walk through it like snow. We walked through drifts of it to do our job. Later some of the children got it, too—from playing with our work boots or sitting on our laps."

From Detroit he sent me a postcard of the Ford plant. Only my address appeared on the back.

The ceremony of burying the dead is ended with tears, wailing, howling, and macerations. They tear the hair, gash the skin.

"Greetings from the Land of Lincoln," the front of the postcard reads in bright red letters, the famed log cabin in one corner, a dark silhouette in the other. "Dow Chemical," my brother scrawls. "Much evidence that Dow knew as early as the mid sixties that exposure to dioxin (Agent Orange) might cause serious illness, even death, but withheld this knowledge and continued to sell to the Army and public."

I have read a hundred times the messages he has scribbled on the backs of these cards. I have looked into the eyes of the fisherman for help, stared at the lobsters he holds to the sky like children. I have read and reread my brother's long litany of betrayal and pain: DES, asbestos, Agent Orange; Lilly, Johns-Manville, Dow Chemical. They lie like scars on my tongue. Then silence—nothing more—a horrible stillness.

There in the distance another Fletcher rises out of murky water. He crawls onto the shore clutching a bayonet. He claws his way into the thick bush where he lies shivering. It could be anywhere: Argentina or Chile, Vietnam or Cambodia. He sits up. It's Fletcher all right. He is hunched over and counting something. Sweat collects on his forehead. He wipes it away with a filthy sleeve. Wasps gather around his head. He tries to bat them away, but they keep coming and coming like helicopters in the endless night. Waves of nausea overcome him. His boots are golden with vomit.

My brother looks so different forced into the brutal postures of war. I barely recognize him at all. He is covered with sores. His legs seem longer, larger somehow. "Best for running, Vanessa," he whispers through the wide leaves. He tears a handful of leaves from a tree to wipe his mouth and brow. Patches of brown and gray and green have grown on his arms. His skin looks tough like a lizard's or snake's. A second skull has grown around his head, hard as a helmet. His insect eyes bulge red.

He has become the kind of person who wants only to survive, only to stay alive. "Nothing else matters, Vanessa," he shouts through the thick foliage. A monkey screams. More planes come. A tarantula is stunned motionless on a banana leaf. The air is filled with snakes. He begins to shake uncontrollably. He does not know where he is.

Trees burst into flames as he watches them. He hears drums, he thinks, in the distance, but perhaps it is his own heart he hears. He closes his eyes. His lids are thick. He covers his face. "You could not do it without the drugs," he says. "No one could." He thinks someone injects the high white clouds with poison. He tries breathing into his hands to keep out the fumes. The clouds mushroom and explode, red and black, igniting the sky. "The sky is burning, Vanessa," he says. He laughs hysterically. His shoulders move up and down frantically as if he were shrugging over and over in fast motion. He is drenched in sweat. He turns suddenly. The brown rice in barrels looks dangerous to him. The sandal of a child makes him weep with fear. Urine flows down his pants leg. "Vanessa," he says, "help me. The sky is burning."

"Fletcher, get up," I try to say. "That lump, over there," but I cannot get the words out fast enough, "is a grenade." If a telegram comes I will not accept it. If a telegram comes I will tell them to send it elsewhere.

Preferring no thoughts to these, I close my eyes, but the fear follows me.

"Fletcher," my mother calls, wandering into the living room of our enormous house in Connecticut one July afternoon years ago. She seats herself in the center of the floor. In the silence she feels the room betraying her.

"I think we'd better get rid of all this," she says miserably and motions to the objects that surround her. It's so crowded, and everything is always moving. She shows him the melting legs of the coffee table, the heavy curtains rustling in the windless air, the stereo that seems to slip from one radio station to the next without anyone touching it. The lamp and the piano chatter. There's whispering among the Waterford. Fletcher's eyes are wide. My mother's perceptions are so real that my brother actually sees the furniture huddling in collusion. The pillows seem to be breathing, in the shrinking room, before his eyes.

"And this rug, too," she sighs, "and these vases—I never wanted them." Now the room seems impossibly cluttered. Fletcher can't believe we ever lived in it.

"And these paintings," he shouts, looking at my mother, then back at the heavy brushstrokes.

"And this couch."

"And the candles," Fletcher says.

"And all these plants," my mother says, gasping for air, and my brother, too, begins to cry.

The enemy is everywhere. It is the chaise longue, it is the love seat.

"Help me, someone," I whisper, closing my eyes in an attempt to dissolve the images with darkness, with words. "Help."

"Who are you?" I ask, squinting, my head tilted to the side. "Who are you really?"

"Why? What does it matter? How could it help?"

"Because I love you."

"You love me? Love yourself first."

"Please, Jack."

"Don't cry," he says. "Keep going. There's no turning back now."

She reaches her arm into the present, into my apartment here in New York. "I always knew you were strong, Marta, but this—"

She hands me an apple.

"Eat this," she says. "Eat this."

"Fool Dog. Three Fingers. Wolf Necklace. Dead Eyes," my brother writes across the last postcard, which pictures Bear Butte in South Dakota.

"Eight miles from Fort Meade," the postcard states in fine print, "is Bear Butte. It can be seen from a hundred miles away. The Teton used to camp on this flat-topped mountain to pray. Here they would wail for the dead of whom the stones are tokens."

The day my mother turned eighteen and was awarded a full scholarship to Vassar College and my Aunt Lucy was more or less settled, having become engaged to the life-insurance salesman and on her way to a career in nursing, was the day that Grandpa Sarkis announced in the gray kitchen that he was going home.

The sisters looked at one another puzzled, pretending they did not know what he was talking about, although they both knew precisely what he meant.

"But you are home, Daddy," Lucy said, patting him gently on the back and looking around the room with him.

Already he had changed his name back to the real one, the Armenian one, Wingarian—not Frank Wing, the name he used in the mill.

"I'm going home," Sarkis Wingarian repeated.

But home, the girls knew, was something only in their father's head. You could not even find it on the map. He was going back to the old country, now many countries strewn across the continent. He was going to a place where, he imagined, his own life and thoughts of his wife might be erased by some greater suffering.

"In this country there is only work. You work your whole life and for what?" he muttered. "For nothing." He looked at the seat at the kitchen table where his wife used to sit when she was well enough.

My mother would never see her father again. Only once that I know of did she ask him to come back, and that was right after my birth. I cannot really imagine it—how she found him or what she said or what he said back.

But he might very well have said, "In America they will laugh at me, they will call me a fat man, but here my weight is cause for respect. Here I am worth my weight in gold. In America I would look like an old man, but here old men are respected. Old age means wisdom."

"But, Father, she is beautiful," my mother would have said back. "I want you to see her." Then she would hesitate. "Father," she'd say in a whisper, "she looks just like Mother to me."

This was one thing my grandfather, running across Russia, Turkey, Syria, Lebanon, could not bear to hear. He pretended he did not.

"What good are girls?" he said back to her. "All we get are girls. Always girls! Let me know if you have a son."

"No, Father," she said, and she did not call him when Fletcher was born the next year.

Yet despite everything, despite even his indifference toward me, I cannot help liking Grandpa Sarkis—stubborn as a bull, thick as an ox, fat as the world.

In the old country you can grow silk on trees. In the old country you are worth your weight in gold. In the old country his people were slaughtered like sheep. I miss him, this enormous Grandpa Sarkis. When I get older and begin to gain weight myself, I know I will think of him. I will watch my hips turn to gold. And in the silk dress I someday buy I will see him in Paterson, setting the weave all day and all night for love. As I slip into that smooth dress, I'll think of him, wherever he is, coaxing the silkworms into productivity for me.

"Turks," my mother hisses to the children passing under her window on bicycles, when she does not feel well. "Turks," she screams.

I have imagined the Topaz Bird with talons, curve-beaked, its brutal feathers sharpening into points. It devours mice in front of me. It lands on my mother's head and draws blood.

"Turks," she screams as the grass turns to worms, as her hair catches fire.

When the last Red Man shall have perished, and the memory of my tribe shall have become a myth among the white men, these shores will swarm with the invisible dead of my tribe, and when your children's children think themselves alone in the field, the store, the shop, or in the silence of the pathless woods, they will not be alone. . . . At night when the streets of your cities and villages are silent and you think them deserted, they will throng with the returning hosts that once filled them and still love this beautiful land.

Chief Seattle

Keep going, I think to myself. There is no substitute for pain.

We were sitting on her bed next to her, but she was in the Sung Dynasty. She was in a German forest. She was blossoming under her dress for a man we could not see. She was next to us again, then far away. She was escaping from the Turks. She was in the center of the waterfall. Her hands fluttered in front of her face. She closed the book from which she was reading our bedtime story. I don't know where she was.

"But what's the ending, Mom?" we said and tugged at her golden robe.

"And then the children plucked the chocolate bonbons from the tree and put them in their pockets."

"What tree?" we asked, thrilled, confused.

"What bonbons?"

The story she had been reading to us had been of a flock of migrating birds.

She smiled. "And the stormy sky turned blue, and the ocean became still. Swim off to bed now," she whispered, "my minnows. Press your bellies into the sand and sleep."

"Good night, Mom," we said, our arms undulating by our sides.

I had just sunk down, it seemed, into my fish position when I saw her, first through water but then clearly. She was coming toward my bed in her white nightgown and holding a compass. Though I was frightened a little, I longed to be with this fluid, fragrant, beautiful creature. She seemed so wispy and strange, a figment of herself, as she walked closer.

"Mother," I said finally, for she is my mother, my beautiful mother, my recklessly beautiful mother. "What is it?"

She points, she looks at the compass, she whispers into my ear. "Everything's all right now, sweetheart," she says, tilting the compass so that I might see its thin needle. She has done this before. She will sit there next to me all night, moving now and then from one corner of the bed to another, hardly ever looking up from the compass, and saying over and over, "Everything's all right," until the sun comes up and she disappears in light.

"Children," she screamed, "get up, wake up! Come quickly! Get up. Hurry!" she cried, calling us from our sleep. "No questions, now," she said, "just hurry." And with some superhuman strength she picked us both up and ran down the hallway with us to her room. She was crying. "Sit in the middle of the bed," she instructed, "way far in the middle, away from the edges.

"My children are not safe," she said, picking up the receiver of the phone and speaking into it. "I would like the Department of the Interior in Washington," she said. "Hurry." She dropped the phone to her side, lifted it to her ear again. "Jesus Christ, this is an emergency, I don't have all day," she said into the dial tone. "There's no time." She dropped the phone, opened a drawer, turned it upside down, and spilled everything onto the floor. "Don't move!" she yelled to us. We huddled in the center of the bed. "Just don't move!" Papers, scarves, jewelry covered the floor. She opened another drawer and turned it over, rummaging through its contents.

"Mom, what are you looking for?" Fletcher asked. "I could help you."

"No, don't. Don't get up. Just hold on one more minute. I'm coming." The Topaz Bird swooped down. She screamed. It woke my father who had fallen asleep downstairs in the chair in front of the fire.

"I've found it," she said. "Everything's going to be OK." In her hand she held a large bolt of twine, the kind used for mailing packages. My father came in as she knotted the string around the first bedpost. She looked over to him. "Go and help the children," she said.

"Oh, Christine," he said, nearing her.

"Don't touch me!" she screamed. "I have to work fast. Go to the children—please—please."

My father came and sat in the center of the bed with us and forced our heads down into his arms. "Don't look," he whispered to us. But I could see her unraveling the bolt of string and tying it around the second post, then the third, and then the last, then circling the bed again and again until we were completely fenced in by it. My father's arms were shaking but he held us tightly to him. When my mother was finally finished she grabbed China, the cat, and jumped over the railing of string and onto the bed.

My father opened his arms to take her in. His face was wet as if he had been crying or sweating, but his gaze was even and calm.

"There now," he whispered. "There now, Christine. We're all here now. We're all all right."

My mother sighed. "Yes, I know," she said. My father loosened his grip. We were a pile of arms and legs and hands and paws on the bed. It was hard to tell whose arms were whose, whose legs, whose hair, we were so tangled in each other.

Only her voice hovered above us, separate. "We've escaped," she said. "We've done it."

Was it fire this time she had saved us from? Or flood? Was it a plague of insects or something less comprehensible? The phone, off the hook, was making loud, piercing sounds. My father moved to hang it up.

"No, Michael, no," she cried. "You'll be eaten alive."

Slowly the bed began to move, slowly, slowly, as we sat huddled together in its center. The desk floated by, the chair, the clothes in the closet moved back and forth, back and forth.

"Mom," I whispered, finding her at the center. "Mom," I said, "we're moving."

She nodded. "We're safe now, Vanessa," she smiled. "We're all here and it's big and it's white and it's taking us somewhere so beautiful!" she said.

"This ship is so beautiful, Michael," she sighed. "It's huge and it's white. And the land is disappearing and it's getting cooler and cooler but it feels so good."

"Yes," my father said. He looked so sad. He did not move or speak again.

"Listen, oh, just listen." She heard a muffled foghorn in the distance, but he heard nothing and sat in silence.

After a long while she took out her compass and showed it to me. It caught the light of the moon. She smiled and closed her eyes finally.

"They can't hurt us now," she said. "They can't hurt us now," she whispered in my ear as we moved through dark water, all night, the four of us, on our sad, lonely voyage—north—somewhere.

Sibelius. Nielsen. Grieg.

She slides into her seat and rubs her back against the back of the chair as the maître d' pulls it out and then pushes it to the table for her.

"Thank you," she says. Her eyes are violet in this light. She taps her finger lightly on the table, brings a finger to her mouth, rubs her head against her shoulder, and smiles.

"Michael, a martini," she whispers and edges her hand across the table to his. He puts his large hand over hers in protection. I would save you if I could, his immense hand says. His wedding ring catches the chandelier's light. Fletcher and I stare at the ceiling, then at our parents, not knowing where else to look. My brother and I are not brave enough yet to see clearly what is obvious: neither of us matters at all to them at this moment as my father puts his forefinger and thumb around her wrist and gently massages it.

I notice there is still a trace of dirt under her fingernails from her long day of suffering. In the morning we had been banished to the garden and spent the whole day weeding and watering, mulching, digging, and transplanting. The house was turning against her, she said, waking me at 5:00 A.M. and, taking my hand, we had fled. "There's evil in there," she said, pointing to the house she loved. "I don't know why, but it's there today," she said, kneeling on the ground. "Don't go near it, Vanessa," she said in agony. "Believe me," she said and sunk her nails into my arm. "Believe me."

I believed her. I knelt next to her. Side by side we pulled weed after weed together, hour after hour, our backs turned away from the dark house. "I can't decide where to put these lilies," she said, and we uprooted them and moved them from one section of the garden to another. "What about this lilac bush?" she asked, and we dug it up. "And the daffodils," she said, "let's try them over there. I can't decide where to put the lilies," she sighed, and she moved them to yet another section of the garden. She was searching for the secret design of flowers that might dispel darkness, evil, fear.

"These need more light," she said, pulling up the poppies and replanting them over and over as she followed the sun across the sky, every few minutes changing the pattern of the great garden. "The work in a garden is never done," she told me. "There's always something to do in a garden," she said, holding the strangled flowers in her hand, burying them in the ground finally, only a wilted petal visible here or there.

"Shit," she cried. "I've killed everything," and she turned and looked accusingly at the house. "Let's clear out the roots, honey. Let's start over." She began digging, and slowly I could see her garden turning in on itself, the earth giving way. "We'll get rid of the roots, it's the only way." "It's the only way," she kept saying. "We'll get rid of the roots."

I let her keep going, swearing into the ravaged earth, laughing hysterically as she excavated marbles and the arms of dolls from the ground. She began lining up all the things she had found on the slate path. "My treasures," she said, smiling. I let her keep going. Father came home from work. He looked at me. I was old enough to know better.

He spoke very quietly into the ditch where we stood. We were waist high in dirt.

"Please don't read tonight," he said to her. "I'll call and tell them that you won't be able to come."

"Oh, but I must, Michael. It's our only hope," she said in her high voice. "It's the only thing that might work. Bring me my clothes, Vanessa. My black dress, my rings, my textured stockings, my new black shoes, and my manuscript, the one that is open on my desk. I will change next door. Call Sonia. Tell her that I am coming."

My mother spoke calmly now, crouching in the dirt, fingering the marbles she had lined up.

As many times as my father saw her this way, he never got used to it.

"I've made dinner reservations," he said softly, "for six o'clock, near the Guggenheim. We should probably leave soon."

My mother laughed out loud. "I'm reading at the Guggenheim Museum," she said. "How odd. Vanessa, my dress. But be careful in the house. Hurry through it, do you understand? And stay out of the shadows, my darling."

I carried her voice carefully, lovingly, as if it were a child, into the house. "My darling," I said, wanting to make her unafraid somehow. "It's OK, darling," I said to her, going through her closet to get her clothes, climbing the stairs to her attic room to get her poems. "Darling," I whispered. "Darling."

My father lifts his hand finally from my mother's. The drinks arrive. She gulps down her martini, interrupts my father as he orders dinner, and says, "Another martini, please, Michael." Then she looks to me. "Vanessa, do you want one? Fletcher, you're still too young to drink." Fletcher was thirteen. I was fourteen.

She finishes her second drink. "I'd like another, please," she smiles, as dinner comes.

"Not wine with your dinner? I've ordered a nice Beaujolais-Villages," Father says.

"Another drink," she says to the waiter. She stares at the food before her.

"You'd better start eating, Mom," Fletcher says. "Remember the reading." She touches his cheek and smiles vacantly.

"My little big man," she says. "My love, my love."

"I think that Fletcher is probably right about your dinner," my father says.

"Don't condescend to me, Michael," she snaps. "Just don't do it."

Nothing can stop us from moving in the direction we must move. I want to stop this dinner scene now or alter it. If there must be this restaurant, then I want her to sit with us peacefully, to eat her dinner and tell us a story, to be sweet and happy.

And if there must be this garden and there must, if there must be this ditch, then let us lie down together holding each other's hands. May we be covered over with dirt. May it all stop. Stop. I would like to stay there with her and her collection of smooth stones and marbles, ladybugs and worms, exotic caterpillars. Let us then be covered over, smothered with earth. Let it all stop here.

"Stop it, Michael," she says, pulling herself up from the ditch, the table, martini in hand, her manuscript under her arm. She walks across the floor away from the tables and into the dark bar. She opens her manuscript. She rubs against a man's gray shoulder. She's so beautiful. He turns toward her and runs his hand up her textured leg. I can see all this, Fletcher; I suppose Father sees it, too.

"Eat your dinner now," he says to Fletcher and me. "It's going to get cold." We cut our meat for Father. We put vegetables in our mouths. Dessert comes. We spoon soft puddings into our mouths though we think we will be sick. My mother's hand rests between her legs. She is shifting on the bar stool, but the bar is dark and I hope I am the only one who notices this movement. She rubs the neck of another man. My father buries his face in his hands. "Leave me alone," my mother says to the man. "Just keep your fucking hands off me," and she walks back to us.

She bends down and gently kisses my father on the cheek. "Oh, Michael," she whispers. She hurries her tongue into his ear. She wraps her arms around his shoulders. "Christine, stop it," he says. She turns from him abruptly, rubs my back and plays with my hair, pushing it to the top of my head.

"Fletcher," she says, sliding next to him, "would you do something for Mommy? Would you please, please?" She tilts her head.

"OK, Mom," he says. "OK."

"Pick out the prettiest woman in this restaurant for me."

He is afraid not to do what my mother asks. "I don't know, Mom," he says, and he looks at his shoes. "I can't pick."

She sighs and he looks up finally and says, "I guess she's pretty, Mom." He points to a tall, thin, dark-haired woman who sits with her boyfriend. She must be about twenty.

"Ah, you've got very good taste," she says, smiling at him. "What's the matter, Michael? Do you think I won't? Do you really think I won't do it?

"Fletcher, get up," she says, staring the whole time at my father. She takes my brother with her and introduces herself to the young couple, and because she is so commanding and confident, so powerful now, at the height, in fact, of some strange power, they are seated in seconds next to the young woman and her boyfriend. My mother smiles. Fletcher looks over at us. My mother takes a cigarette from the woman's pack, lights it, and hands it to her. She lights one for herself. My father's eyes swell as my mother, two tables from us, admires the woman's dress.

"Mommy," I say, "don't do this. Please come back." My father looks at me. There is no stopping her, his eyes say.

"They say I am one of the greatest living American poets," my mother says suddenly in a loud, agitated voice. "Come to my reading," she laughs, leaning into the woman, "and make up your own mind. There will be a party afterwards," she says, moving her hand toward the woman's. "There are always parties." The young man is entranced with her, too. The woman blushes. My mother is irresistible.

We walk down the street to the Guggenheim. "God damn it," she yells. "Fuck. Oh, fuck," she calls into the posh evening air. "Oh, Christ." She is crying. She is wrestling with something right before our eyes. She focuses suddenly on me. I reach for her hand and she slaps mine.

"You don't love me at all," she screams. "You don't care if I live or die. None of you! No, neither do you, Vanessa," she cries, pushing me away from her. "Don't pretend you're any different from the rest of them. Go to hell. Go to hell," she shrieks, running way ahead of us. "And don't come in with me. Don't you dare."

We wait out on the sidewalk for what seems a long time. "OK," my father says in a voice which is hardly a voice at all, and we step into the outer room of the museum where others who could not get tickets into the auditorium stand. There are loudspeakers set up. The young woman and her boyfriend are there. They wave to us. Fletcher waves back weakly, then stares down at the ground. There is silence over the public address system, then a buzzing, then footsteps, my mother's shoes, an adjustment of the microphone, a few coughs from the audience, a bit of rustling, then silence. I imagine my mother just stands there in front of the microphone and stares out into the audience. It seems like forever. My father closes his eyes. We hear the rustling of pages, silence, then her voice, finally her voice. She begins without introduction, and as she reads the first line her voice grows—grows and grows with each word—loud, secure, catching fire, furious and pure.

"You don't love me at all," my mother rages. "You don't care how much I suffer. You don't care if I live or die! None of you do! Neither do you, Vanessa. Don't pretend you're any different!" She is throwing things around the house, shoes from the window, books, jewelry. "You'll be sorry," she screams. "You'll all be sorry someday. Especially you, Vanessa Turin. Go to hell," she shrieks, exploding into a million pieces.

"No, Mother," I say, standing up, sobbing now. "Who do you think you are? Come back here," I demand, "right now. Do you think you can just disappear like that? Come back," I yell. "Mother," I shout into empty space. "Do you think you can explode into a million pieces and disappear?" I scream into the silence my voice makes, into the horrible void that is everywhere.

Anything would be easier than seeing her this way, I think. I turn away again in my hard bed and watch the mist as it moves in on the wings of morning like an angel, like a dove.

On the day of the Bicentennial, July 4, 1976, my grandmother got up unusually early, about 4:00 A.M., unable to sleep. The country would be celebrating its two-hundredth year this day in a grand way, and she had felt some of that excitement in the nursing home where preparations had been going on all week. Banners had been made. Songs had been practiced, the tenors and baritones and the multitude of sopranos getting together to rehearse their parts. Tiny flags had been purchased to decorate wheelchairs, and red, white, and blue crepe paper, to be threaded in the wheel's spokes. The kitchen staff had made little strawberry shortcakes and had dyed the whipped cream blue. And my grandmother, the first one up, was making her own preparations, it would turn out—a different sort of independence.

In celebration, tall ships would be sailing down the Hudson later in the day. There would be elaborate fireworks displays in the evening. We asked Father if he would go to the festivities with us, and, liking water and ships of any kind, he agreed. "But we should go see your grandmother first," he said with a certain resolve. He did not like to visit her alone. God doesn't send us a cross heavier than we can bear, she had always said, but in the years since my grandfather's death she had seemed to stoop further and further into the ground with the weight of it, growing more and more bitter and resentful of everyone but particularly of my father, who was not my grandfather and never would be.

"Sure," we said, and so we went early that Fourth of July to visit Grandma, sometime near dawn.

I drove. I was just learning to drive. "Use the low beams in mist," Fletcher said from the back seat. Though Fletcher was younger than I, it was clear that he had been driving for a long time. The early morning mist was thick and I followed his instructions. Slowly we plowed through the haze to Grandma.

I was doing well: adjusting the lights, using the brakes and the blinkers, but nearing the nursing home I saw such a bizarre image, a picture of such eeriness in the fog that I had to wipe my eyes to ensure I was awake, and, lifting my hands from the steering wheel, the car swerved. Fletcher leaned forward to help.

"Look," I said, pointing. "Look." Father stared straight ahead and said nothing. Fletcher looked up.

In front of us through the early morning mist we saw what seemed to be an old, old woman, or the ghost of a woman, dressed in a strange, elaborate costume and posed on the large front lawn of the nursing home.

"That's Grandma," I said.

"No," they said, "it's not." They did not recognize her this way.

"Yes," I whispered, "that's Grandma."

"How could it be?"

She was tiptoeing about the grass now, checking her stage, testing the light, bending and stretching in preparation. She waved to us and smiled. "My family," she said. We stood at the edge of the lawn and waved back—Father, too. "My family," she smiled.

I looked closer, still not trusting my eyes. A red rosary hung around her neck. She wore a long skirt. Beads and other trinkets were sewn into it—beads from necklaces my grandfather had given her and she had never worn: crystal beads, beads of ruby-colored glass, mother of pearl. She wore a white peasant blouse, made hurriedly from a sheet, probably secretly. She had pulled the hair away from her face and made braids that she pinned up on top of her head. Attached to the braids were red and white streamers that flowed behind her when she moved. She looked like a little girl.

"Vanessa," she said, and she made a full turn for me slowly so that I might not miss anything: the intricately sewn costume, the beautiful hairdo with streamers, the red rosary. I wiped my eyes again. She turned once more and what I saw this time was the girlishness in her motion, the joy, the thrill; yes, it was joy I saw in her turned ankle! She pranced to one corner of the lawn, picked something up, and brought it back with her. It made a lovely sound. It was a tambourine she had made from tin pie plates, yarn, and bells.

"How inventive you are, Grandma! We never knew!"

She was humming something softly to herself—a beautiful, melancholy melody. I trembled, freezing suddenly on this July morning. She hummed louder and then began to sing. Her feet seemed to lift off the ground completely as she began her lilting, graceful, lighter-than-air dance. She took three steps to the right, slowly raised the tambourine and tapped it lightly, then three steps to the left, then a twirl. Instead of her regular black tie shoes she wore ballet slippers. When I saw her tiny feet in those slippers, I felt like going up and hugging her, but I did not dare disturb the dance; I was afraid that she might turn back into the old Grandma if I moved even one muscle. I held my breath.

"I never dreamt it would all come back so easily," she said, and there was a lightness in her voice, a giddiness we had never heard before.

She moved more quickly now, having been bitten, I imagined, by the tarantula of Italian folklore, the spider with a venom so potent that it had made her people crazy for centuries with the irresistible urge to dance.

"How graceful you are, Grandma!"

She smiled at us. "We used to make our own pasta," she said sweetly in her new singing voice. A weight had lifted from her. "We used to make little tortellini, ravioli. We used to make our own wine and olive oil. There were mountains there."

She was surrounded by home. It wrapped around her finally with large, comforting arms—not our home, bannered and lit with fireworks, but hers.

"Oh, Grandma," we said, "why didn't you ever make us those little tortellini? Or tell us about the mountains? Why did you keep it all from us?"

Strains of familiar songs could be heard coming from inside the nursing home—"I'm a Yankee Doodle Dandy" and "America the Beautiful." There was much excitement inside. Some were dressing to leave for the day—off to backyard celebrations. Others were getting ready for the geriatric parade of wheelchairs and walkers. Sparklers had been promised.

Grandma stopped suddenly and looked directly at us. "Your grandfather never let me speak Italian in the house," she said. "He never let me cook my own food. I missed that so much," she said in the loneliest voice I had ever heard. "He never let me sing you to sleep with the sweet songs from Italy I loved so much." My father put his face in his hands.

I thought of my grandfather as a young man in Italy straining toward some idea of America. I thought of him coming here, his dreams of being a real American—eating steaks and eggs, wearing good shoes, making a life—and then another idea, some time later, something quite different, though unmistakably American, too.

A marching band could be heard somewhere in the distance.

"Oh, Angelo!" she said, looking to the sky. "I could have made an Easter torta for the children. I could have sung them the songs my mother sang. There were so many songs to sing."

"Mom," my father said. There were great tears in his eyes. "Why didn't you say something to him?"

"It was not my place," she said sadly.

"Oh, Mom," he said. He walked slowly to her. "I never knew," he whispered . to her, looking into her darkened eyes.

"Mother," he said, squeezing her ancient hands in his. "We've wanted the same thing all along. Why . . ." His voice trailed off. He kissed her hands and rubbed them against his face. "Why? Why have we fought?" he asked. She shook her head, lowered it.

"My bambino, my beautiful, curly-headed bambino. You had the most beautiful curls."

My father turned to us for what seemed the first time in his life and gestured for us to come forward and enter the circle he and his mother had made with their arms. We hugged each other, all four of us. I ran my fingers through my grandmother's hair and streamers.

"My children," she whispered, "my children." I felt our arms around her. She would die in the afternoon of this embrace. She was making her peace with us and with the world at the last moment—and we with her.

"Grandma," I said, "I like your shoes."

"Oh," she said, looking at them and pointing her toe. "I've been saving these shoes for a lifetime."

"Grandma," Fletcher said, "that's a nice tambourine."

"I made it in crafts," she said. "You know, my people always loved music. My father played the mandolin like an angel."

On hearing this something rose in my father like an anthem and he began to weep uncontrollably and embraced his mother tighter.

"Michael," she said, "I'm so sorry." And he nodded. His head was pressed against her bosom, which seemed larger, more maternal somehow, softer. My father left his head on that wonderful place for a long time; when he finally looked up, her face was lined suddenly with the past.

"We used to eat these," she said, bending over and plucking a dandelion from the green lawn. "We used to like these very much. A simple weed. We cooked it with garlic and olive oil and a few flakes of red pepper. We ate weeds and we were happy."

My grandmother waved her arms above her head in some private choreography now, bending over and brushing her ankles in a wide, delicate sweep, a graceful rhythmic gesture.

She was humming the tarantella again. She separated from us and whirled and whirled, moving one hand to her eyes as if shading them from some brutal Italian sun.

"Piccolini," she said. "The piccolini—" I thought those tiny fish must be tickling her childhood ankles. "The piccolini," she smiled. To whom was she speaking? Not to us anymore—to her mother, I think. There was wonder in her voice, the wonder a daughter has for her mother when they are seeing the same thing for the first time. She pointed into the grass. "The piccolini."

Already explosions could be heard far off. Something would burst in her head as bright, as spectacular as the year's bicentennial display.

She danced now more quickly and continued to sing louder and louder as she whirled from one side of the large nursing home lawn to the other, spinning away from us, further and further away with each gesture. But then she came closer and seemed to focus for one moment, halting the dance with this last memory, arrested by it. She looked right at us. "We used to make little Christmas cakes of honey," she whispered. "We called it strufoli. It was very good." Slowly she began to dance again.

She shook her head with amazement. "I can taste it right now," she said. Her eyes were wide. She stopped. One foot was pointed into the earth, one arm raised toward the sky. "It tastes so sweet," she said, "just like I remember." She closed her eyes and smiled.

Though it is the middle of the night and we are both in our nightgowns, our meeting is formal. She appears in the doorway of my bedroom holding a fistful of pens and pencils as she has so many times. Her hair, as always, is falling from the bun she wears to work. As always she looks exhausted. But this time is different. This time my mother steps forward. This time my mother is going to speak. She sits close to me on the bed. I look into her face and, much to my surprise, I see things I have never seen before, though I thought that surely I had memorized that face. There is new beauty there—or more beauty, though that scarcely seems possible. The moon is out, the stars, but it is Venus that dominates the sky, and I watch my mother intently against that fantastic back-drop. I love you so much, I will love you forever, I think. I watch her put her pencils in her pocket. Her lovely white hand falls to the bedspread.

I am surprised to hear the voice she has when she finally speaks. I expected it to be dreamlike and soupy, but it is not. It is as if she is someone else entirely, not my mother but the woman who gives interviews, the woman who has written six books, the one who gives readings. Her voice is strong, bell-like on a clear day.

I could easily touch my mother, but I do not want to frighten her away or make her feel as if she's trapped. I do not want her to misconstrue the situation or to think that I am changing.

Though I have made no move, she seems to back away, and I feel as if I have taken such care to keep her next to me that I begin to cry. Why must she always be leaving? Her face is pained. Why must she suffer so much?

My mother looks at me as if she sees some weakness of hers in my face and grows fierce.

"No one," she says coldly, putting her hands on my shoulders, "should feel sorry for me. I've had a very good life, Vanessa," she whispers. "Do you under-stand what I'm saying? I'm a very lucky person," she says slowly. "I wouldn't have wanted it any different. No one should feel sorry for me. People *read* what I write. Don't cry for me, Vanessa. Don't you dare cry for me."

She sits back as if she is getting ready to tell a long story. She brushes the hair from my neck.

"Sometimes, you know, when I have just finished a poem or have gotten a glimpse of another, made some connection I've never made before, felt some wholeness that has eluded me and everything falls into place, I think to myself I must be the luckiest, the happiest person in the whole world. It's important for you to know. It's true. I'd never lie to you." She kisses me, hugs me, rocking me in her arms. "Oh, Vanessa, don't you cry for me."

"No crying now, Marta." I bend down to her. Her face is in the pillow. I touch her curly head, its unspeakable darkness. "You'll feel better after this," I say. We have run out of drugs. Everything about the world bruises us—its color, its shape, its sound. It is painful for her even to move. Still she turns to me, ever hopeful.

"Come on," I say, helping her up. She is an old woman, I think. Her footsteps are loud as we walk down the hall. I lead her into the curving white room. "Here now. Sit down, Marta," I say, placing her on the edge of the bathtub and slowly undressing her. The old woman turns into a child. She looks up at me with large brown eyes, all hope, as I run hot water into the sink. She is hunched over. She says nothing, rubs her eyes. Is her head still in the pillow? Is the walk down the dark hallway, the warm water in a sink, my hands that skim the top, is it all a dream? I empty what looks to be green sand into a jar and add warm water. We are little girls playing in mud, in clay. She does not take her eyes from my hands. Her eyes are dark—almost black—beautiful, her long eyelashes, her thick eyebrows. I watch her as I mix the paste in a jar.

"It's the magic of plants," I say.

She shakes her head no in some disbelief.

"Yes," I whisper. "It's henna. It will make your hair beautiful, silky, soft."

She smiles slightly. She can't help being a little amused. She has been awakened for this, she says, forced down the cold hallway into this cold room for this?

"That's right," I say.

"An appointment at the beauty parlor? Jesus, Vanessa—the magic of plants—what's wrong with you?"

"I'm not kidding," I say. "You'll feel better."

I put on a pair of rubber gloves. She just stares.

"This is some outfit," she says. I am standing in my underwear, rubber gloves on up to my elbows.

"Shh," I say, dipping my hand into the warm glass jar, the warm paste of plants. I smooth it on, beginning at the roots and gradually working down.

"I like this," she smiles. "This isn't as bad as I thought."

I rub the henna into her hair. I feel the bones of her skull, the line of her neck. I touch her lovely curving back. I cradle her head, feel its bumps. I find my mind drifting. I find myself thinking that I would like to hold this head forever. I work more diligently.

"This feels good," she says. "Do I get a mud pack next?"

"I wonder how you'll look as a redhead," I say.

"What?"

"Well, will I like you as a redhead? Want to hear a redhead's stories? Want to sing Billie Holiday songs with one? You know."

"You'd better not make me a redhead."

"Didn't they have *I Love Lucy* in Venezuela?"

She grins.

"Lucy, Lucy!" I say.

"Yes, Ricky?" she shouts and then does Ricky's part, too, in the Spanish I love to hear.

She becomes weary, bone-tired, suddenly. "Don't make me a redhead," she says sternly.

"Don't worry. We won't leave it in long."

Her head is nearly completely covered now. The smell of henna fills the bathroom. It smells of luck to me, of long life.

"Shall we henna this?" she says, touching the fine hair under my arms. She laughs. "Let me have those gloves." I submerge them in water. She takes them off my hands and puts them on.

"Will I like a redhead?" she asks as she puts her hand into the jar. "This stuff feels good," she says. Delicately she applies the paste to each tiny hair, and the plant warmth radiates through my body.

"I think I will like a redhead," she says.

"It tickles," I say.

"It's not working if it doesn't tickle," she says. I step back for a second.

We are so at ease with each other at this moment, so happy, so much ourselves here, green everywhere, so natural, that we almost forget that this all must be strictly timed, that we must watch the clock, that it cannot go on forever.

She turns to me abruptly as if she can read my thoughts. Her hands are covered with henna. I'm turning away from her when she grabs my arm, leaving her large handprint. Her eyes are black and fierce. Her hair is plastered to her head, a warrior's ancient helmet. She's hurting me. "Don't make me love you," she says bitterly. "Vanessa, please—don't make me love you," she begs.

Part Five

On the train home, on the way to the last Christmas in that string of Christmases, where was the sign, the clue? The impossible blizzard, the closed road, the red bird in the snow, the man in the black coat? Where was the symbol that in its perfection would have told us to prolong our gazes, extend our thank-yous, hold our embraces a moment longer?

We were all students on that train, it seemed—exhausted students, silly students, students in love—nothing unusual, and as the train pulled out of Poughkeepsie and followed the frozen Hudson toward New York, some talked of the exams which in their minds they were still taking, again and again, perfecting each answer. Others slept. Some must have dreamt of home. I was thinking of Marta who was flying now into a different winter. Henna still stained my hands and arms. I had made no attempt to get it off. It would be a month's separation.

Snow had begun to fall. The snow wrapped around the old train like the wings of an angel, and my thoughts shifted to my mother. I was flying headlong through the December night into her favorite season. It was the only time of year when she could lift herself out of the pull of her work and become for a month someone quite different. Some star rose up in her, a perfect, luminous shape, and she seemed to us intensely happy as she shopped and baked and wrapped presents and mailed cards. We had seen it many times now. Each year my father would follow her around asking her not to push herself so hard, begging her to rest, reminding her how easily she tired. December was almost always followed by a January filled with misgivings, depression, lack of focus, lack of feeling sometimes—sometimes worse. She never listened to my father. "It's Christmas!" she would say, as if that explained everything, and she would continue her frenzied preparation. "Shoo!" she'd say to my father as he persisted. "Shoo, Michael." These words always bothered me, the way she batted him away, the way she wiped her brow, though it has taken me a long time to figure out why.

For one month each year my mother and my grandmother would become friends. They sat side by side, putting cloves in oranges, hanging boughs of pine, discussing the Christmas Eve dinner. Each December my mother tried to assume some of those practical, worldly mannerisms. There they sat, the two of them, contented, shoulder to shoulder in our kitchen one week before Christmas—my grandmother laughing with the woman who had ruined her son's life, and my mother festive, manic, in a flowered apron, asking my father, of all things, to be sensible. Journeying in opposite ways around the world, each year they met for a month on some magic, neutral ground where they embraced and forgave. My mother must have missed her own mother very much; she clung so tightly to my grandmother's rigid life.

There were other miracles: the dark house transformed magically into a house of happiness and light, a place where gingerbread men walked from the warm oven in happy rows, a house that rang with laughter and music and bells, a house where a perpetual fire burned, giving a dramatic warmth, the smell of pine flooding the whole living room.

The star that rose up in my mother at Christmas seemed to hang over our house, protecting us. We were all happy, I am sure of it, even Father. He would sit for hours at the piano and play the songs of the season, asking for requests.

"We Three Kings," Fletcher shouted from another room.

"Un Flambeau, Jeannette, Isabelle," my mother cried.

"Oh, please play 'White Christmas,'" I would sigh. I would sit on the piano bench next to him and turn the pages when he nodded. Often he would slow at the hard parts to ensure he touched the right notes. His touch was tentative, as in life. I watched his hand as he reached his long finger up to a black key where it lingered for a moment and then pulled back. For hours I would sit next to him, watching him, listening to his halting Yuletide songs.

"We're quite a team, you and I," he would smile when he was finally done, touching my back lightly, applying just the slightest pressure. He looked into the other room, lost in some melancholy melody—"Away in a Manger" or "Silent Night." I could feel the snowy bones of his hand still on my back even as I was losing him. I looked into his eyes, those remote, cold fields. I studied him hard as I tried to comprehend the mystery of love, for, as we sat there on the piano bench—my father, far, far off and then back, then far off again, then returning to discuss his ideas for a hot punch with port—I loved him fiercely, unreasonably.

"Come on," cried Fletcher, "it's almost done."

Even as a little boy Fletcher liked to assemble the crèche. In the early years Grandpa had assisted him. First they put together the barn, then carefully unwrapped each Hummel from its tissue paper. They had been bought by my mother's friends Florence and Bethany, one by one each year, and given to Fletcher and me as Christmas presents. It was only last Christmas, with the youngest shepherd taking his place far left, that the scene completed itself.

"The wise men," my grandfather said, his eyes shining. "These, children, are the wise men." We stared at the kings, purple robed, dark skinned, holding wisdom in their eyes and gifts for the baby in their hands. I looked at the baby, just a regular baby really, then back to the wise men, then to the baby again, then up to Mary. Her bowing head, her glowing face seemed happy and sad at the same time. Her open hands were shaped like hearts. I turned to Joseph. My eye lingered longest on Joseph usually, standing off to one side. I studied every wrinkle in his rough robe, touched his face. He was so lonely, I thought, so separate from the rest—lonely as faith itself. I touched his sandaled feet with my thumb. He faltered. His pain was unspoken, difficult to name, his carpenter's hand raised in front of him as if he could not view this scene, could not view his wife and child except in this way. He never moved. I have thought of him many times throughout the year in that large box in the basement labeled "crèche." Wrapped in tissue paper, his one hand raised, slightly open, he looks through his fingers in awe.

Fletcher put the young shepherd next to the elderly man who bends over with balding head, and the scene was complete. We looked at the assemblage quietly, knowing already the rest of the story: the afternoon of agony still to come, the betrayal, the rising up on the third day.

I would like to believe that Fletcher carries inside him now into the center of the country the whole of this scene. But it is only Joseph's uncertain position, somewhere between hope and despair, belief and disbelief that I have been able to keep.

There were times when I had gone off with Grandma, that skeptic, to Mass, where weekly I could witness miracles, babble in Latin, denounce Satan, chant to the dead. Blood flowed down those aisles. God was a white bird called the Holy Ghost and a baby and a man and a father, all at the same time. Trees sang. Bushes burned. There was a living water, an eternal fountain inside us that we thirsted for. There were Barnabus and Ignatius, Perpetua and Agnes, Anastasia. I grew dizzy in the sound of it all: the strange songs, the bells, the incense, the wailing for forgiveness, the cross, the apostles and all the martyrs, the saints, Felicity and Cecilia, the blood no doors could hold back.

But slowly, as I sat there with my doubting grandmother beside me, the church changed: the bells became faint and then were gone. We did not beat our breasts, we did not chant ourselves, in another language, into knowledge. Things were explained, reduced. Some of the saints were demoted. The huge pipe organ became a guitar. The words *relevant* and *rational* were murmured like prayers. And the Holy Ghost became the Holy Spirit because it was supposed to be less scary.

Leave them alone, the rivers of blood, the bread from the sky, the wine at the wedding, the saints. Leave Him, the man on the cross dying for love. The church puts words in His sweet mouth, simple feelings in His complex heart. I will not listen; its English is as flat as unrisen bread.

Leave Him alone, the man on the cross dying for love. The church has Him turn his face away from Natalie. The church has Him disown Marta. The church makes Him say He cannot love Florence or Bethany; he cannot love Sabine—ever.

In Italy, Florence and Bethany say there are steep steps that seem to go to heaven itself, leading up to an altar that you must climb up on your knees in devotion. I don't know for sure, but I have a feeling you can walk up those steps now on your feet.

Each Christmas Florence and Bethany told me stories as we grated the various cheeses for the soup or for the brussels sprouts or whatever it was that year. Invariably I would get my fingers caught in the sharp grids of the metal grater, my flesh becoming more and more mangled and bloodied as I continued my task. What was I trying to feel? Whom was I punishing?

Just last year Bethany held my shredded hand under water and shook her head. She talked to me softly as she wrapped my hand up, then hugged me to her as if I were a child. How fond I am of them, my mother's friends, Florence and Bethany, companions for life, generous and kind, unchanging year after year, not even aging, it seems. How I miss them now—those gentle, large-hearted women, those solid citizens, satisfied, intelligent, calm, like no one I have ever known. I cannot remember a Christmas without them—flown in from Italy or Spain or Greece, wherever they had spent the year before, with gemlike stories from an exotic world and news of Sabine.

They blend together finally, each Christmas one spirit, one great sensual procession of friends and family. My grandmother and grandfather sit at one end of the large lacy table. My brother is next to my grandfather, then my aunt, my uncle. My cousin Denise, an insurance salesman like her father, raises a glass of white wine to her lips. Florence brushes the hair from Bethany's forehead. My Aunt Lucy sings for the turkey stuffing in her bird voice, smiling her mischievous smile, so happy. Sing on, Aunt Lucy. Sing now, louder than you ever have. Continue to believe in the life of the family. We need your faith, the faith that turned you from a girl into a nurse as you worked night after night to save your mother's lost life. We need your faith now, your pressed white faith, your bedpan faith, your practical love.

Each Christmas my mother and Aunt Lucy made the same call on the upstairs phone. Their voices were always the same: hushed, excited, childlike. "Sarkis Wingarian," they whispered, all hope. "We'd like to speak with Sarkis Wingarian." He was the only one in our family missing from the Christmas celebration.

"There is no one here who calls himself that," a voice on the other end always said.

Without ever knowing him I missed him. I missed him for them, for those two sisters who turned to one another each time and said, "But Christmas was Mother's favorite season. She loved it so. Surely he doesn't forget that, too."

I would never see him, I thought: Grandpa Sarkis, three hundred pounds; Grandpa Sarkis who read to them from the travel section on Sundays; Grandpa Sarkis who worked so hard, who left his daughters, when they were grown, for the old country and who never came back. "In the old country you are worth your weight in gold. In the old country you can grow silk on trees." In the old country his people were slaughtered like sheep.

Grandpa Sarkis's voice rises from the warm, moist body of the duck in front of us. "Musa Dagh," it says. "Never forget." Fletcher hears it, too. "We will not forget, Grandfather," he says under his breath. Fletcher cannot forget anything. He includes Grandpa Sarkis in his grace, with the hungry and the lonely, with all the world's pain, with the Christmas bombings in Cambodia, with the thousand deaths in Central America. The only grandfather I know nods his head. He is with us every Christmas, even the ones after his death. "God bless you, Sarkis," my grandfather says, lifting his glass.

My mother is decorating the enormous Christmas tree. My father has just put up the colored lights and now lies on the floor watching her. To me this tree seems darker than usual, and I consider that perhaps a few sets of lights have been sacrificed to some project of Fletcher's during the year. My father gets up and moves to the living room where he resumes his playing at the grand piano.

"I'm dreaming of a white Christmas," he starts, then begins again, changing the key. "I'm dreaming of a white Christmas, just like the ones I used to know."

My mother carefully unwraps each ornament from its tissue paper. They are so fragile, so beautiful. One by one she cradles them in her hands, holds them up to the light. She admires especially those that over the years my grandmother has brought to us as gifts. Though my grandmother rarely left Pennsylvania after she arrived from Italy, the ornaments are from all over the world, one more wonderful than the next. Each year is accounted for, every ornament inscribed with a date. It was as if she were keeping time for us, as if without her we would have been totally unaware of its passage.

My mother's hands tremble slightly as she picks up the eggshell-thin ornament from Germany dated 1942. "Frohe Weinachter" is handpainted with precision in an elaborate calligraphy across its center. She tries putting it on one bough of the tree, then another. She already knows that wherever it is finally placed, near the top of the tree or the bottom, near light or away from light, it will always hang in darkness. She knows that whatever creative powers she can summon, whatever aesthetic considerations of shape or color or pattern her eye or heart or imagination can come up with, it will always remain unapproachable, hanging alone, in horrendous, unspeakable shadow.

"Through the years we all will be together," my father croons, "if the fates allow." The melody hangs tentatively in the air. His finger reaches up for the black key but then pulls back. Each word from his mouth stands alone. "Hang—A—Shining—Star—Upon—The—Highest—Bough."

My mother places each ornament carefully, lovingly, on the enormous tree. She steps back now and then to admire her work. She takes two glass fish from their tissue paper and releases them to swim in a piney sea. She moves a straw angel to the front. "Straw is for luck," she smiles.

"Mother," I say, standing next to her, "move those two blue ornaments. Let them float on opposite sides of the great tree. Let their darkness be cast in different directions."

"No, Vanessa," she says, "we must not touch." And she takes my hand. "This stands for something," she smiles weakly and she kisses my forehead.

Behind my eyes now as I sit alone here this Christmas Day in New York, one year later, a deep, red Christmas candle flowers before me, opening itself up, smelly and dark. I cannot see her anymore, I can only hear her voice, coming out of the dark. "Try not to be afraid," she says.

Light the candle, I think. Light it now, Vanessa.

I strike the match in my mind and light the candle there in the dark. In its light I can see everything: the tree, the wreaths, the garland, the crèche; every Christmas, every guest; the china, the cheese grater, the nutmeg, the oranges, the cloves.

"Try not to be afraid, Vanessa," she whispers. "Trust me."

I trust her.

I do not make the candle disappear; I do not change the stroke in my mind that has brought this blossoming, bloody shape to me. I do not alter anything. I hold it now steady in my mind, hold my mother's courage up. It grows larger. The candle opens wider. The flame reaches higher and higher. I do not stop it. There are flames everywhere. I watch my father's piano music slowly curl at the edges and then disintegrate. I smell the charred body of the duck. The punch ignites. The tree crackles and spits. The glass fish crack open. The straw angels hiss and fold into themselves. I destroy everything—the gingerbread boys, the holly, the winter roses. The lead crystal explodes. The piano groans, collapsing in the heat. The strings pop and stretch and melt. The melody my father sings pulls itself apart like taffy. The sisters' sweet embrace dissolves. When they dial the phone it melts in their hands as they strain to hear a disappearing voice. It all turns to ash as I watch, and I know I am responsible for this. My young parents dance into smoke. My mother's organdy dress with wings catches fire.

"Try not to be afraid," she whispers.

"Mom!" I shout, "Mom!" I can't find her.

"Trust me," she sighs, through flames.

My mother left for Maine right after Christmas. The season she loved most had exhausted her. She was like one of those exotic, flowering plants of the season that must be taken away from the light so that it might bloom again some other time in the future.

As we sat at the dinner table she had seemed barely able to lift the scrolled, silver spoon to her mouth. Now there would be time for recovery. She would reclaim the silence; she had begun there at dessert. I could see her going. I tried to detain her—anyone would have—but I knew it was already too late. She was retreating with each spoonful of Christmas pudding, with each lovely laugh, each turn of the head. She looked so beautiful in her deep-green velvet dress and pearls, sitting at the lacy table. She put her spoon down and moved her plate slightly, asked for the cream and sugar, and arranged those two pieces at an angle not far from her plate. She was setting up the rocks. She was seeing it now, the wintry coastline of Maine. Her eyes were graying. She smiled. Her hand settled on her cup like a cloud.

When I spoke to her, my voice turned into the voice of the wind and the voice of the ocean. She could not hear my words now, but she looked at me affectionately and nodded, knowing that I knew. She moved her hand on top of mine and edged it toward her scene. I wondered if I would ever get to that white house. "You've made us such a lovely Christmas," I whispered.

She will meet Sabine there and the gray will give way to a pale, pale rose when she sees her. They will enter the uncluttered room, fling open the large French doors, breathe deeply, walk from room to room, collapse onto the beds, embrace. They will sit hour after hour by the fire, watching the sea, taking each other in in silence. At dinnertime Sabine will throw the lobsters into the boiling water in her delicate way, standing on tiptoe to look into the enormous pot, covering her eyes, peeking through her fingers and holding my mother's hand.

It is New Year's Eve. They will write their resolutions just before midnight. Sabine will resolve to be braver about lobsters. My mother is more serious. Without hesitation, it seems, she scribbles five resolutions on a small piece of paper and tucks them away in some safe place. For the changing of the year Sabine will chop up tiny pieces of herring, which she has heard is the custom somewhere. And they will feed each other twelve grapes as the clock tolls, for luck.

The last time I saw my mother she was standing under the great clock in Grand Central Station, her New Year's resolutions pressed in her hand. She had just returned from Maine where she had spent a month with Sabine. I was on my way back to college for the second semester.

"You don't need all this, Mom," I said, taking jewelry from her arms, her neck.

"You'll miss your train," she said.

Marta was smiling and radiant and waiting for me when I got back to Vassar. Over Christmas something had changed in her, I thought. Natalie had fallen back somewhere, rising only occasionally now in her low voice.

It happens with time, I thought to myself, but as soon as those words formed I knew them to be dishonest. I had wanted to clutch to my heart the easiest explanation, the most available.

"I missed you," I said.

"I missed you, too," she smiled. She put her strong arm around me. She was wearing a T-shirt whose sleeves she had cut off. She was dark brown and muscled and smelled vaguely of coconut oil.

"You look beautiful," I said. I could not take my eyes off her. She was getting better.

Her veins looked good. "Did you bring back any drugs?" I asked her.

"No," she said casually, shrugging her shoulders. "There are always drugs around if we want them."

I felt like dancing, but when I tried I could not lift my feet more than a fraction of an inch off the ground. Seeing Marta this way, I had forgotten for a moment the rows upon rows of gold chains around my mother's ankles as she stood immovable in the station. I felt their weight, too. It was hard suddenly even to walk. I dragged my feet.

"I brought you a present," Marta said, unwrapping it for me like a child who cannot control her excitement when giving, who cannot wait. "It's a dress the Indians wear. You'll look great in it."

I looked up from my mother's ringed hands. It was red and yellow with a design of fish and crabs and sea horses on it, and it had a wrap for the waist of navy blue cloth covered with zebras and trees. I unbuttoned my shirt.

"It must be very beautiful there," I said, looking at the brightly patterned dress. "You must take me someday."

"Oh, yes," she said, looking at me, "it's very beautiful."

I touched her dark face. "You are my brown berry," I said. "Promise to take me."

She took my hand. "Please," she whispered, "don't make me love you."

The next morning Marta began work on her senior thesis; she had been given an extension by the Dean of Studies, who had always been kind to her. I watched her write the first two sentences.

I patted the top of her curly head. "I've got a class," I said. "I'll bring you your lunch afterwards so you won't have to go out." She nodded and whispered in the tiniest voice, "Thank you, Vanessa." She never looked up from the page.

The class met only once a week and so was longer than most others—three hours, I think. It was art history and, looking at slides in the dark, I found myself easily falling into the dreamy apple world of Cézanne, easily blocking out the teacher's comments, which always dissipated my pleasure. I noticed, though, as I sat there that some of the paintings seemed to be losing their color, and the teacher, too, seemed to be fading.

After class I went to the cafeteria. I was happy to bring Marta a lunch not only of carrots and celery and crackers but also a sandwich, a muffin, food that did not crunch; she was eating everything again. Walking down the pine tree path from Central Dining I heard a great commotion. The path was white, as if it had snowed. I decided to ignore the frenzy, not realizing at first that it was coming from the place I was going. I saw a flashing light through the trees, suddenly a stretcher, a car of white, then a siren. There was a crowd of people outside Cushing. And I knew she was dead.

There is a tremendous country house, I am sure of it, somewhere in the heart of France or Maine or Sweden, with so many rooms it's been easy to get lost, it's been easy to be seduced, for each room has seemed more fantastic than the one before it. It's been filled with things we could not have ignored, could not have looked away from. Each table, elegantly set, held great feasts. Music played. Music plays even now, and people dance. Others cry, for they want it never to end. I don't cry. There are so many rooms to go through, it seems they will go on forever—each one different, yet strangely the same. But suddenly we are at the back of the house, and what we see there we have never seen before. At the back of the house, at the place where the rooms end, there is an enormous porch made entirely of crystal, where a beautiful woman sits smiling a most inviting smile. She is patient, for she knows there is no one who can resist her. I have turned my face from her many times, but now I look again. It is Natalie.

Riding in the speeding taxi to Vassar Brothers Hospital, I thought of my mother—how she hated cars, how she hated riding in cars, and most of all how she hated riding in cars that went fast. What she could not bear, I think, was how quickly the world passed before her eyes. She kept wanting to say stop, wait, not so fast. She disliked how objectively the car treated the landscape, not pausing for the barefoot children carrying pails in spring or slowing down for the milkweed pods that scattered in the wind. "Michael," she said one day from the back seat, as we passed a rosy apple orchard and she turned back to look at it, "Michael, my teeth hurt. What shall I do?"

My father just said, "Hmm," and I imagine then he went into a meditation about dentists. There was Dr. Ledbetter who had done that terrible root canal, Dr. Brand who had committed suicide, Dr. Ellis who had run off with a pretty patient. I pictured this seduction: he pressing his white coat, his firm thigh against her legs, lowering his fingers into her mouth, then down into her throat, spraying water on her arms, taking the cotton from the inside of her bleeding mouth, the sound of the drill. How many times did she come back, I wonder. How many noncavities were filled? When did they know it was love?

And pity the poor dental hygienist who had secretly loved Dr. Ellis all along, witness to the whole affair.

All my father said in the end was "Dr. William Wheeler. He's very good. I'll make an appointment for you as soon as we get home."

"But, Michael," my mother said in her swimmy voice, "it's not one tooth, it's all my teeth. They hurt. The actual teeth themselves hurt!"

My father knew to pull the car over then, and as we took a long walk in the woods my mother's pain began to subside. It had been her way of stopping the car. I think she hated what the speeding movement of the car suggested to her about life—that it was all going so fast and that we were doomed for the most part just to take glimpses, never really to see.

Very often my mother developed a physical hurt of some sort when she got into the car. I always thought she did this for us. We could understand a physical malady better than a mental one; it was a way to suffer the way other people did.

A loose tooth falls through time into my lap as I race to the hospital to Marta.

Picture her dead, I kept telling myself over and over. Picture her dead.

Racing through this January, I understood finally that my mother's physical symptoms were very real because, as I flew by children dragging sleds through snow, I felt nauseated and dizzy. Pain cracked like ice in my head. I wanted only to stop, to examine the birch's silver, to lose myself in a flurry of birds, in a community of ants, to skim the thick sleep of the woodchuck and rest there for a while.

By the time I got to Vassar Brothers Hospital, Marta had passed through the doorway into the last room, where she stayed, sleeping, able to see Natalie, I suppose, but not with her yet.

"She slit her wrists," the doctor said, "like a pro. She knew exactly what she was doing. . . ." His voice did not fall like it naturally does at the end of a sentence, and I knew there was more. "She took at least thirty barbiturates," he said in a soft voice. "She has slipped into a coma."

Your hair waves a million times toward me—a lovely curling sea. I move close to you and bathe in its soothing motion as it rises and falls on my face. I could almost drown in it. I could almost become its darkness, forget about everything, forget about you, Marta, as you have forgotten about me.

I take one curl and pull it taut from her head. I wrap my finger around it, feel its oily film on my thumb and on the tip of my forefinger. I slip my finger into another curl, then another, let them recoil. I pull one, I pull two, three, tighter and tighter until her head nearly tumbles from the bed and into my lap. You do not protest; you do not object—you have become so unlike yourself.

I pull your curls and they recoil, falling back into their dark nest where fish seem to swim in and out of your tangled tunnels. Snails curl around your ears in tendrils, humming their snail sounds. And there are starfish, too, that dangle at your neck. Marta, in your hair is a whole world. I see as I look closer even the butterfly shrimp in your curls, plodding on, feeding on death, a scavenger like me. I pull another curl, then another. I watch them bounce back. Marta, why? Why? It is beautiful hair, alive on your head.

I, too, fell into sleep, mimicking Marta's half-life, her patterns of breath, her slowing pulse. I tried to follow her into the hallway of death and yank her back to the place where we were up to our elbows in henna. But day after day she slept, beautiful in her repose, not moving, barely breathing.

"You are my brown berry," I whispered to her, touching her smooth, tanned face, "deep, deep inside a bramble bush, far, far off in the heart of the forest." I could not reach her.

Sabine opens the large French windows and breathes deeply as the air of the ocean enters the house. It is strangely warm and cool at the same time. She takes my mother's hand. She feels snow in the air.

They stare out at the smooth breast of the beach, the lovely white belly of the beach. They watch the ships yearning toward shore through fog. The land seems to extend its arm and curve around each hull, offering its pale embrace.

There's a signal out there: a red light, then a white, then another white from the lighthouse tower. Something shines in the distance. Like a sleepwalker, my mother floats out onto the glass porch. It looks like crystal to her.

"An iceberg," Sabine says, pointing to the place my mother has begun to go.

The lighthouse voice is filled with longing. The iceberg emits a ray of bright light. Only my mother can hear its lonely, snow tone.

When the phone call came at three in the morning with its unmistakable ring of death, I thought that it was Marta who had finally passed from the last room to the lovely porch where Natalie sat waiting. I was not thinking of my mother. I think now that I might have warned her that night, might have done something to prevent what happened. I had watched for days the world drain of color, the way it always had when she was going away; but I misinterpreted that blanching badly. I thought it had something to do with Marta, who with each hour was slipping further and further away. I thought the whiteness of the world had something to do with her whom I had begun to love.

My mother died of what they would call severe burns when our 1973 Pinto was rammed by a car at a tollbooth on the Connecticut Turnpike. The Pinto's rear end collapsed on impact, the gas tank ruptured, and the car burst into flames. She was sitting in the back seat where she liked it best. Death was instantaneous.

My mother died of what would be called severe burns, but later Fletcher would say that when he lifted the coffin as one of four pallbearers it seemed as if it was empty. She must have exploded into bits.

Death was instantaneous.

A one-time Ford engineer testified at the trial that the Pinto's design was not balanced. He said that, for cost reasons, it was designed to withstand only a twenty-mile-per-hour crash.

At the trial, the lawyer attempted to prove that Ford was well aware of the Pinto's vulnerability but that after a cost-benefit analysis a conscious decision was made not to install a $6.65 part that could help protect the tank.

It was at the New Haven tollbooth that the car in back, having lost control in the ice and snow, slid into ours. They were nearly home.

From behind closed doors, three loud hurrahs could be heard in the executive boardroom at the Ford Motor headquarters in Dearborn, Michigan.

They had been acquitted.

Death was instantaneous.

The Pinto collapsed on impact, its fuel tank ruptured, and the car burst into flames. My father and brother both received second-degree burns but managed to get themselves out of the front seat of the car. She never had a chance.

Before her eyes the highway opened up like a field and slowly filled with snow. She looked up into the white sky at the dance of flurries. As they neared home in the small red car, the snow fell harder, transforming the landscape. Suddenly she noticed that they were in the center of a blizzard. No one, not even Fletcher, had expected such a storm. He shook his head at the unpredict-ability of the weather. He was no better at it now, after years of study, than he was as a little boy.

"Oh, it's so wonderful!" she gasped, and her voice ached with the beauty of it. Fletcher turned around and looked at her.

"Mother," he said, but he did not articulate his sentence, for he saw that she was not listening: it was beautiful, and it called out to her, and she was not afraid.

Father never took his eyes from the road. He was always a careful driver. "Painfully careful," my grandfather used to say.

"We're almost home," Father said. "The roads are very bad, but we're al-most home."

Home, she thought. How wonderful to be in the center of snow and to be going home. She closed her eyes as Father pulled up to the tollbooth.

I hope that her eyes were closed and that she did not turn around in the last second and, seeing the car behind her sliding on the ice, know what would happen. Did she call out? Perhaps. It was so close to her, she felt she might call out to it and with her voice hold it back. But I hope she was too tired or preoccupied or just too settled in that tiny back seat to look out the window behind her. I hope that her eyes were closed or at least that she stared ahead into the snow, ordered the last few objects left on the landscape, and held that final word "home" in her mouth, and that the word home carried her through the explosion and over to the other side safely.

There could not have been time for my father or brother to have helped her. I hope that is true—that there was no moment in which to hesitate or make a decision, no split second for them to live with for the rest of their lives, wishing they had done differently. No, there would not have been time to have done anything. There are a few things I know for sure: I loved her more than my own life. She was beautiful and wise. She never had a chance.

I do not know, though, whether this death was easy for her. I fear it was not. I fear, like her life, that it was hard, that she suffered exquisitely, that she turned around in the last minute knowing that it was out there in the snow, because she was so good at knowing things like that, and she went out to greet it, to take in its strangeness, and as the headlights came closer and my father took the change from the toll taker my mother knew and sighed, "Oh," as she let death enter her. And he, I'm afraid, turned around to look at her and saw the agony on her face and said, "Christine, what, what is it?" And at that last moment she just shook her head wordlessly, put her head and her hands on Fletcher's shoulders, slumped over, and said again, "Oh," and then, "Oh, my!"

Or was it different from this? Did she sink her fingernails into the car's upholstery right before the end, in terror as the brain in disorder called up random images—an aisle from a drugstore of her youth or a slant of light from her attic study—as she clung to the car and then separated from the world of tolls and cars into horrendous pain. She never imagined it would be like this— death ramming into her, death so hot it turned green and bubbled. Its fingers curled into her back, its sharp teeth sank into her. Pain so hideous the human body has no capacity to hold it, the brain in a fraction of a second casting off everything, everything, the works of Shakespeare, the poetry of Rilke, the music of Chopin, the lives of her own children, she willing to give up every- thing to be released—everything simply to be released.

She explodes. Or no—maybe she burns more slowly. Maybe my father and brother are made to hear the sighing of her burning flesh, smell the terrible flesh stench of death as she disappears slowly in the snow. She shrieks, one last time, only a mouth left now, the brain dead, but the mouth still shrieking in the excruciating heat.

Then silence, but the silence does not last for very long. It is replaced by something unidentifiable at first, barely audible. It is replaced by the sighing of burning flesh. All year long it has been the sound in the background. It has been the sound in the background all year long. And it never stops. No matter how long we live or how far away we go, it never really stops.

Did my father try to find her withered hand? Did he cradle the head with the mouth in it that shrieked and shrieked?

She was my mother. She was probably just beginning her New Year's reso- lutions.

The Ford Motor Company never sent us an apology. Fletcher gathered as best he could information that might be useful in a lawsuit, but he fell apart almost as soon as he began. Neither Father nor I had the heart to pursue it. Retribu- tion was a pallid emotion in the spectrum we were feeling. My father could not see the use of it; Ford would feel nothing and we would be made to sit in the courtroom and gape at giant blowups of the car and the remains of her body. It was Aunt Lucy who pursued the lawsuit finally, displaying the same courage and tenacity I imagined she once did when my mother was so sure she was bleeding to death, long ago.

There was a flurry of excitement among the senior executives at Ford. They had not counted on a distinguished writer being incinerated in their Pinto. If they had thought such a thing was possible, they might have thought twice about what I am convinced they knew was the fatal position of the gas tank. They did not care at all about my mother. They did not care that they had taken away one of the country's most original, most authentic voices. What they cared about was the publicity, the unknown numbers who would remember "the Pinto incident" because of this Christine Wing, whoever she was.

An added nuisance to an already irritating Monday, Charles Walcott thought, closing his briefcase and rushing to a meeting. In the hall he met Sullivan. "And the icing on the cake is this," Sullivan said, "she's got some wise-ass son, some antiwar type who's gonna try to run us right the fuck into the ground."

Mrs. Walcott, at home in Scarsdale, ordered the maid to intercept all incoming magazines and newspapers. Her husband's high blood pressure, already out of hand, would skyrocket with all this. They must do their best to keep it from him. "Christine Wing Killed in Ford Pinto." "Ford Under Scrutiny." "Walcott of Ford Denies Pinto a Safety Hazard."

If it had only been someone else, she thought, there would be a two-inch article buried somewhere near the back of the paper. An insignificant lawsuit would be initiated, and quietly the family would be compensated. "It's just not fair," Mrs. Walcott sighed to Winnifred the maid. "It wasn't Ford's fault, after all." But Walcott, leaving the meeting, saw my mother's face on the front page of all the local newspapers and all the national newspapers, and a barrage of obscenities spewed like exhaust from his mouth. He did not have the imagination or the knowledge to suspect the front-page headlines of the newspapers in France, in Germany, in England, in Canada, in Italy, in Mexico, in Brazil, in Africa, in Russia, in Poland, in Greece, in Israel, in Czechoslovakia, in Norway, in Holland, in Denmark, in Belgium, in Sweden . . .

She was my mother, Mr. Walcott. She was probably just starting her New Year's resolutions.

My mother's wake was filled with flowers. They came from every corner of the earth and continued to arrive all day and all night. They could not be contained by the walls of the room her coffin was in; they spilled into the other rooms of the great mansion, which was the funeral parlor, and filled them. People floated like sleepwalkers from one doorway to another, dizzied by the awful perfumes of death.

The funeral parlor was filled with the people who loved my mother. There were relatives, there were friends, there were reviewers, there were people she had never known but who knew her through her work. They came with stories, they came holding her books. They kept coming and coming, endlessly, in tremendous white clouds of grief. There was so much grief that, even in this place which was made to hold grief, the walls seemed to tremble and the floor to give way. The funeral directors stood against the collapsing walls and charted the unstable weather of the room. To those mourners who stayed long enough, there came a time when they passed through the heavy, cloudlike sorrow to the other side where there erupted a black wind of anger. It swirled around the room in a twisting so great that it threatened to level the funeral parlor with its violence. It blew our hair back away from our faces. It tore our clothes. It circled the room and grew fiercer and fiercer. "Why?" the mourners howled, raising their windy fists, their mouths in horror frozen open, in rage. The circle tightened.

Fletcher and I sat next to the coffin and did not move. Those who had known her from college gave out great cries when they saw me sitting next to it. I must have looked enough as they remembered her from school to confuse them for a moment. Preparing to see her dead, they saw her alive instead, and young again, the way they remembered her best—twenty-five years earlier, and their own pasts, too, came alive through me. They were young women again, their whole lives yet to live. And in my ruined face they saw her face as a young woman looking into some unbearable future that only she seemed capable of seeing. One always had that impression of my mother—that she somehow knew everything in advance. It was true of her in college, probably even as a little girl—that she held the whole of her life inside her. It pained us all terribly to think of it: she had probably seen her own death, maybe even felt it, many times during her life.

"Oh, Mommy," I say into my quiet apartment, feeling finally the burden of her life entire in me, the way I have never felt it before, not even last January at the actual wake, and tears run down my face.

Fletcher patted me on the knee with his bandaged paw like some gentle monster. Fletcher and I sat next to the coffin and did not move. Our father, who stayed with her or what he must have sensed was her, through the entire ordeal, hovered, hanging in space like an awkward dark bird circling over death. He was quite badly burned, Fletcher said. He must have been in a great deal of physical pain. He had followed her from the accident to the hospital where he refused to be admitted, and from the hospital to the funeral parlor where she had been placed in her coffin. He did not leave her side once. When I came in just off the train from Poughkeepsie, he was still wearing the clothes from the accident. I think some of my mother's ashes must have been in his hair.

Fletcher and I sat next to the coffin and did not move.

Once we sat next to our mother on a blazing beach in high summer. "Don't move," Father said to us sternly. "Don't move." We did not realize that we had been appointed her lifeguards while my father went to get the doctor. We did not move a muscle. Once we lay without moving next to her on her bed, hoping that she might forget we were there so that we could stay near her a little longer.

A friend of my parents, one of the first to arrive at the wake, insisted on exchanging clothes with Father so that he would have something clean to wear. They went in the back to change. Fletcher and I sat next to the coffin and did not move. The clothes were too small for him. The jacket sleeves stopped just below his elbows, the pants well above his ankles. Fletcher got up suddenly and went over to him, and, with his bandaged hands, he slowly tied Father's tie, said something to him, and came back. My father stood there and vacantly watched people come up and linger at the coffin. His shoes were singed. The soles had separated into layers.

"Oh, Fletcher," I said, looking away from the unbearable image of my father, "remember that early, early morning that you and Dad and I visited Grandma at the nursing home right before she died?"

Fletcher nodded.

"Remember how she did the tarantella on the front lawn? Oh, Fletcher, remember how happy she was!"

"Grandma never did that," Fletcher said sadly, looking at me and then looking back at the chestnut coffin. "Grandma never did that, Vanessa."

I felt a great pressure on my chest as if all the air had suddenly left the room and some new tremendous wave of sorrow was moving in. I looked to the doorway.

"Fletcher," I said, breathlessly, "over there." And even my father turned around, sensing something enormous through the layers and layers of his despair.

I stood up and moved in front of the coffin. "Grandpa Sarkis," I said to the fat old man who stepped into the room. No coat to fit him, he wore an exotic silk wrap, bloodred and black.

"No," he said, shaking his head sadly, stepping back, not wanting me still.

I sat back down next to my brother and watched this colossal man run his hand hypnotically over the smooth wood, as if trying to conjure something to help him with this. That was his fate: to outlive the child he had held in his arms, the golden girl, the dream child. When he turned from the coffin he had aged decades and could barely walk. He looked at me. "Alice," he said. "What are you doing here?" He closed his eyes and touched my face. "My wife," he said, "this is my wife," introducing me to Fletcher. "How are you feeling, Alice? She's been so sick." He turned away, shaking his head, and slowly left the room.

White flowers grew from the walls. The snow had continued to fall. People who arrived now were completely white when they entered the room: Florence, Bethany.

When they lifted the coffin into the hearse, it was still snowing. I worried she would be cold out there. I worried she would be lost because everything in this weather looked the same. Each tree looked like every other, each field. She would be frightened. I worried she would not be able to find her way back. I worried she would suffocate under so many white flowers. My father must have felt the same way. No flowers, he said, would follow my mother from the funeral home into the cemetery. They might weigh her down. She might never rise up. As I got out of the limousine, there were only white flowers of snow— only snow, the sighing of snow, the sighing of burning flesh in the snow. I stood at the edge of the plot of snow my mother would disappear into. White flowers continued to fall from the sky, the white pressing against us, pressing us to the ground. I looked to my father, stooped with sorrow in the snow in his borrowed clothes. I watched my brother and the others lift the coffin from the hearse up the hill onto a steel platform in the snow—his bandages dragged in the snow. The priest, and Grandpa Sarkis, the press, the friends, the snow— and the terrible hole, the terrible sighing hole.

The knock at the door came just as my mother's chestnut coffin was being lowered into the ground again, as my father pivoted in the hard snow, slipping slightly, as my brother brought his hands to his face, and as I—I cannot even see myself anymore. The knock at the door stopped the weeping, stilled the speech in the priest's throat. The knock at the door lifted the horrible weight of snow from my mother's chest, and I could breathe again for a moment. I wondered whether I had invented the knock, for it not only stopped her descent now but seemed to tilt her body slightly away from the great silence at the center of the earth. I opened the door slowly, unsure whether anyone would be there at all. I thought this knock might be some elegant safety device of the brain, nothing more. Opening it, though, I still wanted to believe that someone might actually be standing there, someone who would walk into the room when invited and smile and sit with me for a while. I still wanted to believe that I might not be destined always to hear and see what was not there, to love that which did not exist, to want what could never be touched.

I opened the door. Over her arm was a dark corduroy coat. She wore a long black-and-white diamonded cardigan, a tailored white shirt, and black pants. Her hair was short and dark with a few flecks of gray in it. Her nails were polished and perfectly shaped. She wore a thin gold band on her right hand. I had given up the idea of ever seeing her.

She stared at me, saying nothing. Her eyes were dark. She was still beautiful. I stepped back from her.

"Sabine," I whispered, and tears flowed down my face. "What are you doing here?"

She extended her arm tentatively. Her hand was shaking as she touched the side of my face. As she touched me she gasped and with that intake, the breath reversing itself, I knew she was real. I could smell her perfume; I could feel her body trembling; her hand was warm.

"I never expected," she said in a thick accent, "I never expected this. I never thought"—her voice trailed off, then came back, "I never thought you'd look so much like her."

"Please," I whispered. "Please don't."

The cat had come to the doorway where we still stood. It rubbed against Sabine's silky leg, then moved in between mine, and then back to Sabine. She bent down and picked it up. "China," she sighed, looking at my mother's cat sadly, hugging it to her, burying her face in its fur. "Oh, China." In her voice was the sorrow of the universe. In her voice was a car being hit from behind and exploding into fire.

"Please come in," I said.

Sabine, though she said nothing, noticed it all. She recognized the desk, the lamp, the chair, the things my mother had had for years. Some of them she had bought with Sabine in France.

"I didn't think it would be this hard," she said. "I should not have come."

"No, Sabine, I'm glad you're here. I've always wanted to meet you. I've always wanted to know who you were, to see, to look at you, to meet you just once. I have all your records," I said shyly, and she smiled. I was nervous suddenly. I felt awkward, ill at ease, shaken; I bumped into things. She smiled again. I felt a great disorder moving in. This is not at all how my mother would have acted in such a situation, and I thought it brought Sabine some comfort to see me separate from her. But she was still saying it over and over, "I should not have come. I should go."

"Please don't go," I said.

She nodded her head.

"May I?" she asked, tapping on the top of the Scotch bottle.

"Please."

I watched this woman who had never been here before take charge, find the glasses, fill them with ice, make the drinks.

"We'll feel better after this, yes?" she said and smiled slightly. She did not sit but did a little pirouette in the center of the room, put her hand to her head, and said, "My cigarettes—ah, yes," and reached into the pocket of her sweater and took out a light-blue package. She lit one and her voice deepened with the first drag as she settled into a more familiar place.

"Ah," she said, sinking into my mother's chair. She watched me very closely as we spoke of New York and of Paris, of the house in Maine, her life, her singing—my mother hovering on the periphery of each subject but not mentioned.

"Do you like it here in Greenwich Village?" she asked. She smiled again, absently, weakly. She stood up suddenly and turned her back to me.

"You are so much like her—so beautiful and so sad." Tears fell in her voice. Tears had been falling in her voice a long time; it was worn by water.

"I should leave."

"Don't go away," I said, touching her back lightly, "please don't go."

With her back still turned to me, she began snapping her fingers, singing very softly in French, and the room turned dark. Berlin, I thought, it's Berlin. In the darkness I heard an accordion, a violin, a piano, a drum. "Oubliez," "regardez," "l'histoire," "déjà," "l'amour," "il ne me quitte pas"—each word was rough-edged and sounded as if it were being pulled from her. She was making the words work as hard as they could, as if she were trying to help herself explain something, as if through these hard, nasal words filled with bitterness something might come clear to her. The accordion faded, and the piano, and I listened to that voice alone in the dark trying to make some sense.

"Jacques Brel," she said, turning to me. "Another drink?"

I nodded.

"We will feel better soon," she whispered. She filled our glasses with Scotch, took two large gulps, precariously put her glass down, lit another cigarette, and sauntered into the bathroom. "We will feel better soon." She began singing again. She reappeared some time later, her eyes heavy with mascara and eyeliner and eyeshadow. Dark lipstick stained her mouth, there was high color in her cheeks. I could not take my eyes off her. She had begun her drunken cabaret dance toward my mother, swaggering to her in the dark. She was posed in the doorway of death, one hand on her hip, one hand on the frame of the door. "Oh, Christine," she said in her gravelly voice, looking straight ahead, then closing her eyes, rubbing her cheek on her shoulder, "oh, Christine."

"Come here," she whispered and took a few steps forward, moved her shoulder toward me and tossed her head, all style now, all nerve. As she stepped forward her voice took on a different tone; it was a great, consoling hug. "Come here. Oh, please, come."

I moved toward her. "Sabine," I said. We were caught in the dance that those who are still alive must do. We were doing what we had to.

"Come here." She was smiling now, laughing almost. "Come here," and under her breath the one word, the unbearable word, the word we could not do without, "Christine. Come here, Christine." Her look was the look of twenty-five years ago, when my mother was my age and she too was my age. I walked to her, I turned away, I moved closer. She was fearless now. I saw her as my mother must have seen her. She was beautiful and strong.

"Sabine," I said. She looked at me with her twenty-year-old eyes. My mother stood before her again as she ran her hand through my hair and the look did not change back.

"Christine, Christine," she whispered. I nodded my head and she touched my dream body. I took her hand in a motion of my mother's, confident, elegant, her lovely hand, her manicured hand, and laid it on my hip where it rested finally. Her soft hand. The trip she had begun thousands of miles away through this long year since my mother's death had ended finally.

I moved her weary hand up my side and onto my breast. She sighed. I wondered what this hand might do with its firm, nostalgic touch.

"Christine," she whispered. "Oh, Christine." I kissed her hand and looked into her dark eyes. She pushed the hair from my face and smiled, tossed her head away from me and looked back, giggling, pouting, squeezing my face in her hands, stroking my head, pressing me to the floor.

"Don't stop," I said as we kissed. "Please don't stop." Her eyes sparkled. Life could be controlled, the world could be managed, true love would not be broken up. Lives would not be wasted, cut short. Things could be held in place. I loved her very much in that moment with her great saving kisses as she pressed her body that suggested everything onto mine. I loved her as my mother must have. Here, now, everything fell into simple order.

A voluptuous sorrow was propelling us now into a darkness so great, so complete that I could feel it entering me even as Sabine slowly unzipped my dress. With each movement we were going deeper and deeper into that darkness where we might be with her again.

"I will see you again," I whispered. I was losing sight. She touched me gently and the silence deepened. My mother was calling us from far off. Her voice came nearer as we kissed long and deep. Her voice moved into my mouth. "Sabine," I said. For a moment she was with us, in me, or I in her, in the center of that darkness where she was still alive, and we talked to her. "I love you," Sabine said. "I've missed you so much, Christine."

She was warm and safe and she put her great arms around us in the dark. "Oh, Mom," I said. "I love you."

But then the light started to come back quite suddenly, in a matter of seconds. "Why?" I said, and I began to cry. Sabine's eyes were closed but she too was crying when she heard my voice and knew. She did not open them for a long time, but when she finally did she saw that I was not Christine and she began to sob. She touched my face, hating what her hands told her.

Our bodies were so heavy with sadness it seemed they might fall through the three floors of the building onto the street. Though we lay perfectly still, I felt my body of lead to be falling.

Sabine lifted herself up slightly and looked at me. "Ah" was her love call in French to the other side of death where we were sure my mother was, whole, smiling, waiting for us. "Ah," she said, lifting my face up and seeing my mother again in my calm, even gaze. She smiled. As she dipped into me her sighs were muffled by my flesh as she took my breasts in her mouth, kissed my stomach, and parted my legs, taking me along to the place where it was safe. We moved very slowly, carefully, deliberately, and the descent offered great pleasure as we burned slowly into a fine ash. To die with her. To be nothing but ash. To mix together. To end.

There was rest in that gray ashen place. We were up to our waists in ashes until our waists dissolved, too, and we were not anything anymore—nothing, no one, ash on top of ash on top of ash with her.

From that ash, the world rose up again and called us back, shaped us, and we could not ignore its round call; we were back in my room and we knew that she was far, far away. Betrayed, I gave out a long, loud wordless cry into the empty space and the tears began. "Sabine," I cried. Her name came back again. I hated it.

"Oh, Sabine," I said. She shook her head sadly, put a finger—for the world insisted on fingers and we could do nothing about it—she put a finger to my sticky, swollen mouth and outlined it.

We dragged our grieving bodies over every inch of my apartment, lost ourselves, saw ourselves differently, changed the ending of the story for a while, but we always returned. Only our lovemaking could relieve the pain and longing that each of us had created in the other. The warm liquid our bodies gave up changed the atmosphere. It was smelly and dreamy and we floated in the world our sorrow made. We explored long into the day every curve, every contour of it.

"Speak only in French," I told her.

"Say nothing but with your eyes," she said.

"Sing me a song."

"Now you sing me one."

"Turn over on your back."

"Put your hair up in a bun."

"Put on your mother's bracelet."

"Let me kiss your ankles."

"Let me drench you in cologne."

"Make it all stop."

"Make everything disappear."

Day turned into night and night gave way to dawn and dawn to day until we were finally able to sleep in the light, entwined. When I woke up it was dark out. She was sitting up in bed smoking. She turned her head toward me.

"How could I help but love you?" she whispered, smoothing down my wild hair with her hand. I smiled. She reached over me and turned on the light. I put my face in the pillow. I felt some peace.

"I fed China," she whispered. "We are old friends. Are you hungry?" she asked.

"No, not really. What time is it?"

She shrugged. "I have to leave in the morning."

"Have you been up long?"

"No," she said.

We spoke very quietly and barely moved so as not to disturb the calm. We thought that if we did not draw attention to ourselves, if we did not alert sorrow, it might not seek us out.

"Why didn't you come to the funeral?" I asked very, very quietly.

"The press," she said, "I couldn't bear to face them."

I nodded.

"It was very hard. Fletcher punched one reporter. I never saw Fletcher punch anyone before." We lay in silence for a long time. Even though we were quiet and did not move, it was coming to get us. I thought of the press, how they described us all, all the things Fletcher said.

"No, that's not really it," she said finally. "The real reason I did not come was Michael. Your father loved her as much as I did. It would not have been fair to him. It would have hurt too much." She looked away. "Fletcher is in New York, too, yes?"

"No, Sabine. He's still in the Black Hills on the reservation. I never hear from him anymore. Sometimes I think I've lost him for good. All my letters have been returned."

Sometimes I imagine my brother's massive, muscled arm pointing those letters back to me, refusing this world.

"C'est bizarre. Je ne sais—"

"I miss him, Sabine."

"Oui," she said, "bien sûr."

She was slipping into French. She looked tired but calm. She sat straight up in the bed now, leaned over me, and looked into my eyes. She had come to tell me this, whatever it was she was about to say.

"Vanessa," she said. "Do you know, Vanessa . . ."

I could see it in her posture. I could hear it in the changed cadence of her speech, in the pauses around her words, the way her voice faltered suddenly. There was quiet, and out of the quiet she finally said, "Your mother loved you so much." The words hung in the night like stars where I could see them shining. "She loved you so much. I wonder if you have any idea at all. She wanted you more than anything in the world." She paused. "Did she ever tell you about that afternoon at the psychiatrist's?"

I shook my head. Sabine could not know. My mother had died. She had told me nothing. She was always so mysterious, a retreating, exhausted figure, deceptively close, but when I tried to talk to her or reach out my hand I could never touch her.

"Christine had just learned she was pregnant with you a few days before. We were in New York together for the weekend and she had an appointment with the psychiatrist. She never talked about what went on there, but she seemed very nervous about going this time and she asked if I would come with her. So, of course, I did." Sabine lit a cigarette. "It was an office on Madison Avenue."

"I know where it is," I said.

"A beautiful view, modern, very chic, the way only New York can be."

I thought of my mother walking into that office with its thick carpets and glass tables and how the objects in the room must have seemed to float before her eyes and how frightened she must have been.

"The psychiatrist came out and told Christine to come in. He was very tall and he bowed his balding head as he spoke. He spoke in a very quiet, reassuring voice. I had never seen your mother so panicked. It was not like her to show it, but she could not control herself this day. 'I will not come in without Sabine,' she said. 'Very well then,' he smiled in his kind, patient way and we both went in. His office was very large and elegant, very beige, magnificent."

I saw my mother, as Sabine spoke, sinking into the beige carpet as if it were quicksand. I, too, minute inside my mother, must have sunk with her as he closed the door.

" 'I've just received the results from your pregnancy test,' he said gently. 'I think that it is important for us to talk about it right away.' Your mother was shaking.

"And then he said, 'I have told you many times that a child is not a good idea for you at this time. I am being prudent and conservative in my judgment, I believe. You are in precarious mental health and cannot go off your medication now. I must recommend that you do not have this baby. I can arrange everything for you. It will be quite painless and it will be safe. I am only telling you what I truly believe is best.'

"Your mother stood up. She was not shaking anymore.

" 'Prudent,' she said, evenly. 'Conservative. Not have this baby.' " And I knew how her mouth shaped to hold that word, *baby*.

" 'I will have children. I will write poetry. There is nothing you can do about it.' "

My mother grows large and rises above the carpet. The floating objects of the room spin into her hands and she smashes them against the great, wide Upper East Side windows, and speaks now from the clarity at the center of her anger. "I will have children. I will write poetry. There is nothing you can do about it."

"She was radiant," Sabine said. She rubbed her belly through her dress and moved about the room furiously like an animal protecting her unborn, snarling at the man in her dazzling anger, in her crystalline, in her jewel-like anger. I will have children, she stated, lucid in the perfection of her anger.

"And she threw the objects of art at the psychiatrist," Sabine said, "and hissed at him until he was silent.

"She could be very cruel, you know," she said.

"Yes, I know."

"But she could never really be cruel to us." Sabine smiled slightly. "She was still raging out on the street, so much so that I was afraid she might lose you, right then, and I said to her, I remember it perfectly, I said to her, 'If you don't calm down that beautiful baby of yours is going to be born angry and fighting.' Your mother looked at me. Her eyes were purple and wild and she said to me in perfect control, 'If she's lucky—oh, Sabine, she'd be very lucky to be born fighting.'

"And here you are now, all grown up."

The sun was rising. It was getting light outside. In slow motion Sabine got out of the bed and began dressing.

She got back under the covers fully dressed and lay next to me. She brushed down my hair, kissed my forehead, and took my hand. "Ah, Vanessa," she said in her quietest voice, running her finger up my arm, my needle-marked arm, the punctured vein, "this would break your mother's heart. Your mother was not afraid to suffer. She never gave up, even in the face of terrible sadness. She was always brave. And she asked that we be brave with her." Sabine turned toward the wall.

"I know," I whispered and hugged her shoulders and kissed her ear. "I know, Sabine."

We lay very still in silence. The sky was white. It had started to snow. I could feel the white struggling to enter the holes in my arms. I crossed them. Sabine stared out the window. With each flake on the pane she seemed to be moving further and further north. When she began to speak again her voice was not audible. The snow had taken it away from her. Only gradually did it become something I could hear.

"It had snowed overnight," she sighed. "Your mother slept late that morning, for her, until about ten o'clock. When she woke I pulled up the shade. She was so thrilled with the whiteness of the landscape. It was a complete surprise. I remember that morning as perfectly as if it were yesterday: the beautiful light in that house in Maine and Christine in her robe looking out the window into the whiteness. She was fascinated, spellbound almost, very preoccupied. She had one of her faraway looks on her face. You know how she could look sometimes." I thought of my mother burying herself in that snow as she looked out the window.

"But then she pulled away from her vision, and, in a voice I will never forget, she said, 'This is what I've wanted all along—this peace, finally. All this,' and she motioned into the air. 'You, Michael, the children—and this calm. This is what I've wanted,' and she looked back into the snow and put her hand in mine. That was the last morning I would ever see her. And now it is almost one year. The last thing I remember her saying to me," and she smiled slightly and said every word slowly like a prayer, " 'This is what I wanted.' "

Sabine closed her eyes. "We were lovers for twenty-five years." I looked at Sabine, her head that had not left my mother's shoulder, the arm that cradled the neck still.

"Did Daddy know?" I whispered.

"Oh, yes, he knew all along. The only thing he ever wanted was that she be happy."

"But wasn't it hard to always love her from such a distance, Sabine?"

She gazes off. Her thoughts are in French. She puts on her coat. I am not really waiting for an answer. I see us differently now, not like before but from what I assume the real angle is, the angle my mother must see us from. I picture us from far above. Sabine and I are very small. I open the door; she kisses me in the hallway and says something that is inaudible from such a distance and turns to leave, looking back at me several times and waving as she saunters down the hall. From that angle we are laughable, pathetic, pitiable. From that angle we don't have a chance. From that angle it is clear we are doomed.

"But wasn't it hard to love her from such a distance?" The question lingers.

"No," Sabine says, walking back to me, and the vision breaks, "it was not really so hard."

There are other angles. There are other ways of seeing.

"No," she says again. She takes my hand and holds it tightly, squeezes it. "Vanessa," she says, and I see her straight on now. She is an enormous, brave figure, this small woman who holds my hand. She is a figure of extraordinary courage.

"Vanessa," she says, and her voice is strong, fierce. "We must learn to love her from here now." She hugs me tightly. "Oh, Vanessa," she says, and a great tenderness floods her voice, her whole body, which I hold in my arms in this last embrace, "we must learn to love her from here."

Marta did not see her at first from such a distance, in the great cold. She had forgotten what a person looked like and was frightened when she saw the ballooning head and heard the terrible scraping noise which came from an open, moving hole. Long, dangling strings fringed the balloon, moving, making noise too, she thought. Arms appeared and the strangeness of fingers. She watched their motion, concentrated on them. She tried to find her own corresponding finger and lift it, but she could not locate her hands and she wondered whether she looked like this figure at all. She was dying. The sounds faded, the mouth closed up, the balloon filled with helium and began to rise. What had been the neck became a long, white string. The fingers, too, floated off, detaching themselves from the hands. What came at her must have been hands without fingers, or maybe arms. Something warm touched her and, though she was bone-tired, she felt a slight curiosity at this warmth, and when she looked once more she saw the head again, the mouth, the teeth, the blue pools that were the eyes, the long blonde hair. And the mouth opened and the voice said, "Marta, Marta, Marta." The sound began to make sense. It was her name. She was not thinking. She remembered nothing, but the word came anyway, automatically, outside time, memory, outside all history; it came anyway.

"Natalie," she said.

"Marta," Natalie said again, and, with that sound—which was, she now realized, Natalie's voice—her old features came slowly into focus and Marta began to remember.

"Natalie," she said. It was the only word she knew.

"I've been waiting for you," Natalie said in her delicious death voice, the voice Marta had tried to recreate in her head many times but could not, then tried to block out but she could not do that either. "Where have you been?" Natalie asked. "I've been waiting for you a long time."

"Where are you?" Marta said slowly.

"Here," she said, "I'm so close. But I can't touch you yet."

Marta must have only imagined the warmth, the arms, the hands without fingers. "Try to touch me," Marta pleaded.

Natalie shook her head. "No," she said, "I can't. Don't you remember? I'm dead."

"Natalie, don't go," Marta whispered. She felt herself sinking back into her body where everything slowed.

"Look at me," Natalie said. "Look at me."

"Why did you have to die?" Marta whispered.

Natalie shrugged. Marta watched her light a cigarette. "You're almost with me now. You're so close. Come on. It's like swimming," Natalie said. "It's so easy."

Marta thought of swimming. "Help me, Natalie," she said.

"I am dead." She held up her palm. There were no lines in it anymore. "I cannot come into life for you. You must come to me. Do not be afraid." She stared at Marta. "In death things fall into place. We could be happy here. We could be together forever. There's nothing to be afraid of. In one second, as soon as you cross over, you stop missing the world. Believe me."

"Are you lying even now, Natalie?"

"No."

"It was so hard to know what was true. It was so hard to love you. Do you forget now everything that went on between us?"

"No, I haven't forgotten, Marta, but it's like seeing from a great distance, a trillion, billion miles away."

"Natalie, you were always so distant."

"I realize now how much living we missed together," Natalie said.

"You are as beautiful as ever."

"No," said Natalie, "it's only because you still see me with the eyes of the living. When you are dead and with me you will see that none of that ever mattered. I do not look the way I did. My body is green, decomposed, bones in a grave somewhere—I've forgotten now, somewhere in Europe. You see the memory of me, not me as I look now."

"You were so distant in life, so untouchable. You were never really mine—though I tried so hard to hold you. I never knew what you were thinking. One minute you loved me and the next minute you acted like you did not know me. I wanted you to be happy. I would have done anything for you."

"I'm not beautiful anymore. I'm different. Believe me. I realize now, Marta, all the living we've missed together."

"I love you, Natalie. I have always loved you. I love you now. I am dying for you. I have spent so many months dying for you."

Natalie began losing her human shape; the cells in Marta's brain fell into disorder, and her body began to break down.

"Die now, then. Die."

Marta's pulse began to slow. It was almost over. She could feel herself leaving her body. She could view the scene from above. She was being pulled down a long tunnel, but there was no light at the end of it. It promised nothing. It felt like falling forever. She stopped falling somewhere midtunnel. She hovered suspended in midair. There was nothing there, only darkness, silence.

"It's so easy." Marta heard a voice from the other end of the tunnel where Natalie was. "It's like swimming."

Swimming.

A great warmth flowed through her system. She felt her blood for the first time in a long while. She felt her blood moving inside her.

Swimming.

She began to think of Venezuela with what must have been the last part of her brain. She went back to an early, early time. She folded herself around these sensations: a wave, a smile, a ray of light, a hammock, a baby crying— bananas, the tops of trees, the heat. She curled herself around it.

Natalie panicked. "Please, please."

"What?" Marta said slowly.

"You don't understand. I was restless. I looked everywhere for a way to feel better—in Florence, in Nice, in Paris. All of this I am sorry for. I loved you and you never knew it."

"I never knew it for sure. You never explained anything. You were always so difficult. You were always saying good-bye."

"Come with me now."

Tears fell from Marta's eyes and dripped into her mouth. She tasted the salt. In Venezuela the natives made salt at the edge of the sea. The air was white some days with it. She breathed in: the smell of fish and salt and sweat, and the wonderful beach. She pictured three white pillars of salt.

"It was so lonely to love you."

"In death you will finally understand everything. Things fall together. Be- lieve me. I didn't mean to hurt you."

"Hush now." Marta began to sing the Billie Holiday song, softly at first. "Don't explain. Just say you'll remain. I'm glad you're back. Don't explain."

"Please don't sing that," Natalie cried. "I'll miss you too much." Already Natalie must have known the ending as the dead must know endings, far in advance.

Marta nodded.

Natalie moved closer to Marta. "Come with me," she begged. "If you ever loved me at all, come to me now."

Marta closed her eyes. "I never thought it would be this hard to die," she said. "Natalie," she cried, "it means giving up everything."

"Marta," Natalie whispered, but it did not sound like Natalie really. "Marta," the voice said. It was Natalie but her voice was smaller, softer. "It's so lonely here," she said. "There's no music or bells. There's no one we know here, Marta. Most everyone is old. There's no brilliant light like we thought— nothing."

In the darkness, her eyes closed tightly, Marta saw for the first time since she had fallen into the coma, not a black void but the Vassar campus, the chapel, the library, her small room in Cushing. And she remembered the story of a woman in a dress made of twilight fluttering across the lawn with another woman, some time ago. Then she saw Venezuela again: a house, a shell, a smooth, white stone, the ocean lapping in her ears, and the lovely clean coast-line of an island in Greece, beautiful, blue and white.

And France, too, not Natalie's France but a different one—a France filled with earnest faces, loaves of bread, bottles of wine; a cat on a fence and some-one singing with a big voice in the street; an alley. And yes, Natalie, too, Natalie was there, too, but she seemed further away and she did not have the pull somehow, and Marta thought, I have her still but it's different. It feels different. And with this recognition, that it feels different, with this letting go came not a release or a feeling of freedom but an unaccountable pain. She could never have imagined the pain that she now felt. It was a sharp pain, a shrill, horren-dous scream of pain as if she were giving birth; it was a birth pain—one body pulling out and separating from the other. She was alive and she could feel everything, even her own death, her own mortality, and she shrieked again over her own inevitable death, not now, but some other time, far in the future.

She could still hear Natalie's voice, but it was getting softer and she could no longer see her. "Natalie," she cried, "Natalie," and she felt the pain of what it means to be alive and, as she surfaced, she gave out a long, loud howl—a horrible, bloodcurdling scream that Natalie disappeared into.

She was alone. As she pulled herself up through oceans and oceans of pain into the air, she managed to say a few words.

"I love you still," she whispered. Her body ached. "I will always love you, Natalie." She was breathing light; she would live.

"Natalie," she said. "Don't look for me. Please don't look. I'm not coming."

In a blink the whole world had turned white, in a nod: the sky white; the church, the steeple, completely white, the cobblestones covered like a thou-sand graves; the butcher-shop window filled with the white heads of sheep, the frail bones of rabbits, white, all white; the cars buried in white like animals in the snow—winter's fleece.

I barely heard the door open or recognized Jack when he came in. He looked different. I touched the snow that bearded his face. He smiled, looking past me out into the white.

"Isn't it lovely?" he asked.

His voice seemed to pulsate against the snow. As I looked out the window I felt myself to be disappearing.

"Jack," I said slowly. I looked at our hands, our faces, our clothes; we, too, were white.

I felt myself giving in. There are days like this in every season, days of such sensual intensity that they threaten to erase all else. They invite us to surrender to a single moment, they invite us to die. And what choice do we have? Trapped in the blood colors of autumn, caught in impossible snowdrifts or drifts of heat that melt men into the pavement and weaken hearts until they collapse, what choice do we have? Ask for courage then, for it is best not to look away, not to close our eyes. It is best to let our temperatures rise with the sun, to lose ourselves completely in the rhythm of rain, to let it in, to push the limits of what it means to be human, to force our boundaries, to change shape. This was such an evening for forcing things—an evening of excess.

Tonight I thought, looking out the window, Jack murmuring something in my ear, that we would never see color again, never smell flowers, never feel warmth or rain.

He was telling me that the cold front had originated somewhere in Canada and was heading north when it suddenly changed direction and now whipped down the east coast. He spoke softly and it sounded to me like a children's story. With the storm came sharp winds and heavy snow. Around Boston it picked up sleet and hail and by New York it had fully matured. Like a cartoon it raced around the skyscrapers, breaking the glass in the doomed Hancock Insurance Building and nearly blowing into the sky like kites the dogs that were out for walks. The storm was so bad, in fact, that it kept prostitutes from the street, moonlighters from the night shift, insomniacs from the coffee shops. "Imagine," he whispered. Couples from the suburbs forfeited their tickets to Broadway plays. Underground the subway groaned to a halt between stations and a Puerto Rican woman with two children began to cry. Men on the Bowery without homes swore at the sky and futilely attempted to make fires. A young secretary took out her bunny fur jacket and laid it on the bed. Old women switched from one radio station to another for weather reports. Children jumped on their beds gleeful at the prospect of no school. Bachelors smiled, poured more wine, and dimmed the lights, knowing their dates would not be able to get home. Jack smiled, too.

Until now it had been a fairly mild winter—sluggish like the South. I thought Jack had begun secretly to prepare for a time when all the seasons would melt together, blurring into one another, impossible to tell apart. A coolish summer would turn into a muddy, green autumn. A snowless Christmas would begin a warm winter, and when spring came he would hardly even notice it. The mind would sleep forever in a homogeneous stupor, unchallenged.

But with this storm some hope for the diversity of the future was renewed in him. He seemed alive now with the possibilities. What had rested so long in him was now awakened. He paced around the room as if I were keeping him on this violent evening from some urgent, private calling.

Early on there had been signs that this would be an evening of supreme winter, irresistible winter, winter the Québecois know, winter the blind man sees. "Prepare," the wind had whispered into my drowsy ear in the morning light as Sabine turned a corner and boarded her plane. "Prepare," its freezing breath had said, but there was no preparing for what was to come. Those who assumed such a stance did so to reassure themselves and to calm those around them. I was reluctant even to feign a pose of readiness. Sabine had felt it, too, I thought. She had come just in time.

"Put on your coat," Jack said finally, going to the closet. He was clumsy in his boots and heavy clothing. Though he knew this place by heart, he bumped into things, as if he'd never been here before. Together we had explored every inch of my small studio. We'd been up against every wall, under every table; wedged between the police lock and the door we continued to reach new heights of ecstasy.

"But, Jack." My voice curled around his chest attempting with its lowest and most seductive registers to pull him toward the bed. "It's below zero."

"I like it," he said, putting his huge hand on the windowpane. "I like it a lot."

"But we'll freeze."

"Put on your coat, Vanessa."

"Where are we going?"

He held out the coat and I put my arms into the sleeves. I knew this was the night that all our other nights together had been a rehearsal for, preparation. Once my coat was on, I sat back on the bed.

"All right," he shrugged. "I don't need this. Don't come. I'll see you, OK?"

"Don't leave me," I said.

"Hurry up, then. Hurry." He dragged out the word as he said it, in some way contradicting its meaning. I recognized the tone of his voice. He had spoken to me a thousand times before as I had clawed at his clothing. "Hurry up," he had moaned, "please." It was the way he sometimes told me to put in my diaphragm. His voice was a whisper, a cry. "Please, Vanessa, hurry."

"Are those real boots?" he asked. "There's three feet of snow out there already, Vanessa."

"Kiss me," I said with such authority that he obliged. As he slipped his tongue into my mouth, I could feel him beneath his coat, growing large. My hand moved through the layers of clothes.

"Not now, Vanessa," he whispered. His mouth was hotter than any mouth should have been on such a night. "Not now.

"This is the night we've been waiting for," he said, wrapping a scarf around my neck. Sure, I smiled, and locked the door.

Jack dragged me like one of those reluctant dogs through the crooked Village streets. "Isn't this great? Isn't this wild?" he kept asking. "This is what we've been waiting for," he said, not without sadness, patting me on the back.

"You're hurting me, Jack," I complained as he pulled me across the icy park, "and I'm cold."

"Don't give up now," he said. "You've come so far already." His breath had shape; I saw three white pillars in the cold. "Let's have a drink," he said, motioning up the block. Light from a sign spilled through the snow. It blinked, "Corner Bistro, Corner Bistro, Corner Bistro." Neon made me sad. It reminded me of people who had lost their way—drifters, the homeless. I was more lonely than I can ever remember being before, standing under that sign in the snow while Jack lit a cigarette. I thought we paused too long under it, and I pulled at his wool coat. I hated to think of that sign lighting the freezing night for no one. It was a small, inexplicable grief, an uneasiness that lingers long after the actual thought has passed and is replaced.

As we walked into the warmth of the bar, the few people inside turned and stared at us. Lonely, they seemed jealous of what they mistook in our faces for love. In the lines of our bodies they read a great romance, but they misread badly. They missed the point. It was something else that had brought us together, something far more immediate than love, less abstract.

Sitting at the bar, I thought I saw disgust, even hate, in Jack's face, but it was only a passing shape. And in my face I knew there was great weariness: I wanted now only to rest.

"What would you like to drink?" he asked.

"I don't want a drink tonight, Jack."

"Are you sure?" he asked. "Are you sure?" In snow light I saw the passion that contoured his face.

"Yes," I said. We slid along the freezing streets, moving more and more quickly. Desire was the terrible friction between our bodies. It syncopated our conversation. It propelled us into places we could not get out of. We followed it forward, dragging ourselves through dangerous terrain.

Who was he, I wondered? Whose life was this that I hung on to so tenaciously? He had refused to tell me even the smallest details of his life—what his real name was, where he lived, where he worked, what his family was like.

Did he have children? "Invent me," he had said. "I will not exist if you do not invent me."

It was snowing harder now and the wind kept changing direction. We were nearing the harbor. Our boots made black tracks in the snow. The ice was smooth and thick and treacherous.

"I can't go any further, Jack," I said, collapsing.

He pulled me up. "Believe me. You can."

The violence of the seasons invigorated him. I pictured him energetic in the brutal heat of the city summer, concentrated in autumn's excessive beauty, sexual in the torrential rains of spring. But we would never see the spring, I thought.

"Come on, Vanessa," he said.

I was up to my thighs in snow. It was exhausting to walk through so much white. I was so tired. "You're leaving me tonight, aren't you? Why are you leaving me?" I said numbly.

He stopped. He was breathing hard. "Oh, Vanessa," he gasped. "Don't you see?" We had reached the water. "It is you who is leaving me."

The wind whirled us in a convulsive dance. We staggered around each other in hopeless circles.

"No!" I cried, looking up at the ceiling of stars.

"Vanessa," he said, weaving, swerving. "I have invented your life so many times. But usually the ending is sad."

"It doesn't surprise me," I said. We neared each other, then pulled away. "I'm not surprised!" I shouted above the wind. We collided. He took me by the arms. "You can change the ending, Vanessa."

We walked out onto the crystal pier. Water rose and fell around us in violent waves. I was freezing to death. I heard the lighthouse's lonely snow tone. Ice floated by. "Look," I said. "I see a white light."

"Where?"

"Out there. I see a white light. A red light. A white light." The water calmed.

"Yes," he said. "I see it now, too."

I was at peace. I turned around. Before my eyes the West Side Highway seemed to open like a field. I arranged the last few objects on the landscape. I looked at Jack. His eyes gleamed like ice.

The headlights of a car came up from behind. "No," I cried. I felt something hug me like a vice. On impact the man in the car must have been hurled forward. I screamed and screamed, feeling some excruciating force enter me again and again in the snow. I was being slammed over and over. "Oh, God!" I cried.

"Live," he said, "or die!"

There were flames everywhere: flames in my mouth, flames in my hair. There was no stopping this. Blue flames, orange, white—everywhere. "Why?" I shrieked with the last part of me before the brain closed down. "Oh, God," I sighed. "Why? Why?"

I grew large and rose above the flames. "Did you think you could kill us just like that, you stupid bastards? Did you think we would just forget?" I laughed. "Did you think we'd be quiet forever?" My voice grew enormous, my body the tremendous body of rage.

"There is no getting away with it. There is no escape. We will speak and bear witness. You can poison us, you can hack us into little bits, you can burn us in your furnaces, and still we will live. We will never stop speaking. We will glitter in the palms of your hands forever."

At some point we must have fallen because when I opened my eyes we were on the ground and covered with snow. All along it was what they had had in mind: Jack on my back with his teeth in my neck, his blue hands like claws curled around mine, my hair stuffed in his mouth, my mouth frozen open, caught forever in the center of a sigh.

"We'll die here," I said, sobbing, crawling from underneath Jack, separating from the beast our bodies made. I stood up and looked at him from what seemed a great distance. "Wake up," I said to him. "Get up." The snow seemed to muffle my plea, but he must have heard me because after a few moments he slowly opened his eyes and it seemed to me that he smiled. "I'm OK," he said. "Go. Run now." I saw myself again for a moment lying in the snow. "No," I said, and pulled myself up, out of my mother's body, which lay motionless in the snow.

I turned and moved away. I was waist deep in snow. I lifted myself out of her. The pain was terrible. I trudged forward through the snow. I moved as fast as I could but I did not know where I was going.

My body ached, my heart ached.

Far off on the horizon I saw something moving through the white on the line of the Hudson. I moved toward it. I gasped. It was beautiful and white and sailing toward me.

"Daddy!" I cried out as he pulled alongside me and I stretched out my hand, which he grasped, and I helped him ashore. "Daddy." We stood together there in the snow. His clothes were singed. He held my hand tightly. He must have tried to find her withered hand and hold it, to touch what he sensed was her.

"Why?" we said together, looking into the white sky. Why? He had seen the car in his rearview mirror, and it had seemed to float into ours as if in slow motion. "It could not have been going more than fifteen or twenty miles an hour," he cried. It had entered her slowly and with a certain grace. But it exploded into fire anyway.

"Why?" we cried into the sky. "Why?" And with our chanting over and over of the word *why*, I saw Marta again, who had first taught me that impossible word. She had placed it into my mouth before I could possibly have comprehended its full meaning. She had given it to me far in advance, and now she too stood with us there in the snow. "Why?" we asked, the three of us.

"Where was the sense in it?" Grandma lifted herself from her shallow grave and shook her fist into the blurry air and asked for sense, demanded it. Surely, I reasoned, if we all stood there together and shouted in unison, *why*, the answer would come clear. Surely we deserved some explanation, something. We might even ask for her back.

And Sabine, too, stood up, up from the snow and walked out of her dress like she once did long ago and said to the sky, right alongside my grandmother, in her large naked voice, "Dites-moi! Pourquoi?" and certainly such a sad and angry chorus of voices in the middle of the snow, in the middle of the night, would have to be answered—if not in words, then somehow. Surely a streetlight would dim for a minute or brighten. Surely there would be some consolation, some solace, some way into this impossible question. Why? Why?

Sabine stood next to me and looked around for the missing one. "Fletcher is in New York, too, no?" she asked.

"No, Sabine," I said, but, hearing her words again, I moved forward, leaving the small band of angry, demanding people for a moment. I dragged myself through the snow. "Fletcher is in New York, too?" I walked through miles and miles of snow, until I reached the glass booth with its phone book. Turin, I said over and over as I made my way to him. There it was, above my name: Fletcher A., West 18th Street.

He shakes his head sadly back and forth as I close the book. He looks so sad. He seems so very sad. "Oh, Grandpa!" I cry. "Please don't look that way."

"Try to forgive them," he whispers.

I plowed toward him through fields of snow. Whatever was about to happen, there was no changing it now, no stopping it. Now it was inevitable. There was no way to step back. He would be there—had been there for some time.

She had been a model of courage once.

I dragged my aching body through the early morning. I was burning hot. I was freezing cold. I had come a long way to this place. It had taken me so long to get here, to travel these twenty blocks to him.

I climbed the steps to his apartment on the third floor slowly. I pushed open the door, which was slightly ajar. He stood turned away from me looking out the window into the snow. His back was huge and brown and muscled; he was naked to the waist. His hair was long and straight and hung to the center of that great back. He looked like a strong, strong man. Only his arms dangling at his sides revealed the degree of his surrender.

He turned to me. His eyes were pale lakes of pain in the dark, rugged landscape of his face.

"Fletcher," I whispered.

"There's been a terrible accident in the snow," he said. "I've been waiting for you, Pale Moon."

"I'm here now."

"I knew you would come."

I nodded.

Now he moved those massive arms and crossed them at his chest. "They've killed our mother," he said, "and they will die for it." He stared straight into the exploding fire he still saw before him. "They killed her as if she were a deer or a jackrabbit or a dog."

"Fletcher," I said.

"You must prepare now," he said gently, "for the dance." There was a long pause. He just stared at me. "God, you look so bad, Vanessa," he whispered, and his blue eyes brimmed and threatened to spill over.

"Oh, Fletcher!"

"We will do the Ghost Dance," he said. "Everything will be all right. There will be sweet grass and fresh water."

He was nearly a hundred years away, the century about to turn; he was thousands of miles away.

He gestured out the window where there was only snow. "The bison and buffalo and elk will return. There will be plenty of food for everyone. The dead will come alive again, and it will be like old times. You remember, Pale Moon." He smiled and closed his eyes.

"Yes," I whispered, "oh, I remember."

"Come on," he said. "I'll help you out of these clothes." They were frozen to me. "I'll prepare the steam lodge for you."

He ran a hot bath and placed large rocks which he had heated in the oven in the room with me. "Breathe," he said in a low voice, "please breathe."

I lowered myself into the hot water. I watched the dead make their first attempts to rise like steam in a dance of heat. "In case you come back disguised as a stone," I cried, and placed my hand on top of a flat, gray rock, searing it.

I settled into the steam. We will see her again, I thought. My heart opened. I was sweating hard. For an hour I lay in the heat.

I stepped finally from the steaming room wrapped in a towel. "Put this on," he told me and handed me a beautiful, fringed tunic painted with symbols: sun, moon, stars. Eagle feathers adorned the bottom. "This is your Ghost Shirt," my brother said. "It is impenetrable to bullets or any weapon. It will protect you from all harm. Go on," he said, "do as I say." He held my shoulders and looked directly into my eyes. "They will never hurt us again."

He sat in the center of the room and blended the sacred paint. "Red ochre," he murmured. He dipped his fingers into it and marked my face, then his, with the sacred symbols.

"Wherever the white man has stepped, the earth aches," he said. "They killed our mother." He took a hank of my hair in his large, rough hand, pressed the scissors next to my skull, and cut—again and again. My hair fell like tears to the floor. He touched my shorn head. "Why?" he cried, as he picked up my hair and brought it to his face. "They killed her like she was a dog or a squirrel."

He took the large scissors to his own head next and slowly, in sections, cut his long hair and threw it in the pile with mine. He put on the headdress. Around his waist he tied the pelts of rabbit and skunk. He took out a large sharp knife and cut first into his arms and then into mine and I wailed with pain. "We bleed for you," he cried. "We bleed. We bleed."

On a drum he began to beat out a rhythm. "Your children cry out to you," he chanted. "Your children call you by name: Brave Ghost, Brave Ghost, Brave Ghost." His voice started high and slowly descended until he reached the end of his breath and fell silent, then began again. He stood up, still beating the small drum, and I rose too and touched his mangled head. He looked out the window. "Brave Ghost," he cried, "we bleed for you."

"Brave Ghost," I whispered.

He waved eagle feathers in the air above his head in time to the chant for our mother. I continued the rhythm on the drum. He swayed and waved in the air the aromatic tips of sage.

"We shall live again. We—shall—live—again."

I took my first tentative steps in the dark. He took my hands. Over the beat of the drum he said, "We entwine our fingers like living vines. We keep the circle.

"We shall live," he whispered.

The chant began soft and low. I followed my brother as he dipped and swayed, moving one foot forward then the other in a slow, perfect motion: simple and pure. I listened to the drum's strong and steady beat. I felt my fear slowly drop away.

Songs seemed to arise from the dance, and we did not know what we were going to say until we said it. The obsessive beat of the drum, the step, one foot then the other, our voices like hearts, our hearts like drums. We were dancing toward her.

We swayed. We tipped our bodies like gliders into the west, into the east. "Help us," we chanted, "help us to live." Our arms were covered with blood. Tears fell.

"Help us to rise," we said, doing the motion of the soul escaping from the body that Grandpa had taught us as children. All was rhythm and out of the rhythm our songs came, changing many times through the days and nights. We became drugged by the dance and the patterns of our own desire. I saw Grandpa for a second, standing on a chair and waving the soul up through the ceiling. "Oh, Grandfather," I said and fell to my knees. "Dreams of Rain!" Fletcher shouted and helped me back up, and we lifted our eagle feathers to the ceiling. "Over here," he shouted. "Grandpa!" he said, and tears ran down his face.

The sun fell and rose and fell again, I don't know how many times. Fatigue found a home in my heavy bones. We moved forward, forward, slowly, slowly, one foot then the other, hour after hour, drugged with sorrow. "We will see her again," Fletcher whispered. I felt as if I would not be able to go on, would not be able to keep standing and dancing. "Help me," I sighed. "Help. Help me to live." And with those words I felt myself lift out of my body and rise, leaving it somewhere far behind. I could feel her near me. "Mother," I cried, "where are you?" I fell to the floor quaking. She was gone. "Do you think you can disappear just like that?" I screamed. It was dark. The blackness surrounded me. I reached for my brother. He took my hand. Blood rushed to my head. At first I saw nothing and I began to cry. "Is there only darkness here, too?" I cried out. Fletcher wailed and wailed with his whole body, as though he would never stop.

"Is there nowhere we can—"

"Look," I say. A great familiar light fills the room. It is the light of morning, a buttery, pale yellow. I can hear frogs in a faraway pond and I can smell sweet grass and running fresh water and clover. The sky is a high blue.

'It's so beautiful here, Fletcher!" I gasp. "It's so beautiful here!"

A warm breeze caresses our faces. We lift our heads. There are fields and fields of chamomile and wildflowers. Near the lake cattails grow. We reach into the clear water and come up with handfuls of silver fish. We feel the fan-shaped leaves of ferns at our ankles. We take deep breaths. There is such sweetness here. On the horizon are rows of luminous, white birches. They seem to bend toward us. We walk through the cool woods. I touch the dark reddish-brown berries that are deep inside the bramble bush. The woods open up and light floods our vision. Corn grows, acres and acres of corn—brave green V's—and pumpkins, and the flowers of squash. I see sheep grazing. I look closer and see buffalo, elk, bison, and doe. I hear crickets and the complex song of the mockingbird. And another song—it is exquisitely beautiful, nearly unbearable to listen to. I look up into the bough of a fruit tree.

"Fletcher," I whisper, not wanting to scare it, "up there." And I finally see it. I see it perfectly. I do not turn from it and it does not fly away. "The Topaz Bird." We are nearly blinded by its brilliant, jewel-like light. And, finally, from that brilliant light she steps. Through the tall grass, she moves slowly to us. I am breathing light, and she is so beautiful and she is dressed in white.

"Oh, Mother!" we say. And we see the flowering of all human beauty, the end of all pain and disease, and men walk like brothers on the great land. Her eyes overflow with love—her whole body. And we too overflow. Who can contain such love, such beauty, such peace as this?

We look at her with our pure eyes of light.

"Oh, Mother," we say finally. "We've missed you so much!"

"My sweet, sweet children," she sighs and pats the tops of our heads.

"My Vanessa," she says, and she puts her arms around me. "Fletcher! How big you've grown!"

She closes her eyes. "Take my hands," she whispers. "Take my hands now." I take her right hand, Fletcher takes her left.

A small wind blows up. "Try not to be afraid," she says. A large white cloud covers the sun momentarily and then passes it. We watch as men and women who have come a long way get off ships. What Drinks Water dreamt will come true. A strange race will weave a spiderweb around the Lakotas. When this happens they shall live in square gray boxes and beside those boxes they will die.

Gray squares now start springing up on the landscape. From the distance men come on horses. Indians lie dead in the snow of South Dakota, bleeding through their Ghost Shirts.

A man falls in the snow. But it is not really snow at all. It collects on the floor of the boiler room. It collects in the lungs of the man.

Tears continue to fall. A mother and father wave to a plane that takes their son to a far-off country from which he will not come back alive.

"There is so much sadness," Fletcher says.

In the tall president's face you can see how his heart has been torn by the war.

In the Bronx a child does not dream but turns over and over all night, starving to death in its sleep.

Far away a young soldier ties off his arm and shoots morphine into his vein.

My father drums his finger on a table. He moves the salt shaker forward slightly. He draws a line in the salt.

My grandfather leans over three cows that have mysteriously died overnight. The vet in the white coat wipes his brow, rubs his chin, and shrugs.

We watch ourselves gather in the dark barn with Grandpa until the thunder passes. Over and over he tells us the stories we love. "This is a wonderful country," he says. "This is still the best country in the world." He looks to the sky.

Two dreamy brothers in North Carolina, intent on flight, work day and night. In the same town a minister and his grandchild work through a peaceful Sunday morning.

A girl in Connecticut plays cat's cradle, knots daisies into chains, makes mud packs of earth and clay.

My father bends his cloudy forehead down and plucks a squash flower from the ground.

Mary picks apples and puts them in her bushel basket.

Migrant workers, so exhausted they seem to sleep as they stand, as they bend over and over in their drowsy, aching dance, cradle each piece of fruit tenderly in their weathered hands, even at day's end.

A young man catches his fingernail in the heavy machine he operates on the assembly line in New Bedford, Massachusetts. Not wanting to stop the machines, his boss gives no lunch break. The noise is deafening. The man would cover his ears if he could.

My father croons in the dark room with Frank Sinatra.

I look at my mother whose hand I still hold. "How handsome you are, Michael," she whispers.

Grace Kelly turns to say good night to Cary Grant at her hotel room.

A boy plays his trumpet in a band at a local club and dreams of Louis Armstrong.

"I still have a dream," the proud angry man says. It is August 1963.

We live in the hands of the family that prays. We live in the hidden valleys folded in hills. We live in the corncrib, in the center of the haystack. We live in the song of the woodthrush. We live in the life of fish, in the trees that lose their hair in winter, in the wildflowers that return year after year after year. We must learn from the land that gives and gives and asks so little in return.

We live in the south and we live in the north; we live in the east and in the west. We live in the past and we live in the present. Let us live in those who wanted only to have a normal lifetime but for whom it was not possible.

"Give me back what you have taken," the DES daughter says from her hospital bed.

"Give me back my life," the Vietnam veteran demands.

"Give me back what you have taken," Black Hawk repeats, turning the television up louder.

Let us live in the mouths of the men who lie, who deny and deny and deny, who cover up their crimes. Let us change the shape of each word as they speak.

I always tried to believe you, Fletcher: that somehow there would be a way to live side by side with the sorrow. I see a young man walking to a podium. May we not be afraid to ask that those who claim to be responsible act in such a way. May we demand answers from those in the position to give them. "We must reclaim this country," the young man says. "Take it back." And that young man is you.

"This is our home, Fletcher. It's ours now, too."

I see Grandpa Sarkis in Turkey, Grandma and Grandpa speaking their last words in Italian, Sabine somewhere, far off in France.

"There's no other place we can feel at home," I say.

The ocean liner changes its chilly course.

Our mother squeezes our hands. Buildings rise on the land. We see a shimmering beautiful city rise up before our eyes. I gasp as I watch the Empire State Building assemble itself, the Statue of Liberty. Chinese step off boats, Japanese, Puerto Ricans, Cubans, and move into the great city. "And over there!" I say, pointing to the shining water. "Have you ever seen anything like it before?" Pure and perfect in its form—it is the Brooklyn Bridge.

We travel, still holding Mother's hands, over the tops of buildings to another city. In that city men in suits sit around a kidney-bean-shaped table in an executive suite and make a decision. "Don't do it!" Fletcher and I shout, but it's no use. They can't hear anything.

Now it begins. The weather grows colder. Our hair blows straight back from our faces. The sky grows dark. I know what will be next. Yes, there are the first flakes of snow.

Now my father wipes inches of snow from the car's windshield. I hear the motor being started up. And still I do not know why this must be. The toll-booth cannot be too far.

"I have to go now," she says.

"Yes," I say. I know it is time.

"Please let me go," she cries. "Let me go now." Her tears fall on our shoulders as if from far away.

"I have loved you," she says, "my whole life." She is crying very hard now. She looks at us sadly and squeezes our hands. Why must it be this way?

"We must give her back," I say to Fletcher.

"We could go with her," Fletcher says. "She's been calling to us this whole time."

"No," I say, shaking my head, knowing what we must do.

"We can't come yet, Mommy," I say to her. "We must live." And she knows it is true.

I pick up the bag of black cornmeal. It is the heaviest thing I will ever hold. I pour it into Fletcher's left hand, then into mine. We let go of her hands and four times pass the black cornmeal around our heads and then cast it away.

"Now the white," Fletcher says. We sprinkle it. "Rest now," we say. "Rest now. Be safe."

Fletcher lights the pine incense, then walks to the windows. With his massive arms he strains to lift each one. "Open the door," he says.

I open it wide. "I love you," I whisper, and I know she can hear me. Fletcher and I hold each other tightly. "Be happy," we cry. "Good-bye, Mom," we say, looking up to the ceiling, looking up to the sky. "Good-bye."